Praise for
OMEGA DAYS

"When people ask me to recommend great zombie fiction, one of the names I consistently mention is John L. Campbell. Nobody writes an urban battle scene quite like he does. The pace of his storytelling will leave you breathless, and his characters are so real and so likeable you will jump up and cheer for them. *Omega Days* is, hands down, one of the shining stars of the zombie genre. Do yourself a favor and move this one to the top of your to-be-read pile right now. You can thank me later."
—Joe McKinney, Bram Stoker Award–winning author of
The Savage Dead and *Dead City*

"Characters as diverse as a priest fallen from grace to a prisoner who finds his heart are all in this story of terror . . . Campbell is good with characters . . . It's stories like *Omega Days*, with a setting in a popular city that most people have heard about, that can take an average story and make it unique."
—Examiner.com

"An impressively convincing vision of a world suddenly gone insane . . . The maelstrom that Campbell creates is a somber portrayal of the human capacity for both selfishness and, more rarely, altruism. He effectively builds a mood of terror that sweeps the reader along in this powerful example of the zombie thriller genre at its best."
—*Publishers Weekly*

"A highly entertaining read with a style that grabbed me from the very first page . . . There are creepy echoes . . . of masters like King and Koontz . . . If you want highly entertaining, escapist zombie fiction with plenty of action, peopled by rich and interesting characters, you couldn't do better than *Omega Days*."
—*SFRevu*

Berkley Books by John L. Campbell

OMEGA DAYS

SHIP OF THE DEAD

SHIP
OF THE
DEAD

AN OMEGA DAYS NOVEL

JOHN L. CAMPBELL

BERKLEY BOOKS, NEW YORK

THE BERKLEY PUBLISHING GROUP
Published by the Penguin Group
Penguin Group (USA) LLC
375 Hudson Street, New York, New York 10014

USA • Canada • UK • Ireland • Australia • New Zealand • India • South Africa • China

penguin.com

A Penguin Random House Company

This book is an original publication of The Berkley Publishing Group.

Library of Congress Cataloging-in-Publication Data

Campbell, John L. (Investigator)
Ship of the dead / John L. Campbell. — Berkley trade paperback edition.
pages cm. — (An Omega Days novel ; 2)
ISBN 978-0-425-27264-0 (paperback)
1. Zombies—Fiction.   2. Survival—Fiction.   3. Virus diseases—Fiction.   4. Horror fiction.
I. Title.
PS3603.A47727S55 2014
813'.6—dc23
2014016670

PUBLISHING HISTORY
Berkley trade paperback edition / October 2014

PRINTED IN THE UNITED STATES OF AMERICA

10 9 8 7 6 5 4 3 2 1

Cover images: Omega symbol © Morphart Creation; Ship © Jorg Hackemann;
Texture © Sanexi; Zombies © TsuneoMP—all Shutterstock.
Cover design by Diana Kolsky.
Interior text design by Laura K. Corless.
Title page art © iStockphoto.com/trigga.

This book is dedicated to the men and women of the United States Navy and especially to the officers and crew of CVN-68. For all you do, so far from home and family, thank you.

And for Linda, always.

ACKNOWLEDGMENTS

This book would not have been possible without the assistance of Charles Liebener, USN, who helped breathe life into the *Nimitz* and who gave me a polite smile and nothing else when I asked classified questions. His enthusiasm for my endless queries is surpassed only by his passion for the special work he does on our behalf. Any errors found within regarding Navy operations or ship specifics are entirely the author's responsibility or were intentionally fictionalized to fit the story.

Additional thanks go to Amanda Ng, Alexis Nixon, Jennifer DeChiara, Dominique and Anna for their outstanding work in San Antonio, and to my family and friends for understanding the time and isolation required to complete this novel.

Finally, for all the readers who waited so long for this sequel, thank you for your patience and support.

A GATHERING
OF SOULS

ONE

Rosa Escobedo should have stayed with her partner, should have been there to protect her mother. She should have tried harder to report to her unit. She did none of that and instead ran to save her own life. It hung on her as heavy as a cross, one she had carried since that terrible day.

That was the night Jimmy Albright punched the siren, blasting a high-pitched *WHOOP-WAAH* as he hauled the ambulance left, then snapped it hard right again, neatly cutting around a BMW that hadn't bothered to pull over for the flashing lights. The rig sped after a pair of San Francisco Police Department Crown Vics, slashing through traffic on the Embarcadero.

"All I'm saying is something's gotta give, Rosie." He was smoking in the rig, a supreme violation for Emergency Medical Service crews, the butt clenched between his teeth as he maneuvered the heavy vehicle like a sports car. His red hair was closely trimmed, and he was tall and rangy, thin but with ropy, muscled arms. "You're gonna burn yourself out."

The two cruisers split right and left around an Alhambra water truck, and Jimmy came up on its flat back end with sirens blaring, puffing cigarette smoke out the corner of his mouth before he cut right. He cleared the truck's bumper by six inches at forty-five miles per hour. In the seat beside him, Jimmy's partner didn't flinch. After three years together, Rosa was immune to his driving.

"I got it under control," Rosa said. She was twenty-five, dark-haired and attractive, something noticed by every cop, medic, and fireman she encountered. Most of them asked her out. "If it gets to be too much, I'll quit something."

"Yeah, sure." He stomped the brakes and flung the ambulance down an exit ramp.

Even in mid-August the evening was pleasant enough to let the open windows cool the cab, and Rosa cocked her right arm outside and watched as the city flashed by. "You just want me to quit dancing." She didn't look at him.

The rig's tires squealed as he yanked it left, passing under the highway and chasing the two cruisers through the twilight streets. "We're not going to have one of *those* conversations, are we?" he asked. "Because that's not where I was going."

She shot him a look. "That's exactly where this is going."

Jimmy flicked the butt out the window and made a disgusted noise, the kind people make when they are yet again starting down a much-traveled and worn-out path. "If you're asking me if I want you to stop stripping for strange men—"

"Dancing!" Beneath the pressed white uniform shirt and dark blue cargo pants was a dancer's body, firm and full-figured, without the silicone enhancements employed by most of the girls at her part-time job. Jimmy knew what was under that uniform, although that was over now, which made this topic even more difficult.

"Uh-huh, dancing around a pole and taking your clothes off. You want me to lie? No, I don't like it."

"See? I told you." She flashed a triumphant smile and shook a finger at him. "I told you."

"But . . ." He braked, slowing as he went through an intersection against the light. "I know you won't quit because you make too much money at it, and med school is going to be expensive."

"That's right!" Rosa's face was burning. She didn't like talking to Jimmy about that part of her life. He was too close, both on the job and given their brief but pleasant time together, a relationship they had mutually agreed to end because it was making them distracted at work. And yet he was the only one with whom she *could* talk. It would kill her mother to find out, and her sister out in Sacramento could barely focus on a conversation with five kids constantly howling for her attention. Rosa didn't have a boyfriend; she had no time for one. Secretly, she doubted that a decent guy—other than Jimmy— would have a stripper as a girlfriend. *Dancer*, she corrected herself.

"That's right!" Jimmy shouted back, grinning and punching her arm across the cab of the rig, nearly sideswiping a parked car.

Rosa laughed and punched him back. "You can be so stupid."

"I know. That's why I'm dragging my white-trash ass around in this rig. You, however, are not stupid, and you don't need this job. *This* is what you should quit."

The cab fell silent as Rosa stared at him, and Jimmy followed the cruisers into a neighborhood of four- and five-story buildings with ground-floor shops and apartments above. In the distance, still blocks away, red lights of the San Francisco Fire Department were sparkling. It was a non-fire call with injuries, their dispatcher had told them.

"Jimmy . . ." Her voice was softer.

"I'm serious. Look at yourself, Rosie. You cranked out a bachelor's degree with pre-med in record time, you're about to start med school, and you've told me a hundred times what the workload will be like. On top of it you've got a Navy Reserve commitment. And dancing to pay for it all? You don't have time to be out here with me."

She frowned. This certainly wasn't what she had been expecting. "I get practical experience out here. It keeps me sharp."

Jimmy scowled. "That's a bullshit answer. You should have your nose in a book, Doc. You shouldn't be out here scraping bodies off the street, dealing with gunshot wounds, ODs, and abused kids. Up to your ass in human filth," he finished in a mutter.

She couldn't remember hearing him like this, so passionate and bordering on anger. For a moment her heart acted like it might do a little flip, and then settled. "I like being out here with you."

"Yeah? Maybe you are stupid after all."

They were in the Rincon Hill section, just off Folsom. The rig rolled to a stop behind a squad car just as the officers were sprinting toward a commotion at the front of a building. To the EMS attendants it looked like a crowd of firemen were fighting with a mob of civilians in the street, the white glare of a fire truck's spotlight making a confusion of shadows dance on a brick wall.

"Hold on," Jimmy said, clamping his right hand on Rosa's leg just as she was about to jump out. They watched, stunned, as a civilian grabbed a fireman by the head and bit off one of his ears. Someone screamed, and another fireman hurled himself into the fight, swinging an axe. Cops drew their weapons and fired, making three red circles appear in the chest and belly of a fat man in a bloody wifebeater. He didn't flinch, lumbered right at them and tackled a cop, pinning him with his weight. He bit the cop's ear off before going for the face. The fireman with the axe split a man's head open down the middle. The downed cop's partner executed the fat man with a pistol to the ear, then rolled his bulk to the side, screaming "Medic!"

Rosa was out the right door and running to the back. Jimmy met her there and they opened the double doors together, grabbing their bright orange kits. Jimmy suddenly pinned her to one of the doors and moved close, startling her. "You be careful."

She pulled away from him impatiently. "Let's go," and then she ran to where one cop was crouched over his fallen partner, holding the man's head and pressing a hand to where an ear had once been. He was cursing steadily, glancing between his groaning partner and over to where the fireman with the axe, screaming like a mad Viking, had just put down another civilian. Two more people, both Asian women, were clamped to the fireman's legs, chewing into his knees and thighs. No other cops were in sight, despite the second patrol car.

Rosa pulled on heavy purple latex gloves with a snapping noise and dropped beside the two cops, opening her kit. "I got him," she said, pressing a thick gauze pad against the side of the man's head and shouldering his partner out of the way. That cop stared at her for a moment, blinked, and started walking toward the raging fireman, raising his service weapon.

Jimmy Albright saw the gun coming up and cut left away from it, running toward the stoop of an adjacent building, where another fireman was curled into a fetal position, blood soaking the concrete around him. "I'm coming, buddy." He dropped his kit and knelt, pulling on his gloves.

Rosa's cop was struggling to sit up, gritting his teeth. "Fucking guy bit my fucking ear off. Marco! Where the fuck did you go?"

Marco continued to walk slowly toward the axe-wielding fireman and shot one of the Asian women on his leg through the head at point-blank range. The snarling body collapsed, but the bullet blasted through the skull and shattered the fireman's knee. With a scream the fireman spun and swung the axe, cutting halfway through the cop's neck, making the head flop to one side. As the cop sagged to his knees, the fireman took the head all the way off with a second blow, screaming something unintelligible. The ruined knee collapsed beneath him on the second swing, and the other woman clawed up his body until she was able to bite out his throat.

"Marco!" cried the downed cop, still trying to see as Rosa pushed him back to the pavement.

"He's doing his job," she said, hearing sirens and the beat of a helicopter in the distance. "How we doing, Jimmy?"

No reply.

She looked up and saw Jimmy on his back, eyes wide and sightless as a bloody fireman crouched over him, pulling red insides out of the medic's body and cramming them into his mouth.

"Jimmy!" She bolted to her feet and ran toward them. The fireman looked up from feeding with glassy yellow eyes and growled. Jimmy's body twitched. Rosa screamed his name again and ran back to the cop, ripping the nine-millimeter from his holster as he shouted a protest. She quickly checked the chamber and flicked off the safety, more than familiar with the weapon after a full tour in Iraq as a Navy corpsman assigned to combat Marines. Rosa walked to the thing eating her friend. "Fucker," she whispered, and shot it in the forehead.

Her partner twitched again, and she let out a cry of relief, dropping to her knees beside him. "I'm here, Jimmy." She started to cry. "I'm right here, baby."

An off-key chorus of moans came from her right, and Rosa turned to see the axe-wielding fireman hobbling toward her on a shattered knee, his throat a raw, red void with flaps of esophagus hanging out of it. The Asian woman who had killed him lurched a step behind, and then more shapes, firemen and civilians and one of the cops from the empty cruiser they had seen when they arrived—all of them torn apart—shuffled out from behind a nearby Dumpster and one of the big red-and-chrome trucks. Her attention, however, was drawn to the decapitated cop's head, lying on one ear and looking at her with filmy eyes. Its jaw worked silently, snapping at nothing.

Rosa turned and ran.

The cop Rosa had treated propped himself up on his elbows and saw what was coming. "Holy Christ!" He clawed for the hideout pistol strapped to his ankle and fired four times, hitting and missing, but stopping nothing, and then scrambled to his feet and ran into the deepening gloom.

Rosa jumped into the ambulance without bothering to shut any of the doors, watching the cop run away. She thought of how the Marines she had served with never left anyone behind, how they had ingrained that philosophy into their corpsmen, the Navy medics they all called "Doc." But that was war, and this was some hellish nightmare, a drug addict's dark fantasy.

And yet Jimmy had moved.

No, he couldn't be alive after what she had seen. None of them could.

A moment later a bloody palm slapped against the windshield and she screamed. Rosa wedged the cop's pistol between her thigh and the seat, threw the ambulance into a rocking, three-point turn, and seconds later was roaring away from the scene. She began whispering a Hail Mary as tears ran down her face.

A police helicopter—one of the few remaining since San Francisco decommissioned all but a few of its fleet years earlier—hovered slowly up Main Street. It paused to put a spotlight on the ambulance parked at a curb with its emergency lights flashing and rear doors hanging open. The beat of the downdraft whipped the trees along the nearby sidewalk, blowing leaves off limbs, and then the chopper moved on.

Rosa was in the driver's seat, knees pulled up to her chest and arms wrapped tightly about them, rocking and crying. Jimmy was dead. She had left him there, and he was dead. She had run away. Her sobs filled the cab where there had once been two voices as she pressed her face against her knees, body shaking. Headlights slid by, but no one stopped.

Only a few blocks away from the slaughter, she stayed there for fifteen minutes, until her tears stopped and her hands quit shaking. She called her mother's house, but there was no answer. She got out, closed the rear doors, and returned to the driver's seat.

The radio was going mad. Calls to 911 and chattering code filled the airwaves, excited voices calling for more units, for Life Flight, for police and fire. Gunfire sounded in the background of some of the calls. And screams. The dispatcher called for Jimmy and Rosa's unit, eager to send them on another call. Rosa ignored the radio.

Main was a one-way street, and she took it up across Mission, leaving the emergency lights on and banging the siren built into the rig's horn to clear traffic. Around her, all appeared normal, people out at night unaware of the madness she had left behind. At the intersection of Market, however, she came to a full stop. SFPD was setting up yellow sawhorses, their cars crowding the street, all of their attention focused on the wide, brightly lit entrance to the Embarcadero BART station. Every officer seemed to be carrying a shotgun. One of them saw her at the corner and waved her in.

Rosa had no intention of getting involved in whatever this was, so she eased forward slowly, maneuvering around a sawhorse, aiming for the street on the far side of the intersection. She was a third of the way across when bodies spilled out of the BART station entrance, hundreds of them, mostly dressed in business attire that had once been pressed and sharp but was now bloody and torn. They staggered and lurched, pressing forward even though most had great chunks of flesh torn from their bodies, others with limbs twisted at painful angles or missing altogether.

A pair of tear gas canisters was fired into their midst. The crowd pushed through, more flowing out of the station behind them. A bullhorn command was given, and Rosa jumped as a volley of shotgun and pistol fire exploded into the crowd.

They didn't slow.

More firing, and then the crowd was spreading out, tipping over barricades and pawing their way down the sides of police cars, cops falling back as the torn and bloodied commuters slammed into them like a wall, moaning and clutching and biting. Rosa stomped the accelerator and shot across the intersection. A young woman in what had once been a smart gray business suit—now with half her face torn away and her lower jaw missing—stumbled in front of the rig as Rosa hit the gas. She bounced off the grille with a thump and went flying. The medic bit her lip and kept the accelerator down.

The traffic headed her way in the opposite lane was stopped and backed up as Rosa traveled down Drumm Street, then took a pair of lefts until she reached Pine, another one-way that cut straight across the city. Straight toward home. Voices on the radio were still calling for help, a few of them even crying, and the dispatcher was demanding that all available units respond to a police and National Guard emergency on Market, not far from where Rosa's ambulance was racing away in the opposite direction.

She shut the radio off.

A traffic accident appeared in an intersection ahead, and she swerved around it, keeping her eyes fixed forward, refusing to look at the dazed, bloody faces watching in disbelief as she drove past without slowing. At Montgomery Street a pair of SFPD cars were blocking cross traffic while uniformed soldiers uncoiled barbed wire across Pine. Rosa tapped the horn and bluffed her way through. She passed a park on the right a few minutes later, and saw shadowy figures stalking through the trees in pursuit of a homeless man struggling to push a heaped shopping cart over grass and tree roots. They were gaining on him.

Just past the Stockton Tunnel she rolled up on the back end of stopped traffic, the flames of a fully engulfed apartment house half a block beyond turning the early evening orange and red. Rosa used the siren again and bullied her way to the next intersection, driving with two wheels on the sidewalk, and then cut up two blocks before circling around and coming back to Pine, on the other side of the fire.

Her mother's phone continued to ring unanswered, and she redialed three times with the same result. A minute later the chirp of an incoming call caused her to quickly hit the Answer button without looking to see who it was.

"Petty Officer Escobedo, please."

"Speaking." She was startled to hear a man's voice, not her mother's.

"This is the CINCPAC watch officer. Your reserve unit has been activated, and you are ordered to report immediately to Oakland Middle Harbor, USNS *Comfort*. Acknowledge the order, Petty Officer."

Rosa took a deep breath. "Report to USNS *Comfort* immediately, Oakland Middle Harbor. Understood."

"Very well, Petty Officer." The call disconnected.

Rosa resisted the urge to throw the phone at the windshield, cursing softly. The ambulance reached the Pacific Heights neighborhood and she turned north, shutting off the emergency lights and quickly reaching her mother's block. She slowed as the headlights revealed the scene.

Luggage, clothing, and cardboard boxes littered the pavement and sidewalks, and there was only empty curb on a street where it was normally difficult to find a parking space. The well-kept, three-story row houses blazed with light, but there was no movement in any of the windows. Most of the front doors stood open.

Rosa stopped in front of her mother's building and got out, tucking the cop's automatic in her back waistband. In the distance she could hear sirens and the thump of a helicopter, but this neighborhood was quiet. She climbed the steps and went into the first-floor apartment. That door was standing open too, and a note was waiting on the kitchen table.

Rosa,

The Army is putting us in trucks to keep us safe from the rioting. We are going to the Presidio, and should be home soon. My phone is dead, forgot to charge it. Will call you soon.

Love, Mom

Rosa went back to the street and stopped on the sidewalk when she saw a soldier standing near the ambulance's front grille, arms hanging limp, swaying from side to side. He didn't have a weapon or a helmet and the headlights revealed that one of his hands was nothing but ragged, chewed stumps instead of fingers. His uniform was charred, and even at this distance she could smell fire.

The soldier lifted his head, blank eyes glistening in the headlights. He made a mournful sound and then started toward her. He moved the same way as those she had seen at the scene where she lost Jimmy, and the word *plague* popped into her medic's mind. Rosa ran into the street to the right, the soldier turning to follow her, stumbling on the curb but keeping his footing. Once she had enough distance Rosa pulled the automatic and took a shooting stance, gripping it in two hands. "Stay back."

The soldier moaned and kept moving.

Rosa fired twice, hitting him center mass. The soldier twitched with the impact but didn't slow. She fired again, aiming right at the heart, and still the soldier lurched forward, faster now as he raised his hands and emitted a ragged hiss.

Body armor, she thought, raising her aim an inch and shooting him in the face. The soldier dropped immediately and didn't move. A moment later Rosa was back in the rig heading north on Divisidero Street and following the most direct route to the closed Army base at the Presidio. Whatever was going on, she had no intention of entrusting her mother to some half-assed refugee camp.

Four blocks later she realized it didn't matter.

The convoy of four trucks and an escorting Humvee was stopped in an intersection, three of the big vehicles burning and lighting the neighborhood in a ghastly orange hue. A dozen bodies lay sprawled on the pavement amid scattered shell casings, the brass reflecting the jumping flames. Dozens more bodies blackened by fire or stumbling about with missing limbs and mortal wounds filled the street.

Other shapes were floundering amid the fire in the back of one of the trucks.

One of them tumbled out and hit the ground, hair and clothing lit like a torch, blackened skin blistering as it pulled taut. The thing crawled toward the ambulance and raised its head, the heat peeling its lips back from its teeth. It reached with one hand, and in the headlights Rosa recognized the silver charm bracelet her mother had refused to take off since her daughter gave it to her at the age of fifteen.

. . .

Rosa's apartment was only six blocks from her mother's, and by the time she got there she had almost convinced herself that it hadn't been Marta Escobedo falling out of that truck, crawling as she burned. It couldn't have been. That would mean Rosa had driven off without even trying to help, and she would never have left her mother like that. So she simply turned those thoughts off. It was a skill she had developed on the pole at the Glass Slipper Gentlemen's Club: the ability to put aside the most unpleasant parts of life, to dismiss the hungry faces and drunken offers from the edge of the stage, to turn off the shame she felt every time she danced.

This neighborhood was quiet too, the streets and sidewalks empty. Rosa left the ambulance running out front while she went in. There was no roommate to disturb—she lived alone—and she quickly changed into her uniform: blue camouflage and cap, combat boots, the insignia for a Navy corpsman pinned to her collar tabs. Her sea bag was already packed and waiting in the closet, filled with clothes and toiletries, and minutes later she was back in the rig. She didn't bother to lock her front door. She suspected she wouldn't be back.

Rosa's 2007 Toyota Corolla was tucked in a small garage behind the apartment, but she left it there. The lights and siren of an ambulance would get her past obstacles the Toyota couldn't. She headed back across the city, toward the Bay Bridge.

The civilian radio channels were jammed with breaking news, talk of rioting and looters, and there were reports of savage attacks across the city. Police spokesmen assured the public that they had the situation in hand, but as midnight approached and Rosa drove through the heart of San Francisco, she saw things that strongly contradicted that statement. Buildings were on fire and no one had shown up to put them out; squad cars pushed past car accidents, leaving dazed victims waving in the street, just as she had done; looters were already at work, small groups but sometimes larger crowds smashing windows and kicking open doors, carrying their prizes into the night.

At one point Rosa was forced to stop for another accident, looking for a way around it, and a teenager with a knit cap charged the ambulance with a can of spray paint in each hand. He slid to a stop in front of the windshield, shaking the cans as he waggled his tongue and screamed something she couldn't make out. He managed to spray a single red line down the passenger-side glass before Rosa leaned out the driver's door with the automatic and fired a round into the asphalt near his feet. The kid yipped like a kicked dog and skittered away.

Near Fell Street she had to stop again, this time the way completely blocked by a stopped garbage truck, the driver on his hands and knees beside one of the tires, crying and vomiting. A body was pinned beneath the tire, a young man hopelessly mangled. But he was still moving, his mouth opening and closing as the fingers of one hand groped at the truck driver's shirtsleeve.

The driver saw the ambulance. "Help him!"

On reflex, Rosa grabbed the door handle to jump out. Then a body dropped from a building on the right, hitting the roof of an Altima, crushing it and blowing out the windows. The broken figure rolled off onto the pavement and started belly-crawling toward the truck driver. Two more bodies dropped from above, one exploding in bone and blood on the sidewalk, the other slamming down onto the sobbing garbage truck driver, killing him instantly with the impact.

Rosa reversed the rig and found another route.

Her ability to switch off her thoughts went into overdrive, trying to keep her from facing the how and why of what was happening. She knew this was a childish and foolish way to deal with a dangerous reality, but another part of her insisted that to face it would lead to madness. Instead she locked thoughts of Jimmy and her mother and the rest of tonight's horrors into a room deep inside herself and focused on getting out of the city. She would report for duty in Oakland and lose herself in her work, safely immersed in the structure of military authority.

At the entrance to Highway 101, her access to the Bay Bridge, she was handed a reality check about her ideas of safety and structure. Traffic was bunched up in every direction, people flashing their lights and leaning on horns. At the on-ramp, a desert camouflage M1 main battle tank was backing off a flatbed tractor-trailer behind a sandbag barricade still being erected by hurrying soldiers. To the right, police and fire lights spun as a team of firemen trained a high-pressure hose on a crowd of people trying to reach the bridge. Bodies fell and tumbled away from the stream. To the left, an eight-wheeled armored vehicle with a small turret, a Marine LAV-25, armed with a twenty-five-millimeter Bushmaster chain gun, rolled slowly toward the roadblock.

A bloody man and woman staggered in front of it. The LAV rolled over them without stopping, crushing their bodies beneath its big tires.

Rosa hit the emergency lights and sirens, thinking she might get the stopped traffic to part, bluffing her way through another roadblock. The cars didn't move, but the turret of the battle tank rotated in her direction even as the armored vehicle backed off the truck, settling the cavernous muzzle of its 120-millimeter main gun on Rosa's windshield.

The sight of that death-bringer nearly released her bladder, and she reversed quickly, turning and heading back the direction she had come, finding her way to Mission Street. She headed for the water and the ferry plaza, just off the Embarcadero.

It was after 1:00 A.M. when she pulled into the packed lot, and she left the rig in a fire lane as she grabbed her sea bag and hurried inside. Rosa immediately saw the troops and cops, heard sounds from the main terminal room with which she was familiar: cries of the wounded and calls for help. The high-ceilinged chamber echoed with shouts and groans and smelled of blood and antiseptic.

A man in green-and-gray camouflage with brushy silver hair and a doctor's coat saw Rosa, spotted the medical insignia on her collar, and pointed at her. "Corpsman! Over here, now!"

Rosa dropped her bag and dove in.

TWO

"How long were you there?" Xavier asked.

Rosa guided the harbor patrol boat across the bay, windshield wipers slapping against the rain, her eyes moving between what lay ahead and what was revealed on the green surface radar mounted near the wheel. She was surprised at the way she had opened up to this man she had just met. He was in his forties with close-cropped hair, his upper body a V of imposing, packed muscle, and his brown face was marred by a long, cruel scar. At first glance, he was someone to be feared. His eyes, however, held a gentleness that pulled her in. He reminded her of Jimmy in subtle ways, his ability to truly listen, not just wait for his turn to talk like most people did. Attractive women could easily tell when a man was listening and when his mind was elsewhere. Xavier listened. He made her feel that nothing in existence was more important than what she had to say. It was a trait she had experienced with only one other person in her life, a beloved uncle long since passed, thankfully before all this.

"Weeks," she said. "I lost track of the days; they blurred together." She thought about the big ferry terminal, transformed into a trauma center. "It was a nightmare. We tried to help, but nothing could turn back that fever. Every single person who got bitten died, no matter what we did, and then they turned. All of them. We lost medics and doctors to our own patients before we figured it out."

Xavier tried to picture what she was describing. The horror of it was easy to imagine. More difficult was imagining going through the experience without being scarred, as she most certainly was. How could she not be?

She went on. "For a while the soldiers just started executing anyone coming in with a bite. The doctors went crazy, ordered them to stop, and one Army surgeon even pulled a sidearm. We almost had a war right there in the terminal. It didn't matter. We couldn't save them, not the bitten ones."

As the boat thumped over low swells, Rosa's eyes keeping on the alert, she told him about the horrors she had witnessed. Xavier just listened, keeping his own horrors to himself. Rosa talked of seeing men in biohazard suits, soldiers gunning down looters, buildings on fire and cars exploding, even watching as a helicopter suddenly dropped out of the sky and crashed somewhere in the Telegraph Hill neighborhood, its fireball climbing above the rooftops. She spoke of seeing the exodus of ships and smaller boats from San Francisco Bay, about how she and a few others had tried to signal from the roof of the ferry terminal, and how none of the boats detoured from their escape.

Rosa spoke of the dead, sometimes thousands of them in the street, crashing into the terminal in relentless waves, soldiers firing out every door and window to the point that she thought the gunfire would never end. Yet other times they were scattered or gone altogether, leaving the barricaded survivors with no answer as to their whereabouts. She described the eerie sight of their silhouettes moving within the fog, lonely moans echoing through empty streets.

Her cheeks were wet by now, and Xavier rested a big hand gently on her shoulder. She didn't pull away. "Little by little there were fewer people at the terminal," she said. "There were casualties during the attacks, of course. And when the streets were clear, cops and soldiers would go out to gather supplies or look for survivors. Most never came back. The doctors began slipping away in the night too, taking food and weapons and sneaking out." She wiped at her eyes. "Except for that older doc, the one who first called me over to help, the same guy who pulled his weapon on the other soldiers. He was a colonel. He didn't sneak away. He found a janitor's closet and put that pistol in his mouth to make sure he didn't come back."

Her voice shuddered at the edge of more tears, but she fought them back. "After a while there were only a few of us left." She nodded at the pregnant couple and Darius. "There were a few patients too. When they turned, I took care of them."

Rosa didn't speak for a while, and there was only the growl of the motor and the whispery thump of water on fiberglass. Xavier didn't speak, only stared out at the bay and felt ashamed for the times he had pitied himself these past weeks, as if he were the only one who had lived through the nightmare.

The young woman suddenly brightened. "One of my patients was a cop, a horseback officer, or whatever they're called. He and his unit had been doing mounted crowd control, and they got hit by a wave of the dead. It ended up being hand-to-hand combat, and he got some of their blood in his eyes. He had the fever, all the symptoms, but by then the doctors weren't letting anyone kill them until they turned."

"If he was down with the fever," Xavier asked, "how do you know what happened to him?"

She smiled. "Because he made it! He pulled through. That's when the doctors started talking about something they started calling the slow burn, when we discovered that sometimes a person who had been exposed but not bitten could survive. Most of the time they didn't, but it could happen."

Xavier thought about that. Was it cause for hope? Or a setup for even greater disappointment and grief?

Rosa laughed. "Do you know that when he came out of it, the first thing he asked about was his horse?" She laughed again, but it turned into a choking sob.

Xavier kept his arm firmly around her. "What happened to the officer?"

There was a pause, and when she spoke her voice was flat. "As soon as he could walk, he left. Said he had to find his wife and kids. He made it fifty feet into the street before they took him down." She pulled away then, though not abruptly. "They tore him to pieces, and all I could do was watch."

The harbor craft hit some steeper waves, rising and falling more sharply. Alameda grew in the windshield before them. Above, the sky was a brawling mass of black and charcoal clouds, and the rain began to fall faster and with more strength. The new intensity of the downpour was more than Darius and the pregnant couple could tolerate, and now that the newcomer on the boat appeared to pose no threat, they hunched against the slashing rain and moved between Xavier and Rosa, going down into a small cabin in the bow.

"How did you come by this?" Xavier asked, rapping his knuckles against the fiberglass.

"We've only had it since this morning," she said. "It was adrift and just floated into one of the ferry berths. There was no one on board, just a lot of blood and a half-full fuel tank." She shrugged. "I guess all that basic seamanship training is finally paying off."

The priest gave her a small smile. "Lucky for me. Thanks again." After losing Alden—the schoolteacher with a heart condition and Xavier's last friend in the world, it seemed—Xavier had quickly become cornered by the dead at a San Francisco marina. Corpses had swarmed toward him down a narrow dock, trapping him at the end, and it looked like he would go down swinging a tire iron. Then Rosa had appeared with her boat, saving his life. Of course once he was out of the water and on the deck, Darius had tried to take his life, but the shotgun was empty, and Xavier had been spared a second time.

"Finding you was an accident," Rosa said with a shrug. "We were looking for a fuel pump, and then we were going to try for San Jose. There was talk of a refugee center down there." She pointed forward. "An actual helicopter sighting trumps a rumor, though, don't you think?"

"No argument."

"Are you really a priest?" She wanted to say that his size and frightening scar made him look more like a gang enforcer, but she didn't want to be rude. She held back a smile. Even at the end of the world, being polite was still important.

"Yes. . . . I guess." When she raised an eyebrow at that, he pushed on. "Are you really a paramedic and Navy Reservist about to enter med school and paying the bills with exotic dancing?"

She laughed. "When you put it all together I guess it's a lot. You sound like Jimmy. He's—was my partner on the rig." Rosa looked sideways at him. "Are you going to lecture me about how my dancing is a sin and all that, Father?"

"Let's stick to Xavier, okay? I'm not the person to judge another on what she does to survive. I'm more interested in your medical training." He told her he had been a Marine in Somalia and said the grunts had nothing but respect for the corpsmen that went into combat with them. He did not tell her that while over there, he had shot down two boys not even old enough to be out of elementary school. They had AK-47s and meant to kill Xavier and his squad so it was considered a justified shooting by many, but that was small comfort for a young Marine overcome with guilt. His inability to reconcile himself with the killing had ended his military career.

Rosa told him her unit had spent a year in Iraq, and that although female medics weren't allowed out on the patrols, an aid station she was operating in a supposedly "secure" town was suddenly hit by insurgents, and she found herself firing back right alongside the men.

"Did the Navy give you your Combat Action Ribbon?"

She nodded.

"Well, then Semper Fi." That made her smile, and the priest smiled back. "So why don't you try to call me Xavier?"

"That's going to be tough," she said. "I'm Catholic."

Xavier nodded at that. "Do your best. I'll call you Doc, if that's all right?"

"Sure," Rosa said. She pointed at the landmass ahead of them in the fading light, a darker strip against a turbulent sky. "The helo set down on the west end of the island, where the naval air station used to be. Somewhere up ahead are the piers where the ships came in, where the *Hornet* is now. I figure we can dock there, and go on foot to the airfield."

Xavier nodded. "And the dead?"

"If it doesn't look safe at the docks we can cruise the water's edge," Rosa said, "maybe tie up at some rocks and force our way through the perimeter fence."

"That sounds good. And if the dead get too numerous . . . ?"

"Then we haul ass back to the boat," she finished.

"Okay, Doc, what do you need from me?"

"Tell Darius to give you that shotgun and the extra shells. No offense, but it's better off in the hands of a former Marine than with a sociology professor who can't manage to kill a man lying on the deck in front of him," Rosa said, recalling the moment Xavier had climbed out of the cold waters of the bay. He had been shaking and Darius was convinced it meant that the man was infected. He aimed and pulled the trigger on his shotgun, but hadn't realized he had fired his last shell. Xavier took the weapon away from him, and Rosa thought the man showed tremendous restraint by not giving the professor a beating or simply throwing him over the side. She winked, revealing that there was still some humor and life left in her. "After your little moment together on deck," she said, "I don't think he'll give you a problem about it."

Darius didn't. He handed over the weapon, half a box of shells, and another round of apologies. Xavier gave him a smile and told him to relax, which seemed to make the man feel better. When the priest returned to the deck, Rosa pointed to ten o'clock.

"We're not going to be alone," she said.

Ahead were the Alameda naval piers, marking the entrance to a sheltered bay Rosa had described. The silhouettes of retired cruisers and destroyers were overshadowed by the much larger shape of the USS *Hornet*, a World War II aircraft carrier permanently moored at the piers and transformed into a museum.

Approaching the small bay from the left, staying close to the shoreline, was a barge coughing out a cloud of black diesel. At their present speeds, both vessels would reach the mouth of the little bay at the same time. The barge's flat deck was packed with people crowded around a blue truck. All of them were looking at the patrol boat, their weapons raised.

THREE

Evan Tucker piloted the crowded maintenance barge along the south-
ern edge of the old naval air station, scanning the rocky shoreline for
a suitable landing spot. Twenty-five and good-looking, he had blue
eyes and black hair down to his collar. Dressed in faded jeans, a denim
jacket, and work boots, he looked the part of the wandering writer,
traveling America's roads as he dreamed of crafting the Great American Novel. In the weeks since the outbreak he had gone from vaga-
bond loner to leader.

Out on deck, Calvin and his Family hunched against the rain,
many seeking shelter behind the mass of the armored Bearcat riot
vehicle. Calvin, a fiftyish hippie with an Australian bush hat and
heavily armed, had thus far managed to keep the Family alive. The
Family was his collection of free-spirited relatives and friends living
a gypsy lifestyle. Their lack of dependency on modern conveniences
had made them all the more resilient in what had become of the world.

Maya pressed close against Evan, resting her head on his shoulder.
Her silent reassurance was calming, and he needed that now. She was
a few years younger than him, with long dark hair and sapphire eyes.
Maya had been deaf and mute since birth, but she and the young

writer had no trouble communicating their feelings for one another. Her father, Calvin, approved.

The barge was rocking hard, taking the rhythmic surges of the bay full along its right side. They were exposed to more powerful waters out here, a forceful wind hammering them with rain and sudden, unexpected gusts, and yet again Evan was reminded that the long, flat vessel had never been intended for more than puttering about a placid harbor. He was forced to slow down for fear that a wave would tip them over, just as his imagination had pictured, and that action prolonged their exposure and increased the odds of catastrophe.

Though it had occurred less than an hour ago, their narrow escape from the relentless horde of the walking dead on the Oakland pier felt to Evan as if it had happened in another lifetime. For him now there was only the struggle to keep the barge level and on course, and to keep watch out the wheelhouse windows, praying for something more than rock and fence and windblown weeds.

After another hour of achingly slow chugging, during which time Evan's arm, shoulder, and neck muscles had begun to cramp from his fight with the wheel, shapes in the distance began to materialize out of the rain. As the barge drew nearer, the shapes resolved into a pair of huge concrete piers with vintage gray warships and an old carrier tied to them. Evan let out a laugh, and Maya hugged him from behind. To the left of the piers was a large, rectangular lagoon notched into the Navy base, framed by a cement wall. A buoy floated near the entrance with a rusty yellow sign on it reading *SEAPLANES* above an arrow pointing into the lagoon. Evan slowed further as voices out on deck started shouting. With the armored van parked beside the wheelhouse he couldn't see the cause of the commotion, but a moment later Calvin's brother Dane, wearing a blond ponytail to the center of his back and armed with a lever-action rifle, appeared at the window.

"There's a boat coming in from the right. It looks like a police boat."

"You guys will have to handle it if things go bad," Evan said. "I'm heading for that lagoon."

"Got it." Dane disappeared.

The rocking lessened as Evan passed the buoy and angled into the lagoon, aiming for a long, newer-looking dock—empty of boats— leading back toward shore and a cluster of white buildings around a small boatyard. The only vessel in sight was a weathered charter-fishing boat perched on metal stands in an extreme state of disassembly. What appeared to be its motor sat on a plywood worktable nearby, taken completely apart.

Dane returned to the window. "It's definitely a police boat, but I don't think they're cops. There's only a few people on deck, and they started waving when we got close to each other. They're following us in."

"Keep an eye on them," Evan said, still not quite comfortable with giving orders. "And get some guns up front. I'm going to bring us in slow, and I want a warning if anyone sees drifters. I'm not taking us into another death trap."

"Calvin's already on it." He disappeared again.

Evan scanned the approach. The old warships were far to the right now, and ahead, an access road appeared to run beside the concrete lip at the water's edge. Derelict buildings with peeling paint lined the other side of the road, each identical to the next. He saw nothing moving on shore, and no one called out. It was small comfort, and he thought of the elderly zombie he had seen rattling the fence. The old drifter wouldn't be the only one of his kind here.

He throttled back and guided the barge along the side of the dock, hitting it harder than he intended, the impact throwing several people off their feet but thankfully none into the water. The barge made a long scraping sound as it slowed, causing the dock to shudder and splinter in places, and Evan cursed, certain he was going to tear the entire length of boards and pilings apart. He wished for brakes and killed the engine. The left bow struck a sturdy piling and stopped the barge with a wrenching blow, resulting in alarmed cries. In seconds a handful of hippies were tying off, others with rifles leaping onto the dock and going ahead while parents helped their children off the barge.

"We'll take care of your hog," Dane shouted back to the wheelhouse, and immediately a group of men muscled the Harley Road King onto the dock, another carefully walking it ahead toward land. Evan and Maya walked out onto the deck, preparing to join the others.

Carney, one of the two escaped San Quentin inmates on the barge, caught up to Evan and stopped him before he could follow. They had spoken only briefly back in Oakland. "I didn't get your name. You in charge of this group?"

Evan shook his head and pointed at Calvin, who was helping his wife, Faith, with their kids. "I'm Evan, just tagging along." He introduced Maya.

"Uh-huh." He pointed to an enormous, muscled Viking of a man covered in prison ink, with long blond hair, his cellmate of many years. "That's TC. I'm Carney." He left out their last long-term address. "We're going to need this," he said, jerking a thumb back at the Bearcat, its idling engine still knocking.

Evan looked at the truck, then at the narrow dock, feeling foolish. "Right. There's got to be a boat ramp around here. I'll beach this thing and you can drive off." He failed to register that the side of the vehicle said *CALIFORNIA D.O.C.*

Carney nodded and went back to the truck. TC stood on the deck, smiling at the writer. Evan didn't care for that smile, though he couldn't say why. He helped Maya up onto the dock and then started untying the lines that secured the barge.

"I'll ride with you," said Calvin, standing near the bow, wrists draped comfortably over the assault rifle hanging around his neck, rain dripping from the rim of his outback hat. He had noticed what was on the side of the truck and easily made the connection with these two big, tattooed men. "If these fellows decide to go their own way, you won't be left walking by yourself." Calvin was looking not at Evan as he spoke, but at TC.

The smile slid off the inmate's face, and his eyes glittered with something unpleasant.

On the other side of the dock, Rosa and Xavier had pulled in shortly after the barge, the Navy Reservist bringing the patrol boat in smoothly. They tied off as their passengers hurried to join the hippies on shore, ducking against the rain.

"I'm a little worried about leaving the boat unguarded," Rosa said softly, glancing at the crowd of unexpected company.

"So take the keys," said the priest. "If all goes well with the helicopter, we won't be back anyway." He slung the shotgun and climbed off. Rosa hung a bright orange nylon satchel over her shoulder and followed.

On the barge, Calvin spotted the bold red cross on the side of Rosa's bag. "Hey, are you a doctor?" When the woman shrugged, he pointed at the armored Bearcat. "There's a really sick girl in there. Could you take a look at her?"

TC gave Calvin a look that Carney noticed from the cab of the truck. It was a look he was familiar with from their days at the state prison, and it never meant anything good for the person on the receiving end.

"I'll go with you," Xavier said, and followed Rosa onto the barge. Carney climbed out of the cab and took them to the rear doors, opening them and gesturing to the young woman bound and gagged on the floor. Calvin joined them. The barge's diesel fired, and Evan backed slowly from the dock.

The medic looked inside to see a girl—a woman, actually, probably not even twenty—lying on the floor, hands, feet, and mouth secured. She wore a mix of fatigues and civilian clothing. Rosa climbed in and crouched beside her, looking over the gag and zip ties to be certain they were secure. She recognized the restlessness and sweating, felt the heat coming off her. "When was she bitten?"

"I don't think she was," Carney said. "She got brains and blood in her face, definitely in her mouth, probably her eyes too."

"No bites?" Rosa pulled on rubber gloves and produced a pair of surgical scissors, cutting away the girl's clothes. She didn't see any bite wounds. "When did this happen?"

"This morning," said Carney, "in Oakland. We got her out of a church where she was playing sniper." Then he remembered the many bodies in the street, and the accuracy with which she killed. Perhaps *playing* wasn't the right word. "She's been like this since."

Rosa checked her watch. It was hard to see as the storm chased the last of the daylight from the sky, and the rear of the truck didn't have a dome light that came on when the doors opened. She figured maybe nine hours. "Any vomiting?"

"Not that I've seen," said Carney. He looked around for TC. The man was nowhere in sight.

Rosa shook her head. "It's unlikely. If she'd done it with this gag in place, she'd have choked to death."

Carney looked back into the truck. "She's sick, probably the virus." He pointed. "That gag stays in place."

"No argument," said Rosa. She lifted the girl's eyelids one at a time. The right eye was clear and white, but the left had a milky, yellow tint, and the pupil was both enlarged and a cloudy blue, like a cataract. She wrapped the girl in a blanket she found draped over a cardboard case of peanut butter. "We'll know in another twelve to fifteen hours," she said, climbing out of the truck. "She'll have to be watched. If she starts to vomit, we'll have to get that gag off and clear her airway."

Carney shook his head. "I don't know why I saved her in the first place, and I sure don't know why I've kept her with us this long. She's going to turn into one of those things. What's the point?"

"Doc, what will we know in twelve to fifteen hours?" Xavier asked.

"Whether she's going to pull through," said Rosa. "It could be the slow burn I told you about, exposure to infected fluids from something other than a bite. Inside twenty-four hours the victim either comes out of the fever, or turns."

No one spoke as that sank in, the sway of the barge rocking them all gently.

"You mean she could live?" asked Carney. "What are her chances?"

Rosa shrugged. "Not great. I saw only a few cases, and only one that lived." She glanced back at the girl. "I'll stay with her, if that's okay."

Carney nodded.

"What's her name?" asked Xavier.

"I have no idea," said Carney, walking back along the side of the truck. The priest, medic, and hippie exchanged glances, followed by introductions. Calvin quickly filled them in on their odyssey into Oakland, and how Evan had come to be with them. Xavier found that he liked Calvin at once, attracted to his easygoing, confident manner. He was clearly a person to whom people looked for answers and guidance, and the priest suspected he would be a good man to have around in a crisis.

The journey to a nearby boat ramp took only a few minutes. "Coming in now," Evan called from the wheelhouse, and a moment later the barge shuddered as its hull slid up onto angled cement. Carney soon had the Bearcat riot vehicle they had taken from the prison on the access road beside the lagoon.

The large hippie family joined them minutes later, having paused to break open some snack and soda vending machines back at what turned out to be a yacht mooring, sales, and maintenance facility. A bearded young man named Mercury pushed Evan's Harley up beside the Bearcat, as Xavier and Rosa climbed out to join the group. Carney walked up a moment later, but TC stayed in the truck. Watchful eyes scanned the vacant buildings as evening came on fast under a stormy sky.

"If my sense of direction is right," said Evan, "the helicopter landed somewhere over there." He pointed to the northeast, across the lagoon. Warehouses and hangars stood in gray rows where he was pointing, some with streets between them, all with darkened windows.

Rosa nodded. "The airfield is over that way." When this drew some looks, she said, "I live in San Francisco and I'm in the Navy. I've never been here, but the place isn't a secret. It's huge, though. If we're going, we need to move. It's getting dark."

"Maybe we should wait until morning," said Faith, holding her and Calvin's ten- and twelve-year-old sons close to her sides. "We never travel at night." Her face, worn from years on the road but normally warm and welcoming, had a strained, cornered look.

"I doubt anyone does," said Evan, looking around. Everyone shook their heads. "But can we risk waiting and having that helicopter take off before we get there?" More looks, more shaking heads.

"He's right," said Calvin. "We'll stay close together, guns on the outside, and keep moving." The hippie looked at Carney. "You coming?"

Carney paused, then nodded.

"Maybe you could drive slowly ahead of us, let your headlights show us what's coming?"

Another nod.

Calvin nodded back. "Couldn't help but notice the firepower you've got in that truck. Spreading it around could—"

"We're not drinking buddies just yet," said the con, his lip curling. "You keep your people close to the truck, and we'll see what happens."

"I'll scout ahead," said Evan, climbing onto the Harley with Maya. Xavier and Rosa returned to the back of the Bearcat, and minutes later the group was moving slowly through the abandoned naval base, the taillight and engine noise of Evan's Road King vanishing in the thickening gloom of twilight.

In the cab of the rumbling Bearcat, Carney glanced at his cellmate. TC just grinned at him, planted his boots on the dashboard, and cracked open a Red Bull.

FOUR

Naval Air Station Alameda—now called Alameda Point—closed in
1997. Before that, its 2,500 acres had served naval aircraft and provided a berthing for Pacific Fleet ships since before World War II. It
was made up of over thirty miles of road and three hundred buildings,
from hangars and machine shops to barracks, administration facilities, and on-base housing for military families, as well as the infra-
structure to support them: shopping, theaters, barbershops, food
service, laundry, and recreation centers.

Over the years since its closing there had been several attempts
to create modern housing developments. It was, after all, prime waterfront real estate in a densely populated area. In each case, developers
had withdrawn—or been asked to—and so throughout the base were
signs of partial demolition and halted ground clearing. Many places
were still occupied by silent heavy equipment parked next to towering mounds of gravel and broken brick. Repurposing the base had
met with numerous complications. There were issues of soil and
groundwater contamination as a landfill in the southwest corner had
been found to contain PCBs and was the subject of a Superfund proj-
ect, as well as concerns over flood plans, local wildlife, and legal

issues. There were existing leases to consider, and a stubborn historical society that had hired some expensive lawyers and planted its feet, determined to hold its ground. The Naval Air Museum, which included stewardship for the World War II carrier *Hornet*, had proven a worthy adversary in the battle to reclaim the valuable property.

The old base wasn't entirely abandoned. Some buildings had been converted to fitness clubs, design studios, tech companies, auction houses, and nightclubs, as well as a training facility for the City of Alameda Fire Department. Several reality shows—*Angie's Armory* among them—regularly filmed out on the old runways when working with explosives. A plane crash had been staged there for one movie, and still another film company had actually constructed a great looping road around the airfield in order to film a car chase.

Most of the three hundred buildings, however, were vacant and decaying in the sea air. Cavernous hangars were home to pigeons and gulls; two- and three-story barracks sat behind dead, brown lawns while weeds grew unchallenged up through sidewalk cracks and asphalt. Vandals had had their way, broken windows and graffiti marring what had once been clean, uniform structures.

Back when it was a naval facility, a high, sturdy fence topped with razor wire had encircled the base, well maintained and regularly patrolled. Now, decades after the closing, the fence was in disrepair: cut or pulled aside in places by curious explorers, rusted and sagging in others, or missing altogether to permit demolition and the passage of bulldozers and dump trucks. The roads into the vacant blocks of the on-base housing sections were closed off only by sawhorse barricades and *No Trespassing* signs.

NAS Alameda was not secure. Despite its empty and remote nature, it was not free of the dead.

Calvin and his group followed the slow-moving Bearcat on foot as it traveled through the evening streets, keeping close together. They stopped only once, when they found a trio of landscaping trailers parked along a curb, loaded with lawn mowers and tools. They collected whatever they could find: spades, hedge clippers, long-handled limb saws, and scythes. Ragged and armed with these primitive weapons, they resembled a small, medieval army marching behind a siege engine, heading off to war.

In the rear of the armored truck, Xavier sat on a bench watching Rosa as she knelt beside the infected girl on the floor, cooling her forehead with a damp rag and checking her pulse every so often. He knew he should be praying for the girl, but he wasn't. He had told Rosa he was a priest, but was that really true? While ministering to Alden as he died, Xavier had thought that maybe he hadn't lost his faith after all and could possibly reclaim what he thought he had forsaken. When the dead had him cornered on that San Francisco dock, he had begun to pray, but did that mean anything? Was it only reflex, a habit? There had been no stunning revelation of faith, no sense of God's return to his life. As Rosa had pulled the patrol boat into the Alameda dock, he had stood ready with the shotgun not because he feared he would be facing the dead, but because of the armed strangers arriving on the barge ahead of them, his fellow man.

No, still not a priest. And now he was a liar as well.

He wondered what would become of the girl on the floor. She would turn, most likely, and have to be put down. Who would do it? Could he? Not if he had any hopes of regaining God's grace. He wondered about the men up front too. They didn't feel like corrections officers, and they had almost certainly come across this van and made it their own, filling it as they scavenged on the move. There was a hardness to them, a dangerous feeling with which he was familiar, and he decided it was more than a little likely that both they and the riot vehicle had come from the same place. They would require watching.

The seat rumbling beneath him, Xavier thought again about the God he had served for most of his adult life. Had He done all this and ended mankind? That was what he had been taught to believe, that everything was God's will, whether it made sense or not to men. It was all part of the mystery. But this . . . this nightmare. It flew in the face of the idea that He was a loving and merciful God. But then didn't most terrible events do that? School shootings and genocide, war and famine, even the gut-wrenching poverty and homelessness he had seen in the Tenderloin. Now this, the eradication of mankind at the hands—teeth—of the walking dead. It was enough to make a faithful man doubt. What chance did he have, a man with no faith at all?

The Bearcat rolled slowly through the base.

In the cab, TC glanced into the back, then leaned toward his cellmate, speaking in a whisper. "What the fuck are we doing?"

Carney glanced at him. "Looking for a helicopter."

"We're supposed to be looking for Mexico, remember?"

"Yeah, I remember."

"So what the fuck?"

Carney looked at him from the corner of his eye, still keeping his attention on the road ahead. "What are you talking about?"

TC glanced in the back again. "It's supposed to be you and me, putting distance between us and high walls, man. How did we end up babysitting all these motherfuckers?"

"TC, you been sleeping this whole time? You know goddamn well how we got here."

"We're supposed to be free," the younger man pressed. "On the road and taking whatever we want. We don't answer to nobody no more. Now you're taking orders from that hippie like you were his—"

Carney's eyes turned to slits as he stared at his cellmate. "Say it. Go on, call me his bitch and see what happens."

TC looked away and said nothing.

Carney shoved the back of TC's head hard. When the younger man whipped back around, Carney bared his teeth. "You little punk. You think you're strong?" His voice was a snarl. "You think you'd even be alive if it wasn't for me? You'd still be cuffed to that bar, as dead as the rest of them."

TC started to say something, but Carney cut him off. "Any time you want to try me, boy, you just jump. Any . . . fucking . . . time."

The younger man looked back out the passenger window, his head down. When he spoke, it came out as a whine, but didn't quite sound genuine. "It ain't like that. You're my bro, and you know I appreciate everything you done for me, inside and out. But, you know, I'm just worried that you're gonna forget."

"About what?"

"Me. That you won't need me around."

"Oh, *bullshit*. Just keep playing with me, TC. I'll fuck you up for the fun of it."

The younger man looked at him then. "I'm afraid you're gonna forget that you can't trust *none* of them. You get that? These are the people who put us inside, these straight-up, law-and-order mother-fuckers. Just don't forget that they don't give a shit about people like us, man. Don't you ever forget it." He looked at his feet.

It had to be the most Carney had heard his cellmate say at one time that wasn't nonsense or just brainless chatter. But the dog was pulling hard at the chain, and Carney worried what would happen if it broke. "Look at me." TC did. "I run this show, boy. If I decide to give them our food or guns or any other damned thing, I'll do it. If I decide to drive away or steal that helicopter or waste the hippie, that's my deci-sion. It's my show. If you don't like it, you can get out right now."

TC looked back at his boots.

"And the next time you act like you want to throw down with me, you get ready to bleed. Now don't talk for a while."

Carney watched the headlights crawl down a vacant street that a sign at a corner identified as Avenue F. He suppressed a shudder, relieved that his cellmate was properly cowed once more, at least for the moment, and reminded himself to never forget what TC was: an animal, violent and dangerous, and most of all unpredictable. He could go from smiling to rage in a finger snap, and despite his hot-tempered challenge to the younger man, Carney wasn't at all con-vinced that if they went to war, he would come out on top.

And then there was the matter of what Calvin had told him, that he had interrupted TC when he was alone with the girl. Had something happened? Carney had warned his cellmate to stay away from her, threatened retribution if he didn't. How far was he prepared to go? He decided now wasn't the time, and besides, the girl was safe. That black dude with the scar looked like he could give TC a good fight if it came to that. And as for the girl, Carney still wasn't sure why he felt so protective. Was it because she was about how old his own daughter would have been if she hadn't choked to death as a toddler? No, he hadn't even known her. Was it because, inside, Carney had never been able to abide seeing the helpless have no one to take their side?

Bullshit, he told himself, curling his lip. Who was he to even try on high morals like that? Wasn't he the one who left a row of helpless men chained to a bar so they could be eaten by the dead? And hadn't it been him with that baseball bat in his hands, beating two people to death while they slept? Right, Bill Carnes, champion of the helpless. He wanted to spit. He was a killer and a convict, nothing more. Better to keep things in the short term, stay alert and stay alive, and figure things out as they came. Leave the philosophy to people who could swallow it without choking.

Ahead, the kid and his girl were sitting on their motorcycle, surrounded by enormous aircraft hangars and stopped in the street as it made a turn to the right, waiting for them to catch up. When the Bearcat trundled up to them, the kid gave a thumbs-up and motored down the new street, apparently the last one before the hangars gave way to the airfield beyond.

Carney checked his side mirror, saw that Calvin and his people were still behind him, and followed.

"A re these people with you?" Vladimir asked, looking across the airfield toward the single beam of a motorcycle and the lights of a larger truck behind it. They were several hundred yards away. The Russian helicopter pilot felt exposed, and wished he were airborne.

"I don't think so," Margaret Chu said slowly. "Elson! Jerry!" Standing near the white seniors van and the vintage Cadillac, the two men—one a lawyer, and the other, a rotund, stand-up comic named Jerry—retrieved a shotgun and handgun, and came to stand beside Margaret and the Russian near the helicopter. A high school–aged girl named Meagan, who didn't speak much and avoided direct eye contact, joined them. She carried a lawn mower blade as a weapon, and had refused to be parted from it since the day Angie West found her during a scouting trip and brought her into the group. The blade was stained red, and Meagan would not wipe it away.

Sophia, the self-appointed keeper of orphans, remained with the children in the van, and the others stayed close to the vehicles. Learning that the Black Hawk was not part of a larger force and was out of fuel had been crushing to every survivor who had come together under Angie's protection in the Alameda firehouse. They had left their sanctuary in hopes of rescue, but they had also been forced to leave because of one man's treachery.

Vladimir slipped his small automatic into his hand and held it low, just out of sight behind his leg. Extremely tall and homely, nicknamed Troll by his now-fallen military comrades, he towered over the small Asian woman beside him.

Margaret Chu checked the breech of her shotgun and put it to her shoulder, muzzle pointing at the pavement ten feet in front of her. In a short period of time she had gone from a passive, everyday person mildly afraid of firearms to a leader capable of more strength than even she thought possible. People looked to her for guidance and responded to her commands. Together, she and a man she had just met waited.

The Harley's powerful headlamp revealed the helicopter, two vehicles, and the people lined up between them. Evan slowed to an idle as he approached, stopping within shouting distance and climbing off with Maya.

"Who are you?" a woman yelled.

Evan held empty hands out to his sides. "My name is Evan Tucker; this is Maya. We saw the helicopter land." Headlights and the metallic banging of a sick engine approached from behind. "Those people are with us, families and children, mostly. We came from Oakland." He wasn't sure what else to say.

There was some conversation among the people by the chopper, and then a short woman with a shotgun and a tall man in a flight suit walked toward them. "I'm Margaret Chu; this is Vladimir." No one shook hands. "We have children with us too, so we need to make sure everyone is respectful and careful with the firearms. Do you understand my meaning?"

Evan nodded. No one wanted a mistake or sudden misunderstanding to end up in a close-range gunfight in front of a bunch of kids. "I'll tell the others, if that's okay?"

Margaret nodded, and Evan squeezed Maya's hand before jogging back toward the armored truck. Minutes later it was parked beside the Harley, and shortly after that Calvin's hippies and Rosa's boat refugees were mixing with the firehouse survivors. After some initial awkwardness, conversation took over. There was no aggression or suspicion, just frightened people finding others like themselves, relieved at the comfort that came from being in a large group of people with shared experiences. There was even some laughter, nervous at first, then genuine. Children from both groups found one another, and adults, strangers, stood together watching them play and interact, quietly marveling at their resiliency.

Hungry people from Calvin's group were given food from the Cadillac's supplies, and the few refugees who smoked drew off to one side to share their own unique camaraderie. There was a naturalness to it all, almost a feeling that such a reunion with other survivors had been expected, and welcomed. Xavier stood to the side watching, and felt a small measure of reaffirmation in his fellow man's capacity to care for one another in times of crisis. It was something he hadn't seen in a long time.

Xavier saw Carney, the armored truck's driver, and his big friend TC speaking with the helicopter pilot. TC slumped his shoulders and shuffled away when he got the bad news. It was the behavior of a child, Xavier thought, at odds with his size and dangerous presence, and it worried the priest.

"We need to tell them about the girl," Rosa said, coming to stand beside him. "We have to tell them one of us is infected, or we'll risk destroying this trust."

"How is she?"

"The same. Fever, delirium. The condition of her eye bothers me." Rosa checked her watch. "We'll know in a few hours."

"I'll tell them," Xavier said, "when I think the time is right." They were happy at that moment, sharing a breath of relief, all of them unsure of how long it would last. He wanted them to have that moment.

"I'm going to get my bag," the medic said, "start checking everyone over, Calvin's group as well as these new folks. Will you keep an eye on the girl?"

Xavier said he would, and went to the rear of the truck as Rosa carried her orange medical bag toward a cluster of people. The priest checked on the girl, saw no change, and parked himself on the truck's rear bumper. He realized the downpour had ended. In the excitement of this new contact with other survivors, he hadn't noticed. It was only misting now, and overhead the cloud cover had just begun to break up. He listened for a while to the conversations around him, people telling their stories, and then beginning to discuss their situation.

Footsteps approached, and a group assembled around him at the back of the Bearcat: Calvin, Evan and Maya, the Russian pilot, and the woman named Margaret. Carney stood at the edge of the group, half turned away and watching outward with his rifle in his arms.

"Your medic said you're someone to talk to," said Evan. Xavier started to shake his head, but Evan cut him off. "We need to figure things out, decide what happens next."

The priest nodded slowly.

"We need to find a place to hole up, get all these people indoors," Evan continued, "and make some plans. Margaret says one of her group is still out there."

Xavier rose from the bumper and put his hand on the truck's rear door handle. "First we need to talk about this girl . . ." He didn't get a chance to finish.

"Drifters!" someone shouted, and the cry was followed by a woman's scream. Everyone spun to see a dozen figures lurching toward them out of the dark, and then Carney's M14 rifle began to fire.

FIVE

Faith and her brother-in-law Dane were standing at the rear of the white Cadillac, watching the kids play tag in the headlights. She smiled. Kids out late on a summer night, having fun. The young man called Mercury stood a few yards away, holding an assault rifle and straining to see into the darkness. The row of large hangars was no longer visible, and the cloud cover had yet to dissipate. Without city lights, it was as dark as a country night. Mercury was nervous; they were making a lot of noise, a lot of light, and seemed to think they had reached some point of safety where those things no longer mattered. It felt careless. He wanted to say something, but he was not a professional sentry; he was young and quite junior in the whole scheme of things, trusting in the wisdom of the elders in the group that had kept them alive this far.

Dane watched the kids play. "Nice to see that they can just forget it all for a while."

Faith nodded. "Even a little while is a good thing." She looked at Calvin's brother. "I'm sorry about the hospital ship. Sorry I brought us here."

Dane shook his head. "We all wanted that ship to be there, and it was. You were right. How could we have known it was . . . dead?" The vision of the long, white USNS *Comfort* tied to an Oakland dock and swarming with the dead was something both were certain they would never forget.

"Cal didn't want to come, tried to talk me out of it. I forced him into it." Faith started to cry. "I led us here."

Dane took her in his arms and held her.

"My kids are going to die because of me," she whispered through her tears, and that set off more sobbing.

Mercury looked back at them, wishing he could do something. Faith was a mother to all of them, and it broke his heart to see her like this. With his back turned to the darkened airfield, he didn't see the trio of corpses galloping at him out of the night.

The first one threw him down and fell on top of him, knocking the wind out of him. The second dropped as well, pinning him. Gasping for air, Mercury couldn't even scream as they started clawing and biting flesh out of his arms and belly. The third corpse went past, intent on different prey. Dane looked up at the sudden stench in the air in time to see a rotting face sink its teeth into Faith's bare shoulder. She screamed as blood sprayed into her brother-in-law's face, as rotting hands pawed at her eyes and mouth.

"Drifters!" Dane screamed, punching the corpse in the face as hard as he could. There was a wet, snapping sound, and his fist plunged through a decaying nose, collapsing it and the eye sockets inward, his hand suddenly buried in a cold, sticky mass. The thing's teeth didn't let go of Faith's shoulder, however, and it sank its fingers into one of her eyes as the filthy, broken nails of its other hand wiggled into her mouth, searching for her tongue. She tried to scream, fought to stand.

Dane clawed at the pistol he wore on his hip, his now-slippery hand unable to close on the grip. Shots were fired from somewhere as the corpse pulled Faith down, embracing her from behind, ripping at her shoulder until the white of bone appeared. She thrashed against it.

Finally Dane had the pistol in hand and aimed for its head, not wanting to risk hitting Faith, aware of the sound of running feet approaching. He also didn't see the creature that had detached itself from Mercury and scrambled toward him on all fours. It bit him in the back of the knee just as he squeezed the trigger, making the gun jump in his hand.

The bullet caught Faith just above the right eye, at a range of three feet.

Dane screamed at both the pain and what he had just done. Faith's attacker took no notice of her sudden stillness and continued to chew into her arm, groaning.

Calvin got there first, stumbling to a halt at what he saw, letting out a wail. Evan came in a second later with his hatchet and buried it in the back of the head attached to Dane's knee. The creature made a sighing noise and collapsed to the asphalt. Margaret strode to the drifter feeding on Mercury, blew its head off, racked another round, and did the same to the dead hippie. Xavier stomped a foot on Faith's attacker until its head came apart and its hands fell away from her. The woman stared up with one intact eye, her tongue torn out and still between the zombie's fingers, blood from her massive head wound pooling about her on the tarmac.

"Baby," whispered Calvin, dropping to his knees and cradling her. "Oh, baby, no."

Maya fell to her knees and hugged her father, crying silently, as Vladimir quickly moved to intercept the children racing toward them. Carney's M14 cracked several more times and approaching corpses fell. TC arrived and grabbed a flashlight from the back of the truck, panning it through the darkness as Carney tracked the light with his rifle. A drifter appeared in the white glow, a woman green with rot wearing jeans and a T-shirt. Carney put her down.

"Faith!" Dane cried, collapsing on the wounded leg but trying to pull himself toward his brother's wife. "Faith!"

Rosa came on the run, dropping beside Dane with her bag. "Lie still," she ordered.

"Faith!" Dane raised the pistol, pointing it at the corpse with the crushed head.

"Father, get that!" Rosa shouted, and Xavier quickly took the waving gun from Dane's hand. Rosa pressed the man to the cement as a pair of women arrived to hold his shoulders down, smoothing his hair and repeating his name. Rosa pulled on her gloves and used a small flashlight to inspect his knee. She cut away his pants leg and looked again, then cursed.

They all saw the ragged bite, except for Calvin, who saw only his dead wife.

Evan took Xavier by the elbow. "We *have* to get these people inside."

The man had ambushed and murdered her uncle, intentionally let the dead into the firehouse that had become their fortress, and stolen the van full of weapons. Now Angie West, former reality show star and professional gunsmith and shooter, was going hunting.

She figured Maxie would have tried to put distance between himself and the firehouse before going to ground. After radioing her intentions to Margaret and breaking contact, she drove a mile before starting a grid search, street by street. There was no way he could have gotten off Alameda, she knew, given the conditions of the bridges and approach roads, but finding him would still be long odds. All the son of a bitch had to do was pull the van into an open garage and close the door. In addition, driving slowly through the neighborhoods would not only stir up the dead but provide a nice target for the now heavily armed Maxie.

She didn't care. If he took a shot, he had better put her down, because she wouldn't miss when she returned fire.

Brother Peter rode in silence beside her as she cruised Alameda a block at a time, wiper blades thumping against a slackening rain and headlights revealing streets containing empty cars, dropped possessions, and drifting corpses. He sneaked little glances at her, figuring that she was in her late twenties, maybe ten years younger than him. She was lean and athletic, hard-looking with breasts on the smallish side. He preferred his women softer, with more curves, but there was still something arousing about her. He imagined that taut body bucking beneath him in a wicked little fantasy involving handcuffs, moans of pleasure, and ending with him using the box cutter to slit her throat at the moment of orgasm.

His box cutter. That lovely metal tool, cool to the touch, that he had used to open a woman's face in order to leave her for bait as he made his escape. Now, as he sat filthy and coming down from amphetamines beside a woman who had threatened to kill him and then changed her mind, he stroked the box cutter hidden inside the pocket of the ratty, soiled hoodie jacket he wore.

Peter felt himself stiffening and tried to suppress that as well as a smile. "We're hunting a man?" he asked. "The one who killed your uncle?"

Angie said nothing.

"He's dangerous. Can I have my pistol back?"

Still nothing.

Brother Peter fingered the box cutter like an Irish worry stone. "Wouldn't it be smarter if we were both armed? Look at how the dead are coming into the street. The truck's noise attracts them, probably the lights too." He looked at her. "How about that pistol?"

Angie stomped the brake, throwing Peter against the dashboard. "Get out."

"Hold on, I just—"

She gripped the butt of her automatic in its shoulder holster. "Get out," she repeated.

Peter raised his hands and ducked his head, his voice turning to a whimper. "I'm sorry, I'm sorry! I'm just scared, and you're not talking to me. I'll shut up." Oh, how it sickened him to demean himself to this woman. It was necessary, though. It was his way in.

Angie looked at him for a long moment, and then the Excursion was rolling again. Block after block passed and the last of the light was gone from the sky. They traveled through streets filled with broken glass and burned cars, houses with doors standing open, and lots of closed garages. No sign of Maxie. The dead staggered down steps and out from behind cars, reaching and pounding on the SUV as it passed. Many staggered into its path only to be run down, and many of these were left broken on the pavement, struggling to drag their crushed bodies after the departing vehicle.

The Excursion's dashboard clock ticked past midnight, then 1:00 A.M. Peter fell asleep, his head leaning against the window, unable to stay awake despite the increasing thump of dead hands on metal and glass. It had been a long, long day for him: trussing Anderson to that pipe, preparing to eat the young male staffer, carving up Sherri, and running, running, running. The escape from the airport, wandering the golf course, Alameda, and meeting lovely Angie made for such a busy day. He began to snore lightly.

Angie was exhausted too, her eyes raw and dry. It would be easy to tuck the Excursion into a garage of her own, secure her hitchhiker (she had a handful of police zip-tie cuffs in the center console), and catch some sleep. She wouldn't, though; she had to find Maxie. She was still undecided about her passenger. He had pointed a gun at her but surrendered it easily enough and said he was scared. He was creepy and he smelled bad and asked annoying questions, but did that mean he was dangerous? Her uncle Bud had said at the beginning of this, *We put down anything that's a threat.* Did this man qualify? She had been collecting strays for weeks, but of course none had pointed a weapon at her. So far he was behaving, so she decided to let him stay, at least until she had more reasons to put him out.

As the small hours of the new day crept on, she began to consider how impossible this hunt would be. The dead were increasing in number by the hour, and soon the streets would be impassable; the massed strength of corpses would be able to stop and tip over even the heavy SUV. She couldn't stay out here. Maxie might be an evil bastard, but he was far from stupid. He wouldn't just show himself in order to make it easy for her to—

The Excursion's lights revealed Angie's van sitting half a block away.

It was midway up the street, crooked and crunched against a fire hydrant. The driver's door stood open, and a corpse was on its hands and knees on the ground below it, face pressed to the asphalt. The van had come to rest in front of a small tavern, an unlit neon sign over the door showing a shamrock and reading *Lucky's*.

Angie pulled to the curb and killed the headlights, searching for signs of movement, the glow of a flashlight, anything. It was dark and quiet, and the corpse near the van appeared to be the only such creature in the immediate area. At this distance she couldn't tell if it was Maxie. She looked at her sleeping companion. Dangerous? Trustworthy? She couldn't assess those things at the moment, and she certainly didn't know him well enough to take him with her.

She retrieved a pair of hard plastic, prelooped zip-tie cuffs from the console and slipped one over Peter's left wrist, jerking it tight and hauling him over to the steering wheel. He snorted and sputtered as he was yanked from a deep sleep, slow to resist. In seconds both hands were tightly cuffed around the steering wheel.

"What . . . ?"

Angie got out, bringing her Galil assault rifle, tossing Peter's .45 and clip into the rear cargo area. She shoved his hunting knife in her belt and pulled the keys. "Don't make noise, don't hit the horn, or you'll attract them." She held up the key fob and locked the Excursion with the button on the driver's door. "If you do anything to let him know I'm coming, I'll unlock the truck from a distance so they can get in and eat you."

Peter said nothing. His sexual fantasy had distilled down to just the throat-slitting part.

Angie closed the door and jogged up the street toward the tavern, assault rifle to her shoulder, eyes roving for threats. There was still only the one, but that could change quickly. The ghoul at the van's open driver's door had been licking and biting at blood on the pavement, its lips ragged and front teeth broken or scraped down to nubs. It looked up at the soft boot treads on the sidewalk, at the metallic snap of Angie clicking the Galil's built-in bayonet into place, and let out a growl. A sharp thrust and the bayonet plunged through its eye, piercing its brain.

She used a small flashlight and inspected the van. There was blood on the driver's seat and spattered on the inside of the windshield, several ragged buckshot holes piercing the van's skin where Margaret said she had shot at it, but no one was inside. The weapons and supplies in back appeared untouched. Had Maxie crashed the van and been pulled to his death by corpses? She prayed it was nothing as simple or merciful as that.

Pausing to listen first at the tavern's door, she eased it open and was immediately hit by the odors of cigarette smoke and something sour and rotten, different from the scent of the dead. Flashlight gripped tight against the Galil's front stock, she held the weapon firmly to her shoulder and went in.

A candle was glowing in a red jar on a table near the bar, an open bottle of whiskey and a cigarette smoldering in an ashtray beside it. Maxie's .32 rested on the scarred wood beside the candle. The man himself sat in a wooden captain's chair, leaning back from the table and rocking on the rear legs. His shirt was stained a dark red down the entire right side, and in the candlelight his face had a lumpy, jaundiced appearance.

Angie advanced quickly, rifle muzzle pointed at his face, and swept the hideout pistol onto the floor. "Tell me why."

Maxie made a croaking sound and leaned forward heavily onto the table, one hand reaching for the cigarette, the other the bottle. He looked up at Angie. His right eye was swollen shut, the lower right side of his face a big, infected lump. Pus dribbled down his neck, which was swollen as well. He grimaced as he swigged from the bottle, then took a drag off the cigarette. Smoke hissed out from between clenched teeth.

"Chinese bitch," he growled, unable to properly open his mouth. "Saw her in the side mirror, blastin' away with that shotgun." He chuckled, a deep, wet sound, as if the infection had spread to his throat as well. Maxie was that sour rot she had smelled.

"Lucky shot," he said. "Piece of buckshot caught me below the ear, still in there. Smashed my jaw, messed me all up." He set the bottle down and took another drag, groaning with the effort. "Funny, don't you think, Miss Angie? Survive the zombies, get killed by a woman don't even know how to shoot." He tried to smile, exposing a single, gold-capped tooth. Even that small movement was painful.

Angie leveled the rifle muzzle at his forehead. "Why did you kill them? Why Bud?"

Maxie laughed, and then cried out. He raised his fingers to the swollen buckshot wound and winced, then looked at her with his good eye. "Ain't got no nice, neat answers for you, missy. No Scooby-Doo wrap-up. Some folks is just bad."

Her finger tensed on the trigger.

Maxie closed his eye. "Go on, now. Do what you come to do."

The shot didn't come, and Maxie opened his eye. Angie's rifle was lying on the table, but she was no longer standing across from him. Then a hand gripped his hair from behind and jerked his head back sharply, making him scream through his teeth.

Angie whispered in his ear, showing him the blade of Peter's hunting knife. "I've got a better idea."

Maxie opened his eye and looked around. Through an open door he heard a screech of metal as Angie's van backed off the fire hydrant and then rumbled down the street. Not that he was able to define any of this, exactly. It all indicated food, though.

His eye looked around, vision slightly cloudy. The floor below him was wet and red, and just beyond, a motionless body was slumped in a chair at a table, clothes bloody, another corpse squatting beside it, feeding on one limp hand. Maxie wanted to be there. His eye rolled in its socket and fell upon the seated body again.

It had been decapitated.

From its new resting place on top of the bar, Maxie's head glared out at the feeding corpse and rasped in frustration. He was so *very* hungry.

SIX

Positioned at the edge of the airfield where the base's buildings began, the hangar was large enough to have once housed a B-52 bomber. It had since been converted into a nightclub, featuring a long bar, booths and tables, a large dance floor, and a stage for live bands. A row of windows down one side looked out at a lot where the Bearcat and Harley were now parked beside a white van and Maxie's Cadillac.

Near the stage, speakers and lighting equipment in rolling cases remained where they had been left by a band that would never play again. The quilted packing blankets used for the equipment were now being used as bedding for sleeping children. Adults curled up where they could, in booths or against walls, heads in each other's laps. It had been a long time since any of them slept, and almost everyone collapsed as soon as the group got inside.

A perimeter check uncovered a few fire exits—closed and secure—and showed that despite the area occupied by the nightclub, more than half the hangar remained open and unused. Fortunately, no drifters had been discovered in the echoing space. There was no power, of course, and the only illumination came from moonlight through the windows as the clouds finally broke apart.

Carney sat in a chair near the windows, dozing with his M14 across his knees, and Jerry, the big comedian, slept lying down in front of the entrance doors, a shotgun beside him. Before he went to sleep he joked that if a zombie was strong enough to push his mass away from the doors, the group had bigger problems. There were smiles, but no laughter.

TC sat on a stool at the bar, staring at his shadowy image in a mirror on the back wall, still without his shirt. He liked the way people looked at him when he was bare-chested: the men with nervousness, the women with curiosity. He had waited until Carney nodded off before helping himself to the tequila, and now one hand curled around the bottle, the other a shot glass.

Darius, the sociology professor rescued by Rosa, and who had failed to kill Xavier, quietly went behind the bar to look for bottled water. He gave TC a smile and nod—which was not returned—and began checking the cold cases. TC poured a shot and raised the glass, inspecting the golden liquid before downing it. He smacked the glass on the bar and let out a gasp.

The professor glanced at him and then the bottle, seeing how much was already gone. "Maybe you should go easy on that," he said softly, not wanting to wake the others. "We're all going to need clear heads."

TC cocked his head, and the corner of his mouth twitched upward. "Is that right?" He poured another shot, then leaned his elbows on the bar, holding the glass in both hands and dropping his voice to a matching whisper. "You remind me of someone."

Darius smiled and waited.

"Yeah, a little bitch I punked out at the Q. I used to rent him out for smokes."

The professor stiffened as if slapped.

"What do you say, dark meat? I like those pretty beads in your braids. Why don't you come sit on my lap?"

The sociology professor ducked his head and hurried away, and

TC watched him go in the mirror, chuckling. "Maybe later, chocolate," he murmured, downing the shot.

In an office against one wall of the hangar, Margaret Chu slept in a chair, her shotgun leaning in a corner. The sick girl was still bound, lying on the carpeted floor near a desk. Wrapped in a packing blanket, her face glistening with sweat, the young woman tossed and mumbled through the gag. Rosa had made the girl as comfortable as possible, and Margaret volunteered to stand watch and deal with her if and when she turned. Contrary to Xavier's concerns about group panic over an infected person in their midst, there had been little argument. Everyone was too tired. Margaret wished she knew the girl's name, but she would probably never find out. She knew what was coming.

In the adjacent office, Rosa Escobedo finished giving Dane a shot of Demerol and placed a Band-Aid over the puncture. The bite wound at the back of his knee was freshly dressed with a clean bandage, and he sat propped against a wall, unspeaking and unable to meet anyone's eyes. Maya stood near her father, rubbing his back, and nodded her thanks to the medic. Rosa closed the door on the way out.

Xavier and Evan were waiting in the darkness of the big hangar, and the three of them moved off to sit on the back of the stage. They were all exhausted and said nothing for a while, just stared into the dark and listened to the silence.

"We're not safe here," Xavier said at last. "It only feels like that because it's quiet and nothing's happening. That's going to change. They're going to find us here."

"And it's too hard to defend," said Evan. "Too many doors, all those windows."

Rosa sighed. "Those aren't the only problems. Food and water are going to be an issue. It didn't take long to scavenge through this place. We found some soda and bottled water, some bar snacks, but it won't last long. There are supplies in that armored truck, we saw that, but only if those guys decide to share, and even then it's going to run out quickly with this many people."

Xavier nodded. The group now numbered just over fifty.

"People are going to start getting sick," Rosa continued, and shook her head when the two men looked quickly at her. "Not the virus. But hygiene is a major problem for all of us, and there's not enough water to drink, much less bathe. Then there's poor nutrition. Most of us have been living on canned food and crap for over a month. It's going to start taking its toll."

The priest knew she was right. Before the outbreak, he had been careful about his diet, exercising regularly and boxing four or five times a week. He had lost weight, noticed the loss of muscle tone and a growing flabbiness. He itched all the time and was developing boils from a lack of adequate washing. The others were experiencing the same.

"Living outdoors all the time," the medic said, "poor nutrition, poor hygiene . . . even the people who were in good health before this are going to decline, and then there's that elderly couple from the firehouse. The man has MS and the woman is on oxygen, which will run out soon. Two of Calvin's kids are diabetic. . . ." Rosa shook her head.

There was the scuff of a boot in the darkness, and they turned to see Carney walking toward them, rifle slung. He rubbed at his unshaven face. "Mind if I join your meeting?"

Xavier nodded. "I think it's important you be here. I didn't want to wake you, though."

"What's on the agenda?"

"Bad news," said Evan.

Carney chuckled. "Is there another kind?" He squatted and rested his arms on his knees.

Rosa tipped her head toward the offices. "That man is going to turn. The girl too, probably. We'll have to handle it fast."

"And quiet," said Evan. "Gunfire attracts them."

Carney nodded. Before he dozed off, he had seen at least a dozen of the walking dead drifting past the hangar on their way to the airfield. None seemed interested in the group's hiding place, but he knew that was only because they didn't know there was food inside.

"How long does insulin last if it's not refrigerated?" he asked. "It's been two hours since I had to shut the Bearcat off, since that cooler shut down. I see that Calvin brought it inside."

Rosa nodded. "He's just taking precautions, because he doesn't know when he'll ever find more. Insulin can last at room temperature for about a month, and in fact that's how you want it to be when you inject it. I've heard cold insulin hurts like a bastard. If you have an extra supply, though, you should keep it cold."

Carney chuckled and shook his head. "I was afraid it was like shellfish." That got a soft laugh from all of them. He looked at Evan. "How did he keep that thing powered before? They couldn't have just let a car run indefinitely."

Evan shook his head. "Calvin had a generator in the back of his van. They'd fire it up when they were camping or stopped for the night." He looked at the others. "They've got a lot of gear in that caravan we abandoned in Oakland, stuff we could really use."

Xavier looked at the inmate. "And you've got a lot of gear in your truck. We were just talking about food and water." The priest let the sentence hang there, and the others watched and waited for a reply.

Carney looked back at them. "It doesn't seem like there's a choice. I'm not that big of a prick that I'm going to keep it all for myself, but with this many people it's not going to last more than a few days. We better have a plan soon."

Xavier smiled and nodded his thanks.

"How's your partner going to feel about that?" Rosa asked.

"I'll deal with him," Carney said, already knowing how TC would respond.

The woman looked at him. "Who were you, before all this, Carney?"

The man didn't respond, and the silence went on so long it didn't look like he would. Then he stood up and folded his arms. "For the last seventeen years I've been an inmate at San Quentin for double murder. My wife and her lover were drug addicts who let my daughter choke to death, and I killed them both in their sleep. I'd do it again." He looked at their faces and nodded. "More than you were expecting. Careful you don't ask questions when you're not ready for the answers. Is this going to be a problem?"

Xavier looked at the man, at the years of grief that tried unsuccessfully to hide behind hard blue eyes. "Are you going to be a problem for us?"

"No," Carney said, delivering the word without hesitation.

Xavier wasn't ready to ask the same question about the man's partner, however, for it was now obvious where the two had met. "People change," the priest said. "Your word's good enough for me."

The inmate pursed his lips. No one had *ever* said that to him. He turned to look at the medic. "I answered your question, Doc; now I have one. What is all this?" He waved an arm. "How is it, exactly, that the dead are walking around wiping us out?" It was *the* question, one with which they had all wrestled, yet for the most part they had been on the run and fighting to survive too often to care about the answer. Now here it was.

Rosa shook her head. "I'm not a doctor."

Carney laughed and sat down on the stage beside her. "Oh, no, Doc, I'm not letting you get away with that."

"Look," she said, "I got my degree and finished pre-med, but actual med school hadn't started yet. I'm just a medic."

"And that makes you the closest thing we have to an expert," Carney said. "So let's hear it. You must have a theory." The others looked at her as well.

Rosa hesitated, and then shook her head. "I can tell you what I heard and what I saw, give you my opinion, but that's all. You need a virologist."

They nodded for her to go on.

"Okay. We've been calling it a virus, but that's just an assumption based upon how it acts. It could actually be something hidden in the genetic code. I don't know if anyone's done any lab work on it, so I can't say. Let's call it a virus for now."

"The Omega Virus, that's what the news called it," Carney said.

"Right," Rosa said, nodding. "But it's more complex than that. There's something else at work, maybe even a separate strain of OV. The virus is acting like a blood-borne pathogen in the sense that fluid exposure can give you the disease, almost certainly *will* give you the disease, but if it's not through a bite, it isn't always fatal."

They all thought about the girl in the other room.

"How is that even possible?" asked Evan. "Fluid is fluid; if it's infectious it wouldn't matter where it came from in the body."

The medic shrugged. "I didn't say it made sense or that it's right. It's just a theory based on what I've seen, both in the field hospital and out there." She waved an arm. "Maybe it has to do with the carrier, some mutation in the walking dead. An autopsy on one of them might explain more."

"But even if one of the dead doesn't kill you outright," said Xavier, "the bite eventually will."

"Yes," Rosa said. "The bite triggers the fever, and it's always fatal. But it's not what turns you."

"Bullshit," said Carney. "You get bitten, you turn. Simple."

The medic shook her head. "Wrong. You get bitten, it kills you, and *then* you turn. Death is the problem here, and that's why there has to be something else at work."

They stared at her.

Rosa looked at each of them. "Ever see someone turn who hadn't been bitten?"

They nodded, Carney with a startled look on his face. He remembered the overweight corrections officer guarding them who'd gone down with a heart attack, only to rise again minutes later. Xavier remembered the San Francisco cop he'd seen who had been lynched, and probably died from the hanging. Yet there he was, dangling by the neck and jerking about.

Rosa saw the realization. "It's death," she said. "The doctors at the field hospital speculated that OV was already inside all of us, leading some to believe it was in our water supply, or more likely, airborne.

Either way, it lies dormant, without symptoms, waiting for a specific trigger, which appears to be death." She dug a water bottle out of a cargo pocket while the others experienced a brief crawling sensation as they imagined the corruption lying silently within them.

"Again, I'm not a virologist," Rosa continued, "but the theory isn't science fiction. We see all the time where a deadly element sits waiting in a person, harmless until a specific series of events takes place. It could be environmental, pollution, or pesticides." She shrugged. "Theories."

"Where is it hiding?" asked Evan, unaware that he was hugging himself and rubbing his upper arms.

"I would think the brain," Rosa said. "The brain must feed it, keep it alive."

"That's why a head shot puts them down and keeps them down," said Xavier, nodding, "or stops a living person from coming back. We've all seen the suicides."

They looked at him.

Carney was shaking his head. "That doesn't make any sense. They're dead, rotting, which means the brain is dead and rotting too. How can it support anything?"

"Plenty of organisms live off dead tissue," Rosa said. "That's not what you're asking, though, is it? You want to know how it's possible for a corpse to still be mobile. For the dead to be not only walking around, but in possession of senses like sight and hearing and smell, maintaining motor function and rudimentary problem-solving skills like how to turn doorknobs or climb steps? To have hunting instincts?" She gave them a weak smile. "I don't know, and I'm sorry. Maybe you can tell me why they're driven to eat, even though they clearly get no nutritional benefit from it, even after they no longer have any sort of gastrointestinal system left. Can you answer that question?"

"Not my field, Doc," said Carney.

"Well it's not mine either," Rosa said, louder and sharper than she had intended. "I'm sorry," she quickly said.

Carney gave her a nod to let her know it was okay.

"How long do you think they'll last?" asked Xavier. "They're rotting. In fact most of them should have fallen apart by now."

"You would think so," said Rosa. "And they are decaying, which could lead you to believe you could just outlast them. Find a hole and wait it out, right? It makes perfect sense, but beside the fact that *none* of this makes sense, there's a problem with that thinking."

Xavier listened. That was *exactly* what he had been thinking, and still was.

Rosa explained the process of decay, beginning with autolysis. She told them how the enzymes contained within the cells went into a postdeath meltdown, a process that was sped up by heat and slowed by cold. This caused putrefaction, and thirty-six hours after death the corpse's neck, head, abdomen, and shoulders turned a discolored green. Bloating followed, the accumulation of gas caused by bacteria, and it was most visible around the face. The eyes and tongue began to protrude as the gas pushed them forward. Fluid-filled blisters appeared on the skin, and hair began to fall out.

They watched her, listening. All of them had seen what she was describing.

A process called marbling followed, a description of the skin tone when blood vessels in the face, chest, abdomen, and extremities became visible as the red blood cells broke down and produced hemoglobin. The entire body would then turn a blackish green, and fluids would seep from a corpse's mouth, nose, and other orifices. Body tissue would begin to split, releasing gases and more fluids, and by seventy-two hours rigor mortis would be gone.

"Bodies in water decay at twice the speed of a corpse aboveground," she finished.

"I've seen all that," Xavier said, "but not in all of them. Some show those early signs, others are further along, some are withering like mummies. It's not consistent."

"Right." Rosa drank from her water bottle. "That's the problem. It's been more than a month since the outbreak. Most of them should be piles of muck and bone by now, but they're not. Some even look fairly fresh." She looked at the priest. "You said it. They're not consistent."

Carney was nodding slowly. "If they followed the biology you described, Doc, then in a month or so you wouldn't have to worry about fluid exposure. They'd be dry as a bone. But most of them are . . ."

"Still juicy," said Evan. "You're both right, it doesn't make sense."

"Neither does the fact that they're dead and still hunting us," said Xavier.

"Are you suggesting," Carney asked, "that they're somehow stabilizing wherever they happen to be in the decaying process?" The inmate looked at Rosa with a raised eyebrow.

She huffed her frustration, not at his question, but at her lack of information. "I don't know. I can't explain what they are or why they do what they do, or even if what we've seen is normal for all of them. There could be other . . . varieties, I guess, with different levels of senses and motor skills. We don't know if they adapt, or if they can learn." She let out a shaky laugh. "Jesus, I hope not. I certainly don't know where OV came from, if it's man-made, a freak of nature, who knows. It has to be something recent, though, or we would have seen it a lot sooner than August."

"And that makes it man-made," said Evan.

Carney nodded. "Some asshole cooked it up, and some other asshole let it out, on purpose or by accident."

Rosa shrugged. It was as good a theory as any, and this imposing man who admitted to committing two murders had just phrased it more succinctly than any of the doctors she had been around. "I wish I could tell you more. I wish I knew if any of what I just said is true, but I can tell you we'd be foolish to think we understand anything about it."

Xavier squeezed the woman's shoulder. "You did just fine, thank you."

Carney gave her a nudge. "Yeah, thanks, Doc."

She nodded and left to find a place to sleep. They heard a bottle break, followed by a string of muffled obscenities, and Carney went to handle his cellmate. Xavier and Evan sat quietly for a while, then wandered over to the row of windows in the hangar's wall. Everyone was sleeping and there were no sounds other than Carney's low voice and TC's drunken one, as the older man forced his companion into a vacant booth and ordered him to sleep it off.

The clouds were scattered now and a partial moon reflected off wind-shields, turning the hangar across from them white and casting pools of absolute shadow in places the light didn't touch. A corpse lurched through the parking lot on its way to the airfield, a man in some sort of uniform, missing an arm. Xavier and Evan froze. It didn't look toward the windows, and if it had it would probably only have seen its own reflection in the glass, but still they held their breath until it passed.

When it was gone, Evan looked at the older man. "So we just heard a medical explanation. I don't know about you, but it doesn't sound like science is going to give us all the answers."

"It never does," said Xavier, looking out at the night.

"Where's the military in all this?" Evan leaned his palms against the window frame and stared up at the moon. "Where's all the Special Forces guys? The pilot . . . Vlad? He said his base fell apart, but there must be others. How is it that we're alive, and those guys aren't?"

Xavier looked out the window with him. "I don't think we're special, if that's what you mean. We've just been lucky with the math. Statisti-cally, some of us would live, at least for a while. There're others out there, you can count on it." He looked down. "How long we all last, that's a different question, and the numbers probably don't work out too well."

"And the military?" Evan pressed.

"They're sure to be out there too," Xavier said, "at least in places, but they're probably in no hurry to leave whatever fortified position they've managed to hold. The rest were overwhelmed. You've got to realize that the average person had the luxury of running away. The military, the cops and firemen, they had to go into it head-on."

Evan looked at him. "But their firepower, the technology, tanks, and aircraft . . ."

"I'm sure they didn't see it coming any more than we did," the priest said, "and it's not like there's a contingency plan for something like this, unless you're a conspiracy guy." Evan shook his head, and Xavier smiled. "As for firepower, what good is a tank against something that has to be shot in the head? And when that something turns into hundreds of thousands, millions of somethings? How do you deal with that, when most of the people you rely upon are stumbling around dead with all the rest?" Then in an even softer voice he said, "I think pinning your hopes to the government sending in some kind of military rescue is foolish, though."

Evan shoved his hands into his pockets.

"Besides," Xavier said, going back to looking out the window, "it's more about how our society has always been vulnerable to plagues, with no good way to combat a fast-moving outbreak on such a large scale. No one could respond in time, even if there were a way to respond at all. Now it's just about survival."

"I have to tell you, I'm a little surprised to hear you talking this way," Evan said.

Xavier turned. "You don't even know me. Why would you say that?"

Evan smiled to show he meant no offense and said, "Out on the airfield earlier, after Dane was on the ground waving his gun, Rosa called you *Father*. You're a priest, aren't you?"

He sighed. "I wish there were a simple answer for that."

"There is," Evan said. "You are or you aren't and I take it from that answer that you are. That being the case, you must have a theological perspective on this. I'd like to hear it."

Xavier said nothing for a long time. Finally he looked at the writer. "I'd like to give you some comfort, some sort of understanding. I should be doing that, and I know exactly what words to say to make you feel better. But they're hollow to me, Evan, and I don't want to tell you something I don't fully believe myself. Not the answer you were looking for, I know."

Evan was looking out the window again. "My mom died a few

years back. It caused a rift between my dad and me, not that we had been buddies before that, but Mom always kept everyone together. When she was gone, we sort of fell apart."

"I'm sorry."

Evan didn't seem to hear the words of sympathy. "More than that, her passing made me look at what matters. All the shit I thought was so important just evaporated like smoke. It put things in perspective for me."

Xavier nodded. He had heard this during grief counseling many times.

"This," Evan said, gesturing at the window, "is like that, but on the biggest scale you can imagine. All those things we argued about and hated one another for, all the relationships we sacrificed pursuing *stuff*—the way we lived our lives so wrapped up in ourselves—what did it matter?" He yawned and rubbed at his eyes. "I'm beat and I'm babbling. I doubt any of this is making sense."

The corpse of a woman in a torn dress walked stiffly through the parking lot, moving toward the airfield like the others, one arm reaching. She looked like a mother in pursuit of a runaway child, and this illusion was reinforced by the fact that a dead two-year-old stumbled across the pavement ahead of her. It wore little overalls and sneakers that flashed red when they struck the ground, and on its back was a harness that looked like a stuffed monkey with a tail that doubled as a leash dragging across the ground behind the child.

"What does any of it mean when you see something like that?" Evan said softly. Then he turned to Xavier. "Perspective, Father. I asked you if you were a priest, and you dodged me. Whatever you are, you have what people need. Call it leadership, hope, even faith, whether you want to believe it or not, whether it sounds hollow to you or even like complete bullshit. More than any of us, you could help these people. They need a lot of things, but what they need the most is for someone to be stronger than they think they can be by themselves."

The young man smiled and gripped the priest's shoulder. "I'm going to sleep." He walked away, leaving Xavier alone in the moonlight.

SEVEN

Angie's van and the black Excursion sat side by side in the parking lot of a small upholstery factory, not far from the road that led to the main gates of the naval air station. She slept locked in her van, and Brother Peter lay curled up on the backseat of the Ford. He should have been sleeping, but he couldn't.

God wouldn't shut up.

Angie had come out of the tavern covered in fresh blood, a flat, emotionless look in her eyes. She took several shotguns and Peter's automatic from the back of the Excursion, placed them in the rear of her van, and returned to the front seat of the Ford, where Peter was still zip-tied to the steering wheel. He had considered using the box cutter to free himself, and would have if things had gone wrong, but he resisted the urge. He wanted to play out the game.

"I'm still pissed about the gun," Angie said.

"I know. I'm sorry."

She stared at him. "I'm going to link up with my group. You can come if you want to, follow me in this." She tapped the steering wheel.

"No problem," Peter said. "Look, Angie, I'm really sorry about before. I guess I haven't been around people for a long time. I forgot how to act."

She considered this. "Stay close and drive where I drive. If you decide to take off instead"—she shrugged—"then you'll be on your own. No one will try to find you or help you."

"I'll follow you. I want to be around people again." He meant it, but not for the reasons she might think.

Angie had cut him loose with his own hunting knife, then taken the radio off the dashboard and spoken briefly with Margaret again, telling her she was coming in. Margaret sounded sleepy. Minutes later they were rolling, and Brother Peter struggled to control the Excursion at first. He realized it had been years since he had gone anywhere without a chauffeur. It came back quickly enough, though at one point he got too close to the back of Angie's van and rubbed the bumper. She stomped the brakes, and for one fearful moment he wondered if the bitch would march back to the Ford and shoot him.

The dead were out in strength, hundreds in the street, pawing and banging on the two vehicles when they got close enough. Brother Peter watched his rearview, seeing them turn and shuffle slowly after the Excursion as it went by. It gave him a chill. Angie did some circles and backtracking, which he assumed was intended to throw them off and not lead them directly to her group. After they parked and she walked to the Excursion, explaining the strategy, he had nodded, told her she was smart, and pictured raping her while he shoved a gun into the back of her head.

"I talked to Margaret, told her we were going to wait off base and get some sleep. I want to go in during daylight so we can see what we're up against."

"Do you have any food or water?" Peter asked.

"Right, sorry about that." Angie retrieved several bottles of water and some packaged food from the van. "Get some sleep. I'll wake you when we're ready to move."

The streets were bathed in moonlight, allowing them to see quite well. None of the walking dead were in view at the moment, so apparently her methods had worked, at least for now. Peter watched her return to the van, rifle slung over her shoulder. "Sweet dreams," he muttered, fingering his box cutter.

Now, when he should have been sleeping after the effects of the amphetamines had worn off, making him want to crash hard, he could only curl up miserably on the rear seat of the Excursion and cover his ears with his hands. "Please let me sleep," he said. It wasn't fair. After all that he had said to the unwashed masses, the claims in his books and televised sermons, the speaking engagements and seminars at his Bible college, Peter Dunleavy had never actually heard the voice of God. And now, when He finally spoke, Peter was too exhausted for the conversation.

But then, had he ever really believed it all? Really *believed*? Perhaps once, when he had been young and naïve, easily swayed by powerful words. But now? Peter Dunleavy was the one who spoke powerful words now. This was a hallucination brought on by stress and fatigue, nothing more.

Besides, God's voice would be booming and majestic, filling him with glory and awe. Not . . . not *this*.

"*I'm a hallucination, am I? You sound like a little bitch, Pete,*" said God.

"I'm not a little bitch. I'm tired. Let's talk in the morning." No, it was not what he had expected.

"*I don't care if you're tired. Look at me when I speak to you.*"

Peter sat up. God was in the front passenger seat, turned to look at him. The minister blinked. God looked just like the shrink who had kicked him out of the Air Force, uniform and all.

"*You have lost your way, Peter. I'm very disappointed.*"

"What do you mean? I love you above all others."

"*Oh, save your bullshit for the sheep. You've fallen, grown confused, become an unbeliever.*"

"This conversation isn't real," Peter said.

God reached back between the seats and slapped Peter hard across the face, His ring from the Air Force Academy at Colorado Springs bloodying the minister's lip. *"How was that? Real enough?"*

Peter let out a little cry. "Wait, don't—"

Another hard slap, stinging his other cheek. *"Unbeliever."*

The minister held up his hands. "I'm sorry!"

A third smack, this one on the top of his head with the Air Force ring.

Peter began to cry. "Please, stop!"

"I despise whining," God said. *"Pull yourself together."*

Peter wiped furiously at the tears.

"You tried to tell the Air Force the truth about their nuclear warheads, but you used the wrong words and they were taken away from you," God said. *"You founded a global ministry in my name, but you screwed that up too, and it was taken away."* God looked over the top of His wire-rimmed glasses. *"Then you gathered a new flock, led them underground with some half-assed idea of forming a new ministry. That turned into a clusterfuck of cannibalism and forced sex. Very, very disappointing, Peter."*

The televangelist was about to speak but caught himself. He didn't want to be slapped again.

"Now here is this woman. Your head is filled with dark and lustful thoughts, and you talk as if you will enslave her, bend her to your will. Do you do it? No, you grovel and scrape and say things to please her." God made a disgusted face. *"Has my prophet degraded himself for a harlot?"*

"No!" Peter's cheeks burned, and the tears began to flow again.

"Will you serve her as a dog serves a master?"

"No!" He would walk right over to her van, rip her out of it, and use her right there on the asphalt, he would—

"WRONG!" A thunderous slap rocked his head to the side, the Air Force ring chipping a tooth.

Peter covered his face with his hands and wept, shaking his head. "I don't understand."

"*That is because you have strayed from my grace. Do you wish to return?*"

The minister hesitated before nodding. Had he ever actually *been* in God's grace? Wouldn't the real God know him for what he was?

"*Then hear me. I know* exactly *what you are. You've become a screwup, Pete, a confused, dirty little screwup who people distrust and avoid on sight. Look at yourself. You're about to reenter the company of other people, of whom you are not in charge and whom you cannot push around.*" God looked over His glasses again. "*They don't know and don't care who you were.*"

"What should I do?"

"*You will pull it together. Clean yourself, stop sniveling, behave like a normal person.*"

Peter sniffed at his runny nose. "I can do that."

"*Put on the charm that seduced millions into emptying their pockets for the horseshit you were selling.*" God smiled. "*I have faith that you can do it, Pete. Who's a bigger liar or fraud if not you?*"

"Right." Peter smiled back.

"*Ingratiate yourself, be the Peter Dunleavy we all know and love.*"

"I will."

"*And most importantly,*" God said, "*don't let them find out.*"

"Find out what?"

God fingered one of the medals on His uniform for a moment before looking up. "*Don't let them find out that you're dangerous, and batshit crazy.*"

"Okay." Peter nodded. "Good idea." He wanted to chuckle. He was certainly one of those things, maybe both. Oddly, the idea didn't bother him.

"*I still have a purpose for you,*" God said, resting a hand on Peter's knee. "*I will reveal it in time.*"

"Will I see you again?"

"*I think we should meet again,*" said the Air Force shrink, and Peter heard the words like an echoing memory.

"Thy will be done." It sounded like the right thing to say to the Almighty, even if He was a dream.

God nodded. "*Think what you like, Peter, but tuck your lustful thoughts away, for now. They're a distraction. You'll get what you want eventually, as long as you do what I say.*"

Peter licked his lips. "Will I get to have the woman?" He looked toward the van where Angie slept.

"*Pete, my boy, when the time comes, you're going to get to fuck them all.*"

EIGHT

During the weeks that followed the initial outbreak, each of the Alameda survivors had encountered and observed the behaviors of the walking dead, and formed opinions about what they could and could not do. Father Xavier Church was convinced that they could not see long distances but had good hearing. He was wrong on the first count and underestimated them on the second. The dead had exceptional hearing. As to their vision, it was not only as acute as a man's, it was even better at night.

Angie West did not fully appreciate their herd mentality. Often, when one started moving for whatever reason, others within visual distance would do the same, perhaps instinctively believing that food was in the area. Angie was correct in the assumption that they could become distracted and confused, but this was not an absolute. Many of the dead, once they started walking, simply kept heading in that direction until they encountered an obstacle and were forced to move around it. Corpses behind them would follow, and the corpses behind *them* would do the same.

So it was in Alameda, California, that the undead—drawn by engine noise and distant gunfire—began moving west through the city, toward the old naval air station. Like cattle, block by block those behind followed those in front, ever backward, across the bridges into Oakland like a long, moving chain. The dead in that city slowly noticed the movement and soon over a million corpses joined the herd, shuffling toward the bridges. Flowing down the I-80 corridor and across the Bay Bridge from San Francisco, millions more steadily joined the slow-moving but unstopping horde.

To the south, the undead mass from Los Angeles marched north through central California like a swath of ravenous locusts. Nothing survived their passage; vehicles were shoved to the side or tipped over, fences were trampled flat, crops obliterated as fields were packed down to hard dirt by millions of shuffling feet. Scattered refugees were forced from their hiding places, cornered and devoured in fields, rooted out of basements and pulled screaming from cars. The crowd of L.A. refugees that Vladimir had flown over eventually fell to the relentless, pursuing dead, pulled down by the thousands, rising minutes later to join the host.

Along a lonely stretch of road that passed through a thousand acres of farmland, several families of migrant farmworkers hid in a drainage culvert, praying for the horde to pass. They were torn from each other's arms and eaten alive. Soon the L.A. horde would reach the overrun Naval Air Station Lemoore but would find it empty. That horde had already moved north.

At 5:58 that morning, just as Angie was beginning to awaken in her van and Brother Peter was tossing in a fitful sleep, every walking corpse within two hundred miles of western Oakland slowed and stopped. They stood motionless, breezes ruffling hair and torn clothing and flaps of hanging skin. Heads lifted slightly. They did not moan or growl, remaining still, silent.

At 6:01 A.M., the Pacific and North American plates of the Hayward Fault, which ran through Oakland, Berkeley, and Richmond, released a small amount of stress in the earth's crust. The few monitors left in California, sitting in vacant rooms but still drawing power, registered a magnitude of 1.7. The event lasted only four seconds and was hardly noticeable.

As soon as it ceased, the dead began moving again.

NINE

At dawn, Angie and Brother Peter arrived at the hangar. There was a sad reunion with the firehouse group as they spoke of Bud's death, and how they had been forced to leave their shelter. As for her uncle's killer, Angie quietly told them that Maxie had paid for his treachery and said nothing more on the subject.

Angie was dismayed not only at the lack of fuel for the helicopter but at all of the new mouths to feed. That the hangar was poorly secured and would be difficult to defend made matters worse. She was pleased, however, to see that a medic had joined the group and quickly paired her up with the medical supplies she had scavenged and carried in the Excursion.

Peter was a perfect gentleman: subdued, well spoken, and apologetic for his filthy condition. He washed as best he could with baby wipes, shaved, and gratefully accepted a change of clothes offered by one of the firehouse group. His visitation from the Lord felt more and more like a dream with each passing hour, but the advice—to act like a normal person—was sound. There were sheep here, unsuspecting and desperate, easily hurt. And Peter Dunleavy had decided that he liked to hurt the sheep. He transferred his beloved box cutter to the pocket of a new pair of jeans.

Outside the hangar, more and more of the dead drifted through the parking lot. Everyone was careful to stay quiet, and the quilted blankets used as bedding the previous night were now hung over the windows to prevent notice from the drifters. It made an already darkened space gloomier, but there were no complaints.

Margaret returned to the back office to check on the infected girl. As she entered, Skye sat up and growled behind her gag, one milky blue eye glaring at her.

"Angie!" Margaret racked a shell into her shotgun. The sound of running feet came from behind her as she watched the girl thrash against her bonds, trying to stand. Angie appeared in the doorway, pistol in hand, as Margaret leveled the shotgun.

Rosa crowded in beside the reality show star and Skye's head snapped to the door. She growled again, still fighting her restraints. Rosa saw the milky eye, but then noticed that the other one was clear.

"*Wait!*"

Margaret let the pressure off the trigger just one foot-pound before it went off. The medic pushed past and went to the girl, crouched, and pulled off the gag.

"Doc, don't!" yelled Margaret.

"Let me go!" screamed Skye. "Take these off me!"

More figures appeared in the doorway, straining to look as Rosa pulled the scissors from her belt pouch. "Relax," she said, "don't fight me." Skye made a gagging sound, and Rosa called for water. "I'm a medic, I'm here to help you."

The young woman shook her head like a wet dog. "Why can't I see? What's wrong with my eye? Take these off!" Her voice was like gravel, and Rosa helped her drink, going slow so she wouldn't choke.

"I'm going to cut these straps off you, and I want you to lie back and be still for a minute, okay?"

Skye's body was trembling as she looked at her, and she managed to nod. Rosa cut the zip ties, and Skye let herself be gently pushed back to the floor, rubbing at her wrists. "Where's my sister?"

"I don't know, honey," said Rosa, fitting her stethoscope to her ears and checking the girl's pulse. Elevated, but not dangerously so, and not like before. Her skin was cool and dry.

"They're in the church! Where's my rifle? We can't stay here, we have to relocate."

"Shhh, we will, honey, we will. What's your name?"

It took a few seconds. "Skye Dennison."

The medic smiled. "Nice to meet you. I'm Rosa."

"What's wrong with my eye?" Skye was touching it, her breathing moving toward hyperventilation. Rosa kept shushing her, speaking softly. Margaret handed off her shotgun and left the room, hands shaking. Sophia was waiting in the hangar and quickly held her friend as Margaret began to cry.

Rosa told Skye that she had been sick, had been exposed to infected fluid and down with a fever for almost twenty-four hours. She had already heard the story about the church rescue and repeated it to the girl.

"You went through what we call the slow burn. You're lucky to be alive."

Skye's voice was a whisper. "My sister is dead."

Rosa went past it. "The fever must have done some damage to your eye. You can't see out of it at all?"

Skye closed her right eye, leaving the milky blue one open. "No, just light." She winced. "It hurts. Is it going to get better?"

Rosa frowned. "We'll have to see, honey. Tell me what hurts, exactly."

"My head." Skye closed both eyes and rubbed her temples. "Headache. A bad one."

Rosa handed her the water bottle and dug some ibuprofen out of her kit, then finished examining the young woman. She was thin almost to the point of gaunt, but that was likely dehydration from the fever. Her nutritional intake must not have been sufficient, though it was clear she had been taking care of herself as best she could and kept fit. Was she military? Her heartbeat was settling and her vitals looked good—Skye allowed Rosa to put a blood pressure cuff on her—and other than skinned knees and knuckles and raw skin where the zip ties had cut into her wrists, she appeared healthy.

Carney poked his head in, a look of wonder on his face. "Is she going to be okay?"

Rosa looked at Skye. "I think so. I want her to take it easy, though."

The inmate hesitated in the doorway for a moment, looking at a young woman who had come back from the brink, then nodded and left.

"Who was that?"

Rosa smiled. "He's the one who saved you from that church."

Skye thought for a moment. "I don't remember him. I was in the tower. I remember shooting—" She stiffened. "Where's my rifle? I need it!" Her hand went to an empty shoulder holster and then to an equally empty boot knife sheath. "I need my weapons."

Rosa didn't want her to panic and shushed her again, telling her that she was safe and would get her weapons back, that she needed to rest. She made her swallow a couple of strong antibiotics and drink an entire bottle of water, and then hit her with a shot of Demerol. Skye didn't protest but avoided looking at the people who were crowding into the doorway to stare at her. She was careful to keep her damaged left eye turned away.

"Oh my God, I stink. And my clothes . . ." They were stiff with the dried fluids of the corpse she had killed with her machete and reeked of her own waste.

"I'll take care of that too," said Rosa. "We're about the same size, as long as you don't mind Navy camo. You're Army, right? Special Forces?"

Skye blinked and shook her head. "I go to college, or I was going. UC Berkeley."

Rosa nodded, not sure what to make of it, and stayed close to her until the Demerol hit and Skye drifted off. Then she retrieved her sea bag and chased everyone out of the room. Margaret returned more composed, and together the two women stripped and washed Skye, then dressed her in a set of Rosa's blue camouflage.

Margaret was silent through it all, but then a tear rolled down her cheek. "My God, I almost . . ."

Rosa hugged her. "But you didn't, and she's going to be fine."

Margaret nodded and managed a small smile.

There were no such happy moments in the adjacent office. Dane was no longer sitting against the wall but had slumped to the floor on his side. His face was flushed and beaded with sweat as the fever came on, his body trembling. Calvin sat cross-legged beside him, wiping his brother's face with a bar towel. Maya stood a ways back, covering her mouth with her hands and crying softly. She had not permitted Evan to come into the room. This was family business.

"Remember the way she danced?" Dane said, looking up at his brother. "Nothing but life and light."

"I remember," Calvin said softly, smiling.

"I loved her too. I loved that she was with you. A better person than both of us, man. I couldn't . . . I didn't . . ."

Calvin stroked the man's forehead. "I know. It's okay."

"It isn't." Dane shook his head. "It happened so fast, and I was trying to save her. Then I got bit." He let out a sob. "I'm so sorry."

Calvin rested his forehead against his brother's. "It was already too late for her. She'd been bitten, hurt badly. It wouldn't have mattered." Dane tried to protest, but Calvin squeezed his hand. "She would have turned. She's at peace now. You did that for her."

Dane began to cry, and it was difficult to tell where the sweat ended and the tears began. "I'm sick, Cal. I feel so bad. It's going to happen to me, isn't it?"

"No. I promise it won't." Tears formed in his eyes now too.

Dane looked past his brother and raised a shaking hand to blow

Maya a kiss. "I'm sorry, sweetheart," he mouthed. Maya nodded and cried harder.

Calvin rested his hand on his brother's hot forehead for a moment, then told him he would be back and left the room. He found Angie, told her what he wanted, and she retrieved it for him without a word. When he came back in, Calvin was screwing a silencer onto the end of one of Angie's automatics. Maya fled to find Evan, and Calvin closed the door behind her.

Dane struggled to sit up, fighting the urge to vomit, forcing himself to look at the man he had idolized since childhood. "You get those kids to a safe place, you hear me?"

A nod. "I will. I love you, brother."

Out in the hangar, it came as a metallic cough. Then there was only the muffled sound of a man weeping.

The balance of the day was quiet, people resting and taking stock of their meager supplies, grateful not to be running or in constant fear of attack. Carney gathered some men and made several trips back and forth to the Bearcat, emptying it during moves carefully planned to avoid being spotted by the dead. He assembled the weapons and riot gear on the stage, and asked Margaret and Sophia to oversee the distribution of the foodstuffs. TC didn't put up a fight. He was sleeping off the tequila.

Around midday, Xavier asked Evan, Angie, and Carney to come to the back of the hangar. "I want to show you something I noticed when Rosa was bringing us in on the boat."

Angie and Carney went with the priest toward a metal ladder, and after checking to see that Maya was occupied with her younger brothers and sisters, Evan followed. The ladder led to a series of catwalks and then another ladder, set high on one wall of the hangar. At the top, Xavier took them up through a hatch and out onto the vast, arching roof of the building.

When they reached the apex, they got down on their stomachs and crawled to the edge. It would probably be difficult for a living man to spot them up here, much less the dead, but there was no sense in taking chances. All of them had seen the results of underestimating their opponents.

The airfield stretched out before them, the water of the bay beyond. Several dozen corpses, looking tiny from their vantage point, wandered the fields and runways without obvious purpose. A few were standing near Vladimir's Black Hawk while one was on all fours, face pressed to the spot where Calvin's wife had died.

"What are we looking at?" asked Carney.

Xavier handed him a pair of binoculars and pointed out beyond the airfield. "That aircraft carrier out there. I figure it's less than a mile offshore."

The inmate looked at it through the binoculars. "I see movement on the deck, people, but I don't think they're sailors."

"Not anymore," said Angie.

"It's hard to see in the daytime," said Xavier, "but yesterday afternoon when we were crossing the bay and getting close to Alameda, I saw lights on board, running lights, and on its bridge too. I'm surprised you didn't see it."

Evan took the binoculars. "I was busy trying not to tip over a barge. I can see lights; they're faint, though. What's the point?" He handed the glasses to Angie.

"Lights mean there's power," Xavier said. Then he told them what he was thinking.

His companions looked at him as if he had gone mad.

TEN

"It's an island," said Xavier, "a fortress with high walls and the biggest moat you could imagine."

They were all gathered in the bar, filling every seat, standing at the edges or sitting on the floor in front. Xavier stood at the head of the gathering, and behind him, assembled like supporters at a press conference, were Evan, Angie, Rosa, and Vladimir while Carney stood slightly to one side. Those from the firehouse—Margaret, Jerry, Elson, and Sophia—were seated apart from the big hippie family across the room. Between the groups sat Darius and the pregnant couple from the patrol boat, Peter Dunleavy, the elderly couple with the husband suffering from MS, and a mob of kids. Other folks kept to the edges. In the back, TC nursed a hangover, aided by some of Rosa's aspirin. Calvin sat at a table with all five of his children. He looked aged.

It didn't escape Xavier's notice that the different groups sat among their own. Despite their smiles and courtesy, actual trust wasn't on the table just yet. If they were to survive, if they went along with his plan, they would have to work together. His job was to make that happen.

"We can't stay here," the priest continued. "It isn't safe, and there's no food. We can't live on pretzels and canned chili, and we're running out of water. That thing will have everything we need."

Mercy, a woman from Calvin's Family, asked, "Won't the food be spoiled, like everyplace else?"

"Not if it still has power," said Evan. He had immediately seen the brilliance of Xavier's idea and was already all in. "The Discovery Channel did a series on aircraft carriers, I watched it. There's enough food on board to feed thousands of men for months." He looked at their numbers. "It could last us years, if necessary."

Xavier nodded. "Food, high walls surrounded by water so nothing can get on board. There have to be military units out there somewhere, and the carrier will have communications."

"Which we don't know how to operate," said a man named Tommy, another of Calvin's Family.

Standing with his arms folded, Vladimir said, "It will have JP-5." When he got blank looks, he said, "Fuel for the Black Hawk."

Brother Peter, looking miles more presentable than when he arrived, stood and said, "If the government is still standing, they'll want that thing back. If we're on it, we'll be rescued." There was some murmured agreement, and the minister quickly sat back down. Subtle seeding, nothing more just yet. Of course he didn't actually believe a word of what he'd said, but that wasn't the point, and in his career as a televangelist, it never had been.

"We should just stay here," a woman named Lilly said, "keep scavenging like we always have."

Angie shook her head. "It's not safe here. You've seen the dead, there's more every hour." She glanced at Calvin, who looked ashen. "The fence line is compromised in dozens of places."

"And fences," said the Russian, "are no assurance of safety. I have seen this."

"We've essentially trapped ourselves on a peninsula," said Angie.

"What we really need to talk about is the dead," said Jerry, his mass perched on a bar stool. "That ship is going to be infested. Let's talk about that."

That started multiple, heated conversations as people considered a ship packed with walking corpses.

"Why can't we just get back on the road?" said a hippie named Tuck. "Most of us survived that way for weeks, didn't we?"

A big man with the unlikely name of Little Bear shook his head. "We'd never get off Alameda."

"What about Alcatraz?" offered Eve, a woman seated next to a seventeen-year-old named Stone. "It's an island; there could only be a handful of drifters there."

Stone shot a response back immediately. "No food, no power."

Darius, the sociologist, addressed his comment to the leaders at the front of the room. "You said the aircraft carrier is just sitting out there, and leaning a little, as if it's damaged. What if the reactors are damaged too, and it's leaking radiation?"

A voice like a bowl of dust spoke from the side: Skye, sitting in a chair with a bottle of water clenched in both hands. She looked at the gathering with one eye brown and the other glazed. "Do you think that's more dangerous than staying here and being eaten?"

There was silence then, as her words sank in.

"There can only be so many on board," she said, "with no way for fresh ones to follow. Each one we kill lowers their numbers and brings the odds more in our favor."

"Unless we're the fresh ones!" Darius laughed nervously and looked around. "You don't all think we can do this without some of us dying?"

Skye's voice was a rasp, and she looked right at the professor. "We'll take care of the fresh ones too."

Angie looked at the young woman and wondered what hell she had been through, out there alone.

"Why not go back to the firehouse?" Larraine, the old woman who required oxygen, offered. "There will be fewer of them, and Angie stocked it up nicely for us."

Angie shook her head sharply. "The firehouse is out; it's completely overrun, and the supplies there would last a group this size a week. There're more dead in the street than ever before. We saw it when we were coming in." No one had asked any questions about her hunting trip.

"Angie's right," Brother Peter offered. "We probably couldn't even get to that firehouse now. But I'm worried about how much longer we can afford to stay *here*. The question should really be about *when* we go, not if." Angie threw the minister a supportive nod, and he smiled back in humble thanks. The images in his head, however, were dark and featured Angie being left for the hungry dead.

More questions followed, most of the debates directed at one another instead of the leaders. *Good,* Xavier thought, *we've got them thinking.*

A man named Dakota asked, "How do we get on board? Won't it be dark?"

This question unnerved Eve, and she asked, "How will we find our way once we're in?"

"We're not soldiers," said a skinny hippie called Juju. "We don't know how to *attack* anything. We stay alive by running, and we only kill drifters when we have to." There were nods at this.

"What happens if we fail?" a man named Freeman asked quietly. He was seated near Calvin and was about the same age as his leader. "Who goes, who stays, and who decides?"

"And what do we do with the kids?" Sophia wanted to know, the little orphan Ben seated on her lap.

Elson, the lawyer from the firehouse, stood and cleared his throat. "For what it's worth, I think it makes sense, because I can't think of a better option. It scares me, make no mistake. I'll go, I'll volunteer right now, but I'm afraid." He looked around at them. "If we do this, people are going to die. We shouldn't fool ourselves. The alternative is doing nothing, and I think in that option we *all* die."

This sparked another half hour of debate as people assessed the pros and cons. Xavier looked at them, at their rising enthusiasm, and wondered if he was talking them into their own destruction. Evan seemed to sense this and gave his shoulder a reassuring squeeze.

Finally, Big Jerry raised his voice so it would be heard above the others. "Let's talk about what we'd be up against. How many do you think there would be?"

Xavier looked at Rosa, who stood. "I'm Navy," she said. "But I've only been on a carrier once, and only for a few days. It's tight, a maze of passageways and doors, and it's easy to get lost. Aircraft carriers have about six thousand personnel on board. It's a floating city."

There were gasps and frightened looks, people shaking their heads.

"If the air wing left the ship like they do when they're heading home," she continued, "the numbers drop to about forty-five hundred. We would have to clear it to be sure we're safe, and that means every corridor, every room, root the dead out of every possible space, and that's going to be dangerous." She glanced at Xavier. "He's right about the supplies; it will have everything you could ever need. I wouldn't worry about the reactors; there's plenty of safety measures for them, and if one was damaged they'd shut down automatically. The carrier will have fuel for the helicopter, comm gear, weapons, and if the system is still working, it can make its own fresh water. Most importantly it has power, and a state-of-the-art medical unit and pharmacy. That also means the freezers should still be running, and that equals meat, frozen vegetables, food that's far better for us than what we've been eating."

Calvin stood slowly at his table, hands resting on the shoulders of the two boys sitting on either side of him. "I've heard enough. I need a home for my kids. This place isn't safe, the road's not safe. I'm in." Every one of his extended family looked at him with trusting eyes, and with that, more than half the people in the room signed on.

"Like I said before, we're going to need a solid plan," said Carney. "And it has to happen sooner rather than later. The dead aren't going to leave us alone."

Rosa nodded. "The carrier I was on had a swimmer's platform at the stern. We can get aboard there, and if not, we can climb up through the aircraft elevators. The platform would be better. I'm thinking the barge stays behind to evacuate anyone who doesn't go, in the event the dead show up in force, and we'd need one more boat for the assault."

Carney snorted. "Doc, if boats were that easy to find, me and TC would be in Mexico by now."

Plenty of nodding from the room, but then Xavier told them what he had seen at the boatyard in Mission Bay where Rosa had found him: at least one boat sitting up on a storage rack, shrink-wrapped in white plastic as owners did when they put a boat away for the season. He suggested that the boatyard would surely have the equipment needed to get it into the water.

Rosa nodded. "We'll make a trip over and find out."

Tuck, one of Calvin's men, stood. "All those vehicles we left on that Oakland pier are full of supplies we could use, and weapons too. We'll need the firepower." He volunteered to go get it, and a few others stood up with him.

"Another boat trip," said Rosa, nodding.

"Excuse me," Sophia said, moving to sit with the kids on the floor in front. "Couldn't he just fly people in on the helicopter?" She looked at Vladimir. "It must have some fuel left in it, right? You all said it's a short distance."

The Russian smiled. "I do not know if I could even get it off the ground. And if I could, the fuel would probably run out halfway there, and *whoosh*!" He waved his arms. "One helicopter and one pilot on the bottom of the sea. You would not wish to be on such a dangerous aircraft, would you, young lady?"

She blushed and shook her head.

He grinned. It didn't make his homely features any more handsome. "But when we have fuel, I will take you on the first ride." He winked, and she added a smile to her blush.

Xavier smiled too. *We're still okay if we can flirt with one another,* he thought to himself.

"How do we figure out who goes and who stays?" asked Elson.

"It would have to be voluntary," Xavier said. He looked at Vladimir. "You would stay. You're the only one who knows how to fly, and we can't risk the loss."

"Or the medic!" a woman shouted. "I'm sorry, I forgot your name."

Rosa shook her head. "I would have to go. I'm the only one with even a little experience on a ship like that, I'll be driving one of the boats, and I'd need to be there if someone got hurt. I've been in combat before; I'll be okay."

Voices rose at that. "No!" said Lilly. "You're the closest thing to a doctor we've seen since this started. We can't risk you getting hurt." Others were shouting their support.

"You should be close to the kids," Juju added.

Rosa held up her hands. "Listen to me, please. There are dangers inside that ship other than the dead. Live munitions, plenty of places to trip and fall or crack your head open. And there's no telling what condition the ship is in, but it's clearly been damaged." She looked at the gathered faces. "People in combat get hurt in lots of ways, and I can be there to help them. Maybe keep them from dying and turning." Now she looked only at the women and softened her voice. "If your men are in there, wouldn't you want that?"

The statement appeared to hit home, and argument on the issue died off.

There were many other details to work out, they knew it, but by now they were all in. Xavier listened to their many conversations and saw that they were happy to have a common goal, feeling like they were in charge of their lives for the first time in a long time. He also knew, having been in combat himself, that they were like any other green recruits heading to war: excited about a great adventure, with absolutely no idea of the nightmare that was waiting to meet them. Those who had spoken had been right; people would die, perhaps all of them. He had no question about where the responsibility for those deaths would fall.

Xavier didn't dare utter a prayer yet, but risked a question. *Lord, am I doing the right thing for these people?*

God had no reply.

ELEVEN

The harbor patrol boat bounced across the bay, Rosa at the helm. Although there was no power for the pumps at the yacht dock, they found the access port for the buried tanks and found it still held fuel. Using a hand pump, they topped off the boat before heading out.

On board with Rosa were Xavier, Angie West, the inmates, Darius, and two of Calvin's hippies. Everyone was armed. Angie wore twin shoulder holsters, one side carrying her uncle's automatic, recovered from Maxie. She'd had no interest in taking the .32 hideout that had been used to murder Bud. She also carried her Galil, a combat shotgun, and a harness of ammo pouches for both. Carney had distributed what riot gear he had, and most of them now wore black body armor and helmets. Only he and TC had biteproof gloves.

During the ride across the bay, TC sat close beside Darius, moving closer every time the man edged away. Eventually the professor rose and moved to the other side of the boat. TC lifted his helmet visor and blew the man a kiss. Darius looked away quickly, his hands clenched into shaking fists.

If Xavier was right and there were usable boats in a storage rack in Mission Bay, they knew the fuel tanks would have been drained.

It was almost certain the boatyard tanks would hold nothing but vapor, considering the waterborne exodus Rosa had witnessed. For those reasons they had filled a pair of red plastic jerry cans with gas and strapped them down on the deck of the patrol boat. A heavy tow rope was on the deck in case the fuel wasn't enough.

There was little conversation during the crossing, only the rush of wind, the growl of the motor, and the rough hush of water on fiberglass. It was overcast, the sky a flat, even shale, a muted sun lurking somewhere behind it. All eyes were fixed on the dead city looming in the west.

Fires had taken their toll, and now many of the once impressive towers were blackened and riddled with great patches of broken glass, looking at a distance like trunks of worm-eaten trees. A few had collapsed from the intensity of the fires and leaned against one another at angles, while others stood without any glass at all, only gutted shells. No traffic or trolleys crawled the famous hills and boulevards, no bustling throngs of tourists and locals packed the sidewalks or rode along in tour buses. It was a city of shattered lives and shadows, heartbreaking in its emptiness, and yet impossible not to look upon.

They all knew San Francisco was by no means unoccupied. It now crawled with something else.

"Coming in," called Rosa, slowing the patrol boat as it neared the docks and commercial boatyards where she had rescued Xavier only yesterday. Pairs of binoculars went up, and eyes scanned the shore.

Xavier looked at the dock where he had been prepared to make his stand. It was empty. Then he checked the water, expecting bobbing, snapping heads, until he remembered Rosa's lecture on corpses. They would have sunk, and without gases inside them, they would not be coming up. Were they down there still? Trudging through the silt and slime among the pilings, moving slowly through the murky water? Or had the tide carried them away?

"Drifter," said a hippie.

They looked to where the man was pointing at a lone figure wandering along the wharf, moving toward a large restaurant on the right. "I've got another one," said Carney. A thing in the orange coveralls of a city trash handler stood near a small icehouse where fish were unloaded, staring out at them and swaying side to side. The coveralls reminded Carney of his former life, and he clenched his jaws without realizing.

They watched for another ten minutes, the engine idling as the boat rocked gently. Nothing else moved on the waterfront or among the trees beyond, the green area separating the high-rise condos of Mission Bay from the shore. If anything haunted the boatyard, it was out of sight. Rosa brought the boat in and they tied up at a dock.

"Like we discussed," said Xavier, and everyone nodded. Rosa would stay with the boat and cast off. The rest would go ashore, splitting into smaller groups if necessary. Angie carried her walkie-talkie, and the other one sat on a map ledge over the patrol boat's wheel. The shore party set off, moving in single file across the planking, the only sound the sloshing of water against the pilings and the distant call of gulls.

The thing in the orange coveralls moved toward them immediately, and they slowed to let it come, watching it stagger out onto the dock. The bearded hippie named Little Bear, a huge man in a Grateful Dead T-shirt, cargo shorts, and hiking boots, advanced in front of the group to meet it. He carried one of the long-handled limb-cutting tools they had scavenged, but the saw had been replaced with a sharpened blade from a pair of hedge clippers. Little Bear waited until the thing stumbled into range, and then he lunged forward like a castle pikeman. His impromptu polearm caught the thing in the mouth, and he thrust, the blade exploding out the back of the creature's head. It went instantly limp, and Little Bear let it sag to the side, slipping off his weapon and dropping into the water.

Carney nodded. "You look like you've done that before."

Little Bear shook his head. "First zombie. But I worked a summer on a farm when I was a kid. It's kind of like forking a hay bale."

Angie gave him a pat on his broad back as she moved past, her Galil up and ready. TC brought up the rear, the visor of his helmet up as he frequently turned to watch behind them. Xavier told Angie where he had come from and ended up, telling her about the mob of corpses that had emerged from the boatyard, and where he thought he had seen the boat racks.

There were corrugated metal sheds used for workshops, small warehouses, fenced-off service yards, frozen storage buildings for fresh seafood—the spoiled reek had thankfully passed by this point—charter and sales buildings: lots of places for the dead to hide. Darius let out a shriek and almost triggered his shotgun when a mottled gray-and-tan cat burst from between two buildings and streaked across their path, but TC jerked the weapon away from him in time.

"Let me hold that for you, sweetheart," he said softly, winking. Darius took a deep breath as if about to say something, saw the smile that didn't match the menace in TC's eyes, and turned away.

They quickly found the place Xavier had spoken of near the back of the boatyard, a warehouse-style construction of heavy metal racks. As the priest had seen, there was not only one vessel resting on the top level, wrapped in white plastic, but another one beside it.

They were canoes.

Everyone looked at the priest, and he felt the heat in his face. He didn't bother trying to rationalize that he had been on the run, pursued by the dead, and had only caught a glimpse in the twilight. He felt like a fool.

"Let's attack an aircraft carrier with a canoe," TC said, laughing. "What a fucking waste of time."

"Let it go, TC," said Carney.

The younger inmate sneered at the priest. "Good job."

"Uh, before we rush to judgment, folks," Little Bear said, pointing. Beyond an empty, fenced yard where boats would have been stored on their trailers was a row of trees with a service road just on the other side. Sitting on that road was a flatbed eighteen-wheeler tractor-trailer. Perched upon that, strapped down for transport, was a thirty-two-foot black-and-white Bayliner boat. It too had its deck shrink-wrapped in white plastic.

Xavier glanced skyward and shook his head.

"You got lucky," muttered TC, as they all walked toward the prize.

"There must be something wrong with it," said Darius. "Why would it still be here?"

Angie shrugged. "People were in a hurry to get out. They probably didn't see it back there."

Carney shook his head. "It would have been hard to miss. They probably couldn't figure out how to get it off the truck and into the water, which is going to be our problem too."

"It probably doesn't have an engine," said Darius.

"Hey, Mary Sunshine," said TC, putting an arm around the professor's shoulder, which the man immediately shrugged off. The inmate put a gloved finger to his lips. "Sweetie, shhh . . ." he whispered.

Xavier hadn't missed the tension between the two men, or the younger inmate's suggestive behavior. "They have to do this all the time," the priest said. "There must be a big forklift around here." He stepped between Darius and TC and looked at the professor. "Can you go with Little Bear and see if you can find it?" The professor nodded and headed toward a warehouse with Little Bear and a hippie named Lou at his side.

"I'll give them cover," said TC, winking at the priest and turning to follow.

Xavier caught hold of the inmate's arm. "How about you stay and cover us while we inspect the boat?"

TC gave him a crooked, knowing grin, then jerked his arm away and trotted after the three jogging figures. Xavier felt a simmering anger as he watched the man leave, and yet short of shooting TC in the back, he realized there was nothing he could do. Angie and Carney were headed toward the tractor-trailer to see if the professor's predictions of doom and gloom were correct, and after a moment the priest followed. They made sure to check among the trees and in the shadows beneath the trailer for lurking zombies.

Climbing the tail of the trailer gave access to the molded Plexiglas stairs at the stern of the boat, and a quick slit with a blade created a flap in the plastic through which they could enter. It was warm inside the shrink wrap and a little claustrophobic for everyone but Carney. He was long past having any issues with tight spaces. The inmate pulled out a small flashlight.

The Bayliner smelled new. Its large deck offered white upholstered seating, and a fiberglass radar arch curved overhead. The flooring was polished teak, rich with its own aroma. Below, the Bayliner featured spacious forward and midships berths, a good-sized head, and a modern galley with stainless steel fixtures, a fridge, microwave, and stove. It was all trimmed in teak as well. An entertainment cabinet in the main compartment was packed with high-end audio equipment and an LCD flat screen.

"What the hell does something like this cost?" said Carney, running his fingers over the polished wood.

"New?" said Angie. "Probably a hundred thousand. I'm not sure."

The inmate shook his head. *For a boat,* he thought.

They went topside again and began cutting away the plastic, letting in the day's gray light. For a moment, each of them expected to find the eighteen-wheeler surrounded by the hammering dead, but they were alone other than a few birds chirping within the nearby trees.

"These things drive like a car, right?" said Carney.

Angie nodded. "Sort of."

"So it's going to need a key," the inmate said, and the other two stopped and stared at him, then each other.

"Shit," said Angie.

They began searching the cockpit area, spreading out across the deck, opening compartments and looking inside elastic pockets on the backs of the seats. Carney jumped down to check the cab of the truck, just as the crack of gunfire broke the silence, and the biggest forklift any of them had ever seen raced toward them across the boatyard.

TWELVE

"Where did they all go?" Evan whispered. He and Calvin were crouched behind a pallet of crates bearing Korean markings, peeking over the top. Out of sight on the barge below the edge of the pier, four men and women from Calvin's group waited with rifles and shotguns, each additionally armed with a hand-to-hand landscaper's weapon.

"Who knows," said Calvin. It was two of only a dozen words the man had spoken since leaving Alameda.

Evan was nervous about the thousands of corpses that had been on this dock only a day ago, worried about where they might be now. He didn't dare allow himself to think they had all conveniently walked off the pier and sunk harmlessly to the bottom. He was also worried about the people back at Alameda. Both boats were out, and if an evacuation became necessary they would have to pack into that handful of vehicles and try to drive out. Survival would be unlikely. He thought of Maya.

What worried the writer the most, however, was the girl kneeling behind a stack of crates next to them, sighting down her rifle. Skye had retrieved her combat gear, rifle, and ammo and climbed into the Bearcat with the others for the ride to the docks and the boats. She hadn't spoken, and simply climbed onto the barge.

Angie had given up her aviator sunglasses as the young woman winced frequently in the light and rubbed her temples. Though he was a little ashamed of it, Evan was happy not to have to look at that horrible, cloudy left eye. *She's damaged,* he thought, *and not just physically. Now she's packing an automatic weapon.* He tried not to stare.

"Pull the barge down the side of the pier until it's even with the vehicles," Calvin ordered. "We'll empty them fast, throw everything down onto the deck."

"I'll take watch," Skye said, her voice cracked and husky. Without waiting for a reply, she jogged forward, rifle up. Calvin and Evan followed slowly, while the barge's diesel coughed and moved the craft alongside the wharf.

Skye moved past the line of cars, vans, and SUVs, rifle muzzle tracking everywhere she looked: under them, inside them, between them. There was no sign of the dead. A white headache was settling behind her blind left eye, making her grit her teeth, and she knew that if she hadn't been clenching the rifle's front grip so tightly, her left hand would be trembling like a Parkinson's victim. Her depth perception was off too, and although she didn't think it would impair scope shooting, it made quick movement a challenge.

You were stupid and careless, and now you're weak.
Unacceptable.

She reached the end of the row and knelt beside the left rear tire of a Ford Escape SUV, settling into a shooting position, removing her sunglasses and aiming downrange. The wharf stretched before her, lined on one side with ships, each with a bright yellow hazmat symbol spray-painted on the hull, their gangplanks torn down. The wharf itself was cluttered with cargo containers and heavy equipment, and a sprawling industrial park stretched beyond it.

Skye's vision was distorted and it felt similar to looking at a 3D movie screen without the benefit of the special glasses. Things looked flat, like two-dimensional scenery props on a deep stage, and they floated in and out of focus. Debris, containers, and forklifts littered the area and created a lot of places for the dead to hide. But she knew they wouldn't hide. They didn't do that. They detected prey and came straight for it.

"Come on, then," she whispered, flexing her index finger in the trigger well, searching through the small world of her combat sight. The headache suddenly drove a white finger into the center of her brain and she closed her eyes, gasping and nearly dropping her rifle. She clenched her teeth and forced open a watery eye, her vision blurry.

Unacceptable.

Calvin, Evan, and two others moved among the vehicles, opening every door and rear hatch, emptying the contents. They carried cardboard boxes, wooden crates, and plastic totes to the edge of the pier, stacking them or dropping them to the waiting hippies on the deck of the barge. Food, bottled water, clothing, batteries, cans of Sterno and bottles of propane, small grills, coolers and sleeping bags, tents and lawn chairs were all collected.

At the Ford Escape, Skye saw movement: fifty yards out, a shape behind a tangle of metal that had once been a ladderway for one of the cargo ships, a head of dirty blond hair moving slowly. She tracked it, the luminescent green pips of the combat sight wiggling and unsteady. The figure came into view, a teenage girl in clothing so torn and soiled it looked like pinned-on rags, a dead girl walking with a severe limp, one foot twisted backward.

Skye rested her finger on the trigger and tried to put the pips just at the top of her head. She squeezed.

PUFFT. The girl didn't react. A miss.

The suppressor made its coughing sound again, and this time there was a loud *SPANG* as the bullet ricocheted off the tangle of metal. *Christ, that was a good two feet off target,* she thought. The corpse stopped and turned halfway toward the noise, now facing Skye's position. It first cocked its head, then lifted it, turning this way and that.

She's scenting the air, Skye thought. *Searching for me.*

Another figure appeared behind the girl, a tall pole of a man in a once-white doctor's coat now covered in rusty splotches. His scalp had been torn off, revealing a crown of white skull. He too stopped to scent the air. Skye bit the inside of her cheek hard, eye widening with the pain, and let out a long breath. She placed the phosphorescent pips on that patch of bare bone.

PUFFT.

The round blew off a chunk of shoulder, turning him ninety degrees. The doctor corpse walked that new direction for several steps, then angled back in toward the tail end of the line of vehicles. The girl moved alongside him.

Skye wanted to scream. She rubbed a palm at her good eye as the headache turned into fingers that crept toward the base of her skull, probing and white. She felt nauseated, and an involuntary cry escaped her lips.

The dead heard it, heads jerking at the sound.

A hand fell upon her shoulder and Skye leaped forward, spinning, bringing the rifle up. Calvin grabbed the muzzle and forced it away from his face. "Stop it!" His voice was a sharp, angry whisper. Skye jerked the barrel out of his hand and bared her teeth, partially from the pain, partially from something else.

"We're loading the weapons now," Calvin said, his voice still soft as he looked at the two wretches slowly making their way toward them. Skye looked too, but didn't raise her rifle.

"There were so many of them here," Calvin said, no longer really speaking to her. "Why would they leave? Where would they go?"

Skye hadn't seen the hungry mob on the pier, had only heard pieces of the escape story as the hippies relived it with one another. She didn't have an answer for the man. The creatures seemed predictable one moment, like docile cattle, and clever the next, capable of shocking physicality. Not that it mattered, they all had the same value to her. Targets. Tangos, as Sgt. Postman would have said. She rubbed her temple.

"Come and help us," Calvin said. "You need more rest and practice before you can do any good with that thing."

Skye stood and looked at him with that dead eye, then turned and snapped the rifle to her shoulder. *PUFFT. PUFFT.* Both corpses dropped, and Skye Dennison brushed past the aging hippie without a word, slinging the rifle.

The cords on Evan's arms stood out as he lifted a big, hard plastic case from the back of a minivan and lugged it to the edge of the wharf. It was stamped with yellow lettering: *M72 LAW 66mm HEAT QTY 10.* He set it down next to a wooden crate holding forty-millimeter rifle-fired grenades, something he had seen only in movies. Curious, he unsnapped the plastic case and looked inside. A row of tubelike objects was covered in oily brown paper, and he peeled it back to reveal another weapon he had only seen in film.

"LAW rocket, man," said one of the hippies helping him unload the van, a man named Dakota who had spoken out at the meeting. "Light antitank weapon. Cool, huh?"

Evan shook his head, not at all convinced a zombie would care about or even react to being hit by one of these things. It looked like something that would turn one hungry, aggressive thing into *lots* of hungry, aggressive things. "Do any of you even know how to use this?"

A shrug. "Some. The rifles are easy to figure out, and grenades, hell, just pull and throw, right? We haven't really messed with the heavier stuff."

"Where did you get it all?"

Dakota passed an armload of rifles one at a time down to a woman on the barge. "We came across what was left of an Army unit somewhere between Vacaville and Fairfield, strung out along about a mile of highway and off on both sides." The hippie shook his head. "It was bad, man. Those guys must have put up a hell of a fight. There was so much spent brass on the ground you could barely see your shoes. Too many of them, I guess. Drifters, I mean. Not a soldier left alive. Not many left period, most of them out walking." He waved a hand.

Evan tried to imagine how it must have been for them, the numbers needed to completely wipe out a military column with only claws and teeth.

"We were lucky the drifters were gone when we got there. Probably the same horde that took out Travis Air Base." The man helped Evan pass the rocket launchers down to the barge, then straightened and looked at him. "You know, I used to think of those guys as pigs, part of the oppressive military establishment, right-wing morons trying to suppress freedom. All that hippie crap, you know?" Dakota shook his head and made a disgusted face. "What a load of shit. That's not our life anymore, and those guys were never what I called them. They were just people doing a job *I* could never do, fighting while the rest of us ran." He looked across the bay to where a silent aircraft carrier rested at a gentle tilt. "It makes me ashamed."

Evan didn't offer any words of comfort. What had Xavier said about the caliber of those people? Running to the gunfire. The apparently *former* hippie's thoughts had occurred to Evan on occasion too, but he'd never had the courage to face or voice them. Dakota was right. *Ashamed* was the right word.

They finished up a few minutes later. The caravan hadn't actually been a rolling armory—most of it was food, clothing, and camping gear—but the firepower Calvin's people had managed to scrounge would go a long way toward defending the group. Or storming a carrier, if they went ahead with Xavier's plan.

Skye appeared and climbed down to the barge without saying anything. Evan helped Calvin load the last few containers of gasoline, and within minutes the writer was back in the wheelhouse, the barge chugging out into the Middle Harbor. He was relieved, thankful that they had successfully recovered so many supplies without loss of life.

He wondered how the other group was doing.

THIRTEEN

Xavier put his binoculars on the forklift as Angie jumped to the ground and sprinted toward the front of the truck. Little Bear was driving, with TC sitting on the back, firing his cylinder-fed shotgun. Lou, the hippie who had gone with them, was jogging behind at a distance.

The dead followed.

There were over twenty of them, staggering across the yard in the wake of the forklift, more emerging from the sheds and workshops, walking stiffly into the open. As Xavier watched, Lou stumbled and fell, then began howling and clutching at his ankle. Before the priest could even cry out, the dead fell upon the man and began tearing.

"Dear Lord, have mercy," Xavier whispered. He scanned and shouted, "I don't see Darius with them."

Carney jumped down from the cab of the semi holding a large plastic envelope of paperwork. "Found the boat keys," he said, shaking the packet.

"C'mon." Angie jogged past the trees, back out into the open of the yard. The forklift roared toward them as Carney fell in on her left. Angie's Galil and the inmate's M14 came up as they waited for the vehicle to arrive. They cringed at the forklift's blatting diesel engine and the crash of TC's shotgun. Both were certain to summon the dead from a distance. Bear drove past and stopped near the eighteen-wheeler as TC jumped down to join his cellmate.

"What happened?" Carney demanded.

"We found the forklift," he said, grinning and gesturing back at the machine.

"No, with them." Carney sighted down his rifle at the corpses coming across the boatyard.

"Where's Darius?" Angie asked.

TC pointed. "That warehouse down there, the one with the rusty sides. That's where we found the forklift. While the other two guys were figuring out how it worked, me and the black dude went into a back room to look for stuff we could use. We walked right into a nest of them."

"Where's Darius?" Angie repeated.

The inmate shook his head. "They got him. Nothing I could do."

Carney watched his cellmate's eyes as he delivered what sounded like something rehearsed on short notice.

Xavier and Little Bear joined them. "They came out of every-where," the big hippie said, winded.

"Has anyone here ever owned a boat?" Angie looked at each of them. No one had. She thought about what she and her husband, Dean, had learned back when they were considering such a purchase, back before . . . all of this. It wasn't much.

"Let's keep it simple," said Xavier. "Line up the forklift to pick the boat up from the rear, cut the straps holding it to the truck, and then get it into the water somehow. We can figure out the rest once we're aboard and away from them."

"People back boats down a ramp with a trailer," said Little Bear, "and ease it in that way."

There was no such trailer waiting conveniently for them, and Xavier suspected this boat was too big for that anyway. As if to remind them that time was an issue, the dead began to moan. They were closer, and there were more of them than a few minutes ago.

"Use the forklift," said TC. "Just drive that fucker right into the water with the boat and let it sink. It's not like we'll need it again."

They looked at the inmate in surprise, then at each other. Why not? All they would need was a ramp. Angie got on the radio and called Rosa, telling her to scout for one from the water. Rosa acknowledged.

"Carney and I will stay here and hold them back," said Angie. "We're past the sneaking-around portion of this little adventure. You guys get that thing off the truck, and be careful not to crack the hull or this will all have been a waste."

They nodded and headed to the truck.

"And watch the rear!" Carney shouted after them. He turned and raised his rifle. He and Angie opened fire together.

Little Bear drove the giant forklift past the tractor-trailer and turned around on the access road, then approached slowly from the rear. The fork controls took a few moments to figure out, and then he began to creep forward, making small adjustments to the angle of the vehicle and the height of the forks.

TC stood nearby, reloading his shotgun as he kept watch, a faint grin on his face. He hadn't felt this free and satisfied in a very long time, and decided the end of the world was the best thing ever to happen to him. It had become the devil's playground, he thought, words he had possibly heard on TV. *His* playground. A handful of figures appeared on the road behind them, walking slow and crooked, but too far out of the shotgun's range. "Here, kitty, kitty. . . ." TC chuckled and made faces at the lurching creatures.

Xavier moved along the length of the flatbed trailer, examining the canvas tie-down straps holding the boat in place, studying the buckles until he had them figured out. He waved Little Bear forward.

Not every round was a head shot. The Galil's 5.56-millimeter tore holes in chests and throats as well, which the dead did not notice. Most found their mark, however, and a body would drop to the ground. Carney's powerful 7.62s did more damage when he missed the head, blowing away chunks of flesh, breaking bones, even spinning them around or knocking them flat. His on-target shots blew heads apart like rotten fruit. The others just got back up and kept coming.

Two dozen went down for good before they each paused to load new magazines.

As anticipated, more arrived, flowing into the boatyard in a growing stream from the street beyond, drawn by the sounds they associated with live prey. The rifles were keeping them at a distance, but the group as a whole was drawing closer. Angie and Carney knew they couldn't hold for long.

"I think you're good!" Xavier shouted to be heard over the rumbling engine. Little Bear idled forward as the priest guided him with hand signals. *Move to the left. Raise the forks a little. Too much, lower. Come forward.* TC watched them, still wearing his little grin and glancing occasionally at the corpses steadily coming on from the rear. He'd let them get a little closer, just to be fair.

The long forks were designed for this work, both heavily wrapped in some sort of padded carpeting. Little Bear slid them forward carefully, still making corrections as they rubbed against the fiberglass hull. He braked when the forklift could approach no further, and Xavier immediately began unbuckling the straps.

In the boatyard, Carney sighted on a cluster of bodies a hundred feet away. "How many do you think?" He squeezed off a shot, and a middle-aged man in a shirt and tie went down.

"Maybe a hundred," said Angie. The Galil barked, blowing out the back of a woman's head.

"More coming," said Carney. "Not enough ammo for this." He fired again, cursed when his shot clipped off an ear but nothing else. He adjusted and stopped the target with the next one.

"We still need to find a boat ramp," she said. The Galil kicked, and a chubby Hispanic guy in a greasy apron fell over.

At the truck, Xavier finished with the straps and gave Little Bear the signal to lift. The man raised the forks a foot, the vehicle creaking under the weight, and both of them wondered at how it didn't simply tip over. Then he tilted the forks back, felt the tension lessen, and backed up slowly. When Xavier signaled that he was clear of the trailer, Little Bear lowered the boat until it was only four feet off the ground. Xavier trotted over to the shooters as Little Bear drove slowly around the tractor-trailer, leaning far out to one side in an attempt to see around his massive cargo.

Carney and Angie received Xavier's news with a nod and increased the tempo of their firing, wanting to create as much of a gap between them and the dead as possible.

"Oh, no," said Xavier, and the shooters looked to where he was pointing.

It was Darius.

The man was walking slowly into the boatyard, arms limp at his sides, head down.

"Maybe he's just—" Angie started.

"He's dead," said Carney, but Xavier held up a hand and used the binoculars. Darius filled his view up close. The man's beaded braids swung back and forth as he moved unsteadily, looking down at the ground. Xavier saw no blood on the man's expensive, camel-colored overcoat, and none of the savage wounds he had come to expect from the walking dead.

Darius raised his chin. His eyes were smooth and white, the color already draining from his skin. His mouth hung open, moving wordlessly, the muscles of his face slack.

Xavier noticed his neck at once. There, pressed deep in the flesh, were twin bruises he had seen far too many times in the tragic, poverty-ridden tenements of his parish. Bruises in the shapes of thumbs, one on each side of the windpipe, the calling card of a strangler.

"He's dead," the priest choked.

Carney immediately shot Darius in the forehead.

They fell back to where Little Bear was waiting with the big Bay-liner perched on the forklift blades. Carney retrieved the plastic enve-lope containing the keys, and Xavier looked at TC, standing along the side of the access road, cradling his shotgun with a content, easy look on his face.

"Let's head for the water," said Angie, pointing at a space fifty yards away between a commercial fishing icehouse and a corrugated metal storage building. The shimmer of gray light on water peeked from beyond. "Go slow, and do *not* drop the boat."

Little Bear gave her a thumbs-up.

"Carney and I will go ahead and look for a ramp. Xavier, stay close to the forklift and watch them coming in from the left." She pointed at TC. "You come up last and watch the rear." She had already turned away before she could see the man's eyes narrow to slits. He spat on the road, watching her.

The forklift's engine grumbled as Little Bear moved his load for-ward, Xavier helping to guide him while he watched the mob from the boatyard come closer. Soon he would have to use the shotgun and leave Little Bear on his own. Angie and Carney jogged ahead and disappeared through the space between the buildings. Little Bear plodded along with his load, trying to focus on his task but unable to keep from looking at the crowd of corpses on the left, their feet kicking up dust as they shuffled over the ground. The yard was full of them now, and even more shambled in behind them.

Xavier looked back at TC. The man had removed his riot helmet and was tossing his mane of hair, strolling casually behind the fork-lift with his shotgun over one shoulder, smoking a cigarette. Three corpses were angling at him from behind, only thirty feet away.

Murderer.

Hadn't Carney said so in the hangar? Why wouldn't his "partner" be the same? Yet the priest had trouble believing they were cut from the same cloth. Carney had killed, yes, though Xavier admitted he did not know under what circumstances, but the man he looked at now was pure predator.

For an instant, the rage that lived inside the priest crept to the surface and suggested that Xavier should simply walk over to the man, disarming him with a smile, then put the shotgun against his forehead and pull the trigger.

Monster. Kill the monster.

Xavier's body shook as he forced the thought down. He wouldn't, couldn't do such a thing. He suddenly realized he had stopped walking, was standing and staring, and that TC had caught him at it.

"See something you like, *bro*?"

Xavier blinked. "Behind you."

TC nodded. "You too."

The priest turned to see a boy of fifteen with greenish-black skin galloping toward him out of a patch of high weeds, not ten feet away. He cried out and swung the butt of his shotgun at the boy's head as he closed, connecting, making the corpse fall to the side. Before the boy could get back on his feet, Xavier stepped in and took his head off with a close-range blast. Behind him, TC quickly dispatched the creatures that had been stalking in from the rear.

Bear stomped the brakes at the booming shotguns, and the rear tires lifted six inches as the Bayliner carried it forward. "Oh shit," Little Bear said through clenched teeth.

The forklift settled back down with a thump, the boat shifting several degrees to one side. Little Bear let out a gasp and squeezed the steering wheel until his hands hurt. "Are you okay?" he shouted at Xavier.

Xavier stood over the fallen boy, the shotgun trembling just a little in his hands. *It wasn't a person*, he told himself. *It was a monster. I didn't just kill another child.* A wall of approaching dead cared nothing for his guilt and doubt, damaged throats gurgling as they began to move faster, all eyes on the priest.

TC rapped his knuckles on the forklift's roll bar. "Let's get this fucker moving, big man."

Little Bear accelerated toward the space between the buildings, and TC chuckled at the priest before following. In that moment, Xavier had no questions as to who was the real monster here. The forklift picked up speed, and the priest was forced to stop and fire until he was dry, dropping five, missing three others. He trotted behind the departing vehicle, reloading on the run.

Gunfire was coming from up ahead.

A lot of gunfire.

Rosa brought the patrol boat in slowly, the slips and docks to her rear now, a long concrete wharf ahead. It was lined with the commercial fishing buildings she had seen earlier, old tires hanging on ropes along its length, there to provide bumpers for long-departed fishing boats. To the right was the main pier, stretching away toward the restaurant with many windows, a parklike section of trees dividing the waterfront from a row of high-rises.

The walking dead were moving along the pier, stumbling down through the trees, all headed for the gunfire. A breeze carried their stench out over the water and caused Rosa to gag. Out in front of the icehouse, Carney and Angie stood side by side, pouring fire into a crowd coming toward them.

Bodies dropped, some pitching over the side and into the water, more instantly taking their place. The two shooters took turns changing magazines, never at the same time and shouting their actions to one another.

Rosa wanted to help, wanted to roar up beside the pier and use one of the assault rifles on board to add to their fire. Instead she forced herself to look for a boat ramp as instructed. She spotted a sturdy wooden dock far to the right, where a four-wheeled, metal-framed contraption stood with heavy straps slung low between the crossbars. It took only a moment to determine its purpose; motorized and quite clearly intended for larger vessels, it would straddle a boat either on land or already in the water, position its sling beneath the craft, and hoist it out. It looked complicated and time-consuming, and it was on the other side of the dead. She kept looking.

There, off to the left near the end of the pier, away from the shooters and the advancing horde. She grabbed the walkie-talkie. "Angie, the ramp's behind you."

On shore, the other woman didn't react and just kept firing.

Rosa tried twice more without result before realizing the radio was being drowned out by the rifle fire. She grabbed the handset off the dash and flipped the patrol boat's radio switch to PA. Her voice blared across the water. "The boat ramp is to your rear, about fifty yards, near the end of the wharf."

Both shooters began falling back at once, still firing.

The elevated bow of a large black-and-white boat appeared between two buildings, and then the forklift was out on the concrete, Xavier standing beside it. Rosa waved her arms and gestured to the left as if she were a ground crewman directing a plane. Xavier saw her, and a moment later the forklift turned and rumbled toward the ramp with its heavy cargo.

TC was falling back through the space, a wall of the dead advancing into his shotgun. Xavier appeared beside him and added his own firepower for a moment, and then the two of them retreated to where Carney and Angie were waiting.

"Let's go!" Angie shouted, running after the forklift. The others followed. Seconds later, the two groups of the dead, those from the boatyard and those on the pier, merged into one snarling mass and surged after their prey, completely filling the pier.

Little Bear risked a glance behind and realized there would be only one shot at this, and no time for finesse. He leaned out one side of the roll cage, spotted the concrete slope descending into the water, lined up, and floored it. The powerful engine belched diesel smoke as it leaped forward, picking up speed as the pier steadily ran out beneath its tires, the Bayliner bouncing madly on the prongs.

Rosa turned the patrol boat and followed, as her four companions chased after it on shore.

Little Bear's last glance at the oil-smudged speedometer read thirty miles per hour as he pointed at the boat ramp.

He missed.

The giant forklift left the stone pier on an angle a good fifteen feet in front of the slope, plunging straight down; the Bayliner was flung free and forward of the twin prongs, airborne for seconds, then slamming bow first into the water with a tremendous splash, surging up again and coasting away.

The forklift hit the water at the edge of the pier while their newly acquired vessel was still in the air. Little Bear lunged to clear the seat as the vehicle hit the surface. His right boot, however, had slipped under the brake pedal and become wedged. Before he could twist it free, the full impact of water hit him in the chest and face, jarring him back against the seat. He gasped and the water cut him short, several tons of forklift pulling him down fast. The big man panicked, trying to breathe and free his foot at the same time, as the gray light from above quickly turned to ink.

Rosa saw it happen. She cranked the wheel and throttled forward, reversing as she neared the spot where the vehicle had gone under, killing the engine as she coasted in. She rapidly kicked off her combat boots and dropped her sidearm belt, then snatched a yellow water-proof flashlight from a clip on the cockpit wall and dove over the side.

Xavier saw it too and sprinted past the others, dropping his shot-gun and launching himself off the wharf and into the water. The rest of them reached the boat ramp but could see nothing of the forklift, only a disturbance of bubbles on the surface.

Angie snatched the walkie-talkie off her belt and was about to call for Rosa, when she looked up and saw the deck of the patrol boat empty. A horrid symphony of moans came from behind them as the horde drew near enough to break into that awful, predatory gallop. Without a word to one another, Angie, Carney, and TC slung their weapons and jumped into the cold water. They stroked hard toward the slowly drifting patrol craft, pulling even harder when they heard the rippling splash of corpses dropping behind them.

Xavier had always been a powerful swimmer, as swimming was one of the ways he had maintained his boxer's physique into his forties, and now he kicked hard and dug with his arms, clawing into the depths, heading for the jumping, pale beam of a flashlight far below. The pressure built with every stroke. The forklift had settled into the silt nearly thirty feet below the surface, the water cloudy as particles drifted on a lethargic current.

Rosa managed to reach the vehicle, resting tilted at a sharp angle, and gripped one of the metal supports of the driver's roll cage, kicking her feet to help her stay down, aiming the light. Little Bear hung in the water as if suspended, head down and arms floating out at his sides in a parody of crucifixion, his boot still hooked under the brake pedal. Rosa gripped him by the shoulders, shaking him, his body rolling in limp, slow motion. She took him by his bearded chin and raised his slack face.

Little Bear's eyes snapped open, yellow with constricted pupils.

One of his big hands locked on Rosa's wrist and pulled it to his now bared teeth. Rosa tried to pull away, had no leverage, and struggled to bring her legs around so she could brace against the forklift, gain some leverage. Too slow, and a panicked burst of bubbles escaped her lips. Little Bear bit down.

But his teeth clicked together, half an inch from her skin.

Xavier, feet planted on the back of the forklift, had two fistfuls of the big hippie's hair and he hauled the head back, fighting to hold him. Little Bear pulled at Rosa's arm, teeth furiously biting at the water, yellow eyes rolling. Rosa dropped the light and clawed at his fingers as more air erupted from her mouth and panic began to take hold.

Shadowy figures appeared out of the gloom on all sides, shuffling along the bottom, their feet causing clouds of silt to billow about them.

The priest used his right elbow to jam the hippie's head against a roll cage beam, pinning him there, and then used both hands to pry the dead man's fingers from the medic's wrist. Freed, Rosa struggled to kick toward the surface, her arms moving slowly. Xavier pushed hard at the hippie's head and kicked off the forklift, leaving Little Bear still trapped and reaching back over his shoulders. The priest caught Rosa under an arm and propelled them both upward, a crowd of dead white hands reaching up in their wake. Moments later, the pair broke the surface with an explosive gasp.

Within minutes everyone was aboard the patrol boat, all of them soaked and shaking, watching the frustrated dead stumble off the pier with reaching arms. Everyone except Rosa, who clung to the side of the boat and stared down into the water, her gasps turning to sobs.

Xavier took charge, pointing to the Bayliner, drifting fifty feet away. "We don't have enough gas in these cans to get it back, and don't have time to learn to drive it anyway. We'll tow it."

The others nodded and prepared the rope they had brought.

The priest went to Rosa and wrapped her in his arms, saying nothing until she stopped shaking. "We need our skipper, Doc," he said when she finally pulled away.

Rosa nodded, went to the wheelhouse, and throttled their craft toward the wayward Bayliner.

FOURTEEN

The original plan was for the assault group to make numerous trips out to the relatively close *Nimitz*, falling back to Alameda as a base camp for rest and resupply. Like many of the survivors' plans, it fell apart almost at once.

Shortly after the two groups departed for their respective trips to the San Francisco boatyard and to raid the convoy at Middle Harbor, the dead began pushing into the old naval base in numbers too great to ignore and too dangerous to risk having to use the hangar as a point of defense. Their moaning echoed down deserted boulevards and bounced off the walls of abandoned structures, thousands of lurching figures in the streets and parking lots, lawns and parks. Among those left behind, the decision was quickly made to pack every member of the group and what supplies they had into the remaining vehicles and relocate out to the naval piers. They would bypass the docks and drive straight out among the vintage warships, counting on their mass and remote location to hide them from the hungry dead.

They knew there was no way their evacuation would go unnoticed, and they would be followed, the herd mentality eventually bringing the masses their way, out onto a dead-end pier where no boats were waiting.

A hippie named Abel Younger, familiar with both motorcycles and tactics he had seen Evan Tucker employ on their journey down from the Napa region, volunteered to draw them off. He headed out on Evan's Harley Road King, gunning the throttle and laying on the horn for maximum noise, roaring away from the hangar and out toward the airfield. He had grinned as he assured them he wasn't on a kamikaze mission, and once he had as many of the walking dead as he could attract far out at the end of the tarmac, he would double back, leaving them behind to rejoin the group on the Navy pier.

The tactic worked, pulling the dead's attention, those flowing in from Alameda and beyond herding forward in slow but steady pursuit. Within a half hour, the roads around the hangar were empty, and the group hustled into the vehicles and sped away toward the old gray ships, carefully watching their rear for stray zombies that would have to be quickly dispatched. They saw none, and reached the pier in safety.

Neither Abel Younger nor Evan's Harley was ever seen again.

When the maintenance barge returned shortly before the patrol boat and the Bayliner, those on the pier signaled before they could enter the seaplane lagoon and possibly alert the dead. All three craft moored in the massive shadows of the warships. When it was dark, several of them would row the Bayliner silently into the lagoon and pump its tank full of fuel, slipping back out the same way.

The assault would begin in the morning. The rest of this day was spent planning, preparing, and mourning. Most hadn't known Darius well, but he represented yet another hole in their lives. Little Bear, however, had been well loved within Calvin's Family, a central member who had helped keep them all together when the world came apart. He was a man who always had a smile for others and was the first to volunteer for anything dangerous, so that someone else might remain behind in safety. His death today had saved someone's life, and the Family would not forget that.

Plans had changed. The maintenance barge would become their base, loaded with supplies and moored to the pier when the two power boats headed out. Those not joining the assault would remain close to it for a quick exit if necessary. Their vehicles were put into neutral and quietly pushed into position as a barricade that they all knew would not hold back the dead but might at least slow down a mass attack. It was something.

Angie, Evan, and Vladimir stood leaning against a pier cable as thick as their waists, strung between short, broad pilings as a barrier to keep tourists from accidentally walking off into the water. They watched as people tore into the totes and boxes of newly arrived supplies, changing into clean clothes, eating, washing up, and trying to be normal for a while. Evan and Vladimir were sharing a cigarette from their dwindling supply.

"Pray for the dead but fight like hell for the living," Evan said.

Angie looked at him. "Did you write that?"

"No, Mother Jones did. I'm sure she didn't have this world in mind when she said it."

"Should we know who she was?" asked Angie.

"Probably not," Evan said. "She died in 1930, supposedly a hundred years old. She was a woman before her time, fighting for railroad workers, child laborers, and miners. An activist and agitator, some said a terrorist."

"One of your heroes?"

Evan shook his head. "Not particularly. Mostly it's the quote. And she fought to protect those who couldn't protect themselves. I like that part." They looked out at the many children among the supplies and clusters of adults, some of them quite young. Angie nodded without saying anything. Evan spotted Maya and went to her, and Angie gazed over the wide pier.

With the arrival of the contents of Calvin's caravan, the weapons from Carney's Bearcat, and the considerable arsenal from her own van, their little group had been abruptly infused with firepower, a fair amount of it military grade, and none of it secure. She watched a toddler learning to walk while his parents looked on with smiles. The boy edged his little hands along the side of a wooden crate bearing markings for Claymore antipersonnel mines.

Angie grew up around firearms, and joining the family gunsmithing business had been as natural as breathing. With that upbringing came intense and constant training and education, as well as a deep respect for weaponry's destructive potential and the safety measures it demanded. She was intimately comfortable with a broad range of guns, did side work as a professional firearms instructor, and regularly participated in—and often won—combat shooting competitions. The sight of this much firepower in the hands of people with little formal training made her nervous.

Vladimir seemed to pick up on her cloudy expression. "Citizen soldiers now, yes?"

"They're a mob," she replied. "People are going to die, and there's not much I can do about it. We don't have time to train."

"Then why are you here?" the pilot asked.

Her eyes found the toddler again, now taking a few wobbly steps on his own toward his clapping mother. It brought on a familiar ache, and one hand slipped into her pants pocket and closed on her daughter Leah's teething ring, gripping it tightly.

"Evan said it, didn't he? When he talked about protecting those who can't protect themselves." She shrugged. "It's the best answer I have, I suppose." She thought about Evan's words. There were people in need of protection who weren't here, however. Then she looked at the homely pilot. "Why are you part of this?"

He grinned. "Because I have no place to be and no way to get there."

Angie laughed.

Vladimir looked at her, his face serious once more. "I am told you have a family out there?"

Her chest tightened. "My daughter and my husband. They're alive."

"I'm certain."

"They are." Her voice was sharper than she had intended. She touched his arm and softened her tone. "They were in Sacramento while I was filming on Alameda. It was only supposed to be a day trip; I would have been home that night. But then this"—she waved a hand—"all happened, and I couldn't get to them, couldn't call." Her voice caught, and she looked away for a moment. "Dean, my husband, will protect Leah with his life. But I need to get to them." When she looked back at the Russian, her eyes were wet. "They're alive," she repeated.

"I believe you." Vladimir smiled again. "And I will tell you something, Angie West." He gestured at all the activity. "I believe this is a fool's adventure, and the cost will be far greater than we even suspect. Yet it is the only real option, is it not?"

She nodded. Alameda, this pier, they were all death traps the walking dead would find in time, and they would all go down with their backs to the sea, every one of them.

He lit another cigarette and blew the smoke skyward. "None of us will likely survive," he said, and then looked at her. "But if by some accident we succeed, I will fuel that helicopter and take you in search of your family. I give you my word on this."

Angie stared at him, and then the tears fell and she hugged him fiercely. Vladimir laughed and embraced the woman who was so petite against his towering frame. "I told you we're all going to die!" he said. "Don't thank me yet."

She pulled away and stood on her toes to kiss his cheek. "Thank you." Then she left, heading into the crowd. The least she could do was use the time remaining to teach some basic firearms safety.

Vladimir watched her go, then gazed at the clouds, wondering silently to a God he wasn't sure he really believed in if he had just made a promise he couldn't keep.

B rother Peter leaned against a piling on the opposite side of the pier, watching them all. God leaned against a cable beside him, no longer looking like the Air Force psychiatrist. Now He had taken the form of Sherri, the staffer who in her final days had attempted to use sex as a survival technique, and whose face Peter had maimed before sacrificing her to the dead. God's face wore that bloody, ragged slash too, but it seemed to cause Her no discomfort. When She spoke, however, it was with the male psychiatrist's voice.

"You need to be on that boarding party, Pete."

Peter wasn't especially surprised that his hallucination had returned. He had been through a great ordeal, after all, and it would be natural to be suffering some sort of disconnection. It was actually sort of cool when he thought about it. Like having an invisible friend. "Screw that," he said "It's a suicide mission. Let those idiots charge off to their deaths."

"You're being disrespectful, Pete. Don't make me slap you in front of all these nice people."

Brother Peter dipped his head. "Forgive me, Lord." Might as well play along.

"You're going on this trip, and you're getting on that carrier."

"May I ask why it's so important?"

"Because it's all part of my plan. I am the mystery."

God could be frustrating, Peter thought. And now, because of the wound he had given Her, She was difficult to look at as well.

"Maybe next time I'll take on a more pleasing form," God said. "Like your mother."

Peter shook his head. "Please, I couldn't—this is difficult enough."

"Then stop complaining." God threw an arm around his shoulders and lowered Her voice, leaning in. *"Your time is coming. Shall I reveal my plan?"*

The televangelist's heart raced. If God *was* real, and he wasn't ready to really admit that as truth, but if He *was*, then Peter wanted to be a part of His plan. "Yes, Lord." He stared across the pier at Angie West, watching her move, struggling to control a dark fantasy.

"Stay focused, Pete, or I'll set your pecker alight with hellfire."

Brother Peter's eyes snapped open. Now God was the junior high gym teacher who used to keep him in the locker room after the other kids had left, presumably to help clean up, but in reality to satisfy his own twisted urges with a confused, pubescent boy.

"I don't like that form," Peter hissed.

The gym teacher gave him a smile the minister remembered well and still dreamed about on occasion, often waking to find he had wet the bed. Then God became the Air Force psychiatrist again, and Peter's body visibly relaxed.

God's voice dropped to a conspirator's whisper as He pulled Peter close. *"Here's what I had in mind."* As He spoke, a wide, glorious smile spread across the televangelist's face.

All through that evening and into the night, the dead poured into Alameda.

FIFTEEN

It was misting rain, the early-morning sky returned to its flat, shale color, a stiff breeze coming in from the distant mouth of the bay and turning the water to chop. Rosa piloted the Bayliner, and Evan, with his brief experience driving the barge making him the next qualified, had the helm of the patrol boat. Both vessels were overloaded with people, weapons, and gear, so they traveled at an easy pace with a hundred feet between them.

The discussions and decisions as to who would go and who would stay had lasted well into the night; most of the volunteers accepted without argument, but not entirely. Some who elected to remain behind, like the young man with the pregnant wife whom Rosa had rescued from San Francisco, were embarrassed and felt the need to explain their reasons. Others volunteered to be part of the boarding party and were rejected by the group. Most of these were the older kids, fourteen- and fifteen-year-olds. It was Calvin who announced that *no one* under sixteen would be part of the assault. No one challenged his decision.

Maya wanted to go. Evan told her no, she told him it wasn't his choice, he got angry and she got angry. Eventually Calvin came in on Evan's side, explaining to his eldest that he needed her to look after her younger brothers and sisters. She reluctantly agreed but made it clear to Evan that she was mad, and that he wasn't off the hook just because her father had backed him.

Those staying behind included most of the people from the firehouse: Margaret to lead them; Sophia to watch over the children; Larraine and her elderly husband, Gene, who knew they would only be liabilities; Elson and Big Jerry for protection. Several adults from Calvin's group would stay as well, to protect their own children and the others. The pregnant couple would stay behind as well.

Vladimir accepted that he must remain close to the helicopter.

The boarding party consisted of Calvin and eighteen adults and teenagers from his group, along with Evan, Rosa, Xavier, Angie, and Skye. Carney and TC were in, as well as the high school girl named Meagan. Brother Peter managed to include himself, stating that he had electronics training that could prove useful on the aircraft carrier.

Now their destination awaited, a slab of Navy gray a half mile out. The closer they got, the more massive the supercarrier became, and as the fearsome presence of one of America's most destructive weapons of war drew near, Xavier began shaking his head.

"What have I gotten us into?" he whispered.

At the wheel beside him, Evan smiled thinly. "Our future, one way or the other."

CVN-68. The USS *Nimitz*. Her nickname through four decades of service was *Old Salt*. She had taken over four years to build, the first nuclear supercarrier of her class, not due for retirement until 2020. She was nearly eleven hundred feet long—the equivalent of most skyscrapers—and one hundred thousand tons; *Nimitz*'s four-and-a-half-acre flight deck soared ninety feet above the water line, with the superstructure climbing another eight stories above that, the ship a full eighteen stories from keel to mast. The flagship of Carrier Strike Group 11, she carried ninety aircraft that she was capable of launching at a rate of one every twenty seconds. Her twin General Electric A4W/A16 reactors drove eight steam turbine generators that, when combined, put out 8,000 kilowatts, enough to power a small city. These turned four bronze screw propellers, each of which measured twenty-one feet across and could push the behemoth up to a speed of thirty-two knots. Her distilling units produced 400,000 gallons of fresh water per day, the mess halls could serve 20,000 meals every twenty-four hours, and she carried 3.3 million gallons of JP-5 aircraft fuel.

Nimitz had hundreds of ladders and hatchways, over four thousand compartments, and enough pipe, duct, cable, and wiring that if put end-to-end would cross Indiana and back again. The average age of the nearly six thousand serving crewmen of CVN-68 was between nineteen and twenty-one.

Most of them were still here.

Using binoculars, the assault teams spotted them at once. Figures moved on the flight deck, in the openings of the aircraft elevators, wandered along catwalks. Both boats slowed as they came at the great ship from the starboard side, moving to within shouting distance of one another as Evan and Rosa let the boats idle and coast.

The assault plan was simple, necessarily so because admittedly they had no real idea about what they were up against, were not professional military, and were short on time. The dead were sure to find those left behind, and likely sooner than they anticipated. So the plan called for a single circuit around the ship to see if any of the dead could be baited into going off the side and into the water. Then they would dock at the aft swimmer's platform Rosa said would be there. After that? Enter and start killing. It wasn't elegant, and despite their commitment, most had plenty of doubts.

Angie moved to the bow of the patrol boat, kneeling with her Galil and bracing her left elbow on her knee. She sighted on a rotting sailor in the center elevator opening, watching as the target rose and fell with the motion of the rocking boat. She let her breath out slowly and squeezed.

The bullet hit the sailor in the hip, making him stagger.

She aimed again, timing the motion of the boat. Squeeze. The Galil cracked, but the dead sailor didn't move. A complete miss. Angie let out another long breath, aimed carefully, fired. The bullet tore fabric and gray flesh from his shoulder. She slung the rifle and returned to the back of the boat.

"It's like I figured," she said. "We don't have a shooting platform stable enough for head shots with any kind of consistency. We'd expend too much ammo just to get a quality hit."

"How about using the barge?" someone asked. "Would that be better?"

She shook her head. "A little better, maybe, but not enough to justify the ammunition. Besides, they need it at Alameda." She thought about breaking out the fifty-caliber Barrett, the enormous sniper rifle sitting on the deck in its long plastic case, but immediately dismissed the idea. The movement of the boat would disrupt accuracy just as with the Galil, and there was even less ammo for the heavier weapon.

Minutes later both vessels moved off together, starting their circuit. The supercarrier's high, outward-curving steel walls cast acres of shadow, dwarfing the two small craft. It was intimidating, and when those on board thought about what stalked and crawled the passageways within, the feeling turned to an icy fear.

At the wheel, Evan imagined the terror this thing would inspire showing up off the coast of some foreign land, jets thundering off the deck with the promise of destruction mounted beneath their wings and bellies. It was not something a third world despot would care to see, knowing there was little he could do to prevent the ship from raining hell onto his corrupt little empire. An engine of death, now deadlier than ever imagined.

And in we must go, he thought.

As they motored along its length, they saw where radar domes and antennae had been crushed or torn completely away, tangles of dangling cable and wire, mangled catwalks, and what might have once been a large Gatling gun–style weapon, which was now crumpled like tinfoil. *Nimitz* had obviously collided with or rubbed along something nearly as indestructible as she, and there was no doubt part of her hull had been breached, accounting for the list.

Evan's imagination, so useful in his writing, now conjured images of bloated green corpses trapped in water-filled compartments, relentlessly hammering at closed hatches in slow motion. Eternally hungry, trapped forever, until someone on one of these boats opened a hatch and set them free.

He shuddered and tried to keep his mind on his job.

The baiting attempt met with partial success. Upon seeing the boats below, several corpses up on the deck lurched off the sides, arms reaching. One wore a blue jersey and helmet; another was in green. Both fell about four feet before landing in the safety netting that completely encircled the flight deck to prevent a careless sailor from being blown over the side by jet blast. Their arms and legs became entangled, and they jerked and kicked facedown in the netting, still clawing at the prey out of reach below.

A quick sweep with binoculars revealed several dozen more like them along the length of the deck, caught in the netting and flopping like fish. One, a figure in yellow, managed to disentangle itself and crawl to the edge, dropping over the side and falling ninety feet, vanishing into the bay. A moment later it reappeared, its yellow helmet making it easy to spot as its "float coat," the safety vest worn by everyone who worked the deck, kept it on the surface.

Xavier looked at it through his binoculars, watching it bob and gnash its teeth. He scanned the surface. "You would think there'd be more."

Evan leaned forward so he could look up through the windscreen. "Baiting isn't going to work like we'd hoped, not with that netting."

Xavier was still watching the floating creature in yellow when the water around it suddenly thrashed white, the body abruptly plunging below the surface. Several seconds later a dorsal fin slid briefly from the water yards away, joined by another.

"Did you see that?" Xavier asked.

"I saw that," said Evan. "That's why you don't see more in the water. There probably were."

Now it was Xavier's imagination that went into hyperdrive. He hadn't thought about this. How many of the walking dead had gone off docks and piers, fallen from bridges and boats? He had seen them in the murk around the forklift where Little Bear had died, still moving along the bottom. All evidence indicated that animals were immune to OV, so the slow-moving drifters were now part of the food chain.

"There's another one," said Evan, pointing to starboard. A large, white-gray fin slid along the surface fifty yards from the carrier, then slipped beneath the surface like a diving submarine. How many were out here? he wondered. He couldn't help but think about a famous shark movie where the creature devoured a boat about the same size as the one on which they were standing. *I think we need a bigger boat,* the writer thought, glancing at the carrier.

The priest looked at Evan. "Don't fall out."

The younger man grinned. "My luck to survive a zombie apocalypse only to be eaten by a prehistoric animal."

Xavier informed the rest of them about the sharks and announced that baiting simply wouldn't work. Anxious looks were exchanged. They couldn't pick off the dead from a safe distance and couldn't lure them off the ship and into the water. Both would have improved their odds. They would have to do this the hard way.

The opposite side of the ship was much the same: a few shapes within the single elevator bay, several up on the flight deck, and more in the netting. Not as many as they would have liked, however. A lone figure in khaki shuffled along a catwalk high on the superstructure, bumped into a wall, turned, and shuffled back the other direction.

Both boats completed the circuit and arrived at the broad stern of the ship, a flat wall of steel rising out of the water. A vast, rectangular space about halfway up exposed the interior to the outside world, an area used for live testing of jet engines, a place where their fire and fumes could be vented outward. The opening was nearly as wide as the ship but too high to reach. The rest of the stern was covered in radar and antenna arrays, surface-to-air missile launchers, a scattering of catwalks, and an incomprehensible row of vertical piping.

Nestled amid the piping on the starboard side of the ship was a narrow length of steel catwalk riding just above the water, a single, oval-shaped door set in the hull behind it. The swimmer's platform. They tied off on the piping and disembarked, shouldering backpacks and weapons. No one would remain with the boats; everyone was needed, and the group of twenty-eight filled the platform.

Angie had talked them out of bringing along any grenades or LAW rocket launchers, citing that in confined steel spaces, the weapons posed more threat to the living than to the dead. She could only hope no one had quietly smuggled something along in a pack. Skye, in one of the few times she spoke, told them to leave behind the Claymore mines as well. They were useless, and she knew from experience.

Brother Peter nodded along with the rest. He had a pair of grenades in his jacket pockets.

Angie, in addition to her burden of weaponry and ammo, carried the thirty-pound Barrett M82A1 by its top handle. A shoulder bag of spare magazines for the four-foot-long sniper rifle—each fifty-caliber bullet weighing four ounces—put her right at the edge of what she could handle and still move. She wasn't complaining. The shooting would lighten her load quickly, and she knew she would soon long for the added weight of spare ammunition.

Xavier moved to the door as behind him flashlights were readied, magazines and chambers checked, soft words of encouragement offered to one another. This had been his idea, so it was only right that he should go first. A metal wheel was set in the center of the door, and he turned it to the left—*lefty-loosey, righty-tighty,* he thought—expecting it to be locked. It wasn't, and turned easily. He tugged, and it didn't move. Rosa caught his attention and made a pushing motion. He did, and the heavy door swung inward with the softest of creaks.

Darkness and a faint perfume of decay awaited.

Xavier took a breath, raised his flashlight and shotgun together, and entered the USS *Nimitz.*

BELLY OF THE BEAST

SIXTEEN

As Xavier had feared, the lights weren't on everywhere in the ship. Such was the case in the area beyond the swimmer's platform hatch, a space that was little more than a metal box with steep, steel-grid stairways both climbing to higher decks and descending into the bowels of the ship. Daylight from the open hatch revealed a large *02* stenciled in yellow on one wall. Xavier switched on his flashlight.

His nose wrinkled at the air, warm and rich with decay. He doubted that the ship's master computer, running the vessel on reduced power, would consider air-conditioning a priority for areas other than those used for computers. As a result, *Nimitz* had been turned into a humid maze of decomposition. It was something Xavier hadn't considered, and he wished he had brought a bandana to tie across his face.

He stood very still, listening, feeling. There was a vague vibration that traveled up through the soles of his shoes, and a distant knocking of something banging sporadically against metal, though he could not tell if it came from above or below. He panned his flashlight around the room, the hand gripping the shotgun already sweating. A single, oval-shaped hatch featuring a long handle that it could be opened with—a *dog*, he remembered from his distant service days—

was mounted in the center of each wall. Three doors and stairs up or down provided so many choices, none of them likely to be good.

"What do we have?" said Calvin, entering and stopping beside the priest. Others followed.

Xavier moved the flashlight around. "Take your pick."

It had been agreed before they left Alameda that their group was too large to move as one and still hope to be effective. They would jam up in hallways and doors, and in a fight would very likely end up shooting one another. Smaller fire teams had been selected that would split apart as soon as possible, with the simple plan of clearing the ship as they went. It wasn't sophisticated or efficient and they knew they would leave drifters behind them as they moved, but to Skye's earlier point, there were only so many of the walking dead on board, and each kill would lower their numbers. They couldn't replace their losses.

Except with us, Xavier thought.

Communication was going to be a problem, they knew. None of them had any hopes that civilian two-way radios would have any chance of creating a signal that could penetrate the steel walls for distances of any use. The fire teams would be on their own and would have to scavenge what they needed on the move, as they had been doing for weeks.

"Good luck," said Angie, passing the priest without further preamble, her face a grim mask. Skye followed her, along with Meagan. In the weeks since Angie had brought her in, the girl had proven to be a decent shot and was more than willing to face the undead in hand-to-hand combat. In addition to the rifle slung over her shoulder, she carried her lawn mower blade in a leather-gloved hand, one end wrapped in a thick handle of duct tape, the other sharpened like a barber's razor. Angie and Skye would be the sniper team, Meagan their security, and they were headed upward, intending to get as high on the superstructure as they could. From there they would eliminate targets on the open deck.

"Be safe," Xavier called. It sounded stupid the moment he said it, but Angie let him off with a wink as she disappeared up the metal stairway. Behind her, Skye was stone-faced, her M4 in a two-handed grip.

Carney, TC, and half a dozen of Calvin's Family headed up a few minutes later, the older convict in the lead, his cellmate bringing up the rear. Carney had announced that they would try to find the hangar deck, which Rosa assured them would provide an open field of fire. There were no good-byes. Everyone just left.

"This deck looks as good as any," said Evan, stepping up next to Calvin. He approached the hatch in the far wall, listened at it for a moment, then raised the handle with a metallic thud. The hatch swung in, revealing a long, narrow corridor with fluorescent light tubes set overhead at intervals, about one set in every three lit. Openings and doorways lined both walls, and the sporadic lighting created pools of gloom along the hallway's length. It smelled dead in here.

Something in the distance moaned.

The young writer tried to think of some clever parting words, but instead he just swallowed hard and stepped through the hatch, trying to force the shotgun he carried to stop shaking. Another five men and women of Calvin's Family followed, and the aging hippie came last, giving Xavier a nod before closing the hatch behind him.

Xavier, Rosa, and a handful of frightened hippies remained in the room, staring at the closed hatch. Brother Peter stood at the back of the group, his .45 having been returned to him, and now additionally armed with a civilian model twelve-gauge shotgun.

Pistol shots reverberated from behind Calvin's hatch, making them all jump. Rosa started toward the metal door, but Xavier stopped her. "We knew this would happen," the priest said. "We have our own places to go."

The medic nodded and said a silent prayer for her new friends. Xavier gave his team what he hoped was an encouraging smile as he led them down the descending stairway, flashlight beam and shotgun muzzle probing ahead. Reluctant feet shuffled after him.

At the back, Brother Peter rested his shotgun over a shoulder and followed, unable to control his grin. He was already having a fine time.

SEVENTEEN

One landing up from Second Deck, the stairs emptied into an identical room, with three hatches and more stairs above. On the wall here, the letters *MHD* were stenciled in yellow. The daylight from the open hatch below them faded almost at once, and they switched on flashlights.

"Main hangar deck?" Angie whispered.

Skye shrugged, and Angie continued upward, with Meagan moving up to follow close behind. This put Skye at the back, which made more sense anyway. She advanced sideways up the stairs, looking up and down in intervals, panning both her light and rifle muzzle wherever her head turned. Muffled shots came from below and they froze, but only for a moment before Angie got them moving again.

Skye watched Meagan ahead of her, gripping her lawn mower blade machete, wearing hard plastic forearm guards from the prison riot vehicle and additionally protected by a flip-down Plexiglas face shield someone in a wood or metal shop would wear. Meagan had been a student in an Alameda high school, but other than that small detail, she had said absolutely nothing about her life before the plague, or how she had come to be on her own. She and Skye had that in common. Meagan's hatred of the undead even rivaled Skye's own, another thing they shared, but instead of using a firearm, the other girl preferred to get in close.

"That's dangerous," Skye had said to her only this morning, when she learned about the girl's fighting preference. It was one of the few times they had spoken. "The blood spray, it's dangerous. Even with the face shield."

Meagan had only nodded and said, "Who cares?"

They hadn't spoken again, but Skye thought she knew how the girl felt, about living or dying. It was all the same these days, anyway. She wished she'd had that Plexiglas face shield at that Oakland church, though. If she had, she wouldn't be going through this now.

A white headache spike split her frontal lobe at that instant as if to remind her exactly what *this* was, and her blind eye began tearing uncontrollably. Skye clenched her teeth as she sucked in a sharp breath, stopping and catching herself on a handrail. Her pulse slammed in her ears for a few seconds, and then the pain evaporated. She took a deep, shaky breath and wiped at her eye.

"You coming?" Meagan whispered down from the top of the stairway.

Skye didn't respond, only checked behind her with the light and caught up. Another identical room awaited: three more hatches and another set of stairs, a big yellow *01* on the wall. Here, however, the hatches stood open with darkness beyond, and a pair of severely decomposed corpses in blue camouflage lay facedown on the metal floor. The stink was a physical assault, making them all retch.

Angie checked the bodies with her light and determined they had both been shot in the head, probably quite some time ago. The gray walls of the room were scarred from buckshot strikes, and half a dozen empty, red plastic twelve-gauge hulls were scattered on the floor.

Something slid across the floor above: dragging feet followed by a harsh gasp. Angie dropped the heavy Barrett as her Galil's muzzle snapped up to the top of the stairway. Through an open hatch to the left came a hollow choir of moans echoing off metal walls, and the thump of bodies moving close together, their pace quickening.

"Coming in from the left," Skye growled, aiming her rifle and her light. Its white circle revealed a tight hallway crowded with corpses, all in blue except for the one in front, a bald man in khaki. Each was gaunt and torn, dead eyes gleaming in the flashlight beam, and the khaki corpse's skin sagged in loose rolls around its neck.

They surged forward with a snarl as Skye began to fire, *PUFFT-PUFFT-PUFFT*, the stock kicking into her shoulder as spent brass was ejected from the rifle's side port. A belly shot, a shoulder, then the khaki corpse's face and it went down. The others walked over the body. *PUFFT*, a head shot, *PUFFT*, a chest, *PUFFT*, the top of a sailor's skull blew off in a green spray and he sagged to his knees. The others pressed forward.

"Twenty more feet," Skye shouted.

At the stairway, Angie saw a figure at the top of the risers, a young man in dark blue coveralls with one hand chewed down to a ragged wrist stump. He groaned and, as Angie squeezed the trigger, flung himself down the stairway with reaching arms. Angie's rifle, with no noise suppressor, sounded like artillery in the tight space. Her round missed and *spanged* off metal. The corpse tumbled, arms, legs, and head at odd angles as he rolled, and Angie leaped back as he collapsed at the base of the stairs.

The now broken and bent sailor made a gurgling sound and pawed at her ankle, his teeth scraping at the leather toe of her boot. Angie jerked her foot away, put the Galil's muzzle in his ear, and spread his head across the floor with a trigger pull.

More movement and snarling from above, and Angie planted one boot on the bottom step and started snapping off quick rounds, the muzzle flash a strobe revealing a pack of corpses stumbling down toward her. Bullets slashed into torsos and legs, and she adjusted upward quickly, making a head shot.

"Meagan, put your light up here!" Angie shouted.

The high school girl turned and lifted her Maglite, and in doing so put her back to an open hatch. Almost as if it had been waiting for the moment, the body of a sailor in its fifties lunged through the opening wearing only once-white boxers, its chest covered in a huge tattoo of a voluptuous mermaid entwined about an anchor. The ragged bites covering the older man's torso were blackened and rotting at the edges.

The sailor caught Meagan's head in both hands from behind and sank its teeth into her neck with a bloody spray.

She screamed as dead fingers hooked at her face, wrestling her to the floor while the old sailor groaned into the meat of her neck. Meagan thrashed and rolled, breaking free of the bite, and scrambled to all fours, still shrieking as the nearly naked sailor crawled after her. She grunted and slammed the lawn mower blade machete into the drifter's head with a crack of bone. The body collapsed at once.

Angie heard the screaming, saw the beam of light drop away, knowing they had been attacked from behind. She bared her teeth, thumbing the Galil's selector switch from Semi to Auto. A second later she emptied the magazine up the stairs in a chainsaw roar of fully automatic fire, slugs shredding flesh and shattering skulls. Even those not instantly destroyed were flung back by the short-range fury, giving Angie time to drop her empty magazine and slap in another. God, she needed light! She risked a look back.

"Meagan, talk to me. . . ."

Through an open hatch came a muffled sob and the sound of sneakers running on a metal deck, quickly fading. On the floor before her was a fallen creature with Meagan's blade jutting from its head, dark ichor pooling around it. Angie cursed and backed up, grabbing the dropped flashlight and holding it tightly along the length of the Galil's front stock as she switched back to semiautomatic fire.

CRACK! CRACK! Angie advanced on the stairs again, taking the time to sight and drop her targets. Bodies collapsed on the stairs, and as new shapes appeared above, slowing as they climbed over others of their kind, she took them out too.

"Skye, you still with me?" Angie shouted between rifle shots.

Over at the left hatch, Skye had dropped to one knee for steadier shooting. *Hit. Hit. Miss, goddammit. Another miss, fuckers. Miss, c'mon! Deep breath and squeeze. Hit, no, that was a neck shot. Okay, now it's a hit. Hit. Hit.*

The headache spike was scratching at the top of her brain, probing, deciding where to strike. Skye tried to ignore it and concentrated on keeping her own light on the corridor, her sights on target. Every miss allowed them a step closer. She briefly registered Meagan's screams, knew something was in the room behind her, but also knew that was why they had brought the girl, for security. She and Angie couldn't keep up their fire and still keep watch behind. If Meagan didn't protect her area of responsibility, the shooters would be screwed. No sense worrying about it.

Miss and a ricochet. Head shot. Groin shot. Head shot.

Skye dropped an empty magazine and slapped in a fresh thirty rounds. She heard Angie call to her but didn't look back. "I'm still here," she called. "Is Meagan dead?"

"She's gone," Angie said.

"That means she's dead," said Skye, and then both of them were firing. Skye's corridor was quickly filling with unmoving bodies, making it difficult for new arrivals to close on her. They slowed as they climbed over their fallen shipmates, exposing them to Skye's M4. She took full advantage and shot them down.

After another magazine, Skye saw nothing else moving down her hallway and took the time to curse herself and her impairments for all the extra ammunition wasted on misses. Angie had similarly stopped shooting and closed the other two hatchways, dogging them tightly in hopes of avoiding another ambush.

They looked at the lawn mower blade and the dead sailor with his lewd tattoo, a scrap of pink flesh still in his teeth. Then they looked at one another as a silent agreement passed between them, one that compelled them to linger here no longer and move on. Meagan had been bitten and had run off; there was nothing they could do to change that. Both suspected they would see the girl again, but under different circumstances.

Skye closed the hatch through which she'd been shooting and joined Angie at the stairs, now choked with bodies. They listened. Nothing moved above, and the only sound was fluids dripping through the steel mesh of the stair risers.

Angie slung the heavy Barrett, took the lead, and began picking her way up through the dead. Skye stayed with her.

EIGHTEEN

What had it taken, less than a minute? Evan held the hot Sig in one hand, training his flashlight on the two bodies lying facedown on the deck, both men younger than him, wearing reeking, digital camouflage. Evan had been in the lead, and the two drifters had come suddenly through an open hatchway to his right, nearly on top of him. They would have killed him too, but the aircraft carrier's structural design had saved his life. Specifically, the knee knockers.

Throughout the ship, most of the doorways were oval-shaped, a design that helped add steel and strength to tighten the structure, as opposed to simple open door frames. A person passing through was required to duck under the curving top, and because the lower part of the frame was six inches off the floor, also required to step over. It was a skill that required some getting used to. Sailors on their first cruise often fell victim to the knee knockers as they learned how to move through the ship, and the medical corpsmen were kept busy the first month or so stitching up gashes in both foreheads and shins.

In this case, the uncoordinated drifters stumbled while trying to come through the opening, giving Evan both a warning and the precious seconds he needed to leap back and put a bullet in each of their heads.

"You okay?" Calvin called from the back.

"I'm good," Evan replied, "just startled me." He let out a shaky breath, reliving the careless moment when he had been alone in that sporting goods store, when the drifter almost got him. After that incident he had promised himself that *careful* would be his watchword.

And then he got on board an infested aircraft carrier.

On purpose.

Idiot, he thought. He reminded himself again to not be reckless, especially here, where there were so many unexpected openings. Lots of chances to be ambushed.

They were in a seemingly endless corridor: narrow, no more than five feet wide, the ceiling low and completely covered with cables and pipes, many of them color-coded for reasons at which Evan could only guess. It was warm, the air close enough to make him sweat underneath the black corrections-officer ammo vest he was wearing. Beneath the warmth was a dense stink of rotten meat and, below that, the more subtle aromas of oil, fuel, and the peculiar metallic taste of a ship.

A pool of fluorescent light thirty feet ahead showed that section of corridor to be empty, with more openings on the left and right, shadows in front and behind. Nervous breathing and anxious, shuffling feet came from the hippies behind him, and Evan stood still for a long moment, hoping his heart would stop its timpani drumming so that he could listen.

A distant *clang*. The creak of a hatch opening slowly. He gripped the pistol tightly and moved forward, checking openings with both his flashlight and Sig barrel before stepping past.

He thought about Maya, saw her beautiful face, and then savagely forced her out of his mind. Thinking about her would break his nerve and get him killed, and in that moment he understood why soldiers in combat zones sometimes tore up or burned photos of loved ones, even refused mail. It could make them distracted, weak. Evan got it.

His flashlight beam slid over a closed hatch with a sign mounted to one side reading *MATERIALS STORAGE 2.10*. He tested the lever and found it was tight, so he moved past. The crowd behind him—he could only think of them as a crowd, bunched together and making too much noise—followed too closely. *And why wouldn't they?* he thought. *We're a pack of frightened, untrained people wandering a rabbit's warren of the walking dead, surrounded by predators and moving deeper into a slaughterhouse.* Frightened didn't begin to describe it.

They passed by closed tool lockers on the left, a hatch on the right marked *FAN ROOM*, another tool locker—this one open and fortunately only filled with tools—and another hatch marked only with numbers. He stepped in something sticky, and the flashlight revealed it to be a pool of congealed blood with a hunk of scalp in it, a bristle of hair still attached. Evan fought the urge to gag and moved on.

They came to an intersection lit by a single fluorescent light bar, darkness extending in all directions. To the right was a short hall leading to an open hatchway with a sign above it: *BERTHING 2.19. 40.* A wave of thick decomposition emanated from the hatchway, something so tangible Evan thought he should see a green fog, and then from within came the shuffling of many feet.

"On the right," Evan warned, and two hippies hurried to kneel in front of him, their shotguns pointed at the opening.

"Watch the other halls," said Calvin, stepping up next to the writer and aiming his assault rifle.

Evan put his light on the hatch, and the dead poured out.

There were dozens, scrambling over the knee knocker and clawing at one another in their frenzy to reach live prey. Their flesh was a bloodless gray tinged with green, with blackened bites and missing fingers, ears, long patches of skin, and even some entire limbs. Most were male, and the few females were nearly indistinguishable as such due to their rotten condition.

Weapons roared, the muzzle flashes a hot white in the darkness, heads blown apart and off at close range. Bodies collapsed as more rushed past, and volleys of gunfire turned the corridors into echo chambers. The metal walls were spattered with wet green and gray tissue, and a couple of corpses got so close to the gunfire that the muzzle flashes briefly set their shirts on fire.

In seconds it was over, the short hall and hatch so packed with still bodies that the lone figure remaining flailed at the corpses on the other side, frantically but unsuccessfully trying to dig its way through. He was a nineteen-year-old in a red jersey, the skin peeled away from his face just below the nose, creating a toothy, skeletal grin. The boy made a whining noise as he thrashed. Calvin moved in close with his assault rifle, aimed, and fired. The boy stiffened at the new hole in his forehead, and dropped out of sight.

There was a brief pause before the clicking of weapons and magazines being reloaded filled the silence.

Nothing came at them from the other corridors, and so Evan led them left, toward the centerline of the ship. They passed an open hatch marked *AVIATION STORES*, flashlights revealing a pair of workstations and what appeared to be a low-ceilinged warehouse of metal racks and crated equipment, but no zombies. A dozen small offices were on either side of them, most doors open, all of them empty. The overhead lights followed a pattern of one set lit for every three dark as they moved past a pair of steep metal stairs, one rising and the other descending, a few more closed hatches marked with numbers, a water fountain in a recessed alcove, and then they arrived at another intersection.

The intermittent lighting continued ahead and to the left, but to the right was only darkness. The walls here were scarred with bullet impacts, and brass shell casings rattled underfoot. Dark, textured stains were everywhere. On one wall, a metal spool had been swung out on a short arm, a brass nozzle and canvas fire hose lying beneath it in a tangle.

"Fighting here," said Calvin, his voice barely above a whisper.

Evan nodded. "But no bodies."

"Oh, they're walking around here somewhere," the hippie said.

Evan put his light into the darkness to the right, seeing a few motionless corpses on their backs, the rest of the corridor lost in the darkness beyond his flashlight beam. Conduit, cable, and more piping covered the ceiling and walls everywhere he looked, some of it ruptured by gunfire, a few dripping clear liquid. Fresh water or sewage? he wondered. He couldn't tell from the smell, because the stink of decaying flesh not only was thicker here than in places they had been but also reeked of rotting vegetation. The writer tried to make sense of that but quickly gave up. It seemed foolish to wonder about something as mundane as that when he was confronted by the impossible on a daily basis.

"We're leaving a lot of unexplored areas behind us," Calvin warned. "That could be a problem later."

"I know," said Evan. "Should we stop and check every door, every closet and storage room?" He wasn't being sarcastic. He really didn't know. On one hand it seemed the only intelligent thing to do, in order to ensure that they were efficiently clearing the ship and wouldn't be ambushed from behind. On the other, he wondered if it was better just to let the dead come to them.

Calvin peered down the corridors. "I don't know. Maybe we're doing it right. Maybe it's best to take on whatever comes at us, thin out their numbers, and then go back later for a more detailed search." He said this more like a question, and the two men just shrugged at one another. Not for the first time in the last couple of months, Evan wished he had followed his father's advice and joined the military instead of wandering across America. At least he would have had some training when it all fell apart.

Of course he doubted even the military had expected something like this.

From behind Evan, a hippie named Dakota said, "Let's keep it simple and just kill anything that moves."

Evan nodded and Calvin clapped his Family member on the back. A Navy SEAL wouldn't have approved of their tactics, Evan knew, but then any Navy SEAL left aboard was now probably playing for the other side.

They turned left, Evan heading toward what he was pretty sure was the rear of the ship, peeking inside several empty offices and workshops, passing another set of steep stairs and yet another partially unrolled coil of fire hose. He stared at it, a limp canvas snake on the metal deck. They had seen no signs of scorching or blackening from smoke. Just past the hose he saw a fireman's helmet with a cracked plastic face shield, and beside it a yellow oxygen tank with shoulder straps and a rubber face mask. The tank had a rusty smear down one side.

"What the—"

A shotgun blast made him flinch and duck, and he spun to see the men and women behind him turning. A flashlight jerked frantically back down the hall from which they had come, and Evan caught a glimpse of two shapes in yellow firefighter gear stumbling out of the darkness. The shotgun boomed again, pellets shredding the zombie's fire-retardant coat but doing nothing to stop it.

"The head!" a woman screamed.

"I know!" someone else shouted, and the shotgun roared a third time. A pair of rifles fired, and the creature's face disintegrated in a red blur, the second creature taking its place before the body even hit the ground.

Growling came from behind again and Evan turned back to see Calvin on one knee, rifle and flashlight braced and pointing ahead toward an intersection they had been approaching.

"Company's coming," the hippie leader said.

Ahead, a mass of uniformed figures trudged toward them down the main corridor, packed in shoulder to shoulder. At the intersection, more bitten and torn bodies, some bent at crippling angles, emerged from both the right and left hallways, joining the mass. Not ten feet away and to their right, bloodied boots with tucked-in trousers stomped unsteadily down a metal stairway.

Calvin started firing, his assault rifle letting off deafening cracks. In between shots he yelled, "How do we look to the rear?"

Evan turned again to see the hippies unloading volleys of fire, Dakota along with a woman named Mercy and the seventeen-year-old Stone. They were kneeling or standing close together, concentrating their fire on a crowd of the undead that had emerged from the darkness beyond the two firemen and continued to grow, both in numbers and in the volume of their moaning. It looked to Evan that about half their shots were effective.

"Not good," the writer shouted, joining Calvin and adding his shotgun to the damage the assault rifle was doing.

The horde at the intersection pressed in, and now the stairway corpses were tumbling down from above, landing in heaps but relentlessly disentangling themselves and crawling forward, growling and croaking, eyes smooth and filmy in the jittering flashlights.

"We're not going to hold this time," Calvin shouted.

"And we can't go back!" Evan fed fresh shells into his weapon, a difficult job while also juggling a heavy flashlight, but he was unwilling to put it down. He couldn't bear the thought of facing the dead in darkness.

To his rear stood two men who had yet to fire a shot, Freeman and Juju. Both had simply been standing still and staring, and now Freeman began to cry. He dropped his rifle and tugged frantically on a nearby hatch handle. A sign beside it read WARDROOM. "We have to get out!" he screamed.

"Don't open that!" Calvin shouted.

Freeman didn't or wouldn't hear him. He managed to bring the dog handle up and pulled hard. Evan braced for a tide of corpses to spill out and finish them all. When nothing emerged, he saw the hippie duck into the opening, still screaming.

If something got him inside the room, Evan couldn't hear it over the gunfire. He had a wild moment as he remembered standing next to Father Xavier in the hangar as the priest explained to the entire group how taking the aircraft carrier was their only chance at survival. He remembered nodding along with the words, smiling confidently.

"Dad was right," he muttered. "I'm a stupid asshole."

Calvin was switching fire between the corpses on the stairs and the mass in the corridor, and despite the head shots he was losing precious feet of distance. His trigger clicked on a dry magazine. To the rear, the hippies were backing up, bumping into one another as the group became a tight little knot and the firing fell off.

The dead moaned and began to gallop.

"Ah, shit," Evan said, clutching his shotgun and flashlight in sweaty hands. "This way!" he shouted, and ducked through the darkened wardroom hatch after Freeman.

He was bitten almost immediately.

NINETEEN

They heard the ripple of gunfire coming from the open hatch behind them, muted and echoing, one deck up. "That's Angie and Skye," said Carney, looking back. They had parted company only minutes ago.

TC grinned and shook his head. "Hope that girl doesn't get herself killed before I get the chance to fuck her."

Carney turned on his cellmate. "Already tried that, didn't you?" It came out louder than he had intended, his voice carrying down the metal corridor ahead of them. The half-dozen hippies standing nearby looked at each other nervously, then into the darkness. There were wide archways on both sides with a little light spilling out, storerooms of some sort.

TC smirked. "Nah, just jerked off a little. What's got your panties in such a twist?"

The older man stepped closer and lowered his voice. "What happened with you and that guy Darius, the one at the boatyard? I saw the marks on his neck when I shot him."

TC laughed. "Now *him* I tried to fuck, but he wouldn't cooperate." A shrug. "Things got a little out of control."

"You're the one who's out of control," Carney said. "I told you to keep it in line, and I warned you about that girl."

The younger inmate didn't step away or look down as he would have only days ago, just met his cellmate's eyes with that annoying smirk on his face. Carney felt the change at once and understood that their relationship had taken a dangerous new turn. He also noted that the barrel of the other man's automatic shotgun was pointed roughly at his midsection.

"You really want to get into this now?" TC asked, his voice soft, almost seductive. "What if I *do* want to fuck that pretty little thing? You gonna stop me, Carney? You said you would."

No *bro*, no *man*, just *Carney* now.

"You gonna bleed me like you said in the truck?" he asked, and grinned. "You want to do it now?"

Carney didn't move or react. He watched the violence dance in his friend's eyes.

"Right," said TC, his voice still soft. "That's what I thought. Hey"— his voice became jovial once more—"don't worry, I ain't gonna call you a bitch or nothing, cause you're sensitive about it and I respect that." His eyes narrowed then, and the jovial voice took on an edge. "But *I* run *my* life now. The days of you treating me like your fucking dog are over . . . *bro*."

Carney's eyes were dark storm clouds. "It's like that, huh?"

"It's like that," TC replied without hesitation.

Neither man noticed when the half-dozen men and women with them whispered among themselves, casting fearful looks at the two muscled and tattooed men, and then quickly moved away up the corridor, flashlights leading.

TC abruptly flashed a charming grin and tossed his long blond hair. "End of the world, man, new set of rules. You said it yourself. We're all gonna die in here anyway, so what the fuck?" He turned his back, clearly unconcerned that he would be attacked from behind, and propped his shotgun over a shoulder as he walked through an archway marked *CATAPULT EQUIPMENT SPACE.*

Carney watched him go, suddenly more shaken and unsure of himself than he could ever remember feeling. After a moment he realized the rest of the group had left quietly, taking a turn somewhere so that their lights were no longer visible.

From within the storage chamber TC's echoing voice called, "Let's go kill some zombies."

Carney stood in the hallway for a moment and then went inside as well.

Xavier's group descended with the priest in the lead, followed by Rosa and six of Calvin's Family members, Brother Peter at the back of the group. The Third Deck landing was like the landings above, providing choices between hatchways and stairs but empty of the living dead. The thrum of machinery somewhere made the steel deck vibrate gently, and the tang of oil and metal was more pronounced down here.

Xavier took them deeper, down to Fourth Deck, and once again there were choices to be made. The distant echo of gunfire floated down from above, but there was no longer an urge to race off to the rescue. It had been replaced with feelings of dread and the unsettling sensation that the ship had lured them into its maw and was not about to let them go.

It felt different this deep in the vessel. The air was closer, warmer, and more tainted with the heaviness of rotting flesh. Ceilings felt lower, steel walls closing in just a few inches tighter than the decks above, and the cool white of fluorescent bars had been replaced with the dimmer light of wall-mounted bulbs behind steel mesh. Every footfall seemed like the crash of a drum that could be heard for miles, and every shadow was a hiding place for something eager to use its teeth.

Xavier had expected the gates of hell to be crafted from ancient stone and black iron, awash in flames. Instead, they resembled a simple oval hatch with a lever.

His original idea called for this team to begin at the bottom and work its way up through the ship. He supposed that he had imagined pushing through hallways and driving the enemy upward into the guns of the other teams. How simplistic and utterly moronic that plan had been, he thought now. This enemy would never be pursued; it did the pursuing and couldn't be driven like cattle or frightened Somalis running from gunfire.

Some Marine, he thought, and then the heaviness of what he had talked them all into came down upon him with the weight of the very steel tomb they found themselves in. Untrained people. Thousands of the hungry dead. Unmapped, unfamiliar, and darkened mazes of corridors and rooms.

Dear God, he thought, *what have I done?*

He knew the answer, and the bitter word caught at the back of his throat. Pride. Once more he had cast himself in the role of leader, of shepherd, had encouraged others to trust and depend upon him. And once more he had failed, a faithless man leading hopeful souls to their destruction. Oh, how God must despise him and his endless pretending and how Satan must be clapping his hands in delight.

Rosa saw that he was simply standing in front of the closed hatch, staring. She moved in front of him. "Father, what's wrong?"

He didn't reply, and she glanced back at the others, who were watching anxiously. Except for Peter, who only looked back with an unreadable expression on his face. "Father," she said softly, "are you okay? You're scaring me a little."

Xavier looked at the young medic, a woman who, like the rest of them, was filled with fears and doubts, haunted by her own terrible experiences. Yet here she was in this place of death, not falling to pieces, facing her fears out of a belief that she was doing something that would save and preserve the lives of others, not simply her own.

They all were, and Xavier was hit by a wave of disgust for the way he was behaving, had *been* behaving. What would Alden think, the schoolteacher who had literally died in his arms in the lobby of a San Francisco apartment building, a man who even in his dying moments thought not of himself, but of how he could get Xavier to understand who he needed to be. And Evan, during that quiet moment by the windows in the hangar, the young writer all but telling Xavier he needed to be strong, and to give that strength to others.

Xavier Church had been a United States Marine, had been shot at and taken lives in return, faced dangerous opponents in the boxing ring, and through his words and actions, tried to make a better life for the lost and battered children of an urban sprawl. His life had never been one of the easy path, and no one, including God, had ever assured him his journey would be without pain, without loss.

Did he still have his faith? he wondered. Did it really matter now? Priest or not, he could no longer whine to himself about being a poor leader. And what if he had his doubts, his fears of failure? Well then he would just have to fake it and carry on. Time to man up.

Xavier straightened and smiled, taking one of Rosa's small hands in his own scarred paw and squeezing it gently. *Thank you,* he mouthed silently, and then looked back at the others. "Sorry, folks. I just got a little dizzy there for a second."

A young woman nodded. "It's the smell," she offered, hoping that he would nod back and make everything all right.

"That must be it," Xavier said. "Okay, let's start on this deck. We're far enough away from the others that we shouldn't run into them and have any accidents."

There were murmurs of agreement. They all feared accidentally shooting one of their own.

"Try to stay in single file with a little space between each of you," the priest said. "If you see a zombie, call it out and we'll kill it. When they come at us, don't stop firing until you put it down; you'll have to stand your ground. That's about as simple as we can make it." He looked to the back of the group. "It's Peter, right?"

The minister smiled and nodded.

Xavier looked at him, a vaguely handsome man in his thirties, average build, average appearance. He wore a .45 automatic in a clip-on holster, carried a shotgun, and wore a backpack. He looked like everyone else, but there was something else about the man, a nagging something that Xavier couldn't place. Had they met before the plague? Where had he seen this man? Certainly not in the Tenderloin. Either way, now was not the time to ask questions about his past.

"Peter, are you okay watching the rear?" the priest asked.

"Not a problem," the minister said, confident that the priest couldn't see past his pleasant mask and realize how very much Brother Peter hated him. *Pretender. False prophet,* the minister thought, maintaining the easy smile. He couldn't really say why he despised the priest so much. But lately, many things had happened to him that he didn't understand. He'd learned a few new facts about himself, however.

The world had changed, and so had the people. Those who had survived were not the confused masses seeking a guide to lead them out of the darkness. Yes, some were still sheep, but stronger personalities had emerged to lead them, not for gain, but born from a protectiveness that Peter did not understand. He had always been careful to be the strongest personality in the room. He no longer had that luxury. These people—the priest, the biker, the medic, even the hippie—would not be swayed by clever words or wealth or power. The plague had unearthed a strange self-sufficiency in them. Peter recognized that he would never control them.

He was, he knew, a man without friends. So why not give in and accept that God really *was* talking to him, really *did* have a plan?

No, he would never control these people. But he could hurt them, and that was just as good. He decided that at some point before God's mystery was revealed, he would kill Father Xavier Church personally.

"Great," said Xavier, giving Peter a thumbs-up. "I'm thinking that as we pass through and clear an area, we secure the hatch behind us. That will let us know we're making progress, and hopefully keep anything from sneaking up. Sound good?"

They said it did.

Xavier nodded and led off, opening the hatch in front of him. Through it came the hum of distant generators, the heavy scent of oil-based lubricants, and the sickly sweet aroma of death. The hatch led to a narrow corridor lit by single-spaced bulbs, the ceiling packed with rows of pipe and cable. Xavier switched off his flashlight to save the batteries, shoved it in a pants pocket, and gripped his shotgun with both hands. The others followed, and Brother Peter shut the hatch behind them.

The hallway was clear of bodies, moving or otherwise. At first this surprised Xavier, who had an image in his mind of the six thousand sailors on board *Nimitz* crowding every available space, but he realized that this was a very big ship indeed, and six thousand people needed space to move and work. Added to this was the fact that he had often seen the dead moving in packs, following one another like a herd. His real fear was that there might be no happy medium; they would encounter either emptiness or masses of corpses too great to count—or defeat.

As he approached an open doorway on his right, the priest thought about something Skye had said. *Each one we kill lowers their numbers.* Xavier focused on that. Every kill would reduce the opposition and bring them closer to safety, as long as their ammunition held out. The priest tried to tell himself he was being pragmatic, not pessimistic, and turned his attention to the doorway.

It was a machinery room, a tight space filled with pipes and pistons, electrical switches and valves. A paper coffee cup and a clipboard were the only objects on the floor, the rest of the space clean and well maintained. He wasn't surprised. Some chief or petty officer had been in charge of this area and, machine room or not, would never have tolerated grime. Most importantly, there were no dead sailors in here.

"Clear," Xavier announced, emerging a moment later and leading the group forward. There was no hatch to close behind them.

They inspected two more chambers nearly identical to the first, these having something to do with propulsion, then explored a water heating and cooling section, spaces for hydraulic pumps and filtration for fresh water, tiny offices with desks and computer workstations, small workshops and another large space for air-conditioning. It was hours of tension, moving slowly, listening and opening doors carefully while expecting an attack at every turn, but the area was clear of the dead.

Until they found the girl.

It was inside a workshop that appeared to specialize in pipe cutting and fittings, lit by a pair of mesh-encased bulbs throwing shadows into the corners. The back third of the room was filled with a row of steel tool and supply cabinets, divided from the rest of the workshop by a floor-to-ceiling wall of chain link, a gate set in the center. Someone had put a padlock on the gate, ensuring that the girl would remain inside.

Xavier and the others entered and approached the fence. She was young, maybe eighteen, and dressed in blue work coveralls, her hair still tied up in a neat bun, a name tag over her breast pocket reading *SIPOWITCZ*. Her skin was slate-gray, mottled with dark blotches, and her eyes were a cloudy shade of maroon. A dark patch on her left thigh showed where the bite bled through the material.

When she saw them, she began making a soft whining noise.

She had found or forced a small gap between the chain link and a support pole and forced her right arm through it up to the shoulder. The edges of the steel links acted like a cheese grater and, as she pushed through, efficiently shredded the sleeve of her work uniform and the flesh underneath. Now that arm, thrust outward with the fingers grasping at air, hung in tattered ribbons of gray and black, revealing bone. The girl shoved her body against the fencing, still trying to get through, face pressed against the links and jaws working slowly.

"Someone locked her in there instead of killing her," Xavier said.

"Someone who cared about her," said Rosa. She didn't see hunger or malice in the girl's face, only a pathetic sadness. "This was somebody's daughter."

Eve, one of the hippies, rested a hand on Rosa's shoulder. "You've seen them before, hon. They were all special to someone. But now they're just . . ."

"Monsters," said a hippie named Tommy. "It's only the first one we've found on board. When they start coming for us you won't feel so sorry for them."

Eve gave Tommy a reproachful look, then lowered her voice as they all stared at the thing on the other side of the fence, still reaching, still whining. "We can't think they're human anymore. They don't respond to compassion or anything else, and this one would kill you if she had the chance."

"She's right," said Xavier.

Tommy retrieved a long metal file from a worktable and walked to the fence. "I'll do it."

"She can't get to us!" said Rosa. "She can't hurt anyone in there."

"And leaving her like this is cruel," the priest said, nodding at Tommy. Rosa walked back out into the corridor as the hippie quickly stabbed the long file through one of the girl's eyes and punctured her brain. She stiffened and collapsed, but not all the way to the floor, her trapped arm leaving her sagging against the chain link. Xavier offered a silent Hail Mary before turning away.

They moved on, resuming their cautious inspection of every opening and door, Xavier still in the lead. By the time they reached a room marked *GENERATOR CONTROL*, a long narrow chamber of electrical boards, gauges, and workstations, the priest estimated that they had crossed to the port side of the ship. Here, more corridors led toward the front of the ship, even more sporadically lit than those previously, and now the ominous openings of stairwells were added to the many hatches and doors.

They cleared another row of small offices and a room filled with lockers before they began to smell a new odor steadily growing stronger, something unpleasant, a chemical smell. As they traveled the main corridor the odor began to dominate all else, covering the fragrances of machine oil and rot, causing a few of them to squint their eyes and cough. Xavier was about to turn them back when Rosa gripped his upper arm.

"What's that?" she whispered, pointing past him. "Up there. Is that a leg?"

The priest pulled his flashlight and trained it ahead. It was indeed a leg, sticking out of a hatchway ahead on the right, wearing a rubber boot and a pant leg made from heavy yellow material. The corridor lights beyond the leg were out, a tunnel of blackness with some kind of liquid pooling on the floor and spreading slowly toward them. The chemical odor was much stronger here, making them wince and cover their mouths.

"My God, what *is* that?" said Eve.

Xavier moved toward the leg, Rosa close behind, and he let his shotgun muzzle lead as he came to the opening. His shoes splashed through the fluid on the floor.

A sailor in firefighter's gear with an air tank and face mask lay in the opening, stretched out on his back. A single bullet hole pierced his mask, the Plexiglas cloudy with congealed gore, the body appearing deflated as body fluids had exited through the openings in the fire-retardant suit. The smell was foul enough to compete with the chemicals in the air. Two more similarly dressed bodies were crumpled on the deck in the compartment beyond the opening. Someone had shot some zombies, and apparently quite some time ago.

Everyone in the group was coughing now, trying to cover their mouths and noses, squinting and waving at the air as if that might drive the odor back. Xavier swept his flashlight across the floor, seeing empty shell casings scattered across the deck in the spreading fluid. His eyes burned as he looked at the straw-colored liquid, his light tracking to the left wall and upward, seeing that it rippled down the steel in a thin stream. At the corner where the wall met the ceiling was a cluster of pipes, purple, white, and blue, all of them ruptured by gunfire. The yellow liquid was coming from a purple pipe.

Rosa saw it too and gripped Xavier's arm. "On carriers, anything having to do with JP-5 is purple," she said, her voice strained.

"What?" The priest rubbed at his stinging eyes.

She looked down. "We're standing in jet fuel."

And that was when the dead began to gallop out of the blacked-out corridor ahead.

TWENTY

Evan looked down as the others scrambled through the hatch behind him. It had only managed to bite into the thick heel of his motorcycle boot, and it was only a rotting, decapitated head with a crew cut. He had nearly stepped on it.

"*Yaah!*" he cried, booting the head across the wardroom like a grisly soccer ball.

Calvin slammed the hatch behind them and held down the lever as dozens of fists hammered at the steel from the other side. Flashlights swept the room, illuminating a shadow on the far side, darting among the tables and chairs. The boy named Stone shot at it and missed, and the bullet sparked off a steel bulkhead.

Across the room, Freeman, the hippie who had run in, threw up his hands and screamed, "Don't! No, don't!"

Evan pushed the muzzle of the boy's weapon away before he could fire again, and across the room Freeman began crying like a child. Fists pummeled at steel, and the hatch's lever suddenly shot up. Calvin grabbed it and forced it back down. "They know how to open the doors!"

Several of the group ran to his aid, while others scoured the room, one of them returning with a metal folding chair that they jammed between the handle and the door. It seemed to hold. Evan quickly checked the room, finding a similar door on the far side, as well as Freeman, who had tucked himself into a ball on the floor and was sobbing. Calvin appeared a moment later, crouching beside the man and speaking softly.

"Everyone reload," Evan ordered, feeding shells into his shotgun, the others following suit. When he was done, he located the head he had kicked, nudged it out from under a table with the toe of his boot, and then smashed it with a folding chair until it came apart. He returned to the new hatch and listened at it but heard nothing on the other side.

Calvin joined him. "Freeman's in bad shape," the older man said. "He's in shock, and he isn't hearing me."

Evan glanced at the man on the floor. A woman was now kneeling beside him, stroking his hair. "What do we—?" Evan started.

"Nothing," said Calvin. "We leave him here."

Evan's eyes widened in surprise. This was one of Calvin's people.

Calvin saw the look. "Yes, he's family and I love him like all the rest, but we can't help him, we can't stay here, and bringing him along puts everyone at risk." He looked back at a man with whom he'd shared a life. "I hate it, and if anything happens to him I don't know how I'll live with it, but there's no choice. We'll try to find a way to lock him in here and come back later."

Evan nodded as the other man gathered his people to deliver the news. He realized that despite the title others frequently attributed to him, it was Calvin who was a true leader and had been since the beginning. He was someone who would consider the welfare of the entire group and make hard decisions, even though the outcome might be heartbreaking. And he was someone who, if he asked others to put themselves in harm's way, would not hesitate to stand beside them as well.

The writer listened at the door again, knowing they had to keep moving. How long would it take for the mob outside to stumble across a back way into this place? Surely there was another way in, possibly several in this steel maze. If not, it would mean their little band would be forced to go back out where the dead were waiting for them.

Calvin's people moved Freeman to a couch and covered him with a blanket, then assembled on the door, one of them carrying another folding chair so they could secure it from the other side. It would have to be enough.

Out they went, Evan leading them into a short corridor of empty offices. This opened into a long hallway that appeared to run bow to stern, or if not quite that long, at least in those directions. Doorways, hatches, up and down stairways, and equipment lockers awaited, infrequently lit fluorescent bars providing a little illumination.

Corpses milled about at an intersection a hundred feet to the right. More were lingering to the left, only twenty feet away.

Some were staring at walls or actually sitting on the deck, none of them making any noise, and as Evan looked back and forth between them, he was yet again fascinated by their behavior, even after so many encounters. They seemed almost docile when they weren't agitated. He knew that wouldn't last. Word was passed back, and the group readied itself.

They attacked left, toward the closest knot of zombies, weapons roaring in the close space and rounds sparking off bulkheads or shattering light bars. The corpses became animated at once and lurched into the gunfire. In seconds, a dozen bodies were sprawled across the deck.

"To the rear!" Calvin shouted, and the little group turned as one, those in the back now at the front, opening fire on the creatures shuffling toward them from the intersection. The shooting was an endless, reverberating crash, muzzle flashes lighting the hall and filling the air with gun smoke.

The dead fell and didn't rise.

"Reload!" called Evan, and fingers clicked rounds into chambers, slapped in fresh magazines, or pushed shells up tubes.

They moved forward, reaching the intersection and pointing their weapons in every direction. "On the right!" shouted Stone, kneeling and opening fire. Others joined him as corpses in blue coveralls, camouflage, and khaki filled the boy's corridor. Bullets tore through cold tissue and decomposing organs, blasted dark gore onto the walls and into the faces of other corpses. Tops of heads were torn away, backs of skulls blown out. One creature in khaki, so bloated and green with gas that he looked like a balloon, exploded in a greenish-white mess that Evan briefly associated with spinach dip.

"I got a greenie!" Stone cried.

Evan started to laugh, and then the fresh stench hit him and he began to heave.

Corpses fell, and more clambered over them. The firing dropped off when the shooters were forced to reload, giving the dead a chance to advance. When the gunfire resumed, the dead had gained considerable ground.

"Behind us!" yelled Mercy, the woman who had two young daughters back at the Alameda pier. Armed with an M4 taken from an overrun military column outside of Oakland, she stepped out of the intersection and into another hallway, squeezing off rounds at a cluster of the walking dead emerging from another hatchway. Calvin stood beside her and added his own firepower.

Evan recovered from his retching, the bile bitter in his mouth, and resumed firing next to Stone. He suddenly thought that one of the corpses lumbering toward them looked familiar, a woman in soiled khaki with her head cocked on what could only be a broken neck. Then he realized where he had seen her; she had been galloping at the front of the horde bearing down on them just as Freeman had bailed out through the wardroom hatch. So they had found a way around the wedged door.

Evan shot her in the head.

The firing fell off once more as people reloaded. More figures stumbled over the fallen, still closing the gap between the living and the dead. Back at the intersection, Calvin and Mercy finished off their original targets and backed into the intersection so they could cover every approach. Groans echoed from Calvin's side on the left, followed by a metallic clatter that made a chill race up the older hippie's back.

It was the sound of a folding chair hitting the metal deck.

Before the hippie leader could move, Mercy called out more targets, this time on the right, and they both turned to fire. Shadowy figures in uniform trudged out of the darkened hall, bullets slamming into chests and groins and legs before finding their marks. Bodies tottered and collapsed.

A man's long scream pierced the corridor to their rear, and then was abruptly cut short.

Calvin clenched his jaw and forced himself not to turn, not to break off and run to the sound of the scream, making himself scan their target corridor with his flashlight. One of the bodies on the floor groaned and tried to pull itself out from under several others that were pinning it to the floor. Mercy saw it and used the light to put a round in its forehead. With no more targets immediately in front of them, Mercy inserted a fresh magazine and urged Calvin to do the same.

Back at the main engagement, freshly reloaded weapons began to fire once more as the corridor began filling with mounds of the twice dead. Bullets tore into conduit and ventilation and ricocheted off door frames, and one punched a hole in a fire extinguisher hanging from a wall mount. There was a soft *whumpf*, and suddenly the hallway was filled with a white fog.

"I can't see them!" Stone shouted.

Evan grabbed his shoulder. "Fall back to the intersection."

The group did, backing into Calvin and Mercy. There were six of them in total.

"They'll be coming," Evan said, keeping his shotgun aimed into the white cloud, watching for movement. Any second now . . .

"This way," Mercy said, leading them up the corridor that appeared to run toward the front of the ship, picking her way over bodies. The others followed.

Calvin stayed in the intersection, rifle to his shoulder, facing back down the hallway from which they had originally come. His eyes were wet with tears. "Come on," he whispered.

Evan shouted at him. "Calvin, we have to go!"

Calvin didn't move. "Come on," he repeated.

On his left, the dead stalked out of the fire extinguisher fog, hair and skin now coated in white powder. They spotted the lone man in the intersection and broke into their deadly gallop.

There was a moan then, and Freeman staggered into the sight at the end of Calvin's rifle. His throat had been torn open, one of his eyes dangled and rested on his cheek, and several fingers of one reaching hand had been bitten off.

"I'm sorry," Calvin choked, and fired a single round, putting the man down. Then he pivoted left and emptied his clip into the crowd of surging, white-coated corpses, bullets flinging them back into one another, the heavy caliber doing withering damage at such close range. When his firing pin clicked on a dry magazine, Calvin turned and ran after his group.

TWENTY-ONE

Angie and Skye moved swiftly up through the compartment marked with a yellow *02*, encountering closed hatches and the sailors they had killed from below, and then continued upward. Here, the stairs ended in a room with *03 GALLERY* stenciled on the wall. Three open, oval-shaped hatches gave them a choice, none of which they wanted. Both women had hoped the stairway would take them all the way up to the flight deck but realized it was probably asking for too much.

"Let's go this way," Angie said, indicating the hatch on the right.

Skye moved past her, taking the flashlight out of Angie's hand. "You can't carry the Barrett and the Galil, and still hold the light." Her voice was like the rasp of a file across a cinder block.

Angie nodded, wishing she had left the Barrett behind. It offered an incredible amount of standoff firepower, the capability of reaching out and touching a target at extreme range, but in addition to its tremendous weight, it had a low rate of fire and was really useful only in open spaces at long range. Like the flight deck that eluded them, she thought. Still, she couldn't bear leaving it behind, and so she bore the weight and let the younger woman lead.

The overhead lights were out in the corridor beyond the hatch they had chosen, but Skye's flashlight was sufficient. The hallway was narrow and packed with piping and cables, and multiple hatches on both sides. Signs beside the oval doorways read CAT-1 ACCESS, ELECTRICAL, HYDRAULICS, CAT-2 ACCESS. All were closed, and they did not attempt to explore any of them.

Skye stopped them by holding up a fist, something she had learned from Taylor and Postman, the two National Guardsmen who had rescued and trained her, then given their lives for her. It seemed a lifetime ago. "I feel air moving," she said.

Angie whispered, "You can't smell it? That's outside air."

The young woman breathed deeply through her nose. Nothing. It confirmed something she had been suspecting for days now; in addition to the hand tremors, the headaches, and the loss of vision in her left eye, she was also losing her sense of taste and smell. Wonderful. What would be next?

"I feel the draft too," said Angie.

Skye moved forward, the M4 muzzle leading, and came to a turn. She held her breath and listened, then stepped around the corner, ready to blow away anything waiting on the other side. There was nothing but another ten feet of corridor, which led to a heavy hatch standing partially open. A sliver of daylight fell through the opening, and a puff of breeze accompanied by a soft whistle issued from the hatch. Skye used her shoulder to open it slowly.

The sunlight made her wince and draw back, as the headache spike sank into her brain like white fire. She gasped but shrugged off Angie's attempt to reach for her. Skye fumbled her aviator sunglasses out of a pouch on her ammo vest and went through, Angie close behind.

A soft, salty breeze blew in from the bay as the two women stepped out onto a metal grid catwalk with a four-foot steel-pipe railing. The surface was nearly ninety feet below, reflecting the day's light as above the sun ducked in and out behind a generally gray cloud cover. Both breathed deeply of the clean air.

The catwalk began at the hatch from which they had emerged,

quite near the extreme back end of the warship, and extended ahead along the starboard side. The flight deck directly above them stretched another ten feet out over the catwalk, creating a shady overhang, and both imagined what the noise level would have been to stand here while fighter aircraft thundered so closely off the deck. They could see Alameda half a mile away, and the urban sprawl of Oakland beyond. Nothing could be seen moving on the streets, in the skies above, or on the calm waters of the bay. A dead world.

The movement was much closer, and Angie pointed it out. At the edge of the overhanging flight deck, the line of safety netting jutted out another five or six feet. They had seen it from the water as they circled the massive vessel, and now, as then, several corpses flopped in the netting. Here, a figure in a yellow jersey and helmet, steel-toed boots, and tan "float coat" made the mesh sag as it thrashed facedown, groaning and reaching through, arms and legs entangled.

"Tango," Skye said, and shot the creature under the chin, blowing its brains out through a new hole in the top of its helmet.

"Tango," Angie echoed, tapping the girl's shoulder and pointing down the catwalk. A young sailor in a red long-sleeved jersey was shuffling toward them along the structure's length, one shoulder shredded by an old shotgun blast, a gaping hole in the center of his torso. Liquefied, blackened organs dripped from the wound and pattered onto the young man's boots as he moved.

Skye aimed and fired. *CHAK*. The bullet clipped off an ear. Skye bared her teeth at the headache spike, ticked left, and fired again. *CHAK*. A hole appeared above the sailor's right eye and he collapsed. Skye frowned and looked at her M4, not liking this new, metallic sound it was making.

"Your suppressor's wearing out," Angie said. "They don't last forever."

Skye cursed.

"When we get back to my van, we'll make you a new one," Angie offered. "I have all the equipment we need."

Skye smirked and raised an eyebrow. "You really think we're getting off this ship alive?"

The face of Angie's daughter, Leah, flashed before her eyes. "Yes," she said, her throat suddenly tight, "I do."

Skye shrugged and moved down the catwalk.

Thirty feet past the sailor in the red jersey they came upon a pair of low steel lockers bolted to the catwalk, both of them open and empty. Just opposite, set in a heavy, pivoting mount in the railing, was a pair of side-by-side fifty-caliber heavy machine guns, each with a large ammo box affixed to the side. Both were loaded, belts of long, copper-jacketed rounds snaking down into the boxes.

"This makes sense," said Angie. "They would have been at general quarters. Do you know what these things would do to any boat stupid enough to come within range?"

"Open them up like zippers, I'll bet," Skye rasped.

"You better believe it."

Skye patted one of the heavy weapons as she walked past. "Too bad they don't count for shit against the walking dead," she said. "Making a head shot would be pure luck."

Angie nodded. Skye was right; the twin fifties would tear hell out of small boats and even knock down planes, and against human targets they caused catastrophic damage. In one of the episodes of her show, the fifty-caliber heavy machine gun had been demonstrated, with a retired Army master sergeant there to provide commentary. The man had dispelled the myth that the use of such a weapon against human targets was prohibited, explaining that JAG, the judge advocate general's office, had declared it legal.

A human being hit by full-auto fifty-caliber fire didn't leave much behind to even identify. Unfortunately, Angie knew, against the walking dead it would at best chop them up into lots of smaller infectious pieces, and if it didn't destroy the brain, it would still leave a dangerous enemy behind.

They passed the weapons by, heading for a steep stairwell that would lead them finally to the flight deck. Skye went first, the metal risers taking her up through a rectangular opening. She stopped with only her head exposed in order to assess their new environment.

Skye knew the supercarrier was big, having seen it both from a distance and from the water up close as they made a circuit of the ship before tying off at the swimmer's platform. Their climb up from the depths gave the impression of being inside a large building. Yet it was not until now that she truly had a sense of just how massive *Nimitz* was, and for a moment she was overwhelmed.

The flat deck, covered in a rubberized nonskid coating, stretched away like a stadium parking lot and continued so far forward that from this angle there was no clear definition of where it ended and the drop-off to the water began. There were very few protrusions, which immediately made sense to her, as anything poking out of the deck would be a hazard to aircraft. A pair of low, glassed-in viewports amidships and farther out jutted up a few inches from the surface. She remembered that the people who controlled the launch catapults would be in there, something she had learned from seeing *Top Gun*, but all other equipment, elevator platforms, lights, and arresting wires appeared to be flush-mounted and out of sight.

The superstructure was another matter.

About a third of the way forward, rising on the starboard side—their side—was a haze-gray structure climbing over eight stories above the deck, its uppermost levels ringed with tipped-out, bluish glass windows and ringed with catwalks. Above this towered a high mast bristling with antennae and radar equipment. A large American flag hung from the mast, waving in a light breeze.

Between Skye and the superstructure stood a high crane derrick, apparently used for clearing objects off the deck or even swinging out to recover things from the sea. What appeared to be storage sheds or garages were built into the space between the crane and the superstructure.

Based on what she had seen in a movie that was a hit even before she was born, Skye had expected to see the deck covered in dangerous-looking fighter aircraft, and she was a bit surprised to see that it was empty. But then hadn't someone, that Navy medic Rosa, said that the planes might have already left? Skye decided that if the sailors on board had started turning and eating each other, anyone who could fly would have taken off without a second thought.

"What do we have?" Angie asked from the stairway below.

Skye moved to the side and motioned her up. Angie poked her head out and took it all in. Despite the impressive nature of a super-carrier's flight deck up close, it was the dead that interested them most.

Sailors wearing an assortment of colored jerseys, some with helmets and some without, others in camouflage or coveralls, wandered the deck in their stiff-legged gait, arms dangling at their sides. A few stood at the edge of the deck and seemed to stare out at the haunted cities in the distance. None of them were making noise. As they watched, a pair of creatures stumbled up from a catwalk on the far side of the flat expanse, and another emerged from an opening in the superstructure, tripping over the knee knocker and falling onto its face, only to slowly climb to its feet and shuffle away. On the catwalks high above, another half dozen bumped along handrails and into each other.

"Once we start," said Angie, "it's going to get them worked up and bring them down on us."

"Yep," said Skye, clenching her teeth against the headache that had subsided from a blinding spike to a painful throb, one that flared every now and then to remind her it was never far away.

"I had hoped to get up onto those catwalks," Angie said, looking up. "Elevation would be better."

Skye shrugged. "So we run for the tower, or whatever it's called." Her blind eye was watering again. "You saw the drifter come out, so that's our way in. There must be stairs."

Angie thought for a moment. "Let's thin them out a little first, then make our move." When Skye nodded, Angie led them up and across the extreme rear end of the flight deck at a jog. Skye paused once to drop a drifter in a green jersey who she thought was a little too close. It took three rounds before she scored a head shot.

The two women dropped prone on the rubberized deck, about five feet between them. Angie snapped out the bipod at the front of her Galil and set it before her, along with a bandolier of magazines. Skye similarly laid out full clips close to her left elbow as she settled into a comfortable position.

Still on her stomach, Angie scooted left a few feet and unfolded the steel bipod of the Barrett, lining up stubby magazines of heavy fifty-caliber rounds. She embraced the stock, pulling it close, and put her eye to the large scope, clicking a few adjustments. Her right hand found the pistol grip, index finger lightly locating the trigger. To Angie West, the Barrett was an old friend, and she was an expert marksman with the legendary weapon. It was the same rifle used by Navy SEALs, some of whom she had competed against and had come out on at least a level footing.

"I'll go long," Angie said. "You take the targets closer in."

Skye wiped an unsteady left hand at her weeping eye and pulled the M4 tight against her shoulder. She sighted on a thing in a tan vest and white helmet, a rotting thing with a drooping shoulder, a hated thing of a species that had destroyed everyone she had ever loved. She put the luminescent green chevrons of her optics on its wavering head.

"Let's go to work," said Skye, her voice like the gravel at the bottom of a grave.

They fired together.

TWENTY-TWO

Rosa had no sooner said the words *jet fuel* than three of the hippies opened up on the horde with assault rifles and shotguns. The crash of gunfire thundered in the tight hallway, muzzle flashes reflected in the pooling fuel and splitting the vaporous air.

"No!" Xavier cried, involuntarily ducking, expecting the bright flash that would herald ignition and death.

It didn't come.

JP-5, also called AVCAT for *aviation carrier turbine fuel*, was kerosene-based, a complex mixture of hydrocarbons, alkanes, naphthenes, and aromatic hydrocarbons. It was highly flammable with explosive vapors; those who handled it without proper gear were at constant risk of being incapacitated by benzene fumes. Both Rosa and Brother Peter felt the hallway spin as they became light-headed and had to hold on to the walls to keep from falling.

Because of its nature and the dangerous environment of jet aircraft operating on a busy flight deck, AVCAT had been designed with a flash point of 140 degrees and had to be moderately heated before it would ignite. It was considered a stable fuel, even under fire conditions, and was normally impervious to small-arms fire.

That they had not blown up did not replace the fact that they were all being steadily poisoned.

The hippies at the rear poured fire into the surging dead, trying to pull bandanas over their faces at the same time. Xavier grabbed Rosa and Brother Peter by their arms, choking out, "Come on!" as he stumbled back the way they had come. The other three members of Calvin's Family who were with them—Tommy, Eve, and Lilly—had already run in that direction, flashlight beams bouncing frantically. Those at the back attempted a fighting retreat, battling the overpowering fumes while trying to make their shots count as they backed up.

One of them slipped in the pooling JP-5 and went down hard, striking her head. Another was overcome with benzene and sagged unconscious to the deck. A bearded young man named Tuck, who claimed he could commune with Native American shamanic totems when he did peyote, stood over the bodies of his fallen friends emptying his rifle at the galloping dead, screaming, "Oh, God, oh, God, oh, God!"

The dead slammed into him and took him to the floor. They pursued Xavier no farther down the corridor as they dropped to their knees amid the fallen humans in a savage feeding frenzy.

The priest had neither the time nor the strength to look back at the rear guard. Rosa and Peter were heavy and sluggish, even in his powerful arms, and he barely noticed that he had dropped his shotgun in order to grab them. He was light-headed too, and his vision was quickly shrinking into a constricting tunnel with gray at the edges as a wave of nausea hit him in a rush.

He was going to fall, and then they were going to die.

Xavier stayed on his feet, hauling his companions forward and keeping his narrowing sight on the bobbing lights up ahead. If he could reach them, if he could just . . .

The flashlights disappeared, leaving only a long corridor with a few fluorescents in the distance. Under the lights, a crowd of *Nimitz*'s former crew was headed this way. Xavier stopped to catch his breath, his chest burning as he struggled to inhale, his throat raw and the inside of his nose scorched and red. He gagged, fought it, and then vomited on the deck in front of him. He couldn't tell if there was blood in it, though he expected there would be, then heaved twice more.

The growling and ripping sounds of the feeding behind him filled the hall, and from the approaching shapes up ahead came a long, low moan. He looked at his companions, both on their knees and barely conscious, Peter's shotgun dangling from a strap around his neck and Rosa's nine-millimeter still in its holster. He doubted he even had the strength to retrieve the weapons, much less use them, and as he reached out for the shotgun another surge of vomit doubled him over, bile searing his already raw throat on the way up.

This is how we end, he thought, one arm still outstretched for the shotgun when many hands fell upon him and pulled at his flesh. He couldn't even fight back, could only keep his grip on Rosa and Peter and hope they were too far gone to feel the teeth.

It took all three of them, Tommy, Lilly, and Eve, to drag Xavier into the hatchway through which they had disappeared, into the safety of a barnlike room holding the vessel's emergency diesels. They pulled Brother Peter and Rosa in next, closed the hatch, and secured the dog handle with a three-foot-long socket wrench.

Xavier fell over the corpse of a sailor with a freshly crushed head—courtesy of Tommy and the same wrench that now held the door—and collapsed to the deck. Rosa and Peter were stretched out beside him, both fully unconscious now. The room reeked of diesel, but compared to the gas chamber created by the leaking JP-5, it was like high mountain air. Xavier focused simply on drawing breath, and just before he passed out, he had a moment to consider how cool the rubberized floor felt against the side of his face.

While Eve kept watch over her unconscious companions, worried that they might not awaken from the exposure to the fumes but not knowing what to do about it, Tommy and Lilly conducted a more detailed exploration of the generator room. They returned fifteen minutes later, confirming that they were alone, and that the space had a small attached workshop, several exiting hatches, and an open stairway that led both up and down. Tommy stacked two small pyramids of tin lubricant cans at the entry point of both stairways, hoping that if any of the clumsy dead staggered up or down into their room, they would at least get a warning.

Xavier and Rosa didn't come to for another hour and spent even more time just sitting propped against a wall, not speaking. Brother Peter rose a half hour after that, moving away from the others and leaning against a generator with his eyes closed, holding his head against a pulsating pain that threatened to split his skull right down the middle.

"I thought we were dead," Xavier said at last, his voice weak.

Tommy was squatting in front of him and offered bottles of water to the priest and Rosa. "So did we. You got lucky; the others didn't. I guess they bought us some time." There was no recrimination in his voice, only a tone of resignation. "I think we're safe for now."

Rosa produced two bottles of saline solution from her medical bag and passed them around, insisting everyone flush their eyes. Lilly brought a bottle to Brother Peter and had to nudge him several times to get his attention before he obediently took it from her hand.

After a while they huddled together in hopes of figuring out where they were. It didn't take long before they decided that other than being on Fourth Deck and somewhere near the back of the ship, they were hopelessly turned around. A *thump* interrupted the conversation, the single *bang* of a fist on a steel hatch, and all eyes went involuntarily to the wrench.

"Maybe it's one of the others," Lilly whispered.

Another *thump*, followed by a muffled moan.

"Maybe," said Xavier, "but not as you knew them."

They moved away from the door, in among the towering generators. The priest looked around at the group, seeing a fatigue that seemed to have overridden their terror. He checked his watch, only to find it had been smashed at some point.

"We need to rest," Xavier said. "We need to find a safe place to hide for a while, have something to eat, get some sleep. We're pretty much shot right now."

The others nodded their agreement.

Xavier ran a hand over his face, rubbing at tired eyes. "Trouble is, where can we go?"

The Air Force shrink who was also God stood beside Brother Peter with His arms folded, frowning. *"I saved your life again,"* He said. *"I could have left you for the lions, but I spared your life. Do you still disbelieve?"*

The minister quickly looked around at the others. He had only spoken with the Lord when he was alone or away from the group, but now here He was in their midst. What would the others think? Immediately he noticed that they seemed to neither see nor hear the savior. Did that mean they couldn't hear Peter speaking as well?

"I believe," the minister said softly, glancing around. No one noticed. He said it louder. "I'm not a pussy!" Again there was no reaction from the group, not even the priest, who, of course, believed he could speak with the Lord.

"They are heathens," God said. *"They do not even feel my presence. You are the chosen, Peter, and thus granted special gifts."*

The minister smiled.

"But you're still weak."

Brother Peter's face reddened. "I'm not! Don't say that!"

"Hmm, sounds like you might have a little spunk left in you after all," God said, standing close enough to polish His eyeglasses on the tail of Brother Peter's shirt.

"I'm not weak," the minister repeated in a mutter.

"Okay, cool your jets, tough guy. Don't forget who you're talking to." The shrink shifted forms into the hated, touchy gym teacher, making the minister recoil. *"Naughty boys get punished, oh yes they do,"* said God.

"I told you I don't like that form," Brother Peter said, his voice becoming a petulant whine.

God shrugged and turned into Anderson, Peter's trusted and loyal aide whom the minister had fed to the undead. He was naked and covered in bites and torn flesh, scraps of zip ties dangling from His wrists and ankles. He held up His palms, both with bleeding stigmata. *"WHO ... AM ... I ... ?"* God's voice thundered, making the steel deck tremble.

Brother Peter clapped his hands to the sides of his head. "Stop! Please, you're confusing me!"

Anderson became the shrink once more, adjusting the glasses on the bridge of His nose and chuckling. *"Lighten up, Petey,"* God said. *"I'm just messing with you."*

Brother Peter wanted to lighten up. He wanted to understand why his savior was behaving in such a (fucking annoying) mysterious way. It was making clear thinking difficult. And why was God so (fucking sarcastic) displeased with him all the time? Wasn't he God's chosen (fucking murderer) disciple?

God simply looked at him and frowned.

Brother Peter forced himself to stand straight and rubbed his fists at his eyes like a tired little boy before looking his savior in the eye. "What should I do?"

God gave him a patient smile, the kind reserved for clumsy children, and shook His head. *"You can't be a puppet if you serve me. Figure it out."*

Now it was the minister's turn to frown, and he thought for a moment.

"You wanted me to be on the ship, and I am," said Peter. "You want me to be your avenging sword, the vessel from which you will pour your cleansing fire." He wasn't actually sure if God had said that to him, or if he just imagined that was what God intended. It didn't matter. He knew what God wanted. It was what Peter wanted too.

"Excellent!" said God, shifting from the Air Force shrink to Sherri. Only She hadn't been slashed, or bitten, and She looked, well, Peter thought She looked sort of sexy, and he remembered the things the young woman had done in order to keep herself alive a bit longer. God stepped close and draped Her arms around the minister's neck, tipping Her head back, lips slightly parted. She sighed, and Brother Peter found himself growing aroused, instantly ashamed that he should feel this way about *God*, but unable to control himself. His face grew flushed.

"Or do you like this better?" God asked, becoming Angie West in heels and a see-through black nylon catsuit, just like the outfit his mistress in Cincinnati used to wear.

"Oh, yes," Brother Peter said thickly, reaching for Her.

God slapped him sharply across the face. *"No touching!"*

The minister looked down, face burning. And that was just how the bitch was, wasn't she? Strutting around with that tight little body, throwing it in a man's face, then threatening violence if he should want to give her what she so richly deserved.

God lifted his chin and met his eyes. *"I'm distracting you. Please continue."*

Peter thought about the training class in Omaha, when the Navy instructor spoke about comparative security measures. About the carriers. When he spoke it was with a sense of pride. "It was a highly classified subject. Only the best of us were allowed to attend.

"The Navy was bragging," Brother Peter said, his eyes distant with a memory. "They talked about how easy we had it, how simple it was to maintain security measures so deep underground, and that they had it tougher at sea, which made them so much smarter than us."

God began rubbing Brother Peter's shoulders, slowly, patiently.

"They claimed they took them off the carriers in 1997," the minister said, "and that's why Marines were no longer on board, because there was nothing left to protect."

"But you knew they were lying, didn't you?" God was walking in a slow circle around him now, trailing Her fingertips across his neck.

"Of course they were lying!" Peter said, nearly spitting the words. "I could see it in that commander's face, standing up there in his pretty dress whites. He was bearing false witness. And besides, no matter what they said, no one would really give up that kind of advantage."

"Of course they wouldn't," said God.

"Up-to-go-down," Peter said. "They thought they were so clever with that. Up-to-go-down. They even showed us what they looked like. The arrogance! Showing us photos and then claiming they didn't have them anymore. They thought we were stupid."

"The sin of pride," God whispered.

Brother Peter's distant gaze became focused. "MARS, named after Jupiter's son, the god of war. A wing-mounted weapon fired from the *Hornet*. But instead of blast fragmentation, it carried a nine-kiloton nuclear warhead."

"Praise Jesus," God whispered, and then stepped in front of the minister and gripped his shoulders with two powerful hands. *"And you know where to find them."*

"Ammunition bunker, belly of the ship." Peter grinned. "Up to go down."

God peered into the minister's face. *"Do you still have the skills? Do you still have the faith?"*

"I do," Brother Peter said, standing tall, "and I do."

"Then be my vessel, Peter," God said, appearing for the first time as a tall old man with white hair and eyes filled with infinite wisdom.

"Thy will be done," Brother Peter said, his heart filled with glory.

Xavier looked up from his thoughts to see Peter staring at him with a curious intensity he had not seen in the man. More than ever he was certain he had seen him somewhere before. Maybe he was just tired. "Are you okay?" the priest asked.

"I'm worn out from the gas fumes, but I'll be okay. And you were right, we need to rest." Brother Peter walked over to join them.

"Any ideas?" asked Xavier.

The minister nodded. "With all due respect to your plan . . ." Peter held out his palms deferentially.

Xavier chuckled and shook his head. "You're not going to hurt my feelings."

"Well, I just think being this deep in the ship is the wrong thing to do. It's more tightly closed in, the lighting isn't the best, and it's hard to fight down here." Peter summoned some of the charisma that had skyrocketed him to televangelist fame. "And that leaking fuel isn't going to get better by itself; in fact, it's probably going to poison this entire deck. It may not bother the drifters, but it makes staying impossible for us."

Xavier nodded. He was thinking fuzzy. The man had just made an inarguable point.

Brother Peter pressed on. "There's bound to be food, barracks . . ."

"Berthing," Rosa corrected. "On a ship it's called berthing."

"Right, thank you." Peter smiled, imagining burning the woman with a cigar butt. "We'll find a safe place to rest and recover, maybe some ammunition, and hopefully some others of our group." He gave a small shrug. "I think maybe it's time to retreat, at least for a bit, then figure out how to come back safely later. Go up to go down," he couldn't resist adding.

Xavier found himself nodding, then looked at the others, who nodded as well. "That sounds good, Peter."

The minister smiled. "I'll lead," he said.

Beside him, God smiled and clapped him on the back. *"Good boy."*

TWENTY-THREE

This is stupid, Carney thought. *What made us think we could do this?* The *Nimitz* was a city-sized labyrinth packed with horrors, an unfamiliar and unfriendly territory, and they had thought the zombies would simply line up in neat rows awaiting execution? A professional SWAT or SEAL team would train for months before attempting this, and they would have solid information and logistical support. This was not a task for a bunch of frightened amateurs.

TC was staring at him with a cocked eyebrow and a half smile. They were in a long compartment where the walls were covered in blue, white, and purple pipes; steam valves; and seemingly miles of aluminum conduit. Scattered light bars revealed shadowy mechanical equipment, giant reels of the arresting cable used to stop aircraft as they landed on the deck, and a spare catapult piston as long as a city bus.

"Whatcha thinking about?" asked TC. He had slung his auto shotgun, which looked oddly like a six-shooter only with a much larger cylinder capable of handling many more shells, in favor of a four-foot steel wrench. It looked heavy enough that an average person would need both hands to use it, but the muscled inmate carried it in a casual, one-handed grip as if it were as light as a yardstick. "Something's cooking in there," he said.

Carney looked at his cellmate in annoyance. TC frustrated him, dangerous one moment, charming and likable the next. Carney had to remind himself that it was the dangerous side that ruled the man. "Just thinking, is all," Carney said.

"About Mexico maybe?" TC said, nodding slowly. "We could do it, man. I've been thinking about the boats, that one we took from the boatyard. I bet it's big enough to handle the ocean, or at least the coast."

Carney thought about the big Bayliner, with its full fuel tank and deck packed with supplies. The assault group had loaded both it and the patrol boat with food, water, and ammo, thinking they could use the boats as a fallback position if things got too hairy inside the aircraft carrier. The thirty-two-foot Bayliner *could* handle open water. Fuel would be a problem eventually, but there were sure to be plenty of marinas on the way down the California coast.

"We could just slip away," TC said, moving in close, the trusted cellmate once more. "No one would know. We don't owe these people shit, man."

Mexico, Carney thought. Sun and sand. The idea had really just been something to keep TC's mind occupied, to prevent him from going wild with his newfound freedom. Carney had never actually considered it a serious possibility. Had he?

A distant echo of gunfire made Carney start, but TC rested a hand on the other man's arm. "It's just those assholes who ran out on us, getting into some shit. Let them. It keeps the zombies busy and off our ass."

Carney looked through one of the compartment's wide openings and out into a dark corridor. The hollow booming of a shotgun sounded ghostly, and then it was gone. He took a half step in that direction, and TC's grip tightened.

"Fuck 'em, bro," TC said, his voice taking on a nasty edge. "They split, they don't give a fuck about us. No one does, no matter how much they smile and say they do. It's you and me, bro, always has been. C'mon, let's go to Mexico."

Carney looked at the man who had been his friend and ally for so many years. TC had never been terribly bright, and he acted impulsively, his violent tendencies often taking over and getting him into trouble that Carney had to resolve, often at personal risk. During their time together in San Quentin, it had most often felt as if he were TC's keeper. But how many times had TC been there for him, saved his ass? That time when the young Latin King tried to shank Carney in the yard in order to prove his worth to his crew, and TC had seen it coming, warned Carney in time. The young gangbanger had turned up three days later with his neck snapped and his head nearly twisted around backward. Everyone knew who had done it, and TC just gave them that charming grin that invited anyone who thought they could prove it to please, give it a try. And when the Aryans decided that Carney's refusal to join their crew was the kind of insult worthy of revenge, hadn't it been TC who moved fast enough to push Carney aside and take the blade in his own ribs?

For years he had trusted TC, and he wanted to trust him now. Did Carney really owe anything to the others? To Angie, who had stood by his side, unbreaking as they fired on the dead? To Xavier, who, in his acceptance of Carney's past, appeared to offer a second chance? And what about Skye? He still didn't know what, if anything, she meant to him. Could he just abandon them all, slink away like the untrustworthy convict everyone assumed he would be? And would any of them care if he was gone?

TC watched his cellmate's face closely, the grin spreading wider and exposing teeth. In that moment, Carney saw what was behind those smiling eyes, something he had known was there all along and had been a fool to even consider discounting. It was the snake, venomous and predatory, concerned only for itself, seeing the rest of the world as potential prey.

Even an old friend.

"No," Carney said, pulling away. "You go if you want to." He turned and headed for the opening, muscles tensing for the impact of TC slamming his heavy wrench into the back of Carney's head.

The blow didn't come.

"Whatever," TC said. He cocked the wrench over a shoulder and joined his cellmate at the opening, walking with a familiar, swaying, prison yard gait. "We'll just stay and fuck shit up, then."

Jekyll and Hyde, Carney thought, but the Jekyll was only a mask. If he were smart, he would put a bullet in the back of TC's head at the first opportunity. He should do it right now. And yet, he couldn't. He told himself it was because he needed TC's capacity for violence to get through this, that it was definitely *not* because somewhere down deep he still felt responsible for him, that despite it all, he still considered TC a friend.

They made their way down corridors, some lit and some requiring flashlights, passing berthing areas and doorways marked *AVIONICS* or simply *SUPPORT*. The distant gunfire had since been replaced with a hollow silence broken only by their footsteps and the sound of their breathing. They went by a set of steep stairs and took a careful look—nothing was lurking above or below—and passed a series of closed hatches labeled as assorted storage compartments. If the hippies had come this way, Carney decided, they hadn't encountered anything; the floor was clear of both bodies and shell casings. They might, Carney thought, have drawn the dead away from this area, keeping them occupied, as his cellmate had suggested.

They came to a T intersection with long, low corridors to the right and left, the ceiling festooned with wire and cable, infrequent light bars showing emptiness except for a single body lying on the floor far to the left, one that did not get up and come after them. Ahead was an oval-shaped hatch with *HANGAR* stenciled on it in white letters. The hatch was slightly ajar.

TC pulled it open without waiting and ducked through. Carney followed, his M14 ready.

After hours in tight spaces and hallways, the sheer openness of the place was overwhelming. The USS *Nimitz*'s main hangar bay was 684 feet long and over a hundred feet wide and rose to a height of twenty-five feet. The space ran two-thirds the length of the ship, a vast and airy place. Spaced at even intervals along its length were three immense sets of steel, power-driven floor-to-ceiling doors that could close off sections of the hangar, each several inches thick and ready to be sealed to prevent the spread of fire. They stood open now. Daylight flooded into the cavernous bay through four wide openings where the aircraft elevators were positioned, one on the port side toward the rear and three on the starboard. The deck was spongy, covered in a gray-black nonskid coating. As everywhere else, the walls were crammed with pipes and valves, and a complex fire suppression system was suspended overhead.

Normally packed with Super Hornets, Prowler EA-6Bs, Hawkeye air search radar, and antisubmarine aircraft, the hangar bay was empty except for half a dozen SH-60 Seahawk helicopters—smaller versions of the Black Hawk—and a lone fighter aircraft that was partially dismantled and tucked against a high steel wall. Although it was wide open for the most part, there still remained shadowy areas filled with empty fuel drop tanks, tool lockers and forklifts, and empty bomb and missile carts, as well as a seemingly endless supply of hatches, openings, and ladderways. On the far side of the space, at midpoint, a pair of elevator doors were slowly closing on something caught between them, sliding open, then attempting to close again only to repeat the process.

And then there were the dead.

"Jackpot," said TC, a mad grin on his face.

There had to be hundreds of them, Carney thought, some as close as twenty feet, though these had yet to notice the two new arrivals.

The dead of the *Nimitz* were dressed in blue coveralls and camouflage, khaki, and colored jerseys, and almost half wore yellow firefighter gear. All were damaged to one extent or another, some slumped and limping, others stumbling along with missing or twisted limbs, heads cocked at odd angles or chests and bellies blown open and leaking dark fluids. There were sailors who were bloated and green, others withered and dry, and some with blackened sleeves of flesh sliding off limbs like snakes shedding skin, revealing bone and sinew beneath. They moved, they moaned, and even with the fresh air coming in through the elevator bays, they reeked of death.

Here the spongy deck was covered in spent shell casings, some no doubt from the original battle when the supercarrier was lost, others more recent. Several large knots of kneeling corpses, tearing and scrabbling over fresh meat, explained the sudden absence of gunfire and revealed the fate of the hippies who had broken away from the inmates.

TC started in, but Carney jerked him back. "We can't handle this." The older man's voice was a harsh whisper.

"Fuck that," TC said, pulling free and doing nothing to lower his voice. "This is what we came for. If we're not going to Mexico, then I'm gonna get me some."

Carney grabbed him again, seeing that the dead were turning toward TC's voice. "We don't have the ammo for this," Carney said.

TC jerked away again and gave his cellmate a dangerous look. "Then go find a place to hide, old man," he said, shoving the long wrench through his belt as if it were a samurai sword. He walked toward a dead woman in coveralls who was shuffling at him, staring with milky eyes and a slack expression. "What's up, bitch?" TC said, leveling his shotgun and blowing her head off.

The rolling boom of the weapon caused 347 heads to turn in their direction.

TC trotted up to a sailor wearing camo, body armor with lots of pouches, and a helmet, an M4 dangling around his neck on a nylon sling. As the sailor growled and lunged, TC shot him in the face and then quickly dropped down next to the body to relieve it of its weapons and ammo.

For a moment, Carney considered just closing the hatch and leaving TC to his fate. But then he was stepping forward, M14 to his shoulder as he sighted on a portly man with a crew cut and khakis. His first bullet blew out the back of the man's head.

"Yeah! That's it, man!" TC shouted, slinging his new weapon and ammo while bringing the auto shotgun to bear on a cluster of shuffling corpses. *BOOM, BOOM, BOOM.* Heads exploded while chests imploded from shots that didn't kill but knocked down. TC used his boot to crush the moaning head of one such corpse. He turned toward another moaning crowd. "Get some, motherfuckers, get some!"

Carney braced and fired, round after round, the heavy 7.62-millimeter shredding flesh and splintering bone. Bodies fell, others moved forward, and soon the hangar was filled with the competing echoes of gunfire, and the rising call of the dead.

"Get some," Carney snarled.

TWENTY-FOUR

The Barrett M82A1 had a range of two thousand yards and pushed its fifty-caliber rounds out with a muzzle velocity of 2,799 feet per second. It was capable of punching through engine blocks and light armored vehicles and even reaching targets hiding behind brick and concrete cinder block.

What it did to the head of a walking corpse could never be called clean but was certainly efficient. There was simply nothing left. The missed head shots—the body hits—were nearly as effective. Any creature within five feet of the edge of the flight deck was blown over the side, sometimes even beyond the safety netting and into the sea.

The Barrett fired with a deep thunder that rolled across the deck, the stock kicking hard into Angie's right shoulder. It was the last bullet in the ten-round magazine, and she dropped the empty and loaded another with practiced ease. Her eye once more at the PVS-10 day/night optic, she sighted downrange on a target at the extreme far end of the flight deck, a figure in yellow firefighter's gear with most of the skin torn from its face, watery yellow eyes rolling in their sockets.

The Barrett spoke with the voice of cannons.

The bullet took the sailor in the upper lip, shearing off everything north of that, leaving a lower jaw that sagged open even as the body fell. Angie raised her head from the sight and searched for more targets. She saw only motionless forms lying on the deck, except to the right, where Skye was working.

Skye ticked her sight to the right, squeezed, hit, ticked right again, squeezed, hit. She tracked left to a rotten boy in a jersey, the bullet catching him in the eye. She changed magazines smoothly, snapped the arming handle, fired, hit. A kill. A kill. Shoulder hit. A kill. A kill.

Her targets were primarily emerging from a wide hatch in the face of the superstructure, stumbling out one after another. She could have dropped them right at the hatch opening, where they paused to negotiate the knee knocker, but that would have quickly created a clog and jammed the others inside. So she let them stagger out onto the deck, allowing them to move away ten feet or more before putting them down. She soon clicked on another dry magazine and switched out.

Beside her Angie said, "I'm almost out of fifty-cal. I'm going to use it up and leave this baby right here on the deck."

Skye paused long enough to give her a thumbs-up.

The Barrett banged out six more rounds, these directed at creatures up on the superstructure's catwalks. Five were destroyed, a sixth blown in half. Angie scuttled away from the empty weapon and took up her Israeli assault rifle, adding her fire to her partner's. She didn't let the dead clear the hatch in the superstructure before dropping them, however, and before Skye could shout a warning, the opening was effectively clogged. A few pale arms reached through the tangle of bodies, clutching at air.

Skye made a disgusted noise and rose to her knees, shaking her head. Before she could deliver an edged comment, the hovering headache spike drove deeply, not through the top of her head, but through her milky, blind eye. The pain was searing and Skye screamed, dropping her rifle and clapping both hands to her face as she fell over, curling into a shaking, fetal ball.

Angie was suddenly afraid she was having a seizure. "Skye! Skye, what is it?"

The girl rolled away from her, one pressing hand shaking with palsy.

Angie wanted to put a hand on the girl, to calm and reassure her, but she thought it might make her scream louder. The girl shuddered and wailed, wrapping her arms around her head and rocking back and forth. Angie watched helplessly, and for the first time, perhaps now that they were out in the light, she noticed Skye's skin. It was gray, as if the pigment were steadily leaching out of it.

She did the only thing she could think of that would help, and that was to crouch beside the young woman, rifle held ready and standing watch, hoping the episode would quickly pass. It took nearly forty-five minutes, during which time Skye's screams turned to whimpers, but the rocking and shaking continued. Angie fired her rifle four different times when dead sailors managed to find their way up to the deck from the catwalks below the edge, perhaps drawn by the sound of whimpering prey. She also took a shot at an officer up on the highest catwalk of the superstructure, missing, the bullet dinging off a handrail. The corpse stumbled out of sight through a hatchway before she could fire again, not to evade gunfire, but by chance. It did not reappear.

When Skye was finally well enough to sit cross-legged on the deck, head down and not speaking, Angie handed her a bottled water and let her be, still keeping watch. It was another ten minutes before the younger woman spoke.

"Sorry about that," she croaked.

"No worries," said Angie, "I needed the break. She smiled at her young partner, but didn't get one in return. Instead, Skye dug into a breast pocket and came out with a handful of Excedrin, which she chewed up dry.

"That's not good for your stomach," Angie said, realizing she sounded much like her own mother.

Skye held up a trembling left hand for a moment, and then quickly clamped onto it with the other. "Got bigger problems."

"Do you want to stop?"

"Sure," said Skye, "let's just lie on the beach and read a book."

Angie shook her head, but grinned. "The virus is turning you into a smartass. I think I liked you better as the serious, silent type."

The corner of Skye's mouth twitched up in what might have been a smile. "Let's go." She rose unsteadily and inserted a fresh magazine, her shoulders hunched against a headache that had not fully abated. Angie led, heading toward the superstructure.

It really was like an eight-story steel building, a haze-gray mass rising from the flight deck with slanted windows high above and smooth metal walls between. Enormous white stenciled letters and numbers painted on the flight deck side proclaimed *CVN-68*. Up closer, squadron logos and what must have been representations of campaign ribbons were painted beneath the ship's designation, reminders of the many actions in which *Nimitz* had participated.

Just in front of the superstructure was a low garage, its closed door painted with a cartoon Tasmanian devil in a fire helmet and carrying an axe. Above it was the legend *Fighting 68th*, and beneath the character, *Home of the World's Smallest Fire Truck*.

The two women moved carefully among the bodies, muzzles pointed down in the event one of them wasn't quite finished, and then made their way to a chest-high pile of dead zombies effectively choking off what appeared to be the only access to the tower. Snarling, pale faces could be seen in the shadows beyond the pile, and Skye started to raise her rifle. Before the stock reached her shoulder she gasped and let it swing back down as she pressed a hand to the side of her head.

"I've got it," said Angie, the Galil coming up. Half a dozen quick reports later, the faces and reaching arms disappeared, but additional moans could be heard from deeper within. Angie caught movement at her left peripheral, on Skye's blind side, and turned to see an African American sailor in blackened medical scrubs coming around the corner of the superstructure. His skin pigment had all but vanished, leaving him looking albino, and his hands curled into claws as he focused on the women and broke into a gallop.

Angie dropped him with the Galil and tugged on Skye's sleeve. "C'mon, keep moving." Upon seeing the man in scrubs, the former reality show star realized that a flight deck would not be the assigned station for someone dressed like that, and so the creature must have come from someplace else, likely from below, but possibly the superstructure. As they moved around the corner, Angie leading with her gun barrel and Skye following, still massaging her head, they found a massive drop-off to the left leading not to the sea but down the open shaft of an aircraft elevator. About thirty feet directly ahead, the deck ended with the bay beyond, Alameda seeming close enough to touch. The opening for another stairway down to the starboard catwalk was in front of them. That had to be where Scrub Zombie had come from, Angie thought.

And then there was the ladder.

The forward side of the superstructure rose in a flat gray wall for five or six stories until it reached the lowest of the high catwalks. Affixed to the center of the wall, climbing straight up, was a narrow, steel-rung ladder. Angie eyed the height and let out a little laugh. "Oh, what the hell."

Skye squinted at her partner, and then her good eye tracked upward. "Sure," she said, "why not?"

Angie looked at the trembling hand, at a girl fighting to be strong. "Are you sure you can handle it, kid? Are you tough enough?" She threw the girl a wink.

Skye snorted and slung her rifle, heading for the ladder. "You go look for a wheelchair ramp."

"Big talk," said Angie, following her up the rungs. "Hey, maybe we should get you an eye patch. You've already got the ship, you could be a real pirate."

Skye let out a gravelly laugh. "Shiver me timbers."

Angie laughed. "Not quite."

Together they climbed, a pair of giggling killers.

TWENTY-FIVE

Lavender skies announced that the sun was well below the horizon, and gathering clouds the color of a spreading bruise warned of potential rain. The breeze coming off the bay was cool, making a row of pennants snap along a line running from the top of the bridge up to a radar mast. Other than the fluttering sound, it was quiet.

Maya stood on a high catwalk near the bridge of a World War II destroyer tied up alongside the NAS Alameda pier, directly opposite the *Hornet*. To her right was the seaplane lagoon with the base beyond, and to the north lurked the long silhouette of the *Nimitz*, half a mile out.

The young woman stood alone with a bolt-action hunting rifle slung over a shoulder, peering at the aircraft carrier through a pair of binoculars. She thought she had seen the brief flashes of rifle fire out there, but she wasn't sure and saw nothing now. Maya wondered if shots could be heard at this distance and, not for the first time, was frustrated at the silent world in which she lived. The snapping pennants above were nothing more than soundless movement.

She wasn't up here as a lookout as she had no way to cry out an alarm, but she could no longer stay down on the pier with the other refugees, huddled among the supplies as they speculated about what was taking place out on the carrier. Waiting and not knowing was worse than facing the dead. Besides, there was another lookout posted on the stern of the frigate tied up behind this ship, close to the inland end of the pier and the access road leading here. They had a radio and a voice, a useful person.

Maya tried every day not to feel sorry for herself because of her handicap, and most days she succeeded. Her mood was black right now, though, and that made it easy to entertain self-pity. What made it worse was that she had only herself to blame.

Where was Evan at this moment? Was he even alive? He had gone off with the assault group knowing she was angry with him, she had made sure of that, refusing to even give him a hug. And why? Because he insisted she stay to look after her brothers and sisters and the others. To keep her out of harm's way. It hadn't mattered that her father felt the same way. Maya had put it all on Evan, blaming him for being a typical man trying to keep the little woman out of the way, for implying that she wasn't up to the task. She had survived on the road just fine before he came along, so who was he to push her around like that? She refused to think he had done it out of love, and so she acted like a petulant child, hurting him just before he left to face what could turn out to be his own death.

Maya hated herself for what she had done, and she started to cry again. It seemed all she did anymore was cry: for her mother, her uncle, for her father saddled with so much grief and responsibility. Now for herself, and the man she loved.

Come back to me, she begged, the binoculars crawling over the aircraft carrier. She wanted to see movement, any sign of life that would give her hope. There was nothing, and she lowered the glasses and wiped at her eyes.

Down on the pier, everyone was settling in for the night, clearing the remains of a meal and tucking children into sleeping bags, telling them they were safe and that everything would be okay. Telling the lie every parent knew how to deliver with a confident expression and a gentle smile.

At the edge of the group, Sophia and Vladimir were sitting cross-legged next to the little orphan named Ben, who sat wrapped in a wad of sleeping bag as if he were a baby bird in a nest. The Russian pilot had produced a small toy helicopter from somewhere and given it to the boy, who flew it with a still-chubby hand, entranced by the spinning plastic blades. With the binoculars Maya could see Vladimir's face split in a homely smile and didn't fail to notice that Sophia was less interested in the boy's play and more occupied with sneaking glances at the helicopter pilot and sitting as close to him as possible.

Her heart ached and returned to Evan.

Wherever he was, was he thinking of her? Or had she been so cold as to change the way he felt about her? Her mother had told her men could be that way, that a man in love would endure an unthinkable amount of pain, forgiving nearly anything, but that he could also, without warning, come to a point where he simply switched off. Their hearts turned hard all of a sudden, Faith had warned, and that would be the end of it.

"Be careful, Maya," her mother had said years ago, after having her own sharp-tongued exchange with Calvin. Her eyes had looked concerned. "Men put up with our moods, with our casual cruelties, but don't think for a second that they ever forget a single hard word. They love us, they'll die for us, but they remember."

The spat between Faith and Calvin had been merely a marital squall, blowing in hard and rainy and blowing back out again just as fast, leaving sunshine in its wake. But Maya never forgot what her mother had said.

Did I do that to Evan? she wondered. No, she wouldn't entertain that possibility, even if it could be true. It was the kind of pointless thinking that people gnawed at before jumping from high places. He was with her father, and they were fighting to stay alive and create a refuge for the people on Alameda. He was safe, but too busy to be hurting over a spat. She decided that would be her answer every time she began to doubt and worry. It would see her through.

Maya panned the binoculars out across the old naval base beyond the lagoon. Being this high up on the vintage warship allowed an impressive view of the streets and airfield, of the vacant buildings and overgrown parade ground and sports fields. She swallowed hard and her heart began to thump faster. There were so *many* of them now, the streets and worn, grassy areas crowded with slow-moving figures. They seemed to drift without purpose, wandering in all directions once they reached the base, but more continued to stream in like cattle in a slow-motion stampede, focused on a single direction, then drifting once they arrived. They were all in a hurry to get nowhere.

She checked the road that ran beside the seaplane lagoon and led to the pier. Aside from a couple of strays, it was empty. Loners could be easily dispatched hand-to-hand without alerting the mob. But there were thousands on the base now, maybe tens of thousands, and if they ever discovered that there was prey trapped out on this pier . . .

Hurry, Evan, she thought. *Come back for us.*

And then the warship began to tremble beneath her.

It was a magnitude 5.5 earthquake and lasted a total of eight seconds. It was moderate by earthquake standards—the San Francisco quake of 1989 was a devastating 6.9—but it nonetheless demonstrated a seismic yield equal to 2.7 kilotons of TNT, the equivalent of the energy expended during the Oklahoma City bombing.

The dead felt it coming a full three seconds in advance, and wherever they were within two hundred miles of Oakland, no matter what they were doing, they ceased all activity except to turn and face the epicenter, remaining in that pose throughout the eight seconds of shaking.

Back when there had been scientists to debate the topic, sensitivity to earthquakes had been a controversial subject, made even more so when the suggestion was made that not only animals, but some humans exhibited out-of-character emotional and physical behavior in advance of tremors. The general public had long come to accept as fact that animals often displayed sensitivity prior to earthquakes: chickens clustered together and grew hysterical, mice experienced convulsions, pigs bit at one another's tails, and fish jumped out of the water. There was a little science that supported these actions, claims of *piezoelectricity*—electric charges that accumulated in solid material in response to mechanical stress—or chemical changes in groundwater. Evidence, however, was anecdotal and not much studied. Most considered it pseudoscience.

Some humans had publicly proclaimed their sensitivity, and in the days and hours leading up to an earthquake they had complained of dizziness, ringing in the ears, headaches, and anxiety. These claims of forecasting were often determined to be coincidence or even outright fabrications, but proved accurate (and inexplicable) just often enough to make believers out of some people. Within the scientific community, however, a scientist professing any formal belief in human sensitivity to earthquakes ran the risk of ridicule and professional disregard at best, and at worst, denial of research grants.

The dead were sensitive. All of them.

Not only did they sense impending earthquakes, they were able to determine the direction and approximate location of the epicenter. They were drawn to it. Now the dead from over a hundred miles away in all directions were slowly being drawn to a point where, on the surface, a pair of cracked asphalt streets intersected in the middle of the deserted naval air station.

As before, it was the friction of the Hayward Fault that sent shocks out in a wide, growing circle.

Within San Francisco, the quake had assorted effects. In most places a few windows cracked and some car alarms went off, but other areas experienced more damage. In almost every case, the eyes witnessing the events were dead and uncomprehending, and the bodies in which they resided all faced the same direction.

Near Alamo Square, backdropped by downtown skyscrapers, the row of escalating Victorian houses known as the Painted Ladies—much photographed and appearing in numerous films and television programs—lost two of their number to the shaking. The Ladies first leaned, hung at an odd angle for a moment, and then toppled in an explosion of wood, glass, and shingles. Two zombies standing on a sidewalk were buried in the collapse.

At the Palace of Fine Arts, a dozen corpses dressed as joggers stood and faced east on the bottom of the lagoon near the center's beautiful rotunda. The quake knocked down a row of Greek-style colonnades not far from the lagoon, marble detonating like bombs on impact. The remnants of a grade school field trip, a dozen third-graders all dressed in the same bright-green T-shirts with their name on a laminated card hung around their necks and wearing an assortment of cartoon character backpacks, stood on an adjacent brick path. They were peppered with marble fragments that tore into flesh and would have sent them screaming to the emergency room not so long ago. Now they didn't even notice.

The Castro had already burned. The heart of San Francisco's gay community was a neighborhood of hilly avenues and Victorian buildings, much of it charred and skeletal. The dead rode out the quake standing and shaking in streets filled with discarded bicycles and backpacks, abandoned cars and sidewalk sandwich boards advertising small shops and cafés. One zombie, a fifty-year-old drag queen with a crooked blond wig, torn sundress, and gladiator sandals, stood near a brick wall covered in posters shouting about clubs and political agendas, one of her legs fractured with the foot twisted nearly backward. The heavy makeup clumping on what remained of her face made her appear especially ghastly. Already off balance because of the leg, the creature fell to the pavement when the quake began. Groaning, the drag queen attempted to rise just as a five-hundred-pound piece of masonry from a third-floor ledge broke free and crushed her into the sidewalk.

Haight-Ashbury suffered more than some areas, in part because of uncontrolled fires that had weakened structures, and also because many had not been that well cared for anyway. The neighborhood famous for its 1967 Summer of Love, hippies, psychedelic rockers, and, more recently, street festivals, cafés, and eclectic shops, had lost entire blocks. Rows of brightly painted apartments resting atop bookstores and boutiques simply tumbled out into the streets, burying cars and the walking dead alike. Most drifters survived the impact of falling brick but were too uncoordinated to pull themselves free of the rubble once it was over, and their fellow corpses wandered past the struggling arms and legs, incapable of helping or even realizing that they should.

The fires that swept through the downtown section of the city had been spectacular, the intense flames weakening some skyscrapers and causing others to tip over like rotten trees. The eight-second tremor shook great sheets of glass from high windows, and several-hundred-pound guillotines crashed down from on high, detonating in explosions of deadly pixie dust or cutting immobile corpses completely in half. The quake finished off the worst of the leaning towers, filling the streets with mountains of debris and snarls of bent steel.

Near Fisherman's Wharf, zombies that had been piled up against chain-link fences, moaning at the clusters of barking sea lions out on old piers, stood in packed groups facing east, all shuddering as one. When the quake ended, they returned to their incessant pushing, only to find that the tremor had weakened the fence's footings. As the chain link gave way, several hundred bodies tumbled into the cold waters, reaching out to the distant animals. Within minutes the surface was split by dozens of dorsal fins, sharks drawn in from the Pacific that had been circling the aging docks, now breaking away in a feeding frenzy among the sinking bodies. The sea lions watched, huddled closer together, and stayed out of the water.

At Pier 39, those who had once flocked here for chowder in bread bowls and tickets to Alcatraz now tottered off their feet and rolled on the ground for a while, a few entangled with fallen canopies or cut by broken glass, but none perished. Belowground was a different story. Within the three hundred feet of nearby aquarium tunnels, dead tourists, guides, and maintenance workers stood in the shaking darkness, their eastern focus not even pulled away by the loud cracking coming from the thick glass offering views of what lived beneath the bay's surface. Several sharks cruised past, and in the murky distance a herd of corpses stumbled slowly over slime-coated rocks.

When the observation windows imploded like baritone grenades, the bay made such a violent entry that bodies were smashed against the far concrete wall. The dead didn't even register surprise.

Out on the most central portion of the Golden Gate Bridge, the mindless dead stood staring at the bay amid a river of burned automobiles. At their center was the beige mass of a silent M1 main battle tank. The bridge had survived countless quakes over the decades of its existence, but this time the steel supports beneath a fifty-foot section of reinforced concrete gave way, and that section of road dropped into the waters below. A dozen cars, two dozen zombies, and the tank plunged silently after it.

The damage was more severe on the Oakland side. Sagging, abandoned warehouses and poorly constructed apartment buildings collapsed, and the downtown section, decimated by unchecked fires just as San Francisco had been, saw office buildings crumble like matchstick towers. Just to the north, a refinery pipe that serviced tanker ships ruptured, dumping petroleum into the bay at a startling rate. Within western Oakland, up the length of Peralta, the pavement buckled and split, leaving a jagged, three-foot-wide crack in the earth, one side two feet higher than the other. Cars, trucks, and a pair of city buses slid into the crack and came to rest on edge, wheels tilted upward. More than two hundred zombies disappeared into the crevice as well.

Their absence didn't make a dent in the legion of walking dead moving through Oakland.

Maya was a Californian. She had been through earthquakes before, knew what they felt like, and although this was the biggest she could remember—she had been born after the killer in '89—and eight seconds of shaking was a very long time, she wasn't nervous. Part of this was that for her, it was a silent event, one of sensation. And she recognized that had the warship been floating free and not snugged up tightly against the pier, she probably wouldn't have felt it at all.

Her binoculars went immediately to the crowd of people gathered at the end of the pier. Though she couldn't hear their cries of alarm, she saw their looks of terror as they clustered tightly together until the shaking stopped. When it did, they were none the worse for it. There appeared to be no injuries, and the pier was just as solid as it had been. She turned the binoculars toward the naval base in time to see a hangar at the edge of the airfield silently drop from view, replaced by a rising cloud of white dust. Her breath caught at the sight, wondering if that was the hangar in which they had all taken refuge. If so, it was now a grave marker for her mother and uncle, tightly wrapped in plastic tarps and laid gently in the shadows of a back wall.

She did not notice how the dead stopped moving for the duration of the event.

Thinking about loss turned her attention back to Evan, her father, and the others, and the binoculars sought out the aircraft carrier. It was now a long shadow on the water as the day faded into twilight.

Come back to me, Evan. The words had turned into a silent prayer.

TWENTY-SIX

On the carrier, the earthquake barely registered. Only a small portion of the carrier was dug into the sea bottom near the bow, and the sheer size of the vessel displaced the rest of the vibrations. Down in the hangar bay, Carney had bigger problems than odd trembling. There were just too many of the dead and by the time Carney realized that, he was reaching for a fresh magazine that no longer existed.

The two inmates had managed to push forward nearly half the length of the hangar, drawing even with a space between a pair of giant aircraft elevators on one side, and the first in a row of helicopters against the wall on the other, rotor blades folded back for tight storage. TC had cast aside the empty automatic shotgun in favor of the Navy M4, a weapon that required more accuracy. In his fury he had switched to firing full auto, quickly burning through his ammunition.

The dead fell, but new corpses took their places.

"I'm empty," Carney shouted, reversing his M14 so he could use its heavy wooden stock as a club.

"Me too," yelled TC, thirty feet ahead of him. The younger inmate dropped the rifle and pulled the long wrench from his belt, caving in a corpse's head, rushing another, putting it down, and searching for more.

They were going to be surrounded and overrun. Carney looked around desperately, spotted an open hatch on the wall, headed for it. "TC, this way!" He drove his rifle's butt plate into a gray face, knocking it aside but not killing it. "Now, TC!"

TC swung the wrench like a home run slugger and crushed the side of a sailor's head, just as two more leaped upon his back, making him stagger forward. One bit into the Kevlar body armor; the other chewed into an empty pouch on his shoulder where a radio would normally sit. TC whirled, shaking them off, beating them both down with the wrench.

Carney reached the open hatch, finding a space with sets of rising and descending stairs, and another corridor. A zombie stumbled through after him from the hangar bay but tripped over the knee knocker and fell flat. Carney finished it with the rifle butt.

"Any fucking day now!" he shouted through the hatch.

TC swung, crushed a collarbone and made a corpse's head flop to one side, then ran for the hatch. A dozen zombies lurched after him, hundreds more angling in from the far reaches of the hangar. TC jumped over the body in the opening, boots sliding in gore. "Up or down?"

Carney started up a stairway, his cellmate close behind. In less than a minute the dead from the hangar bay began pouring through the hatch, moaning and clawing at each other in their eagerness to climb the stairs. The inmates reached the next deck, which offered the option of three hallways or more stairs.

Corpses began stomping down the metal risers above them.

Carney took off at a jog down the center passageway, another poorly lit tunnel that looked like every other one on this goddamn ship, passing doors marked *PUBLIC AFFAIRS* and *JAG*, some with an officer's name posted to one side. When he came to the end of the hall, he was facing a door marked *STUDIO*.

"They're coming," TC said, looking back. A mob of shadowy figures pressed up the hallway, their moans reverberating off the steel.

Carney worked the dog handle on the hatch and entered the dark room. TC followed without hesitation, slamming the door behind him. They stood in the blackness, unmoving as they waited for their eyes to adjust, straining to see, trying to listen over their own heavy breathing.

A low croaking from somewhere in front of them said they were not alone.

Carney dropped his rifle and shed his pack, digging through it. He came out with a handful of loaded pistol magazines, a nine-millimeter Beretta, and a heavy Maglite. He switched it on, and not ten feet away was a rotting female sailor galloping at him.

Carney shot her in the face, then let out a ragged breath.

TC rummaged through his own pack. He hadn't brought a pistol, but he produced his own flashlight. Together they panned their beams around the room. There was a blue banner on the far wall with *Nimitz*'s emblem sewn into it, a lectern standing in front of the banner, and a pair of large television cameras on wheeled caddies, cables snaking off toward the walls. To one side was a glassed-in control booth, on the other a row of doors.

A corpse pressed its face against the control room window, smearing it with gore and biting at the glass. Behind them, bodies slammed into the hatch, and TC threw his weight onto the dog handle just as it started to come up.

"Hold that," Carney said, moving into the room.

TC laughed. "Yeah, no shit."

The older man quickly returned with a coil of heavy cable, and they lashed the handle down tight. When TC let go, the handle wiggled a bit, but no more than an inch.

TC nodded at the pistol in his cellmate's hand. "Wish I'd thought of that. Don't guess you got another one."

"Nope," said Carney, "and you wouldn't need one if you hadn't blown off all your ammo like you were Bruce fucking Willis." Carney walked to the door of the control room.

"Yeah, but what a rush," TC laughed. A single pistol shot put the control room zombie's brains on the glass. "Sweet," TC said, grinning and watching pieces of gray matter slide down the window.

Carney checked the other doors. One opened into a long electrical room, the other two into an office and a small conference room respectively. None had exit doors.

"We're in a dead end," Carney said, walking back into the studio.

TC dropped into a wheeled office chair and lit two cigarettes, passing one to his cellmate and tipping his head back, blowing smoke at the acoustic-tiled ceiling. "Fine with me," he said, stretching out his legs. "I need a break anyway."

Carney took another chair.

"We should have cut out for Mexico when I suggested it," TC said, huffing smoke through his nose. "That idea's fucked now."

"I told you to take off if you wanted to," said Carney.

TC tilted back and ran his fingers through his long hair. "Nah, this is more fun."

"Yeah," Carney said, looking at the cabled hatch, listening as dozens of fists pounded against the steel on the other side. "Fun."

TC yawned and dug a can of warm Pepsi and a bag of pretzels out of his pack. "I'm gonna eat, jack off, and take a nap," he said, popping the can and shaking the foam off his hand.

Carney nodded and pulled a pouch of jerky from his own pack, looking at his cellmate. *You go and take a nap, TC.* There was no way he was going to let himself fall asleep in this room with that rabid motherfucker.

But after listening to TC snore for twenty minutes, Carney did just that.

D espite her impairments, weeks of physical conditioning sent Skye up the exterior superstructure ladder like a gymnast with Angie close behind. By the time she reached the opening to the lowest catwalk level, her left hand had stopped shaking and her headache had subsided to a tolerable buzz.

Advancing slowly along the tight steel gridwork, elbows nearly touching the railing on one side and the tipped-out blue glass windows on the other, the women moved to the seaward side of the superstructure.

The view from up here was spectacular. Twilight had at last broken through the clouds, turning both sky and sea a dark pink. A strengthening breeze rustled their clothing and threatened to lift Angie's ball cap off her head. The air was salty and clean, and for just a moment it was possible to imagine the world that was fresh, clean, and not an ever-expanding crypt.

The glass encircling the interior of this deck was thick and polarized, not permitting them to see what lurked within. They used the catwalk to make a complete lap of the tower, finding that on each side of the superstructure was a hatch to the interior and a set of stairs up to the next catwalk, seaward side and flight deck side. The hatches were stenciled *FLAG BRIDGE*. The only zombies they found were those Angie had shot earlier from below, and they couldn't hurt anyone now.

Angie looked at her partner. "You're feeling better, aren't you?"

Skye nodded. "The pain's almost gone. I'm okay."

"Then you decide, up or in?"

The younger woman looked up through the grillework of the catwalk above. "I'm thinking if we go as high as we can, then they can only come at us from one direction."

"You sound like a sniper," Angie said.

Skye shook her head. "Sergeant Postman would chew my ass for putting us in a place with no exit route."

Angie didn't know who Sgt. Postman was, but he was sure to be one of the many ghosts haunting the girl. Didn't they all have more than their share of those? "I think it's a good plan. We'll have excellent elevation for shooting, and we can switch off on security to make sure they don't come at us from behind."

"They'll come," said Skye.

Angie could only nod.

Skye led them up to the next catwalk, a place identical to the level below. Here, however, the hatch on the flight deck side stood open. This was where Angie had shot at the dead officer, who saved himself by accidentally stumbling in through the opening. Skye raised the eyebrow over her now completely white, blind eye. It was an unsettling look. Angie shrugged, and then leaned in through the hatch, rifle first.

Even in daylight, the red battle lights of *Nimitz*'s bridge remained on, as they had ever since the supercarrier came to rest with its ruptured hull mired in the silt off western Oakland. The lights revealed that a slaughter had taken place here, splashes of gore covering the deck and control stations, black in the red glare. There was only one occupant, a short, female quartermaster standing next to a comfortable-looking, elevated chair marked *CAPTAIN*. Her arms hung at her sides, and she seemed to be staring forward, out through the blue glass.

Skye stepped up beside Angie and without hesitation shot the woman in the back of the head. The bullet passed through her brain and exited the front of her skull, punching a small hole in the window, creating a spiderweb of cracks.

"She's alone," said Angie.

Lieutenant (junior grade) Doug Mosey no longer remembered when the ship under his temporary command steamed into San Francisco Bay. He didn't remember ignoring the now-dead—for the second time—quartermaster demanding that he stop staring at a city in flames and attend to his duties. He was already dead and beyond noticing when the carrier first scraped against the rocks of Alcatraz and then, later, rubbed hard against the Bay Bridge.

Mosey didn't remember graduating from Annapolis, the faces of his parents or their home in Michigan, had lost all memory of school and friends and movies he had seen, of Christmas mornings or pedaling his tricycle in the driveway. The passage of time held no meaning, and he could not appreciate the cleansing breeze coming in off the water.

Standing in the small navigator's plot room behind the bridge, he did, however, recognize food standing just on the other side of the open doorway. Forces beyond his control or understanding compelled him to eat, and with a snarl, Doug Mosey lunged through the opening and grabbed the arm holding a rifle, sinking his teeth deep into the flesh, blood splattering what was left of his face.

S kye screamed and jerked away, but the zombie hung on with his bite alone, making a groaning sound deep in his throat as Skye's blood ran down his chin.

"Fucker!" Angie screamed, shoving the muzzle of the Galil against the officer's temple and blowing his brains across the bridge. Mosey collapsed, his jaws still clenched on Skye's left forearm as he fell.

Skye forced the creature's mouth open and freed her arm, then skittered away to the far side of the bridge, her rifle hanging loose by its strap and banging against her chest, right hand clamped down over the bleeding wound. "No, no, no, no. . . ." The girl's gravelly voice climbed octaves, sounding like the shriek of metal on metal. "No, no, no. . . ."

"Oh, God, Skye!" Angie cried, moving toward the girl.

Skye's good eye was wide, darting about, and it came to rest on Angie. "No!" the younger woman cried, pointing at her friend.

Angie froze in place.

Skye's finger wavered, blood from her outstretched arm dripping onto the deck. "Stay there," she said, "you stay away from me."

Angie held up her hands. "Honey, don't, we can—"

"Nothing!" Skye shrieked. "There's nothing we can do!"

Angie's hands went to her mouth. She wanted to cry, wanted to shake her head and refuse to believe it, but she had seen and done so much killing, had lost so many people she knew. The tears wouldn't come. She simply stared.

"Nothing," Skye repeated, her voice dropping to a harsh whisper. She looked at the red, torn flesh peeking between her fingers. Then she bolted across the bridge and through another hatchway.

Angie ran after her, catching sight of the girl's boots as she pounded up an interior stairway. "Skye, wait!"

Skye's voice echoed down from above. "Keep away from me, Angie. I mean it."

Angie stood at the foot of the stairs, heart aching not only for this young woman who had quickly become a friend, but for what would now have to be done when Skye turned.

TWENTY-SEVEN

With Brother Peter in the lead, they climbed, rising steadily from the depths of the ship. They were low on ammunition, some down to a handful of shells or a single magazine. Xavier was armed only with a fire axe he took from a wall bracket. They killed the zombies they encountered, thankfully as singles or in pairs—a mob would snuff them out—and kept moving. Each successful kill cost ammo, however, bringing them closer to being completely defenseless.

They moved vertically up the port side of the ship, taking whatever stairways they could locate, and finally reached the 03 Gallery Deck, just below the flight deck. Here they found no more stairs leading up, and so they pushed forward.

This level of the ship was different from the others, not necessarily cleaner—there was still battle damage and dried gore on the deck—but somehow more squared away. Xavier thought it had a familiar feel but couldn't identify it at first.

Xavier looked at the hatches they passed, each painted with a logo like medieval coats of arms: *Black Knights*, *Death Rattlers*, *Blue Diamonds*, *Argonauts*. He saw *Grey Wolves*, the *Screaming Indians*, and the *Wallbangers*. Boards mounted to walls displayed columns of information, like types of aircraft and incomprehensible tangles of acronyms and abbreviations, like *Teceleron* and *Heltraron*. He stared at the logos, so colorful and out of character for a military operation, where things were usually stark and bare bones. It felt almost tribal to him, and then he realized what they were. Squadron designations. These were places for officers, and in particular, the naval aviators for which this ship had been built. The elite, and therefore allowed special privileges.

But there weren't any corpses in flight suits slouching through these passageways. According to Rosa, the aviators would have all departed when the ship reached Hawaii, and that was a good thing. Had they not, then this was where they would be lurking, and a handful of shotgun shells and a fire axe would not have been enough to keep them at bay.

Officer spaces or not, Xavier thought, the lighting here was just as inadequate as it had been below, and the stench of rotting meat was no less pungent. There were still dead things in this place and so the group moved slowly, nerves strained to the breaking point as they approached each hatch and intersection. Rosa picked up on the tension.

"We need to rest," she whispered to Xavier. "We can't go on like this, we're going to get careless." Her eyes were still burning from exposure to jet fuel.

Xavier nodded and touched Peter's shoulder. The man jumped as if hit with an electric shock, and he whirled with the shotgun. Xavier caught it by the barrel and forced it away. Peter didn't fire.

"Easy," said the priest.

Peter peered at him for a long moment as if trying to remember who he was, and then lowered the weapon.

"We need to find a safe place to hole up for a while," Xavier said. "Let's start looking for one."

Peter's face flashed a brief expression of annoyance, and Xavier saw it. Once again he was struck with the thought that he knew this man somehow, had seen him before. But where?

Peter stepped aside so that Xavier could take the lead, and the big man did, holding his axe in both hands and squeezing his eyes tightly, trying to shake off the dry burning affecting him too. He led the group down a passage, pausing once to prod at a corpse on the deck— a middle-aged officer with a bullet hole in his head—to be certain it was harmless. A short while later he froze when he saw a dead sailor lurch crossways to their corridor beneath a pool of light, unaware of their presence and quickly moving out of sight.

Ten more minutes of creeping brought them to a broad intersection of corridors, with angled walls at each corner forming an octagon. Set in each angled portion was a window and counter, each with a roll-down security gate firmly closed over the opening. Stenciling on the walls proclaimed these to be the squadron shops. Beyond the gates, shelves of merchandise could be seen in the gloom: mugs, T-shirts, patches, all bearing the emblems of the carrier's air squadrons.

"Anyone want a souvenir?" Lilly whispered.

The others decided that stalking the hallways of a dead aircraft carrier would provide memories enough.

Just beyond the shops, the gray tiles underfoot changed to blue. Rosa pointed at the tiles. "This means that we're in officer and combat country now."

Twenty more feet forward brought them to a space with a ladderway on the left and a mahogany door on the right. Xavier stared at the fine wood, so out of place among all the gray steel. He thought it looked like something that belonged in a library or the private study of a banker. A brass plate next to the door read *Jacob Beane, Rear Admiral.*

Xavier pushed at the door with the head of his axe, and it swung open.

It was one of the ironies of sea life that, especially among officers, the higher one's rank, the more spacious and well-appointed the quarters one received, but because of the increased responsibilities, the less time the occupant had to spend there. Admiral Beane's quarters were first class.

The center of the space was a briefing room and private mess filled with a conference table, leather chairs, and sofas. The admiral's small, personal galley was to the left, his actual quarters and head on the right. Both the briefing room and bedroom were carpeted and fitted with wood paneling, and high-quality, solid wood furniture was tastefully matched to framed oil paintings of warships at sea. Brass featured heavily in the décor.

Someone had died in here.

There was a broken lamp, bullet holes in the paneling, gunfire splinters along the length of the conference table. A large, rusty patch stained the thick gray carpet.

"This will do," said Xavier, as Tommy secured the door with the deadbolt before he and the other hippies went off to raid the admiral's galley. They returned with bottled water and boxes of crackers, as well as a brick of moldy cheddar cheese, from which they pared away the green.

"The admiral had lots of fresh fruits and perishables," said Lilly, making a face. "You don't want to open the fridge."

They ate in silence and then muscled a heavy credenza in front of the door before seeking out places to sleep. The hippies took the bedroom while Brother Peter curled up on a short leather sofa near the door, and Rosa and Xavier dropped onto a long leather couch, sinking into its cushions.

The priest couldn't remember being so tired, not even after a long match in the ring, pounding and getting pounded back. He now knew what it meant to be tired to the bones, and yet, as much as he desired it, sleep was elusive. Instead his mind gnawed at the magnitude of what it would take to reclaim this massive ship from the dead. They had only been at it for a day, and already their numbers were down by a third, their ammunition all but gone. He wondered if the other groups were faring better. Had any of them even put a dent in the thousands of creatures infesting this floating maze?

"You know who he is, don't you?" whispered Rosa.

Xavier was pulled from his thoughts. "Who?"

She tilted her head to the figure on the couch across the room, already still and snoring. "You were staring at him."

"Was I?" Xavier shook his head. "I didn't realize."

She nodded, keeping her voice low. "It took me a while to figure it out, because now he looks just like any regular guy who needs a shave. He's different without all the glitz, but it's him. I just now got it."

Xavier wasn't following. "Who? What are you talking about?"

Rosa lifted her index finger and pointed at the sleeping man. "That's the Reverend Peter Dunleavy. Brother Peter, to the faithful." Her lip curled when she said his name, as if she had tasted something foul.

Xavier stared at the man, who was sleeping with his back toward them. "*That's* Brother Peter?" He had to force himself to keep his voice down. "I thought he was in prison."

"He should be," Rosa said. "As big a fraud and crook as Bernie Madoff. Prison's too good for him."

Xavier nodded slowly. Now he remembered the man from television, a well-groomed holy roller with an international following, wealthy beyond reason. Brother Peter, his ministry called him, a slick, charismatic showman peddling salvation at an affordable price. Except it had all come crashing down: charges of tax fraud and illegal real estate deals, witness tampering and money laundering. There had also been claims of inappropriate sexual behavior and even outright rape. Xavier couldn't remember all the details, despite the media's ceaseless attention to the scandal. For Xavier, Peter Dunleavy had been like any of the other celebrities caught up in corruption and vice, desperately insecure people in need of constant attention, who permitted their private lives to be plastered all over the tabloids for the world to see. They were like background noise. It wasn't that

Xavier bore them any ill will or resented their money and fame. It was simply that he had difficulty mustering much sympathy for the dramas of the rich and famous when he was dealing with people who didn't know where they would find their next meal or were afraid to fall asleep next to a violent spouse.

"I met him once," Rosa said, still whispering and looking at the sleeping man. "About a year and a half ago, at the club where I was dancing. He was wearing sunglasses and a fake mustache so no one would recognize him. There were two big thugs with him."

"If he was in disguise then, how did you recognize him now?"

"Because I took off his disguise." She smiled thinly.

"What happened?"

"He watched the dancing for a while," Rosa said, "me and some of the other girls, then he sent one of his thugs to talk to us, tell us who was watching and that he liked what he saw. The reverend had picked out his favorites and wanted us to go back to his hotel with him in his limo. Some of the girls agreed."

Xavier looked at her.

Rosa shook her head sharply. "I'm a lot of things, Father, but I'm no whore. I told his thug to go get fu . . . to get lost."

Xavier smiled. "I know you're not, Doc. And I've heard the word *fuck* before."

She blushed. "Yeah, well, not from me while I'm talking to a priest, you haven't."

"Go on."

"So the good reverend gets annoyed that I turned him down and walks up to me. 'I'll make it worth your while,' he says, and then he squeezed my breast. I slapped the glasses off his face and tore that stupid caterpillar mustache out from under his nose. I think it took some skin with it. He squealed like a little girl."

Xavier struggled to control his grin, and it was not so much for the picture she created as the moment of delight he saw in her eyes. He was chuckling as he spoke. "What did the reverend do?"

Rosa crossed her arms. "He ran out to his limo. I ran to the back, and his thug tried to follow me, but our bouncer, this huge guy named Shy, made him change his mind."

Xavier glanced at the man. "He doesn't seem to have recognized you yet. That's surprising. That's a pretty memorable moment."

Rosa's face darkened. "I'm not surprised. He'd been drinking, and when they do that, most men turn into assholes who think they can do and say whatever they want to the girl on the stage. Besides, I'll bet he's cruised so many strip clubs that all the faces just run together." She looked away.

The priest was silent for a moment and then patted her leg. "That was another life, Doc. There's no shame, and there's nothing you need to go back to."

Rosa looked at him and shook her head slowly. "No shame, huh? Father, you are the strangest Catholic I've ever met."

"Amen."

Her index finger came up again and she pointed, her voice dropping so low that Xavier had to strain to hear her. "You want to watch out for him. He's no good."

"I'll keep that in mind," the priest said. "Try to get some sleep."

Rosa faded out a short while later, but it was a long time before Xavier was able to escape into his own dreams. When he did, he found them populated by endless corridors and shadowy, moving figures.

TWENTY-EIGHT

Time had become an intangible thing down here in the dark. They might as well have been underground. A digital clock on the wall of the berthing space read 03:15, but the numbers meant little to Evan Tucker. His sleep had been restless and sporadic, and now he simply lay in the bunk, looking out toward the hatch where Stone, the seventeen-year-old, was standing watch. The sound of deep breathing came from around him, and Evan envied the others their ability to rest.

Calvin hadn't said much after he put Freeman down, and Evan learned from the whispers of the other hippies that the two men had been friends for over twenty years. Evan tried not to think about this new heartbreak added to the existing load on Calvin's shoulders, and he had taken charge of the group, leading them on through Second Deck.

They had all entered the ship practically staggering under the weight of extra ammunition, and already more than half had been expended. Although they had not run into another swarm as they had back at that lethal intersection, the dead remained plentiful on this deck, and the group left a trail of bodies as it pressed forward.

Staring at the bottom of the bunk above him, Evan thought about their journey. They encountered and shot down three sailors outside the ship's post office, and two more near a long bank of satellite phones. Half a dozen zombies had to be hunted down amid the giant washers and dryers of an industrial laundry, a frightening cat-and-mouse game that ended with the big, white machines punched through with bullet holes and smeared with dark blood and rot. Fortunately, the only casualties had been the already dead.

As they had moved forward, Evan couldn't help but be impressed not only with the size of the carrier but with the attention to detail and the facilities put in place to make the ship a true community. There was a general store, a gym, a large rec room with books and Ping-Pong and TVs with video games hooked to them, a barbershop, and a library. The librarian was a rotting sailor in his thirties still wearing wire-rimmed glasses, and Stone blew his head off. There were restrooms and water fountains, private quarters for the ship's senior officers and department heads, and larger berthing spaces for the enlisted men. It was one of these spaces that they had chosen as their place to hole up for the night.

The enlisted berthing accommodated sixty sailors, the bunks arranged in stacks of three, each with a privacy curtain, a reading lamp, and a storage locker nearly identical to those issued in high school. There was a large head with showers and rows of toilets and urinals, and a small common area with a table, chairs, and a wall-mounted TV. From all that Evan had seen on board *Nimitz*, each berthing was a cookie-cutter replica of the next.

Sleep wasn't coming, so Evan sat on the edge of his bunk instead. He wondered how the other groups were doing, who had been lost, and if anyone was even left alive. Was coming here worth the price? He still believed it was. The concept of an unreachable island fortress was sound, and just from what he had seen so far, the many amenities and the presence of power, made the aircraft carrier a prize worth fighting for. They weren't soldiers, as someone had pointed out, and how long could they expect to live if they were constantly running and scavenging? There were children, people with disabilities, and even those strong enough to run would tire. They were already tired, running out of everything, including hope.

Evan looked around at the berthing compartment. Even something as simple as a bed in a safe room was a dream for most of them. The ship would provide safety, food, and shelter from both the elements and the new species of predator hunting them at every turn. And to Evan, the aircraft carrier represented more than a defensive position and satisfying their basic needs. It represented the chance at life.

He thought of the people in Calvin's Family, of the new people they had met and joined with. He thought of Maya. Life. A chance to close your eyes and sleep without fear, to laugh without attracting monsters, to make plans for tomorrow. The chance to raise children out of reach of the horrors, and to love again.

Nimitz had to be cleared, he thought. There was no other option, and no price too high. In that moment he decided that he was no longer hopeful, that was a weak word. He was resolved.

Evan rose and joined Stone at the hatch, the only way in and out of the berthing space. A handful of light bars cast the sleeping compartment in gloom, and beyond the hatch was a long, dark corridor leading to a lit intersection. A sentry would see danger coming well before it arrived.

"Can't sleep?" Stone asked.

"I'm tired, but I'm having trouble settling down," Evan said. "Doesn't make much sense just to lie there." He looked at the boy. "How are you doing? Want to grab some sleep? I'll take over."

Stone shook his head. "I'm good. I figure I'll let everyone sleep for another couple of hours."

Evan smiled, remembering what it was to be seventeen: tireless and indestructible. He also knew that when the kid finally did sleep, he would drop into a ten-hour coma from which nothing could stir him.

"How are you holding up with all this?" Evan asked.

Stone shrugged the strap of the assault rifle higher onto his shoulder. "I'm cool with it. I've been killing them since this all started, so it's no big deal."

Evan had heard that Stone was one of the best shots in the Family, and calm under pressure. He would probably have made an excellent soldier, and was about the right age for it.

"What was *your* first one?" Stone asked. "The first drifter you killed, I mean."

Evan looked down at his scuffed motorcycle boots. "A little girl in Napa Valley. I threw up afterward."

Stone chuckled. "Mine was a park ranger. It looked like a bear had been at him, and his skin was all gray. At first I thought it would feel kind of good, what with the way rangers always used to hassle us for camping, always moving us on. It didn't, though." He looked out the hatch. "Then I was waiting to feel bad about shooting him, but that didn't happen either." He shrugged. "They're just things. It doesn't bother me."

Evan wished he could be as pragmatic as this boy, and at the same time he felt sorry for a childhood that had been snatched away so abruptly.

"Where are your parents?" Evan asked. The Family was large, and even after all the time he had spent with them, he still didn't know everybody.

"They died when I was thirteen," Stone said, not taking his eyes off the corridor. "Drunk driver got them. I was lucky I wasn't in the car."

"I'm sorry," Evan said. God, how disingenuous that sounded. And yet it was an automatic when you heard something like that.

Stone didn't acknowledge it. "Cal and Faith pretty much took me in, everyone did, but especially them." He was quiet for a while. "Faith was a nice lady. I feel bad for Calvin; he's lost so much."

Evan said nothing.

Stone's mood suddenly brightened. "You're a lucky guy, you know it? With Maya, I mean. She's terrific, and beautiful too."

Evan saw the little crush, and it made him smile.

"You guys got into a fight about who was coming to the ship, huh?"

"How do you know about that?" Evan said, frowning.

Stone laughed softly. "Man, there are no secrets in the Family. It was the right thing to do, though, having her stay back with the others, look out for her brothers and sisters."

"I'm not so sure about that," Evan said. "I'm scared for her back there. I wish she had come."

"No, you don't really want her in this place." It wasn't a question. "She'll be okay. She's tougher than she looks."

"I know it," said Evan.

The younger man looked at him. "Why did you come? You could have stayed back there. Hell, you and Maya could have split at any time."

The writer sighed. "It's hard to explain. I used to think being on my own was the best way, but now I feel differently. It's like I belong to something now, like I actually matter."

"You do," said Stone. "Everyone likes you, and everyone trusts you. Plus it's really obvious that you and Maya should be together."

"If she ever stops being mad at me," Evan said.

"She's got a temper like Faith did," Stone said, "but she'll get over it. You two will be fine."

They watched the corridor in silence for a while.

"Mostly I think I came along for Calvin," Evan said at last. "He's lost so much, like you said, and he's willing to risk his life to make a sanctuary for the people who love him. How can you not follow someone like that?"

Stone looked at Evan and nodded. "That's why I came."

"Calvin's a good leader."

"I didn't follow him, Evan," said the seventeen-year-old. "I came for you."

Evan started to slowly shake his head.

"You're part of the Family," the boy said, "and as much a leader as Calvin. If anything ever happened to him, you'd be the man."

"How can you say that? You've all been together for so long, and

I just wandered in from nowhere. Like you said, I could take off at any moment. That's not a leader."

"But you didn't take off," said Stone, "even when a lot of people would. You've stuck your neck out how many times, always on the front lines, never hiding. You think things through, you make good decisions. Sounds like a leader to me."

Evan shook his head. "Calvin is a leader. He cares about people to the point he's willing to die to keep them safe."

The corner of Stone's mouth lifted in a little smile. "And you're not? Then why are you here?"

Evan didn't have a response.

Stone leaned against the bulkhead, watching out the corridor. "Calvin is like a father to everyone, certainly to me. But sometimes fathers die. Sometimes they just get too old or too tired to carry on. I get that, but I think a lot of people just assumed he would be around forever." He crossed his arms. "The Family never really had a number two. Dane was cool, but he was too flaky. Faith could have probably stepped up, and Little Bear too, but you could tell they wouldn't have wanted the responsibility." He shrugged. "I don't think any of us noticed there was no one to take over the Family until you showed up and made us realize it was you."

Evan began to protest, but Stone shook his head. "People trust you, man. They listen to you. Ask anyone," he said. "Ask Calvin."

They stood watch and spoke no more, Evan thinking about what the young man had said, less frightened about the responsibility of leadership than he thought he would be. He had told Stone the truth; he felt like he finally belonged somewhere, and it was that which gave him an odd sense of calm.

The rest of the group began to stir around 5:00 A.M. People took advantage of the nearby head, ate a light breakfast, and counted their rounds of ammunition. Nervous looks were exchanged when the final count came in.

Ten minutes later, Calvin led them back out into the ship.

TWENTY-NINE

Angie sat huddled against the bulkhead near the starboard hatch, the aircraft carrier's bridge silent around her. She had shut all the doorways and moved from her spot only once, when she could no longer stand the reek of the quartermaster and the presence of the officer who had bitten Skye. She dragged the bodies out to the catwalk and flipped them over the railing, sending them plunging to the flight deck.

Now her only company was the muted starlight beyond the windows.

She sat with the Galil standing upright between her knees, head resting against the front stock, trying to clear her thoughts. It didn't help. Now that the adrenaline had worn off, she felt drained and everything seemed to be catching up. She was finally able to cry: for Skye, hiding on the deck above, alone with her bite and waiting for the change; for her uncle Bud, a man whose life and death couldn't possibly be balanced out by her murder of Maxie; for her husband, Dean, and daughter, Leah.

Her husband and daughter were never far from her thoughts. They were like water in a pool, momentarily displaced by a large object, such as when she was shooting. When the object was removed, the water rushed back in to fill the space. How long had it been since she had seen them? More than a month. Could it be two? Days and dates had become confused, blurring together.

As always, she told herself that Dean had gotten them out of Sacramento and safely to the ranch outside Chico, that her mother was looking after Leah the way only a woman could, that they were all alive. She had to tell herself that, or she would go mad. But it was sounding more and more like a lie.

Are they *so sure that* you're *alive? Has Dean reconciled himself to being a widower?*

She clenched her teeth at the hateful thought. Dean would never give up on her. If he didn't have Leah to worry about, he would be looking for her already, but Angie wanted them to stay right where they were. She would find a way to get home.

But if that was her priority, why was she here on this suicide mission? She barely knew these people, and most not at all. Was it because the Russian had promised to fly her north when this was over? No, she had been pushing for this assault even before the offer. So why?

Bud Franks, that was the reason, and damn him for affecting her life the way he had. Bud had been a man of right and wrong, of simple beliefs, and one of them was that you don't run out on the people who depend on you, not once you've taken responsibility for them. He was a good and honest man.

And where did Skye fit in? Again, Angie hardly knew her, in fact knew nothing about her life before the airfield hangar. And there was no arguing with the fact that Skye was distant and could be outright unpleasant. Most of the time. Yet Angie felt connected to her. She grieved for what the girl had gone through, the changes attacking her body. And now for the bite, a death sentence.

Somewhere in all this she grieved for herself, and for her family, so alone and far away. Angie cried a bit longer, and those tears carried her into a fitful sleep.

Skye finished bandaging her arm with the supplies from her small first-aid kit. The bite was deep but hadn't taken as much flesh as she originally thought. Not that it mattered. It had broken the skin. She treated the wound first with alcohol wipes—the burn of the moisture on the tender flesh was almost as bad as the bite—and then loaded it up with a painkilling, antiseptic cream that would also help with clotting. She covered it in clean gauze pads and wrapped it tightly.

It helped, and both the bleeding and the sharp edges of the pain subsided. At least she would be a bit more comfortable when the fever came for her.

Skye was on the uppermost deck of the *Nimitz*, in an area that a sign designated as *PRIMARY FLIGHT CONTROL*. It was a small room ringed with windows and parked atop the ship's bridge, the only thing above it an antenna farm and clusters of radar and communication dishes. As with the decks immediately below, the room was surrounded by a catwalk. Some sailor had hand-painted the words *Vulture's Row* on the metal piping of the catwalk's handrail, and Skye imagined a row of those birds looking down on something of interest. The nickname made sense to her. The catwalk commanded an all-encompassing view of the flight deck.

There had been no zombies in here when Skye came bolting up the stairs. Now, as she sat in the open air on Vulture's Row with her legs dangling out over the side, there was only one in the making. Fever, sweating, delirium. That was what she knew about the onset of symptoms. The speed with which it hit was different from person to person—her own symptoms had come on very quickly after her exposure to the blood outside that Oakland church—and somewhere along the way the virus took hold and began the change.

She looked at her left hand in the starlight, trembling slightly. The smooth skin of that hand was the color of ash, the same hue that was overtaking the rest of her body. Her left eye was fully blind now, unable to detect light of any kind. Mercifully, the headaches were gone, at least for now. It was bad enough to have to wait for your own execution without the added suffering of a crippling migraine.

Skye didn't remember much of her first duel with the virus. The big man named TC had called her a bitch, and somehow she had gotten into the blue truck. She remembered being afraid of TC, of the way he looked at her, hungry and sly. And then there was a foggy span of dreams and nightmares. Crystal had been there, alive and whole. Mom had stalked toward her, dead and losing her insides onto her shoes, stepping on them. There were teachers and boyfriends, all of them dead, miles of the dead. She thought she remembered someone touching her, not in the way a person touched someone who was sick, with gentle hair strokes and soothing wet rags on the forehead. This was different touching, the kind not allowed without consent. Someone said something about having a party.

And then there was a moment of clarity. She saw herself bound and gagged, helpless on her back, partially undressed. TC crouched above her with his broad face covered in sweat, stroking himself with one hand and crooning as he guided his member to her . . .

"Motherfucker," she whispered.

He hadn't raped her, she knew that, but he was masturbating. And had he been moving as if he would do more? She thought he had, though it remained hazy. There was also a vague memory of someone else being present, maybe even interrupting the man before he could go further. Had it been Carney? The fogginess frustrated her.

What was clear, however, was that he had preyed upon her while she was in the grip of the fever, fighting for her life, and she hadn't known until this very moment. Oh, if only she could have remembered earlier, when they were together! She would have shoved the muzzle of her M4 in his mouth, said, "How do you like it?" and blown his diseased brain out the back of his head.

She sighed. The opportunity was gone. TC was somewhere deep in the ship, probably dead by now, and Skye would never get a shot at revenge. Even if she started hunting now, the fever would claim her before she could get very far. And if he was already a zombie, killing him wouldn't really mean anything. She sighed again, a deep, cleansing breath, and let the anger go.

Skye looked up at the stars and breathed in the salty night air, enjoying the quiet, the calmness in her body. Even knowing what was to come, she found that she was at peace. Not with the world or what had become of it; she would weep for that deep inside, as long as she held on to conscious thought. It was peace with herself. The final, bitter irony was that she should finally come to terms with who Skye Dennison was just as Death was calling her number.

She slipped the nine-millimeter out of her shoulder holster and set it on the catwalk beside her. There was no way she would allow herself to become that which she despised, and it would be wrong to inflict this upon Angie, to put her at risk or force her to fire the final bullet. Angie was a friend, and Skye hadn't had one of those in a long time.

Skye decided she would wait for the symptoms to start, and then she would do it herself. But not yet. She would watch the stars a bit longer.

THIRTY

"I think I went up too far," said Brother Peter, comfortable now that the heathens could not hear him speaking. He was seated on the small leather sofa, watching the priest and the medic sleep on the other couch across the room. As Rosa had predicted, he had no idea who she was. "Up to go down, that was the rule. You can only get down there by starting above, but I went too high. I need to get back down to the hangar deck. That's where they arm planes, I think. That's the place to start."

God, looking like the Air Force shrink, sat cross-legged on the end of the conference table, eyes closed behind His glasses, hands resting on His knees. *"Shh,"* He said. *"I'm in the zone."*

"We need to go back down," said the minister.

God opened one eye. *"You're such a screwup. They won't want to go below again."*

"I'll go alone."

A smile, and the eye closed. *"Do you think you're going to just walk right in and find them? No one leaves nuclear weapons just lying around, not even crazy-fuck Arab terrorists."*

Brother Peter thought. "They'll be secured. I'll need a way to gain access." He chewed on a thumbnail, his eyes distant. "How will I do that?" He thought about how he had been able to move around the silo way back when. Electronic pass card, of course. Why hadn't he remembered that?

"Because you're batshit crazy," said the Lord.

"Pass card," Peter repeated, ignoring the insult. "That's how we did it." Who would have access? he wondered. They would probably still have the card on them.

Brother Peter thought about it. The handling of nuclear weapons, in any service branch, was done by specialists, just as he had been. Since dealing with nukes was usually not an everyday occurrence, however, they would have another job, wouldn't they? Nukes were weapons. On carriers, who handled weapons? Red shirts. They would have access to the magazines, and some of them, the specialists, would have access to the chamber where the nukes were stored. He needed a red shirt with a special access card. He knew how to recognize the card.

"That wasn't so hard, now was it?" God asked, unfolding Himself from the conference table and tousling Brother Peter's hair. *"See how much you can accomplish when your mind isn't boiling over with lust?"*

At the mention of lust, Peter immediately pictured Angie West.

"Same old Peter," God said, chuckling and glancing at His watch. *"Let's get Armageddon rolling, shall we? I have other appointments."*

Father Xavier pretended to sleep and watched Peter Dunleavy through slitted eyes. The man was sitting stiffly on the other couch, staring at nothing. His lips moved slowly.

"Is he talking to himself?" Rosa asked softly beside him.

Xavier hadn't known she was awake too. "It looks that way."

"Is he crazy? He's acting crazy."

"Maybe it's just a stress reaction," the priest said, standing and yawning loudly to get the other man's attention.

Peter's lips stopped moving at once, and the focus returned to his eyes. "We should get going," he said.

Xavier nodded. "How about we let everyone wake up, and put together a plan?"

The minister slumped back into the couch and crossed his arms. Dakota, Eve, and Lilly joined them a few minutes later, and they all gathered around the conference table. Everyone looked at the priest, except for Peter.

"This hasn't gone like I'd hoped," Xavier admitted. "The ship is more complex than I imagined, the dead more numerous. There are so many doorways and passages, places where they can surprise us." He ran a hand over his head, realizing he needed a haircut. Much longer and he'd have an Afro, he thought, which, as a former Marine, was any hair length longer than a quarter inch. "I feel like we've been wandering around without getting much done."

Lilly put a hand on his arm. "We're killing them, like we talked about. Every one we do is a step closer to taking the ship, right?"

The others nodded. Peter stared at the table.

"Thank you," said Xavier, "but I think we can do better. This level of the ship seems to have fewer of them, for whatever reason. That could change rapidly, but for now it's a good thing."

"Do you think they all just stopped in place out there because we took a nap?" said Brother Peter. "That's a little naïve, isn't it?"

Xavier smiled at him. "Probably. But we have an indication that there's fewer of them here, so we'll go on that premise. They'll be more manageable, so I think we should stay on this level."

Peter looked about to speak, then closed his mouth.

Rosa was right, Xavier thought, *this guy* is *an asshole.*

Xavier continued. "We should get back to checking and clearing every room, making a mark on the door after we do."

Dakota retrieved a handful of markers from the tray of a dry-erase board mounted to a wall. "These will do for now, until we find some spray paint."

Xavier gave him a nod. "We also need to be on the lookout for weapons, and especially ammunition. We're not going to live long without either, so if anyone sees an armed sailor out there, we should make it a priority and take him down as a group."

And that was it. There really wasn't much planning they could do, other than try to clear out the dead. No one suggested retreat, but Xavier did convince them that if they managed to find their way back to the rear of the ship and locate the original stairway, they would fall back to the two boats tethered outside in order to re-arm.

As Rosa had said, the blue tiles not only signified officer country but announced entry into areas dedicated to warfare tasks. They inspected a medium-sized compartment marked SHIP'S SIGNALS, a room filled with computer workstations and tall processing units. The only occupant was a decaying female sailor with an old gunshot wound to the temple.

JOINT INTELLIGENCE was a series of connected rooms filled with more computers, projection screens, shelves of files that were intricately color-coded like those in a doctor's office, and what looked like endless rows of maps and satellite images in cardboard tubes filed in honeycomb shelving.

As the group fanned out to peek behind workstations and inspect the long rows, Xavier thought about the security clearance it would have required just to enter this room. Intelligence areas in any service branch were highly restricted, and certainly the average sailor on Nimitz never saw this place. He was willing to bet that he was the first Marine grunt ever to do so.

The zombie came at him from the left while he was looking right.

It was a tall, dark-haired man, bloated and green, fluids dripping from its orifices onto the floor. It gasped and lunged, and Xavier managed only to twist and put his backpack in the way of the creature's bite as teeth ripped at nylon. He could not avoid the filthy, ragged nails of its hands as it groped for his face, and in a second it dug four long, red furrows down his cheek. The priest cried out and tried to spin away but slipped in the mess the creature was leaving on the floor and went down hard.

The creature dropped on top of him, gnashing and clawing, and Xavier jammed the axe handle across its neck to keep the teeth away. Fluids spilled from its mouth and turned the wooden handle slick, and a puff of dead air burped from inside the thing, triggering Xavier's gag reflex.

Rosa ran toward the sound of the fight and slid to a stop in a shooter's stance, her nine-millimeter gripped in two hands.

"No!" shouted Lilly. She elbowed Rosa aside, and the medic's shot went into the ceiling. Lilly kept her eyes on the creature, pointing. "It's green. We've seen what happens when you shoot the green ones, remember?"

Rosa did remember. They popped, and sprayed their foul liquid everywhere. Xavier would be bathed in it.

Lilly poked at the raised forehead with her shotgun barrel. "C'mon, handsome, look at me, look at me."

Xavier was strong, but the thing was wet and heavy, and the cords stood out on the priest's arms as he fought the weight, grunting with the effort. He turned his face to the side to avoid what was drooling from its maw.

Poke, poke. "Give mama a kiss, sweetie," called Lilly, as the others arrived and stared in horror. No one wanted to risk grabbing it and pulling it off, for fear the pressure would burst its taut flesh. The thing wanted Xavier, was struggling to bite at the axe handle and get a solid grip with its hands. Lilly was afraid to poke it too hard, but finally she shouted, "Hey, *douchebag*!" and gave it a solid rap on the head.

The thing looked up with filmy gray eyes, snarled at her, and crawled off Xavier. Rosa leaped away and Lilly danced backward, still calling to it as the creature crawled after her on all fours. Xavier rolled on his side, gagging, and Dakota pulled him to his feet.

"Aren't you a pretty one," said Lilly, keeping just out of reach, backing down a row of files. "Pretty little thing, you look like a bad acid trip, yes you do. Come on, handsome, come on. . . ."

The bloated sailor climbed slowly to its feet, tottering as the fluids sloshed inside it. It moved forward faster, then broke into a gallop, tight flesh straining at its uniform.

"It's going to blow!" Rosa shouted. "You're too close!"

"Not yet," called Lilly, leading it farther away. "Not yet. Wait . . . okay, kill it!" She had reached an opening in the shelving and dove through. Rosa fired, three quick barks of the nine-millimeter. One round punched into some files, one hit it square in the back of the head, and the last hit just above where its kidneys would have been.

It was green.

It blew apart.

The sound it made when it went was almost as horrible as the splattered mess, but was nothing in comparison to the smell that followed. The group fled the intelligence rooms retching, back into the passageway. No one had noticed that Brother Peter had stood on the edge of the action the entire time, watching and doing nothing.

Rosa took the point and hustled them through another hatch into a small, blue-tiled galley and mess, apparently reserved for officers. The stenciling on the hatch said *DIRTY SHIRT*. Dakota shot down a pair of creatures in cook's whites, and Eve found a dead boy of seventeen or eighteen standing and swaying near a stainless steel dishwasher. She used her shotgun.

With the room secured, Rosa broke out her medical bag and went to work on the fingernail gouges down Xavier's cheek, her own face the stone mask of a crisis professional. The priest winced as she cleaned out the wounds, but otherwise didn't complain. Between street fights, boxing, a gangbanger's blade, and now the end of the world, his face had turned into a road map of violence.

Rosa sank a needle into the priest's arm.

"What's that?"

"Antibiotic, hopefully enough to kill whatever's inside you. Unless the virus transmitted through the scratches, and in that case you're fu . . . you're screwed." When he started to say something, she shook her head. "I know, you've heard the word before. Just be still. Even if the virus didn't transmit, his claws were disgusting and even a normal infection could be dangerous."

"Thanks, Doc."

"That's a big dose," she said. "You might experience some nausea."

"After smelling that thing?" Xavier laughed. "How will I know the difference?"

As she applied a square bandage to the wounds, Xavier blinked. He hadn't thought about getting the Corpse Virus through scratches. The medic saw it in his eyes. "Try not to think about it," she said, taping down the gauze pad. "There's no evidence to suggest you can get infected that way. I didn't see a single case of it in all those weeks at the ferry terminal."

That doesn't mean it can't happen, he thought. "You watch me closely, Doc. If it looks like . . ."

"I'll do what I have to," she said brusquely, "but I'm telling you not to worry. Doctor's orders. Now let's go, jarhead."

They got moving with Dakota on point, Xavier at the center of their little band with Rosa close by. Brother Peter stayed in the rear. They searched the officers' quarters and found nothing. The air traffic control center, a large room with rows of radar scopes, held a trio of zombies in yellow firefighter gear. They shuffled forward groaning and snapping behind Plexiglas oxygen masks and went down to head shots.

The Combat Information Center, or CIC, was a low-ceilinged room that would have been black except for the colored lights of computer terminals and the hazy blue glow of screens. A pair of vertical, blue plastic plotting boards split the room, covered in grease pencil marks. The air-conditioning was still on in here, and the glowing darkness made the place look like the bridge of a spaceship in a science fiction movie.

The dead surged toward the intruders at once.

There were more than twenty of them, officers and enlisted men in varying states of decay, galloping forward among the terminals. Rosa, the three hippies, and Brother Peter opened up, standing shoulder to shoulder like a firing squad, and the roar of their weapons in such a confined space was deafening. Heads were torn apart and bodies thrown backward, computer screens exploded in showers of glass, sparking like Fourth of July fountains, and the vertical Plexiglas boards disintegrated.

To the right of the shooters, Xavier advanced on a pair of corpses and buried his axe quickly in each of their heads, jerking the blade free and searching for more.

It was over in less than thirty seconds, the stink of old blood and putrid insides mixing with gunpowder, the air-conditioning doing little to dispel the reek. The group reloaded and moved through the room, out another hatch and into a new corridor. After a short distance they were back on gray tile.

A hatch on the left opened into a vacant dental suite that looked capable of handling a dozen patients at once. Rosa told herself to stock up on supplies until she saw what was up ahead, a pair of white swinging doors. In black letters on each door was the word *MEDICAL*.

Both doors were chewed by bullet holes, empty shell casings covered the floor of the hallway, and the left door was marred by a pair of bloody handprints, now turned a rust brown so dark it was almost black. The battle that had taken place here made them pause, as did the absence of bodies. After a moment, Rosa led them forward, and the little group eased through the double doors.

Rosa and the others were so intent on what awaited them on the other side that they failed to notice Father Xavier was no longer with them.

Neither was Brother Peter.

THIRTY-ONE

Carney awoke to the smell of a burning cigarette. He was slumped in an uncomfortable position in the rolling chair, and he groaned as he straightened, opening his eyes. TC was sitting a few feet away, elbows on his knees, watching Carney. A cigarette dangled from his lips, smoke curling toward the ceiling. There was a slight smile on his face.

"What are you looking at?" asked Carney.

TC puffed and ground the butt out under a boot. "Nothing."

"Then go look at it someplace else."

The younger inmate chuckled.

A fake potted tree in a corner of the TV studio served as a urinal, and as Carney relieved himself he checked to be sure the nine-millimeter was still in his back waistband. It was. "We have to decide what to do," he said over his shoulder. "We're still in a dead end." And there was still a steady thumping at the hatch.

"I got that figured already," TC said from across the room. Carney waited to hear some juvenile plan about opening the hatch and going out hard and fast, but when he turned around, TC was no longer in the room.

"In here." His voice came from within one of the open doors across from the control booth.

Carney entered the narrow electrical room, where he found TC on his hands and knees in front of a two-foot-square opening, a pried-off metal panel leaning against the wall beside it.

"It's some kind of service tunnel," said TC.

Carney crouched behind his cellmate and aimed his Maglite beam down the tunnel. It was tiled, tight, and packed with conduit, breaker panels, and bundles of colored wire cabled to the ceiling.

"How did you find this?" Carney asked.

"I woke up before you did," TC said, looking back and grinning. "Started poking around." He crawled into the tunnel, his big wrench in one hand.

Carney felt an involuntary chill at the idea of TC up and moving around while he slept, unaware and defenseless. He couldn't let that happen again.

TC had forgotten to turn off his own flashlight before they slept, and the batteries were dead. He asked for Carney's, then kept crawling as his cellmate followed. It was extremely tight, especially for two men built as broadly as they were, and at times they had to lie flat on their backs and shimmy to squirm past an electrical box or under a thick bundle of cable. Carney didn't envy whatever sailors had been responsible for servicing this area, but he was willing to bet they had been young, flexible, and small.

After forty feet of crawling, they came to the back of another gray panel. It was secured by screws coming in from the other side and would have to be forced open. Turning in the cramped access tunnel in order to kick it free was an impossibility, and neither wanted to back out just so they could repeat this crawl feet-first. TC shuffled onto his back and began slamming the head of his wrench into the metal.

Carney winced at every strike. If those things weren't already waiting for them on the other side, this would surely draw them. He waited in the dark, gripping the checkered grip of his pistol, smelling their combined sweat.

The panel popped off with a bang and TC scuttled out. Carney expected snarls and reaching hands, but there was nothing. He crawled after his cellmate and was able to stand in another square electrical room. TC's hand was already on the handle of the only door, and he threw it open, lunging through and raising the wrench. Carney rushed out nearly on top of him.

The door banged into a dead sailor in a brown jersey and the creature groaned, staggering back. Two others in brown charged forward from the right. Carney shot the closest one in the face, so close that its forward momentum carried the zombie into him, throwing him into the wall. The second one came on and added its own weight, ripping with its jagged fingernails and snapping its teeth as it tried to reach past its dead comrade and get to the meal.

TC swung the wrench in a high arc over his head, but the ceiling was too low and the head of the weapon was stopped by a steel pipe. The sailor in brown flung itself at the younger inmate, and TC straight-armed it with his left hand. The zombie bit down on TC's fingers, its teeth scraping the protective mesh of the biteproof glove. With a snap of its head it tore the glove off his hand. TC snarled and punched the creature in the side of the head with the fist gripping the wrench. It rocked to one side and came back biting.

Carney heaved against the weight, using the corpse pinned against him as a shield, trying to slide out to the right. The head of the twice-dead corpse lolled bonelessly between them, glassy eyes seeming to stare at Carney as black ichor spilled from its sagging mouth. Carney shoved again, gaining a few inches, and popped free to the right. The second zombie shoved the limp corpse aside and reached, only to have the nine-millimeter go off an inch from its forehead. It collapsed on top of the first.

TC leaped away from his own snapping opponent and swung the wrench sideways, connecting with its ear and snapping its neck, causing the head to slump onto the shoulder. The creature moaned and kept coming, and TC swung again, hitting the same spot, and staved in its skull. A dozen more grunting blows while it was on the deck turned the head to fragmented jelly.

Carney tracked the pistol around the room, a long space with racks of pocketed vests, rows of steel-toed boots, and dozens of helmets with attached goggles. Nothing else was moving.

"TC, you okay?"

The younger inmate stooped to pull the biteproof glove from the creature's mouth. The webbing of his left hand between the thumb and index finger was torn and bleeding, the bite mark a curving series of red dashes marring a tattoo of a cross and swastika.

"I'm good," he said, turning away from his cellmate's view and quickly pulling the glove on over the wound.

They took a moment to catch their breath, then left the room and entered yet another narrow corridor with scattered lighting. The perfume of rotting flesh was thick here, but both had become accustomed to the smell. The hall led them past a garbage disposal area where the hatch stood open, permitting the rich aroma of the ship's trash system to float into the hall. If a zombie had been lurking in the room, the smell would have effectively masked its presence. Carney pulled the hatch shut as they passed.

A steep ladder led them up to a large fan room, where only two of the big units were still turning, creating a hum that made the floor vibrate. A corpse in blue, shot down during the fall of the ship, was sitting on the floor slumped against one of the fans, a scattering of bullet holes piercing the sheet metal around it. The fan blew the scent of its decay through the room.

"Why don't we see rats?" TC asked as they moved through the area. "I thought all ships had rats. This place is one big fucking Thanksgiving dinner for them, man."

Carney shrugged. "It's a Navy ship. You allow rats in your areas and they hand you your ass."

"I hate fucking rats," said TC. "Remember the rats at the Q? Big enough to put a fucking saddle on."

Carney remembered. They were big gray-and-brown Norwegians, aggressive and smart—just like all the other animals in that paradise on the bay. As long as they never showed up in the administrative wing, the warden didn't give a shit. Carney had no good memories of that place, but it didn't surprise him that TC was feeling nostalgic about prison. It was where he had spent most of his life. It was what he knew.

The fan room led to an air filter cleaning shop, and then back into another corridor. To the left was a heavy steel hatch with a small, circular window inset that glowed red. The word *RIB* was stenciled on the steel. Their other choice was a short hall leading to another hatch marked *PARACHUTE BAY.*

TC hefted his wrench and went through the *RIB* hatch, and at once both men were hit by clean air from outside. The smell of decay was absent; a large, rectangular opening in the far bulkhead allowed a view of the water out the starboard side, a still-dark sky filled with stars above. Red battle lights lit the compartment.

RIB stood for *rigid inflatable boat*, as they quickly learned. The boats hung on racks on two walls, black rubber marked with *CVN-68* along with their own number, with bins of life jackets nearby, and a rack of upright, outboard motors to the left. The rectangular opening to the sea was fitted with a pair of swing-out arms, boat davits each with an attached winch. One of the boats rested on the deck near the opening, its bow attached to one winch line. There were shell casings on the floor, and a rusty smear on the side of the boat, but no bodies.

"Looks like someone tried to get out," said Carney.

TC kicked the side of the boat and spit. "Too bad you want to stay. Here's another chance to split."

"Why don't you go instead? I'll help you lower the boat."

TC gave him that uncomfortable smile. "I'm having too much fun. This is where I'm supposed to be."

They left the boats behind and made their way down to the parachute bay, opening the hatch into a long, high chamber hung with white shrouds. The parachutes were suspended from above like long curtains, coils of nylon line at their base.

Carney was reminded of a movie they showed at the Q over a decade earlier, a big-budget Bruckheimer production about World War II, filled with waving flags and a soaring soundtrack. It was really more chick flick than war movie. He remembered a love scene in a parachute hangar, the billowing white silk adding to the romantic setting.

There was no romance here. Zombies moved within the shrouds.

Their silhouettes shuffled behind the layers of silk, slouched and dragging, pawing at the fabric and beginning to moan as they heard or smelled or sensed prey enter the compartment. TC tried bashing one with his wrench, but the parachutes and silhouettes skewed his depth perception, and the wrench puffed harmlessly into the silk, making it billow.

"Up the side," Carney said, leading them along a wall, past a bank of industrial sewing machines and cabinets of supplies. The silhouettes moved with them, boots sliding over steel, silk whispering across rotting bodies.

A woman in uniform, most of her scalp torn away and leaving only clumps of matted hair, stumbled through a gap in the parachutes and grabbed at TC. Carney shot her down, and the gunfire made the rest howl and move faster.

They found the room's corner and followed the wall left. A closed hatch appeared up ahead, and they were nearly there when bodies began tumbling out of the shrouds, decaying sailors with cloudy eyes and snapping teeth. TC bellowed and threw himself into them, swinging the wrench and spraying red and green across the silk. Carney fired until he was empty, slapped in another clip, and fired some more, trying to pick out targets without putting a bullet in his cellmate. In less than a minute the deck was cluttered with motionless bodies.

TC used his sleeve to wipe off his face, smearing it across his forehead, grinning as his powerful chest heaved from the battle. "I love this shit," he said, his voice a groan of pleasure.

Carney just looked at him and inserted his last full magazine into the Beretta, then led them through the hatch. They could travel down either of a pair of narrow corridors or climb a stairway into darkness. The older con switched on his Maglite and took them up.

THIRTY-TWO

"Oh, sweet Jesus," Calvin whispered, peering around the edge of the hatch and into the large room beyond. Behind him, Evan pushed up close so that he could see too.

Both the officers' and enlisted mess halls sat amidships on Second Deck, about a hundred feet of distance between them. Each was served by its own galley, but both depended on the same vast stores: humming banks of freezers, perishable coolers, and large chambers for dry goods. Under normal circumstances, *Nimitz* carried enough frozen and dry goods to feed a crew of six thousand enlisted personnel and officers for ninety days without requiring resupply. In the recent atmosphere of political instability overseas, carrier supplies had been increased to six months, permitting short-notice and long-term deployment. The Navy liked its ships to be as self-sufficient as possible.

Nimitz's galleys could feed up to five hundred sailors at a time, and the mess halls were caverns of long tables and benches, self-serve tray lines and drink dispensers, and long collections of trash and recycling bins. The walls were covered in motivational posters, newsletters and notices, bulletin boards where photos from recent ports of call were pinned, and numerous informational posters about the Navy policy on sexual harassment and fraternization, issues of real concern on gender-integrated vessels.

The galleys were expansive spaces of clean stainless steel tucked behind the serving lines. Rows of ovens and grills, coolers and sinks, dishwashers and deep fryers were arranged according to a Navy planner's sense of order and efficiency. The industrial kitchens devoted entire rooms to cleaning supplies in order to keep floors and surfaces spotless.

Evan thought it had been Napoleon who said an army travels on its stomach, and he decided the Navy was no different. Gathering to take a meal wasn't merely a biological need for survival; it kept people happy and motivated, allowed them to bond over a shared experience. To Evan, more important than navigation and weapons systems would be the mess hall.

Perhaps that explained why the place was packed with zombies.

There were hundreds of them, wearing every conceivable type of uniform: cook's whites and camo, medical scrubs and khaki, coveralls, firefighter gear, and every color of jersey. All were bitten and torn, all were decaying—some dry and withered, others green and juicy—and all were dead. Milky eyes stared out of darkened hollows, little moans and airy wheezing issued from split and torn lips. Most were standing in one place, packed closely together and facing in the same direction like a concert crowd, swaying slowly, as if to the beat of an unseen band.

Somewhere up near the front of the horde, however, was an urgent, rhythmic moaning and the unceasing hammering of many fists on metal.

They're not here because this place was important to them, Evan realized. *They've got something cornered, and they just won't go away.*

Calvin and Evan looked back at their little group, six in all, and told them what they had seen.

"We could just close the hatch quietly and move on," Calvin suggested.

The others shook their heads. It was Stone who said, "This is what we came for. If we can do it, we'll really make a difference, right?"

The aging hippie looked into the boy's eyes, seeing no fear, only determination. "Yes," Calvin said, "we could. But there's a lot of them. We all have to be in."

Nods all around. They were in.

Together they made a plan of how the shooting would proceed, preparing all their magazines and loose ammunition. Then they lined up and moved into the back of the mess hall, single file and quick. They lined up side by side, with Dakota and Juju tasked to watch the hallway and their backs, protecting them from ambush.

Their preparations went unnoticed, the horde facing away and swaying.

The line opened fire.

Stone was reminded of a shooting gallery he had once visited at a carnival. For Evan it was like tossing a rock into a lake and hoping to hit water. The dead were packed together tightly, and, give or take twelve inches, most of their heads were on the same level. Even when they turned to face the gunfire they could barely move, and many of them remained upright even after a head shot, their limp bodies supported by the crush of the others.

Assault rifles and shotguns crashed, bullets and buckshot finding their mark and spraying dead faces with gore. Stone intentionally sought out the "greenies," bursting them at a distance. Slugs tore through chests and necks and shattered collarbones, but most hit the target. In this moment, the crew of *Nimitz* was truly equal, officers dying with enlisted men and women; fuel handlers, technicians, and basic seamen collapsing in tangled piles; radar operators and catapult officers going down next to those who handled mops and haze-gray paint all day. The ship's executive officer, who had been dragged onto the vessel's bridge as it entered San Francisco Bay, already turned and hungry, opened his mouth to moan and caught an assault rifle bullet through the front teeth, blowing out the back of his skull. He fell across the body of an eighteen-year-old discipline case who had spent most of his cruise scrubbing toilets and urinals.

As before, when the symphony of firing was replaced by the clicks of reloading, the dead began to press forward. Unlike in the past, not only were they slowed by their own mass, but a sea of dining tables stood between them and the newly arrived prey. Those who tried to climb over were quickly picked off.

The firing soon returned to its crescendo, gun smoke setting off smoke detectors that went off like high-pitched screams. Brass and plastic hulls carpeted the tiled deck as the shooters rapidly depleted what remained of their ammunition.

Calvin saw a gang of zombies moving left behind one of the serving lines, trying to come in from the side, and he took his time shooting them down, making every precious bullet count. Mercy dropped to one knee and used her M4 to eliminate an entire row, one by one from left to right.

The dead moaned, and died.

Bullets punched into drink dispensers and stacks of plastic trays, blew apart clusters of condiments on tables, put holes in the walls and ceilings and sparked off stainless steel. A bank of fluorescents shattered and its housing crashed down onto the heads of the mob. Another fire extinguisher went off like a baby powder bomb, and the putrid fluids of the deceased splattered across every surface.

"Move forward!" Calvin shouted over the next reloading.

Evan, Mercy, and Stone advanced up the right, feeding their weapons on the move, with Calvin moving left, inserting a fresh magazine. At the door, Juju and Dakota watched the hall nervously, wanting to join the fight, but knowing they played a critical role there. As they moved, Evan and Stone pulled pistols to finish off those that were still alive and writhing, pinned beneath mounds of dead sailors. Calvin and Mercy kept up their rifle fire.

Time became suspended, and for the little group the world shrank to include only the enlisted mess of the USS *Nimitz* and its ghastly inhabitants. Soon they were walking among the dead, picking their way through and climbing over, trying to stay atop the dining tables and still firing. Mercy shot an eighteen-year-old from Oklahoma who had joined the Navy to escape the drugs, teenage pregnancy, and hopelessness of her hometown. Stone put a final bullet in the head of a helicopter pilot who had turned without ever knowing that his pregnant wife was safe at a Texas refugee center. Evan blew the head off a thirty-year master chief who had been afraid that retirement would leave him without purpose in his life. Calvin shot a nineteen-year-old who couldn't wait to get out of the Navy because he couldn't live with the tormenting he received for not concealing the fact that he was gay.

The firing grew sporadic as targets became fewer. Stone ran to one wall and secured a pair of hatches so no new arrivals could flank them. Calvin shouted for Juju and Dakota to secure their own door and join the group.

Mercy, Evan, and Calvin moved into the immense galley to hunt the dead among rows of refrigerators and microwaves, baker's racks and prep tables. When one popped up, they put it down without hesitation and moved forward. Calvin found a short hallway leading to the nearby officers' mess—a quick peek revealed it was empty—and secured the door.

They all came together at what had drawn and kept the horde in this place: a large metal door to a walk-in cooler or storage room, its stainless steel surface so hammered by fists that it looked like crumpled tinfoil. The metal pin securing the handle had been dropped into place, and it was bent from ceaseless pulling and pounding.

Something was thumping at the door from the inside, and a muffled sound—moaning or yelling, they couldn't tell—came from within.

Mercy used the metal barrel of her flashlight to hammer the bent pin out, and as soon as it popped free she pulled the handle and leaped back, Calvin and Evan standing with weapons leveled, tension on triggers. A wave of foul air billowed from the opening.

Five of the dirtiest, most foul-smelling men they had ever seen stood just inside, all of them bearded and in the same clothes they were wearing the night the ship fell. Beyond them was a dry-goods storage stacked high with cardboard boxes, littered with empty food containers and plastic bottles. The men were pale and gaunt, and they slowly raised their hands as if in surrender.

The man in front, wearing blue camo, looked at each of them and their weapons, his sunken eyes darting. "Chief Gunner's Mate Liebs, United States Navy," he said, his voice more of a croak than anything. He slowly pulled a large brass key from down the front of his shirt, hung around his neck on a chain with his dog tags. "I need to get to the armory."

We were falling back," Chief Liebs said, sitting on a dining table and drinking a bottle of water with the others standing around him. The four men who had been trapped in the storeroom with him were washing at the galley sinks, Dakota standing watch nearby.

"It was me, Sanders, and Lieutenant Sharpe, my commanding officer. We were herding some of our shipmates along"—he gestured toward the men washing in the galley—"and were cutting through the mess. We just couldn't hold them back, and everyone was dying. They came at us in here from all sides. We burned through all our ammo and I was using my weapon like a club, had it torn right out of my hands. Sanders screamed and went down." He shook his head. "The lieutenant led us back there, pushed us all into that storeroom. He must have been the one to drop the pin on the handle." He paused. "He saved our lives."

"You've been in there since this started?" Calvin asked.

Chief Liebs nodded. He was in his early thirties, hair already silvering, not especially tall but with a straightforward, pleasant face. The other sailors in his party called the chief gunner's mate "Guns," a nickname of respect.

"August thirteenth, I think," he said. "What day is it now? I tried to keep track, but that didn't last long."

Mercy told him she wasn't exactly sure either, but that it had to be well into September or even beyond. The realization that he and his shipmates had been barricaded in that storeroom for over a month shocked the chief.

"They've been pounding at that door the whole time," Liebs said, looking at the piles of corpses, wondering if the officer who had saved them was here, realizing he probably was. "They couldn't get in, and we couldn't get out."

Chief Liebs told them the storeroom was ventilated, so there was no fear of suffocation, and stocked with plenty to eat and drink. There was no way to dispose of waste, and they had turned a corner of the room into an impromptu head, which of course made the entire space reek. They had fashioned a deck of cards with cardboard and a marker to pass the time. Liebs lowered his voice and admitted that each of them had struggled with having no sense for the passage of time, day or night, and the endless pounding and moaning at the door had been maddening. That one of his men might commit suicide had been his biggest fear, and Liebs had used every bit of his leadership skills to keep them from making that choice. As Evan listened, he decided it had been the man's personality and caring that kept them alive, nothing he had learned from the Navy.

"What's the condition of the ship?" Liebs asked.

"It looks like it ran aground," Evan said, "just off Oakland. It's infested with the walking dead, and you're the only survivors we've found."

Liebs was quiet as he absorbed this: the loss of his ship, the loss of so many friends. At last he looked up at them. "I have a fiancée in New Jersey. Do you know anything about what happened back east?"

They didn't, but told him a little about what had become of California, or at least what parts of California they had heard about.

Mercy rubbed the man's back slowly. "She might be okay," Mercy said. "You can't assume she's not."

The chief nodded without comment. He asked if there had been any Navy activity around the Bay Area, any other ships or aircraft. He frowned when they told him there had been none, and they shared what they had found at the USNS *Comfort*, the hospital ship resting abandoned and overrun by the dead at an Oakland dock.

When the other sailors joined the group, Liebs introduced them to their rescuers. All were young and male. One was a basic seaman, a boatswain's—or bosun's—mate, another was an electronics technician, and the third was a petty officer second class who was an operations specialist, a carrier's jack-of-all-trades. The last in their group was a young man from Colorado, a machinist's mate and petty officer third class whom Liebs referred to as a "nuc," pronouncing it *nuke*.

"You can tell because he glows in the dark," Liebs said, making the boy smile. "He helps run the reactors."

"How are they?" the nuc asked. "At least one must be at reduced power. Have you been down there?"

Calvin gave the boy a smile. "Son, we wouldn't know a nuclear reactor if we were standing in front of it, and no, we haven't been down there."

"Are you worried there might be something wrong with them?" Mercy asked, her face showing a hint of alarm. Next to her, Evan suppressed a grin. The walking dead were trying to eat them at every turn of a corridor, and Mercy waded into them like she was Special Forces, but she was still afraid of radiation.

The nuc shook his head. "I'm sure they're fine, I'm just thinking about maintenance. If there were a problem like you're worried about, you'd already be dead."

Mercy was oddly comforted by the blunt words.

Stone asked, "What's the deal with all the dead firefighters?" When the chief looked at him, obviously not understanding, Stone said, "Everywhere we go, no matter what part of the ship we're in, we find unrolled hoses and zombies in firefighter gear." He gestured at examples among the heaped dead around them. "But there's no sign of a fire."

Liebs got it. "That's because we were at general quarters. Every sailor on board is trained in damage control, and that mostly means firefighting. General quarters is battle conditions, when fire is most likely, so lots of people without combat assignments suit up and prepare to fight fire." He shook his head. "Fire on a ship is no joke. I'm glad you haven't seen any."

Chief Liebs looked into the faces of his liberators. "I can't believe a bunch of civilians got it in their heads to board this monster and take it by force." He shook his head in wonder and respect. "I'm glad you did. I'm just amazed you're still alive."

"We won't be for long," said Calvin. "We used up most of our ammo clearing this room."

"You said something about an armory?" Evan asked.

The chief nodded. "I'm a gunner's mate. We handle ship's security and tactical training, man the crew-served weapons, and maintain the magazines." He produced the key again. "We also run the armory." He looked around at them. "We'll need to get there if we're going to survive."

"Do you know where it is?" Mercy asked, and abruptly blushed at the stupid question.

"Yes, ma'am," the chief said, giving her a smile. "It's only about a hundred feet from here. We just need to get there."

THIRTY-THREE

Angie was awakened by a single, muffled pistol shot.

She scrambled to her feet and yanked open the bridge's main hatch, pounding up the metal stairs to the level above. "Skye?" she called, her heart hammering, eyes already welling up. She went over the knee knocker and into Primary Flight Control, looking around the small compartment at the uppermost tip of the aircraft carrier.

It was empty.

She approached the open hatch leading out to the catwalk overlooking the flight deck. It was still dark, but the sky was lightening a bit. There was Skye, her body seated on the metal gridwork facing away, legs dangling and arms draped over the pipe railing, head slumped.

"Oh . . . Skye," she whispered, walking out to her. "I'm so sorry."

"Why?" Skye asked, lifting her head. "I got him." She gestured with her pistol at the body of an officer lying nearby on the catwalk with a fresh bullet hole in his head.

Angie sobbed and laughed and dropped to her knees, hugging the young woman from behind. "I thought . . . oh, I thought . . ."

Skye hugged at the arms encircling her. "The shot—I didn't think about that." She turned and looked at Angie. Her skin was the color of lead, her left eye a milky orb, but otherwise she appeared fine.

Angie looked her up and down rapidly. "You're okay? What about the fever?"

Skye shook her head. "I've been waiting for it all night. No fever, no symptoms." She held up her bandaged arm. "This hurts a lot; the bastard bit me hard. I hope it doesn't get infected. Human mouths are dirty."

Angie laughed and hugged her again, crying. "That we can deal with."

Skye let herself enjoy the hug, and felt a twinge in her chest she hadn't felt in a long time, a good twinge. She pulled away slowly. "My headaches are gone," she said, then lifted her left hand. It was steady, without a hint of tremble. "That's gone too. Angie, I haven't felt this good in . . . in I don't remember."

Angie stared at the hand, at the girl, and suddenly realized that the gravel quality of her voice was all but gone. Skye had a nice voice. "Are you sure?"

Skye nodded. "I know my body. I'm fine. If it were going to hit me, it would have happened by now, right?"

"I don't want to . . . to get too hopeful," Angie said, "but . . ."

"I think I'm immune. The blood exposure, maybe it was like—" Skye waved a hand, frustrated. "Like a vaccine? Maybe the slow burn worked like that. I don't know, but maybe it's like a childhood disease; once you get it, you can't get it again."

"Rosa might be able to tell us," Angie said.

Skye nodded. "I might still turn if I get killed, I can't tell, but that thing had to have given me a full dose with that bite." She smiled. "Nothing."

Angie liked this smile. It wasn't like the crooked, sarcastic lip curls she had seen. This one was real.

They climbed to their feet, and Skye holstered her pistol. Below them, the walking dead of the *Nimitz* had once more begun to crowd the flight deck, coming up from below.

"Ready to go to work?" Skye asked.

Angie loaded a fresh magazine into the Galil. "You bet your ass."

Skye smiled again, and it made the other woman's heart soar, compelling her to give another big hug. Then Skye touched Angie's arm. "Now that I know they can't infect me, I want a machete as soon as we can find one." Her eyes hardened. "It's fucking *on*."

There was enough starlight, and the quality of their rifle optics combined with their elevated shooting position helped in their work. Nothing that moved on the deck could escape them, and with the superstructure's location just aft of midships, there was nothing they couldn't reach. Brass tinkled down through the levels of catwalk grid and spun through space as below, bodies crumpled and fell. At various points around the flight deck, where stairways led up onto the perimeter, corpses lurched up into the gunfire one after another, bullets dropping them flat or spinning them over the side to sag motionless in the safety netting.

By the time the sun began to peek over the Oakland foothills, their rifles and bandoliers were empty except for pistol ammunition. On the deck below lay two hundred fifty fresh kills.

The women slung their rifles across their backs and checked their sidearms, their next move a room-to-room hunt down through the superstructure. There had been armed sailors who had tried to prevent the ship from falling, and although they had failed, they would still be around, along with their weapons and ammunition. Angie and Skye would find them.

As they left the catwalk and reentered the ship, neither woman looked toward Alameda, and neither one saw it fall to the dead.

WRATH

THIRTY-FOUR

The sky was a cool pink as the sun approached, and beneath its pale glow, more than ten thousand of the walking dead flowed silently down the access road beside the seaplane lagoon and into the mouth of the main pier. Close to the end of her overnight watch, a young woman named America, positioned as a lookout on the stern of a World War II frigate, had wrapped herself in a blanket to ward off the chill, and nodded off. She was asleep when the horde began to move, asleep when they turned the corner and started down the pier, and she was only just coming around when half a dozen drifters made their way up the ship's gangplank and found her at the stern.

She didn't even get a chance to scream.

Among the dead were Alameda natives, drifters from Oakland and Sacramento and some that had crossed the Bay Bridge, along with the first of many that had torn down the fences of NAS Lemoore. Among these was a fighter jock nicknamed Rocker. His flight suit was black with old blood and ragged from many miles of travel, and his head flopped to one side.

Vladimir Yurish was up early, as was his custom, and he stood on the deck of the same vintage destroyer where only last night Maya had been, staring out at the *Nimitz* just as she had done. Vlad stood at the bow, which pointed toward the open bay, and quietly smoked a cigarette as he gazed upon the first touches of light on water. The *Nimitz* remained little more than a silhouette. A light, cool breeze tugged at his flight suit and ruffled the hair of the small boy beside him.

Ben, three years old, stood beside the pilot with his small hands gripping the wire railing encircling the deck, a mere sprout beside the towering oak that was the pilot. He was looking out at the water as well.

Vlad had planned a peaceful morning by himself before the others awoke. When he crawled from his sleeping bag, he walked away stretching and swinging his arms, trying to work out the stiffness from sleeping on hard ground. He quickly found, however, that he was not the first one up. Small Ben was seated alone on the pier thirty feet away from the others, playing with a little blue-and-yellow plastic truck and making engine noises. Vlad glanced back to Sophia, knowing she would panic over the boy's absence. She was motionless in her bag. *Let her sleep,* he thought, and knelt beside the child.

"What sort of truck do you have?" Vlad asked, not expecting much of a response. Sophia had told him about the boy's rescue from the street in front of the Alameda firehouse, and how Angie had run at the dead and laid waste to them with the ferocity of a she-bear defending a cub. Sophia knew nothing about the boy, and he spoke very little. Ben had taken to Vladimir at once, however, sitting in the big Russian's lap without invitation and handing over a book to be read, or standing on Vlad's legs and tugging on the man's protruding ears with his little hands, laughing as if they were the most delightful two things in the world. Vlad put on a show of patient endurance, but he somehow always ended up near the boy, and Ben often wandered into Vlad without seeming to notice, casually wrapping a small arm around one tall leg. Sometimes Vlad would take great long steps with the boy clinging to his leg like a small chimp, and it never failed to make Ben laugh.

"It's a blue truck," said Ben. "And yellow."

"Yes, but do you know what it does?"

Ben nodded. "It's a dumb fuck."

The Russian's eyes widened. "A *what*?"

"Dumb fuck." Ben showed him how the back tilted as if pouring out a load.

Vladimir burst out with a laugh. "A *dump truck*."

Ben looked up and nodded, smiling as if Vlad might not be as bright as he appeared. Then he drove the truck up the pilot's leg. "*Rrrrrrrr . . .*"

Vlad let him play a bit, then asked Ben if he wanted to go for a walk. He did. They headed up onto the deck of the destroyer, Vlad careful to go slow and take small steps to accommodate quick but short little legs.

Now, at the rail with a fresh sea breeze making Vlad wonder if he should have brought the boy's jacket, Ben looked up and said, "*J* is a letter."

Vlad nodded solemnly. "Yes, it is."

"So is *B*. I know some *B* words." The child bounced on the balls of his feet. "*Banana. Bird* is a *B* word. *Big*."

The Russian leaned on the wire railing and grinned down at his little companion.

"*Jelly* starts with *J*. And *juice*. And *giggle*."

"That is a *G* word," the pilot said, making the boy pause and look at him for a moment.

"Is *good* a *G* word?" When Vladimir said it was, Ben smiled. "*Giggle*. I said that. *Go. Google*. That's a computer."

Vlad was looking the wrong way, down at Ben, so he didn't see the horde moving along the pier. He couldn't hear the shuffling feet or whispery gasps over the wind and the song.

"*Dog* is a *D* word," said Ben. "*Danny*. He's at my school. . . ."

The dead flowed past the destroyer's gangplank, moving steadily toward the row of parked vehicles and, beyond them, stacks of plastic totes and dozens of shapes still in their sleeping bags.

"... *Dig. Daddy* ..."

Vladimir closed his eyes for a moment, thinking of his daughter, Lita, coming home from preschool, proud of a new word or song she had learned. She would dance in the kitchen of their tiny apartment, twirling in circles as she sang. His throat tightened, and he wondered when the memories would stop hurting. He thought never. Then he noticed Ben was no longer reciting words he knew, and opened his eyes.

Ben pointed past him. "Monsters."

Vlad spun and saw the horde, thousands strong, about to reach the vehicles. The group slept not fifty feet beyond them. Knowing there was no time for anything else, he jerked the Browning pistol from his shoulder holster—he had upgraded to a bigger frame and heavier caliber—and fired a shot in the air. Ben huddled tight against his leg.

The group was startled awake, sitting upright in sleeping bags, heads turning, seeing the oncoming dead. Then the screaming started.

The creatures at the head of the mass reacted to the screams and sudden movement, and broke into a gallop. People scrambled for their weapons, mothers snatched crying children from sleeping bags, and a few people, those closest to the wall of drifters, panicked and tried to crab-walk backward, tangled in their bags and shrieking.

The dead fell on these unfortunates first, tearing them apart.

Vladimir lifted Ben in his left arm, his right hand gripping the pistol. "We will be moving fast and quiet, my little friend," he said, his voice low. "Can you be quiet?"

Ben nodded and buried his face in Vladimir's shoulder, small arms hugging his neck tightly. Vlad moved, not toward the destroyer's gangplank, for he knew they would be coming to the sound of his pistol shots, and instead jogged down the deck on the side of the ship facing the lagoon. He kept the vessel's long superstructure between them and the horde, staying out of their sight. It took less than three minutes to reach the stern, where a battery of aft-mounted cannon pointed back toward the frigate where the lookout should have been. He crept beneath the long barrels and looked toward the gangplank.

A dozen drifters stumbled up the ramp and onto the deck, dead eyes searching. Seven wandered away from him, toward the bow and where he had been. Five headed in his direction. He could hear them rasping, whining, and in the background, gunfire rippled among the screams.

Shit. He glanced around the deck, looking for something they could hide behind until the dead went past, but the deck was bare, stripped of anything that might trip or impede tourists. Vlad back-tracked down the starboard side, hunting for a way into the super-structure. Ben hung on tight and didn't make a sound.

He found a hatch. It was locked.

Shuffling footsteps on the deck behind him.

Vlad moved farther down the ship. Another hatch. Welded shut. The screaming was climbing like an out-of-control choir, and there wasn't as much gunfire now. The pilot ran for another hatch, this one at the center of the ship. Tugging. Welded like the previous one.

The dead that had gone to the bow discovered this side of the ship, coming around the end of the forward gun battery. They spotted their prey, snarled, and hurried down the starboard side. To the rear, the other five came into view and slouched toward the man and the little boy.

Vlad looked back and forth between the two groups, hefting the weight of the Browning. It was a close-range weapon, and he was no marksman. They would have to be *very* close, and even if he scored a head shot with all five of his remaining rounds, he would be empty before they all went down and would never get the chance to reload.

He thought about the water below. If he lost his grip on Ben, the boy would drown.

He thought about a bullet for Ben, and one for himself.

Never.

And it was that last thought that made him bare his teeth. *God,* he thought, *it is Vladimir again. We will not speak again, you sadistic son of a bitch. But I want you to know that you will not take another child from me. Fuck you, Groundhog-Seven signing off.*

Vladimir hugged Ben close and strode toward the group of five, the Browning coming up. *BLAM. BLAM-BLAM-BLAM-BLAM.*

CLICK.

With the slide locked back on an empty chamber, Air Lieutenant Vladimir Yurish stepped over the bodies of five fallen drifters, each one down with a perfect, black-edged hole in the forehead. He walked to the stern, ejecting the empty magazine and slamming a fresh one home.

"You killed the monsters," Ben breathed, peeking over the man's shoulder.

The Russian's face was hard, and yet tears filled his eyes, his voice a rumble between clenched teeth. "Papa will kill *all* the monsters, little one."

He rounded the aft gun battery and headed down the port side, toward the gangplank, right arm fully extended. A drifter in a janitor's uniform walked stiffly onto the deck.

BLAM. The creature fell.

Vlad reached the ramp, where a teenage girl, whose face would have been torn completely away except for the multitude of piercings holding it together, was walking up the ramp.

BLAM. The head shot spun her right over the gangplank's rail and dropped her into the oily water.

Ben hid his face in Vladimir's neck and began to whimper. "Shh, little one," Vlad said, descending the gangplank, "you are safe in my arms." Below them, a river of the walking dead moved by left to right, an impassable current of teeth and death.

H old the line!" Margaret shouted, standing with Elson and Big Jerry to her right and left, Maya and a few others strung out to the sides. Pistol, shotgun, and rifle fire poured into the wall of the dead as they neared their prey, clutching at air, mouths hung open and moaning. Bodies fell, but not enough.

Ahead of them, the white van from the senior center groaned and tipped sideways from the press of bodies. It let out a long creak and fell onto its side, windows exploding. The black *Angie's Armory* van moved as well, sliding at an angle as the dead forced their way forward, tires dragging across the pier as it was pushed aside, and then leaned before toppling over the edge to land on its roof in the waters between the pier and the *Hornet*, sinking quickly in a gurgle of bubbles.

"There's too many!" shouted Elson, feeding shells into his shotgun, several slipping through his fingers.

"Stand your ground!" the small Asian woman bellowed, pumping rounds into galloping creatures. Some were knocked back by center-mass hits only to rise again, while others were exterminated with faces full of double-aught steel buckshot.

Behind them, everyone was boarding the service barge that had rescued many of them from the Oakland Middle Harbor days ago. Older kids jumped to the deck while adults handed smaller children down before jumping themselves. A pair of hippies helped Larraine and her oxygen bottle to the splintered deck, then two more arrived to help with her husband, Gene, nearly immobilized by his MS. Some of the adults and older kids stood on the barge and used the edge of the wharf as a battlement, firing into the endless mass of oncoming corpses.

Margaret spotted a female zombie half in and out of a sleeping bag, crawling forward by pulling itself along with its hands, teeth snapping. She and the dead woman had shared coffee and stories of their pre-plague life only last night. A breath hitched in Margaret's chest as she aimed her shotgun, but Maya's nine-millimeter pistol did the job first, a single round through the eye.

Maya knew the woman too, and had grown up with her in her father's traveling Family.

On the left side, a gang of galloping corpses broke through the gunfire. Elson turned and fired, blowing one off its feet, and then the rest swarmed him, carrying him to the ground. Snarling, ripping, and biting blended with his screams as he thrashed beneath them.

Margaret saw it, cried out, and began firing at the tangle of bodies devouring her friend.

Big Jerry grabbed her arm. "It's over! Get on the barge!" He pulled hard, dragging her back toward the end of the pier, pushing her to the edge, forcing her to jump. A rotting corpse naked from the waist down galloped at Big Jerry's back, lips peeled back from its teeth. Maya shot it in the side of the head, and its momentum carried it off into the water.

Jerry yelled for those on the barge to "Stand clear!" and hurled his three-hundred-plus pounds off the wharf, landing on the deck with a tremendous thud and a loud *POP* that curled him into a groaning ball as he clutched his knee. Maya leaped down behind him and spun, pistol up and ready, putting a bullet in the face of the first drifter to appear at the edge.

The diesel engine fired, and others had already cast off the mooring lines. Half the people on deck pushed against the mossy surface of the wharf to help the barge move off, while the others began firing at the horde as it reached the end of the pier.

Zombies fell to gunfire. Dozens staggered off into the water, sinking quickly and each replaced at once by another corpse falling into the water. A handful flopped down onto the deck before the barge could gain much distance. More screaming as people tried to scatter from the creatures slowly climbing to their feet.

Maya snatched the handle of a yellow ice climber's pick from an open Rubbermaid tote and waded in, her face contorted by a silent war cry. She planted the pick in a head, kicked the body free, buried it in another. A drifter came in on her side, close enough to bite, but the young man with the pregnant wife rammed the barrel of a shotgun under its jawbone and blew its head apart.

People scrambled clear as Maya swung her pick in a deadly arc, through an ear, through an eye, overhand and down through the crown of a rotting head. It ended quickly, and the deaf girl stood in the midst of a slaughter, chest heaving, wiping blood off her face with a sleeve. Members of her Family moved in quickly to clean her off with disinfectant wipes, while others rolled the bodies off into the water. Maya never let go of the ice-climbing pick.

The barge chugged steadily away from the pier, and many of those aboard were quickly reminded of a scene they had witnessed before: hundreds of reaching corpses stumbling off the end of the pier and sinking beneath the surface, still trying to get to the escaping prey.

Once the barge was away, Margaret and Maya knelt beside Big Jerry as a few others gathered around. The part-time stand-up comic cracked a joke about fat track stars, his grin failing to conceal the pain of his blown knee. They made him as comfortable as they could.

It was quickly decided that returning to Alameda, any part of it, would be impossible. They would head for the *Nimitz*. On the deck, Sophia moved through the refugees making a head count. They had lost four adults, including Elson, and thankfully no children.

Another woman was doing the count with her. "No," she said, "your count's off. We're short."

Sophia counted again. *Okay, the woman was right, she was off by two, but Ben was with Vlad, and Vlad was . . .*

Sophia began to scream.

Vladimir crouched on the destroyer's gangplank, looking at the moving horde. The drifters on the ship behind him were coming, and he knew he had only seconds before he and his small companion were discovered. He saw that the zombies below weren't really packed in shoulder-to-shoulder, belly-to-back as they appeared from above. There were gaps, and if he moved fast enough, he just might make it.

Vladimir hugged Ben and ran for a destination on the wharf,

sprinting into the horde, weaving like a ball carrier in one of the American football games he had come to enjoy, as snarls surrounded him, bodies lunged, and fingers clutched at his flight suit.

The group had left the car out on the wharf, alone and abandoned. He knew what it represented to them and saw the way Angie's lip curled every time she looked at it. Because of their distaste they had, intentionally or unintentionally, separated themselves from it. Now, Maxie's eighties-era Cadillac resembled a white-and-chrome island along the edge of a river of corpses.

Vladimir tore himself away from a drifter's grip, dodged left, then right, shouldered another aside, and reached the car. He tore open the passenger door and hurled Ben inside, then scrambled after him.

Hands caught at his legs.

An arm encircled his waist.

Vladimir turned, lying half on the seat, and shoved the muzzle of the Browning into a snapping mouth, blowing its brains across half a dozen of its kind. The arm dropped from his waist. Another two bullets and his legs were free, and he hauled on the door handle.

A drifter pulled back, trying to rip the door from his grasp. Ben was screaming, curled up on the floorboards. Vlad kicked the zombie in the chest and it fell back. Teeth sank into the rubber sole of his boot, and he kicked that one away too. More pressed in, and with a curse bellowed in Russian, Vladimir slammed the door shut and slapped down the peg lock.

The driver's door creaked open behind him.

Vlad rolled on the seat and brought up the Browning, blasting until the slide locked back, clearing the door. He pulled it shut, locking it, then checked to make sure the back doors were locked. They were.

Fists thundered against the sheet metal, covering it in dents, and horrid faces pressed against the glass, teeth biting and leaving scratches. It sounded like being inside an orchestra drum.

The back window cracked. A side window burst into a cloudy mass of shattered glass, still hanging in its frame.

The Cadillac lurched and slid a foot toward the edge of the pier.

Vlad pulled himself into the driver's seat, reaching for the ignition, keeping his promise and refusing to pray to a sadist who wasn't listening anyway. He found the keys dangling and started the well-cared-for engine.

The car slid another foot, tires at the edge now.

Vlad had never met the man and knew he never would, but he could tell Maxie had treated this automobile well. Now he would see just how much punishment this classic example of American manufacturing could take as he hauled the wheel over and accelerated into a squealing U-turn. Bodies thumped down the sides, banged off the grille, rolled across the hood, and streaked the windshield with gore. The right tires went up and over what felt like a row of logs, making the suspension twist, forcing Vlad to slow down—if they became high-centered it was over—and then bumping back to the ground with a bounce. The Caddy was pointed back toward the access road to the naval air station, and a wall of the walking dead was before him.

Ben crawled onto the seat and tucked into a tight little ball next to the Russian pilot. Vlad gripped the wheel with two hands and said, "Sing me your song again, little one."

He stomped the accelerator.

THIRTY-FIVE

Rosa went in first, her pistol held in a two-handed grip. Her first impression was of something out of a carnival's haunted house: white walls and divider curtains splashed with red, a white tile floor strewn with corpses and streaked with blood, a stuttering strobe overhead. Even on a reduced reactor, *Nimitz* kept the sick bay fully supplied with power, and every light bar would have been lit if not for the battle damage. Now, fluorescent tubes were shattered, metal housings dangled from the ceiling by conduit, and several lights flickered on and off. A few remained intact, which only served to deepen the shadows.

Every footstep sent empty brass casings skittering across the tile, and Rosa moved carefully, watching the decomposing bodies on the floor for movement. Tommy, Lilly, and Eve stayed close behind her, turning on flashlights.

The aircraft carrier's sick bay was like a hospital wing, with waiting rooms and records compartments, X-ray and surgical suites, a full pharmacy, and nurses' stations. To the right was a line of curtained ER cubicles, and up ahead was an eighty-bed hospital ward. At sea, six doctors and a surgeon were assisted by an army of corpsmen and enlisted orderlies, handling everything from garden-variety lacerations and fevers to ruptured appendixes, fractures, and even industrial accidents. In wartime, the facility stood ready to take on combat casualties.

It was the sick bay and the presence of everything she would need to care for the sick and wounded—sterile instruments, bandages and splints, medication, and a lab—that had convinced Rosa to support braving a warship infested with the dead. This facility, combined with someone with medical skills, could be the deciding factor between life and death for the survivors, not only now but in the future. Now that she was here, the medic was determined to take and hold the place.

Combat had taken place here, Rosa thought. Counters and walls were pocked with bullet holes, blood pressure and EKG machines were overturned and shattered, beds were flipped over, and curtains had been pulled down by frantic hands.

Most of the dead were dressed in scrubs; a few were in hospital gowns, and one was in a white lab coat. Near a tangle of bullet-riddled bodies, the corpse of a woman in blue camo sat propped against a wall gripping an assault rifle. She wore body armor and a bandolier of magazines and was covered in bites, one ear dangling by a string of sinew, her dead eyes the color of pewter. A single bullet had pierced her forehead.

Rosa motioned at the armed corpse, and Lilly went to relieve it of its weapons and ammo.

It had been a massacre, Rosa thought as she eased deeper into the hospital. But who had done the killing? How had it started? Something banged against hollow metal down a corridor to her left, and Rosa's pistol snapped in that direction, Eve following with her flashlight. Open doorways in a darkened hall, blood-slicked tile and stillness in that direction. Behind them, Tommy parted bloody curtains with the barrel of his shotgun, peeking into ER cubicles.

"We're not alone," Eve whispered.

"Not since we came on board," Rosa replied.

The two women moved slowly up the hallway, and when the banging came again, they froze, holding their breath. Then they moved forward. As they came upon an open doorway on the right, Eve put her flashlight inside.

"Holy shit," she said.

Rosa turned with her pistol and looked to where Eve's light was pointing. It was a small supply room, with shelves of neatly ordered items stacked in rows: folded sheets and blankets, hospital gowns and robes wrapped in plastic, bedpans, toiletries, slippers, and towels. Several folded wheelchairs leaned against a wall near stacks of red plastic bio buckets. Heaped on the floor in the center of the room, violating the sterile order of the place, was a pile of weapons, boots, and body armor, all of it covered in blood. There were ammo vests and bandoliers, boot knives, grenades, a backpack radio, assault rifles, pistols, and submachine guns. The blood had dried, leaving it all coated in a rusty smear. It looked as if everything had simply been dumped.

It didn't look Navy to Rosa; these were infantry tools, and the odd, personalized assortment of weapons indicated that it was not from a regular unit. The body armor was a digital black-and-gray pattern, as were the backpacks. Rosa looked at the weapons and ammunition and sighed. They had been down to their last magazines.

Bare, galloping feet slapping at the tile made her jerk left. Rushing out of the gloom was a bare-chested zombie muscled like a weight lifter, wearing black-and-gray camo pants and a black bandana. A skull with crossed daggers was tattooed on his left pectoral, the letters S.O.G. inked beneath it.

A Navy SEAL.

Rosa fired, two, three, four times. Two shots went wild, one grazed bone where the thing's right arm had been stripped of flesh and muscle, and the fourth slammed into its groin. It didn't slow, and let out a long rasp.

Eve emerged from the storeroom, put her light on it, and screamed.

Tommy's shotgun went off back in the ER, three shots in succession.

The dead SEAL was twenty feet away, then ten feet. . . .

Rosa fired and the nine-millimeter slug punched through the SEAL's cheekbone. It didn't stop. She fired again, grazing the side of its head, and then it was on her, and she fired point-blank. The zombie's weight slammed into her and threw her to the floor, dark ichor spewing out of the creature's mouth and onto the tiles beside her, oozing out of the final bullet wound through the bridge of its nose.

Eve started to pull the dead SEAL off the downed medic as a corpse in bloody scrubs staggered toward them from the dark corridor. The woman let go of the heavy, limp body and tucked her flashlight in her armpit, racking the shotgun—ejecting a perfectly good shell—and firing. She had to do it three times before her buckshot hit the mark and put the thing down. By then, Rosa had shimmied out from beneath the SEAL on her own.

The medic went into the storeroom and soon emerged with a second nine-millimeter pistol belted around her waist, a full ammo pouch of pistol mags, two bandoliers of rifle magazines, and an M4, the same assault rifle she had carried overseas. She and Eve returned to the center of the sick bay.

Lilly was sitting in a plastic chair wearing a dead woman's body armor, weighted down with her gear and looking pale. She gave Rosa a brief smile, then staggered off the chair and threw up. Eve went to her.

Tommy stood nearby with his shotgun. "I got two more down that way," he said, indicating the direction of the hospital ward. "They looked like patients. I expected a lot more drifters in here, being as it's a hospital."

"It's been a while," said Rosa. "They've spread through the ship. This was probably the site of the initial outbreak. Any hospital would have been the scene of tremendous virus transmission. It would have gotten out of control after it broke here."

Rosa told Tommy about the weapons cache, and he headed in to re-arm himself. Eve first got Lilly calmed down, then reported that she was happy with the shotgun and would take Tommy's spare shells when he upgraded to an assault rifle. Lilly didn't say anything, just nodded that she was okay.

Turning in a slow circle, taking it all in, Rosa was even more convinced that this was where it began, at least for *Nimitz*. Why should this hospital have been different than any other? Wounded personnel had come on board, likely SEALs from what she had seen, which was a common occurrence with aircraft carriers, and they were infected. Medics would have stripped them of their gear so they could be treated, dumping it all in one place so a gunner's mate or master-at-arms could collect it later. The SEALs would have turned, started biting. Their victims would have turned. Security would arrive to find the place overrun, the dead already spilling out of the sick bay and into the rest of the ship. It would have been dominoes after that.

"We need to clear this area," Rosa told the others. We need to lock it down and make sure nothing else is in here with us."

It wasn't until that moment she realized neither Xavier nor Brother Peter was with them.

The door marked *CHAPEL* closed silently behind him, and Xavier walked into a nondescript room with rows of chairs arranged to accommodate about twenty people. Cabinets lined one wall, and a pair of lecterns stood in a corner, one with a simple cross on its face, the other with the Star of David. The walls were unadorned, and as the priest moved to the front of the room he realized that, aside from the admiral's quarters, this was the only other carpeted compartment he had seen. A single fluorescent bar was the only source of light in the room.

He leaned the fire axe against a chair and took a seat in the front row, leaning forward and resting his arms on his knees. The wall before him was blank. He assumed, with the multidenominational nature of the crew, that the celebrant for each faith would have his articles secured in one of the cabinets, bringing them out for the service.

Xavier clasped his scarred hands and lowered his head, closing his eyes. Dozens of prayers and litanies came to mind, meticulously memorized scripture passages, all quickly rejected. His shoulders sagged and he let out a deep sigh.

"I'm not sure I even have the right to speak with you, Lord," he began, his voice soft, "so if it's all right with you, I'll speak plainly. I won't blame you for not listening. I'd be surprised if you did, but . . ."

He was silent for a while, then said, "I want to be able to give them strength, to give them hope, but I'm so very tired. I need you, Lord. I have no right to ask, but I'm asking." Xavier looked at the blank wall, his eyes moist. "I'm a sinner and a killer, and I broke faith with you when I should have placed myself in your hands. I'm so very sorry for that."

He was quiet again, thinking of what it truly meant to be a priest. For much of his faith's history, clerics had sanctioned and planned wars from afar, participated up close, even killed alongside their faithful warriors. All in God's name. It was a part of his church's history that few people were proud of, but it was their history nonetheless. Had those priests been forgiven, they who shed blood? Theirs had been a different time, a different world. Was this not a new world as well, demanding a different sort of priest? A warrior? Or was that just a convenient rationalization? Perhaps, now that the world had gone to hell, it was more important than ever to stand as a symbol for peace, to serve as a model of temperance and love. But how long would such a priest survive in this new world? And who was he to make such a decision?

Xavier looked at the blank wall again. It had nothing to say.

"I've taken lives, and nothing can justify that. But I know that I can still lift others up with your strength. I still want to be a priest,

Lord, and if you'll allow it, I know I can." He lowered his head. "I won't pretend to understand why you've chosen to destroy your world and your children, but I've been angry with you for it, angry and faithless. Let me be a shepherd in this new world. Grant me forgiveness, help me to make wise decisions. I beg that you not punish those around me because of my weakness. Help me to be the priest you need, Lord, whether a lamb or a lion. Let me renew my faith."

Xavier pressed his forehead to his clenched hands and wept.

Oh, listen to this bullshit," God said. He was sitting in a chair at the back of the room, legs crossed as He picked a piece of lint off His uniform trousers. *"Bargaining, simpering. It makes me sick."*

Brother Peter used his fingertips to ease the door shut, then stood in the center aisle next to his savior. There were no more doubts about hallucinations. God was here beside him, as real as any man. "Do you hear his words?" the minister asked.

"Of course. He's sitting right there." God mocked him in a falsetto voice. *"Don't punish them for my failings, let me be your lamb."* He shook His head. *"He makes me want to puke. Hey, Petey, at least you've got some backbone, man."*

Brother Peter looked around at the simple room, intentionally lacking the grandeur and icons of many places of worship. Military order, but with it came a simple purity. "Do you live here?" Brother Peter asked.

The Air Force shrink looked up at him. *"What the hell are you talking about?"*

"It's just so . . . plain," the minister said. "It doesn't need gold and statues and choirs. Can you hear us better in a place like this?"

God sighed. *"Okay, let's just settle down, Pete. Don't get all 'Filled with Glory.' It's a fucking conference room shared by half a dozen faiths who smile at one another and have nothing but hatred for each other."*

God reached up and snapped His fingers sharply in Brother Peter's face. *"Focus."*

"I've broken away from the others," Peter said, his eyes locked straight ahead. "The priest is a threat, and I need to kill him."

God nodded.

Peter's eyes were glassy. "I'm going down to the magazines. I'm going to find the nukes, wire them together, ignite your holy wrath. Praise God." A trickle of drool escaped unnoticed from the corner of his mouth.

The Air Force shrink stood and clapped Brother Peter on the shoulder. *"Good, let's get to it. And by the way"*—God looked back to the front of the room—*"he can hear you."*

Brother Peter blinked rapidly, as if coming out of a half doze. God was gone, and the big, black priest was on his feet not far away, mouth hung open and staring at him. Peter realized his conversation, at least the last part of it, had been spoken aloud.

"Uhh . . ." Peter said, locking eyes with Xavier. Then he pulled a grenade from a jacket pocket and yanked the pin, letting the spoon fly. He dropped it on the carpet at his feet, then bolted out the chapel door.

Xavier was diving when the blast and shrapnel tore the chapel apart.

THIRTY-SIX

Mercy gave Chief Liebs her M4 and what little ammo she had left, as he was the professional marksman. The others spread around their weapons, and everyone supplemented from the big knife racks in the galley. The chief took point, with Evan behind him holding a flashlight and his Sig Sauer.

Liebs advanced with the rifle to his shoulder, muzzle moving everywhere he turned his head. A pair of sailors staggered out of a hatch in the corridor just beyond the mess hall, and the chief put them down with a fast pair of shots, barely pausing as he moved past, setting a swift pace. The others peered through doorways and closed hatches as they went by, but the Navy man was all focus, moving forward.

Calvin fired four times to their rear, dropping a cook and a jet engine mechanic. Liebs killed four more corpses that tumbled into the corridor from a narrow ladderway, finishing them before they could disentangle themselves at the bottom of the stairs.

The group passed through a pair of knee knockers, then came to a four-way intersection with a set of stairs tucked into an alcove to one side, stairs that only descended. The decapitated and decomposing body of an officer was stretched out on the gray tile, his head a few feet away. The eyes rolled and a blackened tongue probed past its teeth.

"That's nasty," said Stone, booting the head down a passageway like a soccer ball.

"No, *that* was nasty," said Mercy.

Chief Liebs held a finger to his lips and crept toward the stairway as the others kept watch down the four corridors. Evan moved up with him, holding his breath, and both looked over the railing. They heard the moans, a low hum coming up out of complete darkness. The depth of the sound indicated that there were many of them down there. Chief Liebs motioned Evan back from the rail, and the group came together in the intersection.

"Let's just go past this," said Dakota, and Juju nodded with him.

"We can't," said the chief, pointing to the stairway. "That's the only way to reach the armory."

Frightened glances from the others.

"Those stairs lead down to a good-sized compartment, sort of like a lobby," the chief said. "To the right is the armory door, with a small service window about four feet to one side. Straight ahead is an office and quarters for the master-at-arms, and left of that is the brig. To the far left is a berthing compartment for gunner's mates, an office for the chiefs, and then chief's quarters."

He explained that the area should be well lit, even on reduced reactor power, and speculated that a firefight might have damaged the electrical panels. He repeated that the stairway—he called it a ladder—was the only way in or out of the section.

"There's twenty or more down there," Liebs said.

"Do we really have to do this?" Juju asked.

The chief looked at Evan, who said, "We're out of ammo and out of time. Even if we passed, we don't have enough bullets to reach daylight again."

"The armory will have everything we need," said the chief. "My men are all trained in basic rifle, shotgun, and pistol. All of us together, plus what's waiting down there, have a chance to take back the ship."

"If we can get to it," said Evan.

Liebs let out a deep breath. "Yes, if we can get to it. I'll go down first."

Off to one side, Stone laughed softly, shaking his head. When the others looked at him he said, "Don't take this wrong, but you guys are really stupid."

Calvin grinned. He had known the boy since he was born. "Enlighten us, wise one."

Stone explained his simple but effective idea. It was brilliant.

They all had to admit that the kid was right, and even Chief Liebs gave him a pat on the back and told him he would have made a fine sailor. It was Stone who snapped them out of their frontal assault state-of-mind, and even showed each of them where they should stand in order to carry out his plan.

Once everyone was in place, Stone said, "Just call me Bait." He jumped halfway down the stairs and shouted, "Dinnertime!" at the drifters waiting in the darkness. Stone backed up the stairs. "C'mon, sexy, that's it, good little zombie. Come on. . . ."

The dead scrambled over one another in their rush to follow the live meat up the stairs. The first drifter to set both feet on the tile of the intersection caught a butcher knife through the ear. The body was still stiffening from its brain being pierced when one of Liebs's sailors rushed it from the other side, half tackling, half carrying the body away and dumping it in a corridor. The chief prepared his knife again, and another sailor stepped into tackle position.

Stone stood ten feet away from the top of the stairs, hooting and tormenting the dead, even turning and smacking his behind at them. The drifters were so fixed on the difficult task of first climbing stairs and then getting to the lively meal that was so very close that they didn't stand a chance against the chief and his butcher knife.

One by one the walking dead climbed up the narrow ladderway to their doom. The chief broke three knives in the process, instantly rearmed by Mercy standing behind him with two fistfuls of fresh blades from the galley. Dakota and Evan joined in the tackling process when the dead came too fast and too close for the sailors to keep up. Calvin saw none of it, facing away from the action so he and his assault rifle could watch the corridors.

It was a smart move. Stone's howling and catcalls echoed down the steel passages, and called to the dead. Calvin took careful aim and squeezed, well aware of the thin supply of bullets, determined to make his shots count. He fired on corpses up the center, down to the left, over on the right, pivoting back and forth. Shuffling figures in blackened uniforms emerged from the darkness, sliding along walls and filling the halls with echoing cries.

The pile of brain-stabbed drifters now nearly filled the opening to the right corridor, limp bodies spilling into the intersection. Live drifters, attracted to all the sound, clawed at the mound from the other side, unable to get through. Calvin didn't bother shooting these, grateful that his area of responsibility was now effectively down to three hallways instead of four.

His rifle clicked on an empty magazine. "I'm out," he shouted.

Dakota handed him a shotgun. Two minutes later Calvin called it empty as well.

"Use the M4," Liebs yelled, stabbing a man he had known for two years. He tried not to think about it, about the fact that he knew everyone coming up out of the darkness, people he had laughed with, whose stories of family were as familiar as his own. The growing fatigue in his right arm and shoulder was a welcome distraction. "I'm going to need a relief soon," he called.

Evan took a butcher knife from Mercy and handed her his Sig. "Give this to Calvin."

He was about to tap Liebs on the shoulder when the chief lunged with his knife. The drifter, moving on a fractured leg, abruptly staggered sideways, and the blade cut a neat slice through its scalp but didn't pierce the head. The bosun's mate was already running, and he grabbed the live drifter around the waist, hoisting it, preparing to run it to the pile.

The drifter snarled, grabbed the young man's head, and bit his ear off.

The bosun's mate screamed and tried to throw the wriggling creature away, but it hung on and bit a large chunk of meat out of the boy's cheek.

Mercy dropped her knives, stepped forward, and with Evan's pistol shot the drifter at point-blank range. The wet blast out the back hit Dakota in the side of the face, and he staggered away, wretching. The bosun's mate flung the body to the floor and clamped his hands to his savaged face, stumbled to a wall, and collapsed.

"Keep up the relay!" Chief Liebs shouted, stabbing the next creature to emerge from below. His petty officer second class moved in, hauling the corpse out of the way.

"There's way more than twenty," Stone yelled.

"No shit, kid," the chief growled.

It seemed to last for hours, but in just over ten minutes it was done. A few more pistol shots from Calvin cleared the halls, and there were no more drifters coming up out of the dark. Flashlights revealed none on the stairs or in sight at the bottom.

Dakota was in a panic, scrubbing blood and brains off his face, and Chief Liebs went to his wounded man, a boy, really, kneeling beside him. The kid pressed his hands to his ear and cheek, blood seeping between the fingers. "I don't want to die, Guns," the bosun's mate cried, looking up and trembling. Mercy knelt down too, trying to replace the boy's hands with gauze pads. "Don't let me die," the sailor said.

Chief Liebs gripped his shoulders. "You're going to be fine, shipmate. Don't you doubt it."

"But the b-b-bite!"

"You're going to be fine," Liebs repeated. "You just stay quiet and hang on. Your chief's going to look after you."

Evan saw the strained look on the chief's face as he turned away.

"We need to get down there," Liebs said, his voice cracking. He took the Sig Sauer, the last weapon in the group that still had bullets, and only four at that, and went down the stairs with a flashlight. The others followed, two of the sailors helping their maimed friend.

The compartment was exactly as described and, because of Stone's plan, free of the dead, except for some thumping and muted moans coming from behind the brig's bolted steel door, which they all ignored. The chief had explained to them that the armory door normally required that it be buzzed open from inside, but both he and the division officer carried a key in the event of an emergency. The armory's solid steel door was the only option for entry, as the service window had been designed to be too small for an adult to crawl through.

"The armory is staffed twenty-four-seven by a pair of gunner's mates. I expect they'll still be in there," said the chief, "so stay alert."

Liebs keyed his way in.

Two dead sailors came at him immediately, and the Sig barked three times before Liebs called, "We're clear." Everyone came in, securing the door behind them.

Liebs hadn't been joking when he estimated that the compartment held enough armament to retake the ship. Even after general quarters had sounded and the security teams geared up before running off to their own grisly ends, the armory was loaded.

There were racks upon racks of M16 and M4 assault rifles, twelve-gauge Mossberg 500s, the wooden-stocked M14s favored by snipers, nine-millimeter handguns, crates of empty magazines, and shelved cans of ammunition for everything in here. There were body armor and helmets, gas masks, pencil flares, spare fifty-caliber heavy machine guns with tripods, and lockers of belted ammo. In another area were crates containing the M240 machine gun mounted in the doors of helicopters.

Everyone but Liebs stood and looked on in awe.

"Guns," said the nuc, crouched beside the bosun's mate near the door.

The chief moved over to his men, kneeling and speaking quietly to the maimed boy. It was difficult to hear, but whatever he said made the boy smile and nod. When the chief stood, he wore a pained expression.

Calvin moved up close beside him and whispered, "I can do this if you want."

Liebs shook his head. "They're my men." He went back to help the boy to his feet, telling him they were going across to the berthing so he could lie down and be comfortable. The armory door clicked shut behind them, and everyone on the other side of it simply looked at each other or down at the floor.

A minute later there was a single pistol shot.

Chief Liebs keyed his way back into the armory and handed the empty Sig back to Evan. "We have a job to do," the Navy man said, his voice thick. He refused to meet their eyes as he pushed through the group and walked into the racks of weapons.

THIRTY-SEVEN

The explosion outside the sick bay got them running, Rosa in the lead, Lilly behind her loaded down with weapons and body armor. They hit the double doors simultaneously, throwing them wide.

Peter Dunleavy was in the hallway a short distance away. He grinned wildly and threw something at them. It hit the floor and rolled between the women, into the sick bay. Rosa had the impression of an olive-drab egg.

"Grenade!" she shouted, leaping forward into the corridor, away from the egg, as Peter sprinted away up the hall. The medic dove as she had been taught in training, and as she had done overseas when an insurgent managed to get close enough to throw one of these things: facedown, head away from the blast, legs outstretched behind and boots clamped together, both hands tucked under and cupping the privates. If she was lucky, the position would get her feet blown off but hopefully nothing more critical.

The grenade went off. It sounded strange, a muffled thump instead of a ripping blast, but enough to make her ears ring and blow apart light fixtures.

Then the screaming started.

Rosa turned over and looked back. One of the sick bay doors had been knocked flat; the other sagged on one hinge. Just beyond, Lilly's torn figure was crumpled on the floor, her body armor ripped from her left side, bloody ribs jutting at odd angles from raw meat, left arm blown off.

Oh God, Rosa thought. *She threw herself on it.*

She wanted to scream, but someone else already was, a female voice high and wailing in agony. Rosa scrambled to her feet, the blast still echoing in her head. Behind her and up the hall, Xavier stumbled out of a doorway, colliding with the opposite wall and bending at the waist, holding his head. His pack was gone, his pants and shirt torn, blood soaking through the fabric and dripping on the floor.

Upon seeing Rosa he shouted, "Which way?"

Rosa pointed past him, and before she could even speak, the priest broke into a run, heading in the direction of the treacherous minister.

He was unarmed, but his big hands were clenched into fists.

Rosa went into the sick bay and saw that despite Lilly's sacrifice, she hadn't smothered the grenade completely. Tommy had a bleeding head wound, and he had to keep wiping a sleeve at it to keep the blood out of his eyes. He was kneeling beside Eve, putting pressure on the woman's chest. Eve was on the tiles, arching her back, her head tossing from side to side as she screamed. There was too much blood.

Rosa slid to her knees beside the woman and clapped a hand over her mouth, forcing Eve to meet her eyes. "If you don't stop, they'll come. I can't fight them and save you at the same time."

Eve nodded, squeezing her eyes shut and gritting back the screams.

Rosa shrugged off her medical bag and unzipped it, looking at Tommy across from her. "Watch the doors," the medic said, "and kill anything that comes through." Then she went to work.

Too high, I went up too high, Peter thought. He was running down an empty passageway, searching for a down ladder. Access to the magazines, deep in the ship, would probably be found in the hangar bay. He had to find it.

A zombie was on its hands and knees up ahead, gnawing on the leg of another sailor slumped dead against a wall. It turned its head at his approach and growled. Brother Peter got close before blowing its head off with the shotgun.

"You don't have time for this," God said, looking like Anderson, naked and bitten and standing a few feet away.

Peter ran past the sight of his once-trusted right-hand man, pausing briefly at an intersection before running straight across.

Anderson jogged easily behind him. *"They better all be dead."*

"They are," Peter panted. "And if not, they will be soon."

"Praise God," said Anderson.

Brother Peter found a set of stairs that only went down. He looked first and saw Anderson at the bottom, waving him on.

"It's safe," said God, *"hurry."*

The minister trotted down the metal risers and into the arms of a walking corpse. It grappled with him, snapping and giving off the odor of spoiled meat. Peter let out a cry and shoved at it with the shotgun, cursing as it yanked the weapon out of his hands and came back in fast. Peter pushed at its chest with both hands, throwing it back, but as it went it jerked its head and snapped, clipping Brother Peter's right pinkie off at the first knuckle.

Peter howled and charged it, hammering with his fists, kicking and breaking its arms, seizing the shotgun and pointing. The creature tried to rise, and clamped its teeth on the muzzle.

BOOM. Its head painted the far bulkhead.

The minister held up a shaking hand, staring at the missing digit with wide eyes. "Thou unclean beast," he whispered.

"Ah, shake it off, Pete," said God, once more the Air Force shrink. *"It won't matter soon enough to make a difference, right?"*

Peter looked at his savior. "You said it was safe."

A shrug. *"So I lied. Wouldn't be the first time."*

"Satan lies," Brother Peter mumbled, beginning to walk once more and rounding to the next descending stairway, finger dripping blood.

"Who do you think he learned it from?" God called from behind him.

The minister moved down more cautiously this time, allowing his sense of depth and direction, developed from his Air Force days working deep underground in missile silos, to guide him. The Gallery Deck had been four levels above the hangar. He had two more decks to descend, and then he would head to port. An empty passage awaited him at the bottom, and he hurried around to the next flight. A sailor in the yellow jersey of a catapult officer was slumping up the stairway from below, steel-toed boots banging against the risers.

"Kill it!" shouted the Air Force shrink, but Peter waited, letting it see him, letting it clear the stairs in its rush to feed. Then he shot it.

"We're thinking for ourselves now, are we?" asked the shrink, descending behind the minister.

"I'm doing what you want!" Brother Peter screamed. "Let me concentrate!"

"Oh, and talking back too. Growing a pair, Pete?"

The gym teacher was waiting at the bottom of the next flight, curling a finger at him. *"Let's see if there's any hair on those new balls, sweetness."*

Peter screamed again and charged the gym teacher, who winked out of sight a moment before the collision. The minister looked around for movement, then headed down a hallway toward the port side of the ship.

"What's wrong?" asked God, no longer in a physical form, now only a voice echoing in the steel corridor. *"Did you go down too far? Are you moving starboard instead of port? Will you burn for eternity if you fail?"*

"I know the way!" Peter cried, ducking through a knee knocker, scraping the top of his head on the metal and ripping away hair and skin. Tears ran down his cheeks.

"You're lost," God said. *"You're lost and you're going to get eaten without carrying out my holy plan, and then you'll be in a world of shit."*

"I know the way," Peter whispered, coming to a closed hatch, pulling up on the dog handle, and swinging the steel oval aside. The hangar stretched out before him.

"*Bravo,*" said God, standing beside him now as Sherri, most of Her flesh bitten away, but the cruel box cutter wound still prominent on what remained of Her face. She tapped out a soft golf clap.

Brother Peter ignored Her and ducked through the opening.

I'll never find him, Xavier thought, standing in a gloomy intersection of corridors. *He could have gone anywhere.*

The grenade blast had blown the rows of chairs out in a circle, adding their own fragments to the destruction. Xavier had been on the carpet in a low silhouette as it went off, and the chairs had absorbed much of the damage. He escaped death but still caught at least six or seven fragments along his right side: his thigh, hip, ribs, and right shoulder. All of them felt like he imagined a knife wound would, the twisted fragments biting with every move, and all were bleeding. The one at his ribs hurt and bled the most. He knew at least one rib was broken, and he suspected the fragment had gone deep, perhaps slashing into an organ. What organs were on that side of the body? he wondered.

He couldn't tell if an artery had been torn, but figured he would find out soon enough. If he collapsed and bled out in the next few minutes, he would have his answer.

The zombie's scratches on his face didn't seem so bad anymore. *Peter Dunleavy. World-renowned man of God and mad as a hatter.*

Xavier could only assume from hearing the man's one-sided conversation that he believed he was speaking directly with the Lord. It went beyond assumption that the man planned to detonate a nuclear weapon inside the ship. Those words had been quite clear.

Did he have the knowledge and the skills to do it?

Xavier had to believe he did. If it was true, there wouldn't be much time to find and stop him. But where had he gone?

The distant echo of a shotgun blast rolled down the corridor to the right, and the priest took off at a run. *Thank you, God,* he thought, praying he wouldn't bleed to death before he caught up to the madman.

I t was a losing battle, and it didn't take long. Eve bled out on the tiles of the sick bay waiting room, letting out a soft sigh before her eyes closed and her body grew still.

Rosa was bloody up to her elbows, surrounded by clumps of red-soaked gauze and trauma instruments. She flung a stainless steel clamp across the room and pounded her own thigh. Tommy stood and stared down at the dead woman, shaking his head. He had stayed out of the way keeping watch, except for when he had to step over to Lilly as she attempted her return from death, putting her to rest with a single rifle bullet.

"We have to find Xavier," Rosa said, slinging her medical bag and not bothering to wipe the blood from her hands and arms. "Can you keep moving?"

The hippie nodded. He had wound gauze around his head to form a thick bandage and it seemed to have slowed the bleeding from what was really just a superficial flesh wound.

"Good. Load up with as much ammo as you can carry, and find a pistol." Rosa walked over in a crouch and began removing the weapons and ammo from Lilly's body.

"Hey, Doc," Tommy said, gesturing at the other dead woman.

Rosa stood, drew her pistol, and put a round in Eve's head. Tommy flinched.

"Let's go," said Rosa.

S omeone had been here, and not long ago, Peter thought. Hundreds of bodies were crumpled on the rubberized deck of the hangar bay, brass and shotgun casings lying everywhere. Whatever creatures hadn't been killed must have moved off in pursuit of the shooters, because the long, high compartment was empty of movement.

God be praised, he thought, expecting some sarcastic remark from his savior as He took one form or another. There was nothing, as God chose to be elsewhere at the moment.

Batshit crazy, wasn't that what the Lord had called him? Was he? No, he rejected that idea. God had said it, yes, but God had also admitted that He was capable of lying. No, it was a test, a test to see if he would falter and break faith, if he would be weak and abandon his holy purpose. Brother Peter smiled, confident in the strength of his belief.

He moved into the bay, feeding the last of his shells into the shotgun, knowing it was less than fully loaded. If he ran into trouble . . . *The Lord will provide,* he thought, looking for a sign. Surely God would provide guidance.

And He did.

Along the left side of the bay he spotted movement, but not the familiar shuffle of a corpse. This was mechanical and rhythmic, the repeated opening and closing of a set of elevator doors. Wide doors, like a freight elevator. Wide, red doors.

Red meant ordnance.

An oval hatch was set in the bulkhead not far from the elevator. It was red too.

The televangelist hurried toward the motion, staying close to the wall like a rodent scurrying for safety. When he got there he saw the zombie, a young man who had somehow gotten himself caught between the elevator car and the opening, his severed upper body stuck in the gap and hanging out, arms reaching as the head lolled and made a croaking sound.

The zombie wore a red jersey the same color as the door, and a plastic card was clipped to his shirt near the collar. Brother Peter used his foot to push the snapping head to the side and plucked the card off the jersey, examining it. He smiled as he recognized what it was.

The card had a magnetic stripe down its back so it could be swiped at a card reader, and sure enough such a unit was mounted beside the elevator doors. On the front was a photo of the zombie when he had been alive, a young man with a crew cut and a serious expression. Beneath the photo it read, *Weaver, R., Petty Officer 2nd*, along with a string of letters and numbers. The bottom half of the card was coated in a film that would change color if exposed to radiation.

"Thank you, Weaver, R.," Brother Peter said, tucking the card in a pocket. Then he stomped repeatedly on the creature's head until it was flat and the moving stopped. He grabbed the corpse under the arms and heaved, straining with the effort. The upper body came free with a wet, ripping sound, and he dropped it at once, jumping into the now-freed freight elevator before the doors could close.

There were only two button choices, one marked *H* and one marked *M*. He pressed the *M* and the doors closed, the elevator car sinking smoothly into the ship.

Brother Peter hummed one of his favorite hymns as it descended.

THIRTY-EIGHT

Carney and TC climbed the stairs with the horde in pursuit, up two floors, ignoring side passages, always moving up. The stairway finally led them through a large rectangular hatch set in the floor above, held open by a pair of hydraulic arms. With barely a glance around the new compartment in which they found themselves, the two men worked together to press the hatch to the floor. It had a rubber seal all the way around it, and as Carney spun the wheel on top, it let out a long, pressurized hiss, locking down tightly.

The moaning from below was cut off at once, and then there was only a dull thumping.

Carney smelled corpses, but also a puff of fresh air. Looking around, they saw that they were in a long compartment with multiple hatches down the left side, more stairs leading up, and rows of shelves and hooks holding colored helmets and vests with numerous pockets. A line of clipboards hung beside a dry-erase board covered in acronym scrawls.

There was also daylight.

In the middle of the right wall was a wide hatch, crowded chest-high with the bodies of sailors, all with head wounds. The top three feet were open to the outside, and a blend of morning breeze and early sunshine passed through.

"I need some fresh air," said TC, shoving the bloody wrench through his belt and setting to work dragging the bodies from the opening.

Carney searched the area instead. All the hatches on the left were closed, and he opened them cautiously, shining his flashlight and pointing the Beretta. Each revealed a small office or what appeared to be a waiting room. By the time Carney was certain no former crewmen were lurking nearby, TC had cleared the main hatch and stepped outside.

The older inmate followed him out of the superstructure and onto the flight deck, and for a long moment both men simply stood with their eyes closed, heads back, breathing deeply and taking in the warmth of the sun. When they opened their eyes they saw that the deck had become a field of fallen bodies.

"Someone's been busy," said Carney.

TC stripped off his body armor and shirt, letting them fall, and stretched his powerful back muscles, rubbing at his chest. "That's better," he groaned.

"You're going to want that back on," Carney warned.

"No need for it," said TC. He turned and grinned at his cellmate. "I'll go Tarzan for a while." He lit a cigarette.

Carney went back into the superstructure, looking through the compartment for anything useful. He found no weapons, only paperwork, flight deck gear, and a tool belt hanging near the hatch. TC appeared silently beside him and made him jump.

"Stop creeping," Carney said. "I don't like it." In fact, he didn't like most things TC did anymore, and decided that the truth was he didn't like TC anymore.

"You're like an old lady, bro," TC said. He started pulling off one of his gloves. "I want to show you something. It'll blow your fucking mind."

Muffled gunfire came from somewhere up above the stairway, pistol shots. They looked up, seeing only gloom.

"What was—" TC started.

"Shut the fuck up," Carney barked, straining to listen. More gunfire, and then the distant voice of a woman cried, "Skye!"

Carney's fist tightened on the pistol's grip, and he started up the metal stairway. He hadn't climbed two steps before TC's wrench crashed into the back of his head. There was a dazzling white, and then Carney plunged into black oblivion.

His cellmate's body collapsed and slid down the steps, back to the floor. TC took the pistol from Carney's hand. "Sorry it ended like this, bro." He flicked away the cigarette. "You turned into a bitch. We should have left when I said so."

Blood pooled around the older man's head.

From above came more gunfire, and a woman called out again, "Skye!"

TC began to stiffen at the sound of the name, and he mounted the steps two at a time, a hungry grin on his face. "Daddy's coming, baby," he murmured. "We're gonna finish our party."

Skye and Angie worked their way methodically down through the superstructure, cautious on the stairs, taking turns at hatches and covering each other's back. Pistols and flashlights probed every corner, every shadowy space.

They found navigation compartments with both digital and conventional chart tables, an entire floor dedicated to meteorology, and still another for radar. An additional floor was packed with a confusing array of communications gear. Some chambers were lit by the red general quarters lights, others with only the glow of computer screens and control boards.

They weren't alone.

In a navigation compartment, a sailor who'd had his pelvis blown apart by an old shotgun blast was lying on the floor behind a chart table. Angie almost stepped on him, and he caught her boot in his hand, nipping fabric from her pants. Angie leaped back and Skye was there with a pistol shot. After that, they were careful to watch where they stepped.

Two ghouls were found seated in swivel chairs in front of radar consoles, seeming to stare at the blank, glowing green screens. They looked up and moaned before dying for the second time.

"I can't figure them out," Angie said, her voice low. "Sometimes they cluster together and stay on the move. Other times they're idle, like these two, staring at nothing."

Skye shrugged, slipping a fresh magazine into her pistol. She despised them and couldn't care less about why they did what they did. They were nothing more than tangos. They killed without mercy, and that was the end of it. In that way, she realized, she at last discovered something they shared. It hadn't taken much time after the end of the world for Skye Dennison to decide that her most effective weapon was, and would forever be, a hard heart.

"Let's go," Skye said, easing out of the room.

Angie stared at the two corpses a moment longer. "Maybe they're dreaming," she said softly. Then she joined her partner.

The next level down was claustrophobic: narrow corridors with a couple of intersections, every wall lined with gray metal access panels. Black numbers and letters were stenciled on each, once holding meaning for something now sliding dead along the ship's passageways or already lying still with a bullet in its brain. The women opened a few of the panels, revealing complicated circuitry and switches. They decided the entire level had to be computer and electrical systems necessary to feed all the technology they had seen in the superstructure. There was no place for the dead to hide in here.

The stairway leading down, located at the far end of the access panel maze, was a different story. A drifter in shredded khaki—a slender, bald man with his throat blackened and torn—stepped up from below as they arrived, and growled.

Skye shot him. The bullet punched through his ruined throat and he galloped forward, reaching. Both women fired together, and he went down face first. More drifters surged up the stairway, clawing and scrambling, their moans long and eerie in the tight space. Angie and Skye stood close together, firing until their slides locked back, and they grabbed for new magazines.

The corpse of a blond girl no older than Skye was on the floor, two others dead on top of her. A bullet had shattered her right cheekbone and orbital socket but hadn't pierced the brain, and she was down only because of the falling weight of her shipmates. The dead girl lashed out with both arms, locking her hands around Skye's calf, and she pulled herself forward with teeth snapping.

"Skye!" Angie yelled, shoving the young woman back, kicking the biting face loose, and putting a round in the back of its head.

"Bitch," Skye said, giving the blonde's head another kick. Then she was firing again, quick shots that were poorly aimed as she advanced, entering Angie's sight picture. Suddenly a corpse had Skye by the shoulders, snapping at her face, and she shoved the barrel of her pistol under its chin and splattered its brains across the ceiling. More of the dead trudged up the stairs, packed in close, and Skye stood her ground at the top, firing until she was dry. Angie was still looking for a shot.

"Skye!" she yelled again.

This time the younger woman fell back, reloading as Angie moved up and fired. She tried to take them while they were still on the stairs, and a few tumbled backward. Others pushed the bodies aside and pressed upward, their growling reverberating down the metal panel walls. Then Skye was back up and firing, and both women pulled their triggers until nothing else emerged from the stairs, and their pistols were empty.

There was grunting from below, accompanied by thuds and cracks. It went on for a few seconds, and they looked at each other.

"Don't shoot," a voice called from below, sounding hollow. "It's Carney." Boot steps on the stairs.

Angie and Skye let out pent-up breath.

The figure that rose from the darkness below was not Carney. This man had stripped himself completely naked; his powerful chest, covered in tattoos and fresh, bleeding bites, was heaving, and the bloody wrench he carried dripped with blood. His other hand held a pistol. The eyes above the mad grin were a cold, wild blue.

"Hey, bitch," TC said, and shot Angie.

Skye reached furiously for a magazine and saw the wrench swinging. She raised an arm to stop it but was a moment too late, and she caught the blow just behind the ear. It threw her against an access panel with a metallic bang, and then there were two TCs, three, spinning and spinning. She sagged limp to the floor, blood coursing down the side of her head.

Angie was down, gasping, one hand holding her chest, the other reaching for her dropped pistol.

"Unh-uh," said TC, raising a boot and stomping on her outstretched forearm with a sickening crack. Angie screamed, and TC silenced her with a second bullet.

The inmate cast the wrench and pistol aside. Grinning, he grabbed Skye by both arms and dragged her a few yards away from the stairs and the corpses, stretching her out flat. Then he crouched over her, drinking her in with his eyes.

TC slipped the boot knife from the sheath at Skye's ankle and quickly cut away her combat vest. Then he slit the knife up the front of her tank top and sports bra, baring her breasts. He touched the tip of the blade to one nipple.

"Now it don't matter if you infect me," he said, beginning to cut away her fatigue pants, stroking himself with the other hand. "Par-ty time . . ."

THIRTY-NINE

They quickly realized that even though it was a mere half mile, the service barge was not designed even for the fringe waters of the San Francisco Bay. It rocked side to side with each swell, and on a particularly large wave it tilted so steeply that people screamed, hugging the deck and each other as plastic totes of supplies and a wooden crate of Claymore mines tumbled into the water.

Maya manned the helm in the small wheelhouse, trying to guide the long, narrow craft the way she had seen Evan do it. The vessel was painfully slow and the aircraft carrier seemed to draw no closer. Another swell cast the barge to the right and more supplies slid off the side. Someone shouted, "There! There!" and heads turned to see a gray-and-white dorsal fin cut through the water not ten feet away.

Maya wasn't distracted by screams or any other sounds. She felt the thumping of the old diesel radiating through her hands on the wheel, felt the roll of the waves with her body. She tried to time her acceleration with the rhythm and remain on her feet.

Something bumped against the bottom of the hull. More fins appeared.

Just ahead and to the right Maya saw a body in an inflated vest wearing a helmet and goggles. The zombie's mouth was opening and closing, but it wasn't reaching. Its arms had been bitten off, and it bobbed slowly past them.

A boy lost his grip when a wave flung the barge to the right, and he slid toward the edge, yelling and grabbing at whatever he could, unable to catch hold, legs going over the side. A beefy hand clamped down on the boy's wrist and Big Jerry, lying flat on the oil-stained deck, hauled him back in.

At last the aircraft carrier did draw closer, and minutes later the barge was in its shadow, a speck of lumber floating alongside a steel behemoth. Maya piloted the craft toward the stern, where she had seen the assault team's two boats tethered and bobbing.

Green and black liquid pattered onto the deck, and all eyes went up. A sailor in flight deck gear was entangled in the safety netting above, reaching through, thrashing. He was swollen and green. People moved to keep out from under it, and a pair of hippies picked up the old man with MS and moved him away. A young man in a leather vest pointed a rifle at the creature.

"I wouldn't do that," Big Jerry said, still lying on the deck and holding on to the boy who had almost gone overboard.

The hippie considered for a moment and didn't fire.

Maya brought them around the wide back end of the carrier, its presence seeming to stabilize the movement of the water around it. She drove the barge in, tried to reverse too late, and crumpled the bow against haze-gray steel, throwing people off their feet.

Evan rammed a dock, I rammed an aircraft carrier, Maya thought. *I win.*

They tied off quickly, and Margaret began getting them together, keeping an eye on another zombie tangled in the netting directly above them. This one wasn't green, but it looked like it was working itself free, wiggling toward the edge.

"Gather food and water, and don't forget flashlights," Margaret barked. "Everyone carries a weapon and as much ammo as you can."

The group moved quickly, stuffing backpacks and shoulder bags. One man opened the crate of antitank rocket launchers, but Margaret told him to fill a bag with rifle ammunition instead. She kept an eye on the creature above. It had freed itself and was crawling over. Margaret readied her shotgun as the zombie hurled itself over the netting.

It dropped, missed the barge, and sank.

Maya had been watching too, gripping her ice-climbing pick. She let out a shaky, silent laugh as it went under.

When she was satisfied everyone was ready, Margaret told them to stay close and stay together. Then she went through the hatch at the swimmer's platform and entered *Nimitz*, followed by a long line of people. One man helped Larraine along as the old woman sucked at her oxygen, eyes wide above the mask. Two others carried her husband, Gene, stoic and uncomplaining, eyes closed against his pain. Some of the women shepherded the orphans, and Sophia walked in a silent daze, not speaking. Big Jerry insisted on going last.

"You don't need a gimpy fat guy blocking a stairway in an emergency," he told them, limping and trying to take pressure off his blown knee, using a shotgun barrel as a cane. "Of course it would take them so long to eat me," he added, "that the rest of you could make a clean escape."

It didn't get any laughs, and Jerry decided that was why he was an *amateur* comic.

There were no messages left for them, no sign of where the assault group had gone. But then they hadn't been expecting the Alameda refugees to follow on their own. Margaret decided to take them up, perhaps reach the open space of the flight deck where at least they could see their attackers coming and have an open field of fire.

Their upward progress felt like an inchworm scaling a redwood. People froze at the sound of a distant rattle or bang; frightened voices rose when a moan echoed from somewhere above. Starting and stopping, backpacks bumping into faces, flashlight beams crawling nervously in every direction.

The smallest of the children were crying.

The adults tried to shush them, to distract them, but it was dark, it smelled bad, the grown-ups were visibly shaken, and even these little ones knew that monsters were real, and they ate little kids. Their cries and whimpering echoed and carried, and this ratcheted up the panic level within the entire group.

The sound was a summons, and it was answered. The dead from multiple levels homed in on it and started moving.

The head of the group reached a chamber where *MHG* was stenciled on the wall, and like those who had gone before them, they had a choice of three closed hatches or more stairs. Wanting the flight deck, Margaret started moving up.

The dead started moving down.

A sailor in a shredded hospital gown descended, gray legs and feet marching stiffly on the risers. The sailor moaned, and the sound was picked up by others behind him.

"Another way!" Margaret shouted, triggering her shotgun. The buckshot shredded the sailor's features and sent his limp form tumbling down the stairs. More followed.

Maya threw the dog lever on a hatch to the left, shining her flashlight down an empty corridor. She went through and waved for the others to follow. Margaret's shotgun roared again, and now all the children were wailing. The adults herded them quickly along as two men joined Margaret at the stairs, firing alongside her. Children covered their ears and hurried through the hatch, one little girl barking her shin on the knee knocker. A mother swept the shrieking girl into her arms and followed the others.

Big Jerry watched them. *Too slow,* he thought, *they're going too slow.* Then he saw the dog handle on one of the other hatches slide up, the metal door slowly swinging open. A gray hand curled around the door frame. The big man planted his wounded leg and charged the hatch, hurling his weight against it. The slam severed four thin fingers, which scattered at his feet.

"Get moving," he shouted, shoving the handle back in place.

Slowly, slowly, the refugees filed into the new hallway, pushing the people ahead of them, urging them to hurry, hurry.

The stairway was jammed with the dead, and Margaret and the hippies took the opportunity to reload. When the last refugee went through the hatch, Jerry hobbled after them as one of the hippies took over his dog handle. Margaret produced a roll of duct tape from her backpack and strapped the handle down, putting on multiple layers.

"My dad says you can fix anything with this stuff," she said through clenched teeth. Then she chased the hippies through the new opening and slammed it shut behind her, going to work again with the duct tape.

Up at the head of the refugee line, Maya led with her flashlight and pistol, checking openings, coming to an intersection. She knew Margaret wanted more stairs, and since she didn't see any here, Maya led them straight across. The intermittent lighting revealed nothing waiting for them up ahead, at least not in the passage, but she didn't accept that as safety. She was careful at every door and opening, thankfully able to avoid the pressure of the frantic voices behind her. She couldn't hear the crying children, but she sensed it in the air, knew that the line behind her was making the kind of noise that would travel great distances in these steel tunnels. It was going to bring the dead down on them. She knew that too.

Her flashlight came to rest on a hatch at the end of the passage marked *FANTAIL*. It was a few inches ajar, and she peeked through the opening. She saw daylight, and lots of it, along with fresh sea air, and a high, wide open space. There were drifters moving in there too, but within her limited view she couldn't see too many. Maya turned to pass along what she had found and immediately felt the heat of frustration in her cheeks. Most of the people here couldn't sign, and even if they could, signing in the dark was pointless.

Maya panned her flashlight over those behind her and saw a man named Clyde who, for as long as she could remember, had been the Family's resident auto mechanic. He was carrying a lever-action Winchester rifle and wore two revolvers like an Old West gunfighter. Maya grabbed his shirt, hauled him to the door, pointed two fingers at her eyes, and then pointed at the opening.

Clyde looked through the hatch, then up at her, and nodded.

Maya made a talking gesture with her hand and waved at the group. Clyde nodded again and went back down the line, sharing what he had seen. Within a few minutes, Margaret and a dozen armed people joined her at the hatch. Maya pulled it open, and they went in firing.

The fantail of the *Nimitz* was a lofty, airy chamber three decks high, level with the hangar deck, and divided from that space by a thick, steel fire wall. Aft was the big rectangular opening seen from outside, sun, sea, and sky revealed beyond, as well as a view of the haunted city that had been San Francisco. The air in here was fresh and untainted, despite the presence of the dead, and there was no need of lighting.

Within the space stood several large metal stands where jet engines could be mounted and test-fired out the opening, two of which held partially disassembled Super Hornet fighter engines. In the center closest to the open air stood a pair of gigantic spools, tightly wound with cable and affixed with what appeared to be long, ventilated steel tubes. The refugees couldn't even guess at their purpose. Small forklifts and gang boxes of tools were scattered across the floor space.

On the wall nearest to the group, and on the far wall, narrow steel ladderways led to catwalks and hatches on all three levels. On the floor level alone, no less than a dozen wall and deck hatches stood open.

There were more zombies in the fantail than Maya had glimpsed through her narrow view, and they reacted to the gunfire at once.

Some fell to the first volley, and the rest began angling in from every direction. More entered the space through hatches, tumbling down catwalk stairs or flipping over railings, rising immediately, unmindful of fractured bones. Those unable to walk, crawled.

Maya, Margaret, and the hippies tried to stay in a line as they moved forward, but they were untrained, and very quickly the attack disintegrated into individual battles where lone refugees reloaded and fired as fast as they could at whatever they saw.

A dozen sailors went down. Then a hippie shrieked as he was pulled to the floor by dead hands. More zombies collapsed, but fresh replacements shuffled through open hatches. Margaret saw this happening, spotted Clyde, and ran to him.

"Find some chain or cable and start locking down these hatches." Margaret had to shout to be heard above the gunfire.

The hippie shook his head. "There's no way! We have to go back!"

Margaret looked over at the hatch through which they had come, seeing crying children being moved into the fantail, followed by two men carrying Larraine's husband. Gunfire and muzzle flashes came from the corridor behind them.

"There is no back," the woman said. "Get moving or we're all dead."

Big Jerry heard the duct tape let go with a ripping sound, and he put his flashlight on the hatch to his rear. The dead had managed to force the dog handle up despite the impromptu lock, and now they poured into a passageway filled with the helpless and sick.

The comic leaned against a wall, tucked the flashlight under an armpit, and opened up with the shotgun, trying to be calm and precise as Angie West had taught him. They hadn't had many lessons.

"Get them out of here," Jerry bellowed to no one in particular, firing three times, cutting down an avionics technician, a basic seaman, and a lieutenant commander. The empty shell hulls rattled at his feet. The line of refugees screamed and moved forward. Jerry fed fresh shells up the tube, trying to think of any jokes he knew about zombies.

What do you call a zombie cow? Dead meat.

His shotgun decapitated a Navy plumber.

That one sucked. I wouldn't even try it onstage.

A blast cut a female sailor in half, and her fellow corpses trampled her torso even as she tried to drag it forward.

Where do zombies come from? Rotterdamned.

Jerry made a face as he blasted a boy in a green jersey, and then another in white. *That one sucked even worse. It was a wonder I got any bookings at all.*

A glance over his shoulder told him the corridor was emptying, but slowly. His knee was the size of a cantaloupe and pulsing, and the dead came on steadily. He fired, racked a shell, fired, racked, fired. Not every trigger pull resulted in a head shot, and the dead were relentless, the misses not slowing them in any way. A couple more shots and he would be empty. They would never let him reload. At least he had bought some time for the others.

What do you call a fat guy who runs out of shells? A feast.

CLICK. The shotgun trigger snapped back empty, and he reached for his ammo pouch as they galloped at him, knowing he would never make it.

Four shots fired in rapid succession went off beside him.

Maya's nine-millimeter bucked in her hands as she appeared on Jerry's right, another hippie beside her who slipped Jerry's arm around his neck and began moving the big man back up the tunnel. Bodies sprawled and moans bounded down the hall as Maya emptied her clip into the horde, slowly backing up. A stray who escaped her bullets galloped at her over the fallen bodies.

Maya jerked the ice climber pick from her belt and spiked the stray's head.

She reloaded the pistol and fought a rear guard action, always backing up as the last of the refugees and Big Jerry entered the fantail.

Margaret realized with a sick, sinking feeling that things had just gotten worse, as she saw the refugees spilling through the hatch: the sick, a pregnant woman, people too scared to even hold a weapon, lots of children. They scattered and tried to hide behind equipment and spare engines, and the dead began hunting them at once.

She spotted Clyde and another man, both carrying lengths of chains, and waved them on. If they could just seal the openings, they might have a chance to wipe out the remaining creatures inside the sprawling room. Margaret fell back toward the refugees, pumping and firing, stopping to reload, firing some more. Out of the corner of her eye she saw Maya wedging a length of pipe through the wheel of the hatch they had all come through, Jerry leaning on a wall next to her and reloading his shotgun.

A man's scream echoed from deeper in the space.

A woman's high wailing sounded to her right.

Margaret and those around her fired.

There was more screaming on the right. She saw the pregnant woman's husband with a pipe wrench, bashing the head of a corpse. Gunfire was suddenly replaced by silence followed by shrieking, and an oxygen bottle with a slender, bloody palm print on it rolled by. Corpses galloped at her and she pulled the trigger, working the shotgun's slide, blowing off a head, an arm, ripping open a belly.

We were safer on the water, she thought, tears in her eyes.

Clyde staggered out from behind a forklift holding a fistful of chain, his clothes bloody, a dead sailor close behind him. "Clyde, over here," Margaret shouted, turning to blast a blond sailor in oily coveralls. A hand gripped her shoulder and the Asian woman turned to see that Clyde's eyes were gray and cloudy, his throat red ribbons of flesh. Margaret's scream was cut short as he fell upon her.

Maya saw it all, saw it coming apart. Hippies went down, Larraine was dragged away screaming, and her husband flailed his arms weakly beneath a pile of ripping and snarling creatures. Then Margaret fell. Near an engine test mount, Sophia had a screaming child by the arm as a zombie tried to pull the boy away by his legs, the woman's mouth open in a scream Maya couldn't hear.

The deaf girl charged and shot the creature in the face, and Sophia gathered the boy to her chest. Looking around frantically, Maya spotted a hatch twenty feet away, open, with nothing coming out of it. She ran to Jerry, slapped him on the shoulder, and pointed to the hatch, making a gathering gesture. The big man nodded and roared for everyone to get to the opening.

Maya shot at the corpses closest to her, thinking that no one would move; they would remain huddled where they were, frozen and unthinking until they were torn apart. But they did move, and quickly. Women grabbed kids by shirt collars, tucked the smaller ones under their arms, and ran for the hatch. The pregnant couple reunited, and Big Jerry hobbled as fast as he was able.

When Maya's pistol clicked empty, she switched to the ice pick, swinging, kicking a twitching corpse away, swinging again. When Big Jerry raised his swollen knee to clear the hatch, Maya broke away and headed for it at a sprint.

She almost made it.

FORTY

The Cadillac was heavy, made of quality Detroit steel. But it wasn't a tank, and it was coming apart.

From the outside it was barely recognizable for what it had been. Every bit of glass was cracked or broken, bent chrome twisted away like stray hairs; the once-white paint job was now red, streaked with green and yellow, and the metal surfaces were hammered like a Mexican copper plate. It rattled on one flat tire, the alignment was out of whack, and the engine knocked.

Vlad ignored the car's condition and poured it on, swerving the wheel left and right, fighting for gaps among the stumbling dead. They banged off the remaining front fender—the other was long gone—and rolled beneath the undercarriage, broken hands grasping at hot pipes and spinning wheels. Ben was a tiny ball shivering against Vlad's ribs. The man's jaw ached from clenching his teeth.

They had made it off the pier, down the access road, and survived the streets that marched alongside vacant hangars and buildings.

Vladimir and Ben had reached the airfield.

The pilot floored the accelerator and shot across the tarmac, honking the weak-sounding horn and waving his left arm out the shattered driver's-side window, shouting in Russian. It got their attention. The dead followed.

The pilot stayed clear of the helicopter, wanting them nowhere near the aircraft, and shot out to the far end of the airfield before stopping. He didn't dare turn off the engine for fear it would object to its punishment by refusing to turn over. Now Vlad waited and lit a cigarette, blowing the smoke out the window.

"Those are bad for you," said Ben, looking up at him and waving a hand in front of his face. "They're stinky."

Vladimir nodded solemnly and flicked the butt out the window. "It is a dirty habit. Will you help me to stop?"

"Yes," Ben said as he climbed to his knees on the seat. "Are we going home now?"

The Russian hugged him close. "Soon, little one," he said. He watched the dead through the starred windshield. There were thousands of them, flowing across the cracked, weed-infested concrete, every shape and size, and in every phase of decomposition. He couldn't hear them moaning over the rattling of the engine, but he knew they were.

He let them draw closer.

"Am I going with Mommy and Daddy?" Ben asked.

Vlad cradled the boy's head in one oversized hand and held it against his side. "If you do, I will be going with you."

The Russian gave them close to twenty minutes, and as waves of California's dead shuffled and dragged themselves closer to the Cadillac, he stepped on the gas. This time he swung far to the left, away from them and picking up speed before he cut back, aiming the space where the hood ornament had once been at the distant Black Hawk. Now his foot sank to the floor, and bodies that turned slowly in his direction blurred by.

A Sikorsky UH-60A was not a car, and one did not simply jump in, turn a key, and fly away. It was a detail most people didn't appreciate but one that helicopter pilots knew without even thinking about it. There was a startup process, and mathematics tumbled through Vladimir's head as he raced toward the aircraft. He didn't like the outcomes that kept repeating.

The Cadillac coughed and a sharp, metallic *PING* made the whole vehicle jump. Black smoke streamed from beneath the hood, coating the windshield with oil and forcing Vladimir to stick his head out the side window in order to see. He held the accelerator down, no longer caring what it did to the engine. They were out of time.

The dead trudged steadily after.

A hundred yards away now . . . seventy-five . . . fifty. The Caddy's engine shifted from knocking to outright hammering, a high-speed knock that made the vehicle shudder. They were twenty-five yards away when an explosive *BANG* shot a piston through the Cadillac's wrinkled hood like a bullet. Power failed, the steering wheel locked, and then they were coasting, slowing rapidly.

As they neared the chopper, Vlad jammed the emergency brake down with his foot, and the Cadillac stuttered to a halt, never to move again under its own power. The pilot tucked Ben under an arm and ran to his bird, buckling the boy into the co-pilot's seat. As he snapped himself in on the left, he didn't bother to look out the windscreen. He knew what was coming.

Vlad switched on the fuel valve, then depressed the starter and the counter at the same time, his eyes on the N1, the gauge for the gas producer turbine. The Black Hawk was cold and had limited battery power. He would have two chances at most to start the turbines, and after that the bird wouldn't have enough juice to start without an external battery cart, and there was no helpful ground crew standing by at the moment.

The Russian watched the gauge and told himself not to look outside. It wouldn't matter anyway; this would work or it wouldn't. He peeked, and realized that battery power or not, if the first attempt failed, he would never have time to make a second.

The corpses he had originally led away with Maxie's Cadillac were coming, but most were still some distance away. They weren't the problem, and this was immediately apparent. The dead weren't moving as a single mass; they were strewn across the airfield, all at different distances from the helicopter, and some had been so far back that they didn't cover enough ground to be drawn away. They were closer, and coming toward the meal they had just seen climb aboard. In addition, new arrivals were walking out from between the hangars by the dozens, the hundreds, closer than those he had led away.

"That wasn't much of a plan," he muttered.

Cold-starting the turbine took about thirty-five seconds. At twenty-five percent on the N1 gauge, the rotor blades should start turning. The seconds ticked by on the counter. Vlad had flown into Alameda on vapors. He wondered if he had enough fuel left in the lines to even start the turbines, much less do what he intended.

Twenty seconds. Twenty-five.

The dead came closer, enough so that he could make out their twisted features.

Overhead the turbines began to whine, quickly becoming painfully loud. It wouldn't mean anything if the fuel ran out. He pulled a pair of ear protectors from the back of the co-pilot's seat and placed them on Ben's head to shield him from the noise. The little boy was too small to see out the windows, to see what was coming, and he patted the protectors, gigantic on his head, and laughed.

The rotors began to turn.

Vlad released the starter and saw the N1 gauge creep past thirty percent. He watched the temperature on both turbines as they spooled up and heated the engine and lubricating oils. It would take another full minute before they would be hot enough to give him green lights, and attempting to lift off in any other condition would almost certainly cause mechanical seizing and an instant crash. The timer clicked steadily, and to him it sounded like approaching footfalls. He was careful to increase his RPMs slowly, because if he overheated the turbines, it was over.

Although the tail rotor was humming nicely, the fifty-three-foot-diameter rotor blades turned ponderously. Considering the noise they made, they didn't move nearly fast enough.

The N1 gauge reached seventy percent, and Vladimir turned on the generator and started flicking overhead switches to power his many electrical systems. At once he was assaulted by a barrage of buzzers, horns, and flashing red lights.

The fuel gauge showed one flickering red bar.

Something bumped against the aircraft's tail boom. Vladimir gritted his teeth, wanting to draw his pistol, knowing he couldn't. He needed his hands now. Another thump, and then he felt something climb into the troop compartment just as his temperature gauges turned green. He prayed for lift as he hauled on the cyclic and collective. The Black Hawk's wheels left the pavement, rising up and forward.

The zombie was wearing a chef's uniform that had been starched white a long time ago but was now a mottled brown. Just as the chopper lifted off, it tried to stand and lost what little balance it possessed, tumbling out the troop compartment door and hitting the tarmac, shattering both legs.

Vlad didn't see it, but when neither he nor Ben was attacked after a few moments, he had to assume the zombie was gone. He took the Black Hawk up to twenty-five feet and accelerated over the heads of the swarming dead, now packing the old airfield, the beat of his rotors blowing the unsteady ones off their feet. Groundhog-7's nose was fixed on the west end of the field, out where the pavement led to weeds, a fence, and then the water.

They were going to go nose-in right at the fence, Vlad knew it. Or they would clear it only to fall into the bay. Somehow the chopper stayed airborne.

Ben, who had never flown before, stared at the pilot with a child's wide-eyed amazement, completely without fear. He laughed and clapped his hands.

Vladimir laughed too, but it came out as a hoarse shriek. He climbed as quickly as he dared, water passing below. Groundhog-7 was now "feet-wet," the term used by pilots to indicate they had left land behind and were now over water. Vlad tried for as much altitude as possible, needing at least a hundred feet to clear the carrier's deck. His pilot's mind quickly calculated airspeed against the half mile to the carrier. Fifteen seconds.

The lone, flickering fuel bar winked out.

Vladimir felt the abruptly starved turbines react the only way they could.

FORTY-ONE

Xavier had followed the yelling when he could, but the blood trail was better, a spattering of small, wet red dots on the steel decking, leading him onward. Brother Peter was wounded. He went through the hatch and entered the hangar bay, catching movement far to the left. There he saw Brother Peter take something off a corpse, pull half of it out of an elevator, and then jump inside just as the red doors closed.

The priest ran.

He reached the elevator, saw the key card reader, and recognized the color of the doors for what it represented. The minister had found a way to the magazines, and he had taken the only way to operate the elevator with him. Xavier wanted to cry out, to curse, to scream.

He took a deep breath. In almost every place he had ever been, elevators had stairs nearby. He looked at the red-painted hatch off to the side and guessed it had to lead to stairs, as it was the only other object around that color. Then he saw the lock plate and keyhole. Of course it would be secured, just like the elevator.

A moan echoed through the hangar. The priest didn't even look. He grabbed the severed upper torso of the ordnance sailor, now with its head flattened, and flipped it onto its back, tearing at its jersey. It stood to reason that if the young man had an access card—there it was, a heavy key connected to his dog tag chain. He snapped it off and ran to the door.

It opened at once, revealing a stairwell lit with red battle lights. Xavier started down.

The magazine was well lit, as Brother Peter would have expected. Turn off the ice cream machine and the lights in the john, shut down TVs and air conditioners, but keep the systems essential for war fully functional. It made sense.

The aircraft carrier's magazine was composed of numerous chambers located off a wide, central hall, each secured by a thick, blast-resistant steel door. There was dried blood down here, signs that even this area had not escaped the damnation that had stalked these passageways, but there were no zombies. He noticed that the red hatch beside the elevator on this level was standing open and peeked inside. Stairs. *The dead things went thataway.*

Peter moved briskly, swiping the key card at every reader, opening the motorized blast doors for each magazine compartment. Lights were on inside as well, and his eyes roamed over racks of missiles, cluster munitions, smart bombs, "dumb" iron bombs, bunkers of ammunition for twenty-millimeter Gatling guns, torpedoes and chaff canisters. There was oh so much firepower aboard this floating tomb, and none of it interested him. Peter was seeking the holy trinity, the black-and-yellow symbol with three triangles that would signal he had arrived.

He found it on the last blast door on the left side. Beneath the radiation symbol was a warning that the area was restricted to a particular security clearance, and that unauthorized access would result in prosecution under the Uniform Code of Military Justice, section *blah, blah, blah.* He opened the door, half expecting to hear angels trumpeting and choirs of cherubs singing his praises. Instead he was hit by a puff of cool, dry air and found a rather small compartment lit with white fluorescents. The walls were covered in more warnings, alongside detailed safety procedures. A single missile rack occupied the left wall.

"Praise God," he whispered.

There were forty of them cradled three high on padded steel racking, and they looked almost identical to the AGM 88 HARM, the high-speed anti-radiation missile carried by the Super Hornets, designed to home in on electronic transmissions coming from surface-to-air radar. Ship killers. Each was thirteen feet long, weighed 780 pounds, and had a range of sixty-six miles. Their smokeless, solid propellant rocket motors pushed them along at Mach two-plus, about 1,420 miles per hour, allowing them to cover that sixty-six miles in short order.

These beauties were different from the HARM. They had yellow noses and measured their punch in kilotons.

MARS. That was what the briefer at the Navy seminar called them. The god of war, blasphemous to even utter, as if there were any other than the one true God.

Who, in fact, was sitting on the top of the nuclear weapons rack. He appeared as a bitten and slashed Sherri, only dressed in the Air Force shrink's uniform, complete with eyeglasses.

"Let's get cracking, shall we?" said God.

Brother Peter nodded and opened a tool locker, quickly seeing that it had everything he needed. Well, almost everything. Peter looked around and smiled when he saw the phone box on the wall beside the locker. *Now* he had everything. Using tools from the locker, Brother Peter opened the phone box and attached the stripped end of a coil of wire to a point inside, playing the wire out across the magazine. Then he used a battery-powered screwdriver to remove a curved panel from the skin of three missiles.

"You still got it," said God.

Peter ignored the voice, focusing on the work.

These were tactical nukes: short range with a low yield. The word *low* was laughable, considering that the Little Boy dropped on Hiroshima in 1945 had produced a yield between thirteen and eighteen kilotons, and each of these much smaller devices packed at least half that punch by themselves. Little Boy had been a simple gravity bomb, but a nuclear warhead could be attached to a variety of delivery systems: artillery shells, cruise missiles, the towering intercontinental ballistic missiles—ICBMs. In the 1960s, the American ICBM of choice had been the Jupiter and Thor, and during Peter's time in Omaha, it had evolved into the Minuteman III.

At its foundation, however, a nuke was a nuke and they all worked the same. Enriched uranium assembled into a supercritical mass. It started a nuclear chain reaction that grew exponentially by compressing a subcritical sphere of material—plutonium-239—using chemical explosives. All were set off by an electrical charge and the resulting implosion was the stuff of nightmares: fatal burns, smoking cities, shadows of ash left on walls by incinerated children.

Hallelujah.

The federal government had not only trained him in how to handle these things but paid him for the privilege. *Glory Be. Three should be more than enough,* Peter thought.

"Three works for me," said God.

Peter got started.

Xavier quickly figured out how this worked. The stairwell was either the primary way down to the magazine or a backup in the event the elevator failed. Regardless, the stairs descended deck by deck into the lowest level of the ship, and there was a locked red hatch at every deck. The same key worked in them all, which at first surprised Xavier. He would have thought that, security in mind, a different key would be needed for each door. Then he realized that would be far too complicated, especially in the chaos of battle. This way, with a single key, any intruder would be delayed as he opened each hatch, or, if someone got careless and left one open, a fail-safe was created with additional sealed hatches. He was thankful for the simplicity of the one key.

The priest traveled down three decks without interference. Then he came to a red hatch where something was repeatedly thumping on the other side.

Xavier had no weapon. He was holding a key and there was no other way down.

He retreated up two flights to where he had seen a fire extinguisher hanging from a wall mount, then returned with it to the thumping. He inserted the key, took a few quick breaths, and hoisted the fire extinguisher as he swung open the hatch.

A rotting face snarled at him, and he caved it in with the red steel bottle. The creature staggered back a few feet, and another corpse with a crew cut pressed into the opening. Xavier smashed it in the forehead, and when it stumbled back, he smashed it again. It went down.

The first one came back at him, and Xavier used the fire extinguisher to shove the dead sailor against a wall. It craned its neck to snap at him. Using the bottle and the bulkhead as a hammer and anvil, Xavier pounded until the skull cracked and flattened. A hand gripped his ankle, and he turned on the crew-cut corpse as it tried to bite his ankle. A quick pounding sent it to join its shipmate.

Xavier hustled down the stairway, and when he reached the next hatch he found it standing open. Had these sailors been in the magazine and tried to flee? Had something caught them on the stairs?

Aware that there would likely be more, Father Xavier descended as quickly as he dared.

FORTY-TWO

Skye was in a dark place with a deep, tolling bell. With every *clang* came a burst of pain that made her head feel as if it would split down the middle. The migraines had returned. She wasn't immune after all, and this was what it was like to die and turn. Pain. Her body was being shoved at, pounded. Something was probably devouring her as she changed, and when she rose she would be maimed like all the others.

Then the darkness grew lighter, charcoal to haze and then brighter still. The bell became a thudding in time with her heart, and this was a small measure of relief. Zombies didn't have heartbeats.

There was pressure, a firm weight on her chest. Was she having a heart attack? No, she was too young, too fit. There was pressure between her legs too, and that made no sense either. The gray turned into a yellow curtain of fog, and it slowly parted at the center. She was on her back, her head a throb of agony, dizzy, feeling like she had to vomit. Her body rubbed against the steel floor, and she saw someone atop her, large, covered in paintings. *No,* her mind said, *those are tattoos.* He was pinning her with one hand in the center of her chest, grunting and thrusting himself forward. His thrusts were hurting.

She knew him, but couldn't remember his name.

And then she did.

And realized that she was being raped.

"Don't . , ." Skye muttered, her voice thick, eyelids fluttering as she tried to swing at him.

TC batted her feeble arm away and slapped her hard across the face, then hit her again, rocking her head back to the left. "Shut up!" he yelled. In his other hand he held her boot knife, and he pressed it against her throat. "You're just a girl!"

The blows sent Skye sliding back toward the darkness, and she was glad to go. Maybe she could stay there. But just before she slipped away, she saw a man standing behind TC, half of his face and one side of his clothing red with blood. He was gripping the enormous crescent wrench TC had used on her.

It was Carney.

San Quentin had saved Bill "Carney" Carnes from TC's wrench. The blow split his scalp, damaged his ear, and gave him a concussion, but most of it landed against his dense shoulder and back muscle, which absorbed the impact and prevented the wrench from crushing his skull. The Q's weight equipment and pull-up bars in the yard had built that muscle.

His cellmate had aimed poorly. Carney would not.

Perhaps it was the squeak of a boot on the bloody floor, a subtle change in the air pressure, or just a predator's natural perception for danger; whatever the reason, TC reacted a half second before the wrench landed, flinging his naked body forward over the unconscious girl. His own powerful muscles took the hit across his meaty upper back. It hurt, made him cough out a whimper as a pair of ribs snapped, but he twisted as quick as a rattler. TC crouched and then launched at his cellmate before Carney had the chance to strike again.

TC slashed the boot knife in a wide arc at Carney's face, the blade catching the older man at the corner of his mouth and slitting it and four inches of his cheek, speckling the wall with red. Carney swung the wrench and TC leaped back, barely escaping having his ribs caved in. He feinted with the knife and drove, but Carney caught his knife hand by the wrist and locked down with a powerful grip. TC grabbed Carney's wrench wrist and twisted, and they came together, faces transformed into primal, snarling things capable of greater savagery than any of the walking dead.

They were chest to chest when they head-butted one another at the same time. There was a thud, a spray of blood, and the men reared back, dazed like a pair of rutting rams. Neither loosened his grip.

Carney saw the fresh bites on TC's chest and arms, but they barely registered.

TC heaved his weight into his cellmate, throwing the older man into an access panel with a hollow *bang*, and then it was Carney's turn, pushing off and slamming TC into the opposite wall.

There were no words, no threats, only growls as they began to spin, fighting to break each other's wrist, hammering each other into the walls as they moved down the narrow corridor, locked in a violent waltz. Then came the litter of corpses, the stairs, and they were tumbling, falling down a wet, padded carpet of the dead. They landed in a tangle at the bottom and instantly sprang to their feet. The knife was lost, the wrench was gone, but true killers are never unarmed, and their powerful hands locked on one another again, clawing for a throat, an eye.

TC jammed his palm under Carney's chin, shoving the man's head back, driving with the fingers of his other hand to blind, to gouge. Carney caught the wrist under his chin and bent it savagely. TC screamed and the pressure came off as he jerked his hand away. Then Carney was hammering at him, and as TC answered with blows of his own, the space was filled with their roars and rage.

They were dancing again, hands catching at throats and squeezing, whirling through a dark compartment in the ship. TC relaxed his elbows and the two men suddenly came together, TC head-butting again, his broad forehead breaking Carney's nose. Their backs were against a pipe railing and they stumbled over the dead before pitching down more stairs. There was a grunt, a crack of bone, then only falling.

FORTY-THREE

Chief Liebs was leading them, a gang of heavily armed refugees and hollow-eyed, bearded sailors, gunning down the dead. Liebs was armed with his favorite weapon, the wood-stocked, 7.62-millimeter M14, Carney's choice as well. He was lethal with the rifle as the high-powered round not only destroyed the brain, but blew out large sections of skull. Everyone was firing, the group pressing steadily forward down passageways, clearing side hatches and intersections. Gun smoke filled the air, and anything that moved, died.

"Up," ordered the chief as they came upon a stairwell. "Up to the hangar bay. It's open space, and we can do more damage."

The group hustled up the metal risers, Evan now in the lead with a Mossberg 500 combat shotgun. As he reached the top he heard gunfire to the left.

And screaming.

And children.

It sounded like a hollow recording of some wartime atrocity echoing down the steel corridor. Calvin and Liebs joined him a moment later.

"Those are our people," said Calvin. "Where does that go?"

Chief Liebs hadn't even finished uttering the word *fantail* before Evan was sprinting down the poorly lit passage. Calvin was after him at once, and then Stone and Mercy blew past. The chief collected the others and followed.

The hatch was right there, Big Jerry's bulk disappearing inside, and Maya dodged a dead sailor coming around a jet engine resting in a maintenance cradle. She went to leap over another corpse lying in her path, saw it moving, reaching.

Michael. Her ten-year-old brother, the youngest. Her heart cried out, but then in a second she realized he wasn't one of the undead. His left foot had become twisted in a bundle of cables and he had fallen, trapped.

"Maya!" he mouthed at her.

Maya nearly went down herself as she tried to stop, skidding on the deck, turning as the dead sailor lunged. With a silent howl she buried the ice pick in its head, jerking it free as the body crumpled. She crouched and tried to free her brother's foot, hoping the ankle wasn't broken, afraid that it was. She wanted to scream at him, demand to know why he wasn't with the others, wanted to cry for joy that he was still alive, cry for fear at what was coming down on the two of them. She couldn't make a sound.

She saw Michael throw his arms over his head and duck, and she spun on her knees, the pick already swinging. A female sailor—little more than a severed upper torso—was dragging herself at Michael, mouth open and drooling fluids, about to bite. The pick sank into her ear all the way to the shaft.

Michael and Maya tugged together, trying to loosen his foot. She felt a vibration in her body that she knew to be a scream, but she did not pause, pulling hard.

The foot popped free.

The zombie that had been Margaret Chu landed on Maya's back, snapping at her ear.

Maya rolled to the side, throwing the woman's weight off even as the dead Asian woman locked her hands in Maya's hair. Three more drifters galloped in from different directions, encircling her. Maya's neck muscles strained to keep Margaret from dragging her by the hair to Margaret's deadly teeth, and she actually screamed, the sound coming out like a ragged wheeze.

One of the charging corpses was blown off its feet, and another's head disintegrated from the jaw up. Another caught a load of buckshot that turned its face into a red sponge, and as it fell, Michael was loose and on his knees with Maya's pick, swinging, spiking Margaret Chu through the top of the head. Gray fingers went limp in Maya's hair as she tore herself free.

Big Jerry was braced against the wall beside the hatch, jacking another shell into the breech of his shotgun, bellowing something Maya couldn't hear but understood. She grabbed Michael and the pick and they fled for the hatch. Jerry was firing, turning, firing, his normally round, friendly face a visage of rage, eyes narrowed as he cut down the dead. Shapes came in from all sides, too many, and then the two of them were inside, bouncing off a wall and careening into a cluster of terrified people.

They were in a small room that was storage for parts and tools. No exits.

Jerry stumbled over the knee knocker, dropped his shotgun, and grabbed the hatch handle, throwing his weight behind it as he hauled it closed.

Dead hands caught the edges, a dozen or more, and tore the hatch from his grip.

FORTY-FOUR

Within the echoing passages, it didn't take Rosa long to realize she would never find Father Xavier. He had run off in pursuit of a madman, unarmed and wounded, chasing a killer into a maze. There were too many corridors, too many stairs and hatches. He could be anywhere. There were only two of them now and remaining below would be suicide. The end result would likely be the same wherever they went, so Rosa Escobedo vowed to see the sun one last time before she died.

The medic moved down a hallway with unsteady lights, the M4 to her shoulder and her eye at the sight. She thought about all of the wounded and dying Marines she had treated in the desert who had hunted insurgents the same way. A shape in a hatch caught her eye and she squeezed the trigger a second before she realized it could be her friend the priest. It wasn't. It had been a rotting petty officer whose brains were now sliding down a steel wall.

She needed a stairway. Finally she found a short one, only four steps to a small landing and a hatch. She and Tommy pulled it open together, sunlight and sea air pouring through, both of them gasping.

There was an outside catwalk beyond, and as they exited they saw an overhang that could only be the flight deck over their heads. Another metal stairway led up to it.

Rosa and Tommy emerged from below and stood on the rubberized decking, clothes snapping against them as a sharp wind rushed across the flight deck. She looked around and saw that the aircraft carrier's superstructure, a steel high-rise bristling with antennae, was on the opposite side of the deck. There were corpses everywhere, all of them down.

There was movement at the superstructure's hatch, two figures locked together, stumbling out onto the deck. They separated; the bigger one's arm moved in a quick arc and the other fell.

TC and Carney.

And then Rosa's attention was snapped away by a metallic screaming and a black shape rushing at the ship from out of the sky.

Vladimir fought against physics, against engineering and mathematics and gravity. He gripped the cyclic and collective so hard he thought they might shatter in his hands, as the fuel-starved turbines sucked the last JP-5 from the lines. The pitch of the two engines howled higher and higher toward seizing. Screaming buzzers filled the cockpit with an unholy noise as Vlad willed the chopper to hang in the air for just a few seconds more.

The Russian saw the wall of the carrier rushing at him on a tilted angle. They would impact right at the cockpit. The Black Hawk would crumple against an immovable, metal mass, folding the cockpit and its occupants in an envelope of torn steel. There would be no explosion—there wasn't enough fuel left to start a campfire—but they would both be dead just the same.

"Ben," Vladimir said, and in that final instant the child looked up and smiled.

.   .   .

The two men lost their grips and fell apart, panting like two enraged animals hunting one another in a gray light, circling. They hunched low, grappling, arms swinging and teeth bared. There was no punching, for this was no fistfight. It was a battle of grips, and he who seized the other first would live.

It was TC who struck first.

Carney lunged, but he was still dizzy from being hit by the wrench, and he misjudged the distance. TC twisted and locked an arm around Carney's head, cranking down with his bicep, forcing Carney to bend with his face to the floor. Hands batted weakly at the muscled arm. TC laughed through bloody teeth, one eye purple and swollen, his forehead split and trickling red into his good eye. He hauled Carney toward the open hatch, and the older man was helpless, choking and deprived of air, unable to keep himself from being dragged along.

They had been here before. There were the racks of vests and helmets, rows of clipboards, and the black nylon tool belt. TC snatched a screwdriver out of the pouch and dragged Carney through the hatch, out onto the flight deck.

As they went over the knee knocker, Carney raised a boot and smashed it against the side of TC's knee. The bigger man let out a cry and sagged away, releasing enough pressure for the older man to pull his head free. A moment later they were locked in another dance, hands gripping wrists, throwing their weight, spinning across the flight deck.

Carney snorted blood and mucus from his shattered nose and hawked it into TC's face. The younger inmate roared and fell back a foot, but in that brief instant of separation he slashed and plunged with the screwdriver. The flat blade caught Carney across the belly, lodging against meat and slipping from TC's hand. Carney staggered and fell onto his back, smacking his head on the deck.

Something was screaming in the sunshine, a high, metallic cry accompanied by a thundering heartbeat, a *THUMP-THUMP-THUMP* that filled the air. Carney's world was spinning, his head ready to detach and float away.

TC dropped onto him, his face red and contorted by a savage lust. The younger inmate ripped the tool out of Carney's gut. "End of the world, motherfucker!" TC screamed, raising the screwdriver over his head with both hands.

FORTY-FIVE

Evan heard the gunfire drop off and stop, immediately replaced by the moans of the dead. His boots hammered the deck as he charged the corridor, spotting a partially open hatch at the end, sunlight glowing at its edges. A drifter was dragging itself over the knee knocker on the way in.

He fired on the run, the Mossberg blowing the thing's head apart from behind, and then Evan was swinging the hatch wide, leaping over the corpse and through, into the open-air fantail. He instantly took in the high space, the daylight and the sun beyond the wide opening. He saw bodies on the deck, fresh gore everywhere.

He saw the dead, all shambling toward an open hatch on the far wall, approaching from all directions.

He marched into them, firing, racking, firing. A moment later a trio of assault rifles joined in with Calvin to his right, Mercy and Stone on his left. Then Chief Liebs was there, the M14 bucking, his men on line beside him, pumping rounds into the dead. Finally Juju and Dakota, blasting shotgun rounds.

The fantail echoed with the unending ripple of gunfire, dead sailors crumpling to the deck, some turning to face the new sound only to be cut down. The group advanced with the deadly calm of professional warriors, changing magazines and feeding shells with precision, hippies and wanderers and boys in dirty uniforms, killers all.

Within minutes not a single zombie stood or crawled, and not one of them had managed to even get close to their executioners.

Evan saw the bloody oxygen bottle on the deck, and then there was no doubt. *Why? Why had they come?* He ran toward the hatch where the dead had been heading and saw a body lying half in and half out. *Why didn't you stay?* he thought, tears leaping to his eyes. Calvin ran with him, making a long, low keening sound.

They reached the hatch together, and Evan went in. The bitter, coppery tang of blood was heavy in the air, mixed with a vile putrescence. It had been a slaughter, and as he saw what was at the end of the room, he let out a sob.

Maya stood with her legs planted in a wide stance, her body heaving as she breathed. Her hair hung damp and limp about her face, and she was bathed in blood. One hand held a glistening ice climber's pick. The floor before her was layered with dead sailors, heads and faces pierced, motionless and staring. Behind Maya, a cluster of adults held children close to their bodies, crying and keeping their faces turned away from the massacre. The pregnant couple was there, and Big Jerry lay on the floor, propped on one elbow and holding an empty, smoking shotgun.

Maya's eyes, hard and deadly, met Evan's and softened at once. With a bloody hand she signed, "I missed you."

Evan made a sound that was both a sob and a laugh and ran to her.

FORTY-SIX

It was the wind, a lovely, stiff wind across the flight deck, a naval aviator's friend. It meant lift.

Just before the failing Black Hawk was hurled against *Nimitz*'s unforgiving side, the wind cradled the bird from below and gave it lift—just enough. With less than six inches to spare, the helicopter's wheels cleared the edge and thudded down onto the rubberized deck surface at the extreme bow end of the ship.

Vladimir and Ben bounced with the hit, and then the pilot was changing the pitch of the rotors, using that same wind to slow his rolling aircraft and bring it to a stop. His hands moved quickly, shutting his systems down as above him the turbines died in a long, sinking whine. The rotor blades began to slow at once.

The Russian stared out through the windscreen for a long moment, heart pounding like the hooves of a running horse, and then he let out a rush of breath. He looked over at his tiny co-pilot, who still wore the oversized ear protectors.

Vlad held out a trembling palm.

Ben laughed and slapped it.

. . .

Rosa saw what was happening at the superstructure, screamed, "No!" and started running at the two men, Tommy beside her. They both knew they would never cross the distance in time.

As TC rose up for the kill, she saw the zombie emerge from the superstructure's hatch. It was female and half-naked, its remaining clothing torn and bloody, galloping at the two men, both arms coming up.

Blood was in Carney's mouth, leaking out the corners, TC's weight crushing his lungs. He looked up at the face, at the man who had once been his friend and was now about to drive a screwdriver into his heart and cast him into darkness.

The sound of the shot came at the same instant the bullet punched a hole out the front of TC's head.

The big inmate sagged off to one side, limp and boneless on the deck. Skye Dennison, staggering and unbalanced from her blow to the head, slashed clothing blowing in the wind, lowered her pistol as she reached the two men.

"No, fuck *you*," she said, pumping three more rounds into TC's body.

She dropped to her knees, then fell to the deck, landing partially on Carney's chest. She closed her eyes and sighed, head resting against the man's heartbeat.

Carney spat blood and choked out, "Skye . . ."

She found his hand and squeezed it, then whispered, "Some people just need saving."

Carney faded.

When the pounding of Rosa's boots arrived, Skye pointed back toward the superstructure. "Angie," she said, and then she faded too.

FORTY-SEVEN

Father Xavier couldn't help but think of passages he had read, both biblical and literary, containing descriptions of the descent into hell. He was living it now, the stairway lit with red battle lights that cast a hellish glow on steel walls and railings. The reek of rotting flesh was thick in the unmoving air, and without air-conditioning the temperature climbed as he traveled deeper. He was sweating, and his hand was slick on the handle of the bloody fire extinguisher. He expected the undead to block his path at any moment, minions of the devil determined to stop him from getting to Brother Peter.

Was the man truly evil, or only psychotic? Did the devil dwell within him, as Xavier had been taught, or was he just a man, violent and deranged, hopelessly trapped within a fantasy? And if Xavier did find him, would he listen to reason? What could Xavier do if he didn't? He had just renewed his faith with God, begged Him to live in his heart once more. Would he kill Brother Peter and, in so doing, ensure his own damnation?

Assuming he wasn't too late. Instead of a soulless, shuffling corpse in his path, it might just as easily be a microsecond of white heat and incineration as the minister carried out his final task in God's name.

Xavier reached the bottom of the stairs and stepped into the main hall of the magazine. There were no minions, no zombies with which to contend. He would face the Beast itself.

The blast doors to every magazine stood open, light spilling into the corridor from within. Xavier moved on the balls of his feet, breathing through his mouth to remain as quiet as possible. He looked into the compartments, eyes falling on the tools men used to destroy one another, silent couriers of death waiting to be employed.

How fitting that he should face the Beast in such a place.

Give me strength, Lord. Be my light in the darkness.

Xavier didn't have to search every compartment. After looking inside only a few, he heard the conversation echoing from the far end of the corridor.

He moved swiftly now.

*W*hen you get to heaven, I think we'll have a luau," said God. The Lord was in the form of a beautiful, red-haired woman with heavy breasts, naked and straddling one of the MARS nuclear missiles a little farther down the row. She looked like the mistress Peter had kept in Chicago.

"Or an orgy," the woman said, stretching Her body across the missile in an erotic pose, stroking the metal skin.

"Don't talk like that," Brother Peter said. "It's not . . . not right. Not for you."

"You're just shy," the woman said, transforming into Angie West, trailing Her nipples across the cold missile. *"I know what you like."*

Her bare hands and feet bled with stigmata, streaking the metal skin.

"Stop distracting me!" Peter shouted, pointing a pair of wire cutters at the figure. "I need to focus."

"Fuck us? Is that what you said?" Angie purred.

Brother Peter clamped his hands over his ears. "Stop it, stop it, stop it!"

God turned to smoke and drifted toward the ceiling as Peter went back to work. The first two missiles were wired to this one, armed and awaiting a charge. He finished arming the third warhead and stepped back from the weapon's open maintenance panel. Peter smiled, looking at his work. Bands of colored wire looped between the three missiles and then connected to the wall phone across the room with a long stretch of red wire.

"Is that pride I see on your face?" Peter's savior was once again the Air Force shrink, standing a few feet away with His arms folded, frowning. *"Is it?"*

Brother Peter hung his head. It was almost over, and then he could sleep forever in silence. "This is for you, Lord. Thy will be done."

The shrink shook His head and began polishing His glasses. *"You're such a schmuck."*

Peter threw the wire cutters down. "Why do you do that all the time? Why do you always make me feel bad?"

"Oh, did I make you feel bad?" The shrink pointed at the minister. *"Go fuck yourself. I can't stand you anymore."*

"Stop!" Peter cried. "You love me! I'm your chosen disciple, and you can't talk to me that way!"

God stared and said nothing.

Brother Peter was crying. "All I've ever done is serve you. But you're cruel. Why won't you love me?"

God began to fade. *"You're a fool,"* He said, and then He was gone.

"But you are loved, Peter," said Father Xavier, standing in the opening to the magazine compartment. He set the fire extinguisher down and held out his hands, palms up. "You are loved," he repeated, walking forward slowly. He saw the missiles, saw the wires and where they ended.

Brother Peter bolted for the phone, and Xavier charged him. The minister got there first, gripping the handset and holding it in the cradle.

"No, no, no, no!" Peter said, pointing a finger at the priest.

Xavier slid to a stop ten feet away. "Don't do this, Peter," he said. "Don't hurt any more people."

"They're not people, they're sinners," he hissed.

"We're all sinners," the priest said. "Isn't that what we're taught?"

The minister sneered. "*You* are, praying to your idols and make-believe saints, bowing and scraping to your master in Rome." He stabbed the air with his finger. "You are! You are!"

Xavier Church was no expert in nuclear weapons, but he knew they needed an electrical charge in order to detonate. If the televangelist had done what it appeared he had, lifting the phone receiver from its cradle would open the circuit. The charge would travel down the wire in a millisecond, and then there would be the slightest instant of searing heat, followed by a vast nothingness.

"This isn't God's work, Peter," Xavier said, easing forward, palms still open and empty. "Wrath is His privilege, not ours."

Peter bared his teeth. "He works through me. I am His instrument."

Xavier shook his head slowly, still gliding forward. "You're a man of deep faith," the priest said. "I can see that. And sometimes a man, a *good* man, can lose his way."

Peter began to cry again. "Stay there! I'm not lost. I'm doing God's work. Just ask Him." He gestured at the room, keeping his eyes on the advancing priest, still gripping the phone receiver.

"We're alone," the priest said gently, a step closer, another. "Just you . . . just me . . ."

"Liar!" Peter spat. "Behold the Lord our God!"

When Peter Dunleavy glanced over to where God should be standing, Xavier Church struck. Peter looked back just in time to see it coming, and Xavier would never know who said the words, him or the minister.

"Forgive me."

Xavier's right fist shot out with the speed and power of a professional boxer, connecting with the minister's chin. There was an explosive *crack* as the force of the impact snapped Peter's neck, killing him instantly.

As the body sagged to the floor, Xavier leaped for the phone receiver, clamping his hands over it and holding it firmly in the cradle as Peter Dunleavy's hand slipped away.

"Forgive me."

This time, Xavier knew that it was he who spoke.

EPILOGUE

Early January, the outbreak now five months past. Life on the *Nimitz* was chilly, and much colder on the open deck as light rains and a regular breeze came in off the bay. It was cloudy most days, but it was still California and rare for the temperature to drop below forty degrees. Everyone wore light, thermal-lined jackets, all Navy blue.

There was little free time, and everyone had a job, some several, and all were important. Everyone traveled the ship armed, and no one went anywhere alone.

In the months following the assault, Chief Liebs wore many hats, and his most important task was organizing and leading hunting parties. By the time January arrived, Liebs had collected nearly four thousand dog tags and compared them to the ship's roster. By his estimation there were still close to a thousand drifters on board. Many were suspected to be trapped in sealed, watertight compartments—where they would remain—but there were countless other places they could be.

The hunting parties went out daily. Other groups in hazmat suits, under the watchful eyes of people with rifles, scoured the ship and placed corpses in body bags, dropping them over the sides. Fire hoses were used to wash down rooms and corridors. Four more people died during the clearing process, including Juju, who opened a hatch without listening at it first and had his throat torn out by a woman in surgical scrubs.

When he wasn't hunting, Chief Liebs gave firearms instruction. Both he and Xavier insisted that everyone age twelve and up learn to shoot. His two best students turned out to be Stone and Mercy, and they accompanied him on every hunting party.

Vlad was happy with his new family. Sophia, who had organized a school for the children on board, shared his quarters, as did Ben. The boy called the pilot "Papa."

The Russian was busy as well. He interviewed and selected four men and women from Calvin's Family and began to teach them helicopter maintenance and fueling. He relearned a great deal about it himself in the process, and he built a ground crew. He also began teaching Evan to fly the carrier's SH-60 Seahawks, smaller and simpler versions of the Black Hawk. There was no shortage of fuel. The Russian was fond of repeating that having a single qualified pilot on board was madness, and despite the fact that Evan was just north of incompetent, he was satisfied with the young man's progress. Evan was bright and picked it up quickly, realizing that the joy of riding his Harley was nothing compared to the freedom of flight.

Maya wanted to fly as well, but her inability to hear cockpit warnings or communicate by radio kept her grounded. Instead she had been chosen as one of those learning ground maintenance, specifically electronics. She wanted to do it as long as she was physically able.

One evening, after work on the carrier's six helicopters was done—Maya had been noticeably absent—Evan returned to the quarters they shared to find her sitting on the edge of the bed.

"You weren't at work today," Evan said. "Are you okay?"

Maya nodded and took his hands, guiding him to sit beside her. "I was with Rosa," she signed.

Evan's breath caught. Ever since he had seen her in that tool compartment, covered in blood, he had feared that she had been exposed to the virus, even months after the battle. He knew it was irrational, because the symptoms would have presented themselves long before now, but it scared him all the same. Losing Maya would kill him.

Maya knew his fears, and smiled broadly, hugging him close. Then she sat back, still smiling. "I'm pregnant," she signed.

It took Evan a moment. They signed constantly, and he had been learning, but the word caught him off guard. Then it hit.

"Oh, baby," he whispered, his hands going to her still-flat stomach. "Is it healthy? Is it a boy or girl? When are you due?"

Maya laughed. "It's early," she signed, "but I'm healthy and Rosa isn't worried." She needed to use a pad and paper for the next part, unfamiliar with how to sign a particular word. "We'll know more once Rosa figures out how to operate the ultrasound."

There were tears and more long hugs. Finally Evan held her face in his hands. "I'm a little frightened," he said. "A baby in a world like this, what kind of life will it have?"

Maya nodded, signing. "I'm scared too. But we made a place for her, didn't we?"

Evan smiled and nodded. "Hoping for a girl?"

She nodded back.

"Well if it is," Evan said, "we'll name her Faith."

Calvin did his best to heal, but he grieved for his decimated Family. They had lost so many. The man was quieter now, taking on less of a leadership role and becoming more of a caregiver, ensuring that everyone was comfortable in whatever quarters they had chosen, seeing that they were well fed and had whatever they needed. He hunted alongside Chief Liebs and the others, dispatching the dead with cold ruthlessness. To Calvin, with every kill and every small comfort he could arrange, he gave people the sanctuary for which so many had died. He thought Faith would approve.

Although her head required seventeen stitches and she lost a molar, Skye recovered from TC's assault and was soon stalking the corridors of *Nimitz* with her M4. Chief Liebs took special interest in her and provided individual shooting instruction. He acknowledged that she'd had a good teacher and also possessed natural talent. He was also very direct in pointing out that she had much to learn and had developed some bad shooting habits. With his tutoring, Skye became truly lethal.

One afternoon in November when they were doing target work out on the bow end of the flight deck, taking a break and looking out at the water, Liebs asked Skye about her original weapons training, and what it was like for her in the days following the outbreak. She didn't reply, and they were quiet for a while.

"Were you scared?" Liebs asked at last.

Skye took her time answering. "Yes," she finally said. "Not so much of the drifters, but I was scared to fall asleep most of the time. I still am, I guess. Sometimes the dreams are worse than facing the actual dead." Then she looked at him with one clear eye—she had covered her unsettling one with a proper eye patch for some time now—and said, "What scares you?"

Chief Liebs, Navy sniper and leader of a zombie-hunting party, looked down and turned red. "Ferris wheels. Tell anyone and you're dead."

Skye laughed until tears ran from her good eye.

After Carney's nose was set as well as it could be, his belly stapled closed, and his slit-open cheek sewn up, he and Skye began spending a lot of time together. At first it was simply hunting the dead. Then it was shared meals after hunting, and working out in the aircraft carrier's gym. They came to enjoy one another's company.

Near mid-November, they found themselves sitting on a high catwalk late at night, having coffee and looking at the sky.

"I dreamed last night that I was fighting zombies with a Wiffle bat," Skye said.

Carney smirked. "How did that work out for you?"

"It was about what you would expect." They both laughed and looked back at the stars. "They're brighter," said Skye. "There're no city lights to compete with. I never realized how many there were."

Carney took a deep breath. "Skye, I went to prison for murdering two people in their sleep. One was my wife." There was a long silence, and he couldn't tell if she was waiting for more, or if he had just completely screwed things up. He plunged ahead, telling her about the murders that had put him there, and about the child he had lost. He held nothing back, wanting to be completely honest with someone for the first time in his life. When he was done, Skye was looking at him in silence. Carney felt an ache he couldn't explain, and his shoulders sagged. So much for honesty.

"My parents were killed right in front of me," Skye said softly, "and I watched my kid sister turn." Now it was Skye who spoke of unspeakable things, and together they talked until dawn. When the sun came up at last, they were sitting close, his arm around her shoulder, her head resting against him.

"I still can't explain why I saved you in Oakland," he said.

Skye liked the warmth of him and pressed in closer. "It doesn't really matter, does it?"

Carney tilted her chin up so he could look into her eyes. "Saving you matters more than anything else in my life."

In the weeks that followed, Carney told her about life at San Quentin, and Skye spoke about the National Guardsmen who had rescued her from the campus, about her solitary days and nights in the weeks following, and how she feared that she was going slowly insane.

They were both torn, inside and out, and might never be fully healed. What healing they did, they did together.

On a night in December Skye came to Carney's quarters and, without a word, undressed in front of him. She let him see the ash-gray skin, the scars, even removed her eye patch.

Carney didn't flinch. "I'm so much older than you," was all he said.

Skye put a finger to his lips and entered his arms.

She kept her own quarters, and they weren't together every night, but it worked. They had no expectations.

Arguably the busiest person on board was Rosa Escobedo, whom everyone simply called Doc, for that was what she had become. Chief Liebs, who outranked her, gave her the respect he had reserved for officers. Rosa had completed pre-med and developed a wealth of skill and knowledge both through the Navy and as a paramedic, but she had much to learn. Most of it was on-the-job training, placing open manuals on tray tables and referring to them as she performed small medical procedures or used the X-ray machine and ultrasound. In what little time off she could find, she studied the many medical texts she found in the ship's surgeon's office. Most of the time she functioned with dark circles under her eyes.

She made mistakes. Carney's abdomen got infected and she had to remove and reapply the staples, treating him with antibiotics. The pregnant couple lost their baby, and she had to learn to deliver a stillborn as the mother wailed with grief. Rosa took it personally.

One afternoon Xavier came to her holding a white coat, looking at her scrubs. "Wear this," he said, slipping it over her shoulders.

"I'm not a doctor."

"It will give your patients confidence," he said, walking out of the room. "And yes, you are."

Rosa did a lot of apologizing at first for her lack of skill, for sloppy stitches or for causing pain as she treated injuries and tried to set bones, for not knowing as much as she should. In time, however, she came to be comfortable in the white coat, and her mannerism became more professional, though no less compassionate. She learned to be stern when she had to be, especially when the patient was a pain in the ass.

Like Angie West was.

It was a constant battle to keep the woman in bed, to keep her from undoing the amateur healing Rosa could provide. It didn't help that they were both strong, opinionated women, and it finally took Father Xavier weighing in on the doc's side before Angie grudgingly relented and promised to be a good patient.

It had long been Angie's habit, even back in her gunsmithing and firearms instruction days, to wear light body armor under a jacket, and she had continued the practice. It had saved her. TC's first bullet hit her just below the left breast, the impact cracking ribs and causing massive bruising, but the body armor had displaced the energy sufficiently to prevent it from entering. The second bullet, fired down at her while she was lying on the deck, had probably been intended as a throat shot. It went wide, clipping the collar of the vest and slowing before punching through the meat of her shoulder and breaking her collarbone, but exiting without further damage. No surgery had been required other than stitching, and the flesh wound and collarbone would heal in a few months.

"The path of that bullet was one in a million," Rosa told her. "Lottery-ticket lucky."

Angie had to admit that the doc was right, and that knowledge helped her to not be too much of a pain in the ass.

The broken arm was another matter, with fractures to both the radius and ulna, but fortunately they were not compound fractures. Rosa set them as best she could and opted for the flexibility of a splint and sling instead of a cast, so adjustments could be made as needed.

Angie was physically fit, a nondiabetic nonsmoker who ate well and did her physical therapy as directed. She would heal quickly, and Rosa predicted three to six months for the bones to knit, possibly a year or more before they were back to normal. The problem was Angie's tendency to overdo it, to try to do too much, too fast. She wanted to hunt with the others, wanted to shoot, wanted to be useful, but she had to rest. It hurt, and not just physically.

Father Xavier visited with her every day, talking about her family, the goings-on of the ship, helping her with her guilt and grief for her daughter and husband, out there somewhere. Sometimes he simply held her when she cried.

Angie did as she was told. The aircraft carrier's computers reunited them all with the passage of time and dates, and Angie watched the days tick away. By the new year she was fit, although the arm ached in the cool, damp weather and wasn't as strong as it had been. Chief Liebs took her on at once, working her back to combat readiness.

With unspoken and unanimous understanding, command of the *Nimitz* and its new occupants went to Xavier Church. He didn't turn from the responsibility, and took on the role of administrator, counselor, father, protector. When the others insisted he take the admiral's quarters as his own, he opted for a single-occupant officer's room, where he spent little time. He was forever walking the ship, checking the progress of countless projects and joining the ongoing hunt when he could, constantly touching base with the souls now in his care.

He limped and had to rest frequently. Rosa had been able to pluck out all but one piece of shrapnel from Brother Peter's grenade, and that one, deep in his thigh near his hip, caused him discomfort. The doc was afraid to go in after it because of the potential bleeding, and thought it might slowly work its way close enough to the surface for her to reach, but she wasn't sure. Xavier didn't let it slow him down, and even spent time in the gym working the speed and heavy bags.

As for what God thought of him, Xavier didn't know. If killing Brother Peter and assuring his own damnation had been the price for saving the people he had come to love, then so be it. There was a measure of solace in that acceptance, he found, and he even began to pray again. He held a mass for those they had lost, and during a Christmas service he asked, on behalf of all of them, for safety, health and peace. Maybe God listened. Xavier hoped He did.

Angie West walked down the passageway so loaded with weapons and ammunition that Xavier couldn't fit beside her and had to walk behind. The priest carried a Mossberg slung over one shoulder, and although this part of the ship was fully lit and had been declared safe, he was watchful.

"You have the Hydras?" Xavier asked.

"I do," Angie replied. "One for me, one for him, and two spares." Chief Liebs had introduced them to the handheld Hydra radios used on the aircraft carrier, powerful enough to penetrate the many steel walls, and if in the open, capable of miles of range. Everyone aboard carried them now. Angie wouldn't be able to communicate with the ship once she got where she was going, but at least she could keep in touch with her pilot if they became separated.

"You know I'll go with you," Xavier said. "I really think I should."

She stopped at the foot of a stairwell and turned. "We've talked about this. Your place is here." She kissed him on his scarred brown cheek, where the claw marks of a zombie's nails were slowly turning from pink to white. "Walk me out."

They climbed to the flight deck, where Vladimir already had the Black Hawk spooling up. Xavier went with a heavy heart, trying to be happy for her, praying that she would find her family alive. During her convalescence, Angie had told him about Vladimir's promise to take her to look for them. The priest believed it was what had helped her to heal so quickly, and now that time had arrived.

Angie wore Leah's blue teething ring on a chain around her neck.

"Chico's not far," she said as they stepped up into the breeze. "We might be there and back before you even miss us."

"I already miss you," said Xavier.

Angie smiled. "I promised Sophia I'd take care of Vlad."

"Take care of you," Xavier said. He took the woman in his massive arms and held her. "I'll pray for you until you come back," he said into her ear. He was unashamed of the tears that blew away in the wind.

The chopper was out on the bow, and they walked there together. Vladimir had installed a new pair of M240 door guns, one on each side, and had prepared the Black Hawk with extra fuel in the form of two drop tanks. As they approached, Angie saw Skye loading gear in through the side door. She was dressed in black fatigues and boots, wore a loaded ammo vest, and was armed with an M4, a pistol, and a machete. Her head was freshly shaved.

"We don't have all day, lady," said Skye, climbing in after the gear.

Angie gave Xavier a sharp look, and the priest laughed. "You don't think *I* was going to tell her she couldn't go, do you?" he said.

Angie shook her head and climbed in. Before she moved up to the empty co-pilot's seat she pointed at Skye's eye patch. "You *do* look like a pirate."

"And the horse you rode in on," said Skye.

"Are we at last ready?" Vladimir asked as Angie buckled in and put on a headset. When she nodded, he said, "Good. Do not touch the controls. I have no wish to die because you have seen this done on television and think you understand aeronautics."

Angie smiled and jerked her thumb in the air.

Vladimir was preparing to lift off when a lone figure came jogging across the deck, armed and wearing a backpack. The Russian held off on the stick as the figure spoke briefly with Xavier, then climbed into the back.

Vlad sighed. "Now are we ready? Or shall we burn more fuel as we sit on this deck?"

Angie gave him the thumbs-up again, and the Black Hawk left the *Nimitz*, rising and banking to the northeast.

"Groundhog-Seven is airborne," Vlad said into the mic, using the bored tone of all aviators. He received an acknowledgment from the ship.

Back in the troop compartment, Skye sat with one boot propped on the hard plastic case of the Barrett fifty-caliber and looked at the late arrival. "Are you lost?" she asked.

Carney grinned. "Nope. I'm right where I want to be."

Father Xavier stood on the deck and watched the helicopter until it was out of sight, then turned and headed back to the superstructure. As he walked, a video-assisted scope tracked his movement from a position across the bay. A man with unfriendly eyes and murder on his mind watched the screen. "See you soon," he murmured.

It was January 11.

The biggest earthquake in recorded history was two days away.

Turn the page for an exciting excerpt from
the next book in the Omega Days series

Drifters

Coming January 2015 from Berkley Books!

DEAD
OF JANUARY

ONE

In life she had been Sharon Douglas-Frye, thirty-three years old and a mother of two. A music scholarship took her to the University of Illinois, where she met Joseph, a grad student with plans for starting a heavy equipment dealership in California. Marriage, house, kids, book club, and Pilates all followed.

Then she had been bitten while sitting at an outside table of a sidewalk café by a little boy wearing an Angry Birds shirt, a wild little thing with no mommy in sight. Not even a real bite, really, more of a nip, which she cleaned and bandaged at home. Joseph was away on business, no need to worry him.

Sharon died of a fever in the master bedroom of her lovely Chico home.

And then she came back. And ate her children—parts of them, at least.

She ate Joe too, when he got home from his trip. The kids helped her with Daddy. Since that day, Sharon had seen none of them, and wouldn't have recognized them anyway.

Now, five months later, Sharon Douglas-Frye shuffled barefoot through a January hay field of brittle stubble, her feet black and torn, the meat worn off several toes. She wore the tatters of a floral print nightgown that drooped off one shoulder, exposing an emaciated body with flattened breasts, jutting ribs, and skin the color of old wax. Her face was drawn and tight, decaying jaw muscles visible through holes in her flesh, teeth clicking incessantly. Her eyes were a cloudy blue shot through with black blood vessels.

The hay crackled beneath her feet and her arms flopped as she walked, following the sound of crows. That sound always meant food, either what the crow was eating or the crow itself, if it wasn't fast enough. The birds were usually too quick and clever to permit Sharon to catch them, however.

A few others of her kind slumped through the field around her. Sharon paid them no mind.

It was cool, the barest of breezes making her knotted hair rustle about her shoulders. She trudged directly through the skeletal remains of a cow, the bones gnawed clean, catching and ripping her nightgown on a thick, upward-curving rib. As she moved past, her left hand banged against the rib, and Sharon didn't notice when both her engagement and wedding rings at last rattled off her bony finger and dropped into the hay stubble.

The crows called, and Sharon kept moving.

To her right, a man who had once sold used cars moved through the field with jerking steps, still wearing the remains of a shirt and tie. His skin was a mottled olive streaked with black, now split and hanging about him in loose, sour ribbons. Strands of a comb-over fluttered about a face so torn it revealed bone, and the car salesman was bent forward and to the side by a pair of fractured vertebrae, grinding against each other with every step.

The three coyotes that had been trailing the salesman for the past hour finally decided he posed no threat. They darted in and took him down at the knees, and the salesman groaned and flapped his arms as they devoured him.

Sharon didn't notice the coyotes. She heard crows.

A sharp, twisted piece of metal severed two toes on Sharon's left foot as she walked through the hay field. She stumbled, then got tangled in a swirl of burned electrical wiring. That made her fall down, and she crawled toward the sound of the crows for almost an hour before she managed to free herself of the wiring and could stand once more.

There were a lot of sharp things in this field, bent shapes and pieces of metal blackened by fire, scattered over a hundred yards. The hay stubble was brittle and ashy where it had been burned, snapping under her feet, and she could still smell the smoke from the fire. That usually meant food too. She fell again, this time tripping over a long, slender length of melted polymer, constructed in a honeycomb pattern. Sharon rose once more, walked on, and at last reached the place with the crows.

Half a dozen of the glossy black birds were perched on the fuselage of the Black Hawk helicopter, which lay on its side in the field. The tail boom was gone along with both turbines, and only the troop compartment and shattered cockpit remained, all of it scorched.

The crows shrieked in annoyance as Sharon stumbled to where the cockpit windscreen had been, a few melted fragments clinging to the edges of the frame. The body of a tall man was still strapped in the pilot's seat, slumped against his belts, his blackened skin picked away to reveal dripping, red meat. His flight helmet and head had been caved in when the cockpit hit the ground nose-first, and so he was not moving.

Sharon moaned and reached inside, tugging at an arm, trying to bring it to her mouth, snapping her teeth. It didn't quite reach, and so she started to whine, pulling herself up through the frame and into the cockpit, tearing her own flesh on jagged aluminum and sharp Plexiglas. Her feet left the ground as she wriggled through, at last stuffing the fingers of the pilot's dead hand into her mouth. Sharon chewed and grunted, and the crows watched.

350

.　.　.

Orlando Worthy was a biter.

The Chico police had long ago nicknamed him Orlando the Impaler. He had drifted into the northern California city at age twenty-six after receiving parole on a seven-year stretch for armed robbery (he slashed a female store detective's face with a fish-cleaning knife on a sidewalk in front of a discount store) and had remained in Chico for the next twenty-two years.

In those two-plus decades, Orlando had bitten nineteen people during meth transactions, bar fights, domestic disturbances, and just because. He bit another nine police officers and seventeen store detectives over the course of fifty-three arrests for petty theft. He bit a cocker spaniel when it barked at him in Bidwell Park. As payment for the biting, he had been hit with nightsticks, pepper spray, Tasers, a beanbag round from a nonlethal police shotgun, two kitchen knives, a tire iron, and countless punches and kicks.

By the time he turned forty-eight—the summer of the plague—Orlando already looked like a zombie, the meth wasting his body and aging his features. He was so distorted by the drug that a twenty-year montage of his booking photos had become one of the highest-viewed online features at Faces of Meth, a dramatic progression of decline that he bragged was his second claim to fame.

His first claim to fame was boosting. Orlando Worthy had been a professional shoplifter for his entire life. Not professional in the sense that he was too good to get caught—he had been caught plenty of times and his face was known by every cop, retailer, and security guard in Butte County—but that he did it for a living and was skilled in using the tools of the trade.

His bony hands could snap off security tags faster than an electronic detacher. When he couldn't break the tags, he used wire cutters or stuffed the goods inside foil-lined bags to defeat the electronic pedestals at the front doors. If a garment was affixed with ink tags, he would just put it in the freezer overnight and snap them off harmlessly in the morning. For the big, cabled Alpha tags, the screamers, he would go in with a large drink from 7-Eleven, dip the sensor until it shorted out, and then clip it off with his cutters. Retailers called this drowning tags. A flat-head screwdriver could get him into locked electronics and jewelry cases, and threats of violence and biting stopped most store owners and at least two-thirds of store detectives from trying to apprehend him.

Some weren't intimidated, and Orlando had taken his share of beatings.

Orlando Worthy stole whatever he could sell, and that was most everything. There were always buyers for Polo shirts, fragrances, Timberland boots, and Under Armour. Anything Apple was a hot commodity, as well as electronic games and learning toys. Shrimp, condoms, batteries, leather jackets, women's shoes, Lego, pocketbooks—everything had a market. He would steal powdered baby formula by the case and sell it to drug dealers who used it as a safe way to cut heroin, or to welfare moms who paid him twenty cents on the dollar. If a woman walked away from her purse at a grocery store, it was his. If someone left their car unlocked near him, they would return to find their GPS and any spare change missing.

Orlando liked to think of himself as the Prince of Thieves. He didn't understand the literary reference to the nickname the Impaler, and no one bothered to explain it to him.

In August of last year, Orlando scooted out of a store with seven pairs of snowy-white Nikes, aluminum foil wrapped tightly around the sensors to prevent the pedestals from sounding. He ducked behind the store, on high alert for signs of pursuit, relaxing only when he realized no one was coming. He was shaking, not just from the adrenaline; the pipe was calling. Not just calling, but singing.

A beefy kid in his twenties emerged from behind a Dumpster, a store detective Orlando knew well, and who knew the meth addict just as well.

"Oh, shit," Orlando said, bracing himself as the kid galloped in and tackled him. As they hit the pavement together, Orlando growled and bit the kid's arm.

The kid bit him back and damn near tore his right ear off.

Orlando shrieked and hammered at the store detective with his fists, squirming beneath his bulk and slipping free. The kid snarled, glassy-eyed with Orlando's blood smeared across his face, and the meth addict ran. He didn't care about Nikes anymore. The look on the kid's face held the promise of death beside a stinking Dumpster.

He made it seven blocks, stumbling along a sidewalk with both hands pressed to the dangling flap that had been his ear, blood streaking his neck and dampening his clothes. A police cruiser slid to the curb and the young officer inside immediately recognized Orlando. He leaped out of the cruiser and slammed Orlando to the ground, cuffing him. If Orlando Worthy was running and bleeding, he surmised, then he had been up to some illegal shit and that was probable cause enough. The young officer didn't want to hear Orlando's protests of innocence, cared nothing for the meth head's claims about a cannibalistic store detective. He took him to Enloe Medical Center.

The center folded within twelve hours.

When Orlando turned, he had a pressure bandage with heavy gauze wound around his head and was handcuffed to a bed rail in the emergency room. He tugged and rattled the cuff for five months before decay finally tightened his flesh enough to pull his hand free.

There was nothing left to eat in the hospital, so he wandered out.

Eventually he heard crows, understood that it meant meat, and made his way to the sound. When he reached the debris of the wrecked Black Hawk, he saw that another of his kind was already dangling out the cockpit as it fed. Orlando Worthy crawled up and in beside her, moaning as he pushed her over a bit so he could also reach the meal in the flight suit.

Sharon didn't appear to mind the company.

They had both been dispatchers for Chico Emergency Services, Patty Phuong and Patty MacLaren. The first Patty was petite to the point of being childlike, the second a solid woman with red hair and a booming personality. Cops, firemen, and paramedics, without exception, called them Rice Patty and Patty Wagon. Neither woman took offense, and they even had coffee cups at their workstations bearing the nicknames.

Friends both on and off the clock, the two women no longer knew one another as they shuffled across the winter hay field, walking together by chance alone. Their uniforms hung in tatters and the flesh beneath was a speckled gray and maroon. Rice Patty had lost an eye and most of the flesh on one side of her face. Big Patty Wagon was missing her left arm at the shoulder, and her meaty body was peppered with blackened buckshot patterns.

The women began moaning as they neared the Black Hawk, spotting the figures already feeding there. Then their attention was drawn to the right as a pair of indignant crows, working at something on the ground, took flight in a flurry of black feathers. Rice Patty and Patty Wagon lurched over to see what the birds had been eating.

It was the lower torso of a woman, hips and legs only, with burned fatigues tucked into combat boots. The crash had pitched this bloody mass thirty feet away from the helicopter. The two Patties dropped to all fours and began to feed, side by side.

Along the length of Mulberry Street in Chico, drifters wandered with arms dangling at their sides, shuffling through blown trash, dropped luggage, and abandoned cars. They moved beneath darkened traffic signals and past houses and businesses with broken windows and kicked-in doors. Spray-painted signs—messages to family members about whether someone was alive and where they had gone—marred walls and pavement. A drifter locked in the backseat of a patrol car pressed its rotting face against the glass and pounded a fist with a steady rhythm. Black, crispy shapes moved through the skeletal remains of a burned movie theater, and things dressed in the baggy clothes and knit caps of hipsters walked stiffly along the paths of Chico State University.

Coyotes loped through the quiet streets. Sometimes they fed, sometimes they were fed upon.

A single rifle shot echoed through the bare limbs of winter trees, and a V of honking Canada geese passed high overhead. The wind blew newspapers and foam cups down boulevards of stopped vehicles and whistled through the space left between a pair of municipal trucks parked nose-to-nose in an attempt to block a street. Drifters wearing summer clothes shuffled around the ends of the trucks and kept going with no particular destination in mind.

Along Vallombrosa Avenue, where it ran alongside Bidwell Park, crows perched on the wooden crosspieces of the tall, heavy crucifixes planted there, picking at the flesh of still-moving corpses lashed and nailed to the wood in a line that stretched for three blocks. Occasionally a crow would get careless and a head would snap over, teeth crunching down on bone and feathers. For the most part, the birds were clever enough to stay clear of the bite.

The wind ruffled the clothing and hair of the crucified, carrying their moans away.

TWO

August—Sacramento

It was two minutes past six when Dean West let himself into Premier Arms, deactivating the alarm and locking the doors behind him, switching on a few lights. Opening wasn't until nine, and Tony and Juan wouldn't be in until eight. The daycare offered early drop-off hours, which worked well as Leah was an early riser, and so Dean looked forward to a couple hours of solitude before the actual workday began. He was restoring an M1 Garand, the standard-issue rifle of World War II GIs, and the quiet would allow him to give the old weapon the attention it deserved.

Dean was thirty-three and fit, hardened by his former military service, and his current regimen of five days a week at the gym, plus racquetball. He had to stay in shape to keep up with his wife, a fitness junkie. Not that he minded her dedication. Angie West was a MILF if ever there was one, though he caught a hard slap on the behind when he used the term. Just shy of six feet, handsome by any standards, Dean had tousled brown hair, dark eyes, and a scruff of whiskers on his angled face that Angie said made him look rugged and sexy. He suggested the sexy came from his biceps and washboard abs. She didn't disagree.

According to their every-other-day rotation, it was his wife's turn for drop-off at the daycare, but Angie was in Alameda today filming a segment with her uncle, Bud Franks. They were showing off the fifty-caliber Barrett. Flexibility, Angie and Dean agreed, was one of the keys to a successful marriage, and since she was traveling, he took up the slack. It would balance out later when it was his turn to be out of town, and he didn't mind, anyway. He was crazy about their two-year-old daughter, and even at her tender age, she knew she had her daddy completely wrapped around a tiny finger.

While thinking of being out of town, Dean reminded himself to check his calendar. He was pretty sure the producers of *Angie's Armory* were planning a shoot for next week involving a "Life at Home" segment, showing Dean and Angie around the house, having dinner, and playing with Leah. He'd have to get a haircut. They also wanted him to do a shirtless bit, but he hadn't yet decided if he would. Actually, Angie hadn't decided.

Premier Arms was a Franks family enterprise, but Dean and Angie ran it. Her dad was semiretired, and contented himself with occasional shifts at the smaller shop he had up in Chico, only showing up in Sacramento for an occasional business meeting or when filming required his attendance. Premier Arms was the big shop, converted warehouses nestled between Sacramento's industrial and commercial areas. It boasted a large store that included the showroom; a public firing range; the machine shop where they fabricated, serviced, and restored weapons; some small offices; a receiving bay; and a pair of classrooms for gun safety courses. There were over forty full- and part-time employees, and they needed six or seven more now that the show had taken off, driving traffic and sales.

Dean walked through the silent showroom and into the back, setting down his coffee and switching on the shop's lights. At his regular worktable, the metalwork of the Garand rested in a pair of clamps. He turned on the iPod nearby, set it to a nineties playlist, and within minutes was lost in the detail work of professional gunsmithing.

"Dean!"

The yell made him jump, and Dean spun to see Juan Vega, one of his senior guys, standing at the end of the worktable. The digital clock on the shop wall read 7:01. He hadn't even noticed the hour go by. He switched off the iPod.

"I been calling you," said Juan, "and yelled at you three times."

Dean shrugged. "The music's on. What are you so worked up about?" He had meant it to be casual, but then he noticed that Juan was worked up. He looked pale, he was sweating, and his eyes darted around too much and too fast. Then Dean noticed that Juan was wearing a big-frame automatic in a belt holster. "You okay, man?"

"Where you been?" Juan demanded, his voice higher than normal. "What are you doing here?"

Dean frowned. "What does it look like? Is Tony with you?"

Juan shook his head angrily and waved a hand. "No, why are you here?"

Now Dean got angry. "Because it's my place. You're not making sense. And why are you strapped?" He pointed to the pistol on Juan's hip.

The other man seemed not to hear him. "I tried calling. I didn't think anyone would be here, but I drove down just to check. I saw your truck outside. Tony isn't answering either. I'm going to pick up Marta and the kids." It all came out in a rush, and Juan was leaning a palm against the worktable as if he might fall down. Dean held up his hands.

"Slow down, buddy. Breathe or you're going to pass out."

Juan looked at him as if Dean were speaking another language. "You haven't heard the radio?"

Dean shook his head and pointed to the iPod.

"You don't know shit, do you?"

Dean shook his head again.

"It's fucking crazy out there," Juan said. "There's rioting, bodies in the streets, fires. . . . People are attacking each other, killing each other with their bare hands. I saw a police car on fire." Juan grabbed his friend's arm and gave him a shake. "Are you listening? I saw a helicopter fly over, and the guy in the door was firing his machine gun down into the street, looked like at a crowd of people." He wiped a shaking hand across his face.

Dean tilted his head. "Don't fuck with me, Juan. This better not be some gag you and the crew worked up, some punking bullshit."

The look on the other man's face told Dean it wasn't. Juan wasn't that good an actor.

"Tony doesn't answer his phone," Juan said again. "I'm going to get Marta at her office, and then we'll get the kids from her mother's. Where's Angie?"

"Oakland. She's with Bud and the film crew."

"You gotta get Leah, man," Juan urged, tugging on his friend and leading him out into the showroom. "You gotta get the fuck out of Dodge. People are gonna come here." He gestured at the locked cases of rifles and pistols. "They're gonna take all this. You can't be here when they do."

Before Dean could reply, Juan went around one of the counters and used his keys to unlock a rifle case and the cabinet beneath it, pulling down a pair of black clip-fed Mossberg twelve-gauges and stacking several boxes of shells on the glass. Dean said nothing, only pulled out his cell phone and dialed the daycare. Busy signal. He dialed Angie and it went straight to message. He texted her, *R U OK?*

Juan quickly loaded both shotguns and came from behind the counter, handing one to his boss along with two boxes of ammunition. "The radio was talking about a virus," he said, "probably terrorism, some kind of biological attack. Another station said zombies . . . fucking zombies, man. I saw some shit in the street on the way over. . . ." He trailed off, looking at the door.

Dean snorted. "Zombies? Brother, if this is some kind of punk, you are so fired."

Juan just nodded slowly, his eyes on the door. Then from outside came a pair of pistol shots, close together, and both men jumped. A third shot rang out.

"Does that sound like a punk?" Juan asked.

"Watch the door," said Dean, going behind the counter and unlocking another cabinet, pulling out a Glock forty-caliber in a paddle holster and clipping it to his belt. "Go get Marta. Call me when you can."

Juan looked sharply at his friend. "You're not gonna try to stay here, right?"

"Hell no, that's what insurance is for. It covers civil disorder, but I don't know about zombies." Dean had said it to make his friend smile, but it didn't work, and that scared him. "Let's go out together."

The two men moved to the front door and peeked outside. In the lot was Juan's white Jeep parked next to Dean's black Suburban. Out on the road that ran past Premier Arms, a tractor-trailer was stopped in the far lane, the driver's door open, no sign of the trucker.

"When I was coming over here," Juan whispered, I saw—" He hissed and pointed. "There! What the fuck is that?"

A woman in a yellow tank top was walking past the Suburban, her shirt covered in fresh blood, most of her face missing, head tilted at an odd angle. She suddenly increased her pace, breaking into a grotesque gallop as she moved to the left and out of sight. A moment later there was another pistol shot, followed by a man's scream.

Juan crossed himself and muttered something Dean couldn't hear.

"Let's go," said Dean, racking his shotgun and pushing through the door. Once outside, Dean took the time to lower and lock the security gate—no sense making it easy for the bastards—before turning toward the parking lot. Juan was a few feet away, staring at a point just past the tractor-trailer. The woman in the tank top was on all fours in the road, kneeling next to a man in gray coveralls. They were ripping at the body of a man in a flannel shirt and work boots, still gripping a pistol. They were . . . eating him.

"Go," Dean said, pushing his friend, "go get Marta."

Juan nodded and walked to his Jeep, moving like a sleepwalker, unable to take his eyes off the grisly scene. Dean jogged to the Suburban and fired it up but didn't pull out until Juan's Jeep finally started moving. In his rear view he could see the two figures devouring the third, and he didn't miss the fact that the sounds of the starting engines made them both look up. Moments later Juan was on the road, and Dean pulled out, heading in the opposite direction.

Sunrise Daycare was five miles away, almost an equal distance between Premier Arms and his and Angie's house. It was a good, safe place where the teachers and kids regularly drilled on crisis procedures. Leah would be okay.

The busy signal that greeted him every time he called seemed to argue the point.

She would be okay, he insisted. But it didn't prevent him from stomping the accelerator and rocketing into the commercial district.